SOROKA

Corin Cummings

AOS Publishing, 2024
Copyright © 2024

Corin Cummings

ISBN: 978-1-990496-78-3

Cover Design: Jessica James

Detail of "Head of Demon," by Mikhail Vrubel (1890-91)

Visit AOS Publishing's website:
www.aospublishing.com

This is a work of fiction. Any names or characters, businesses, events or incidents appearing in this work are fictitious. Any resemblance to actual persons or actual events is coincidental.

msh

Principal Characters of Soroka:

Alex - Boris's brother & driver (See also 'cousin Alex')

Anton - Former friend Connor met as an exchange student

Artur Losha - TV-N staff, journalist, local legend

Baba Yaga - Character in Russian folklore; dwells in a hut that stands on chicken legs

Bogdan - TV-N staff, host of 'Blue Door'

Boris Mikailovich Vodopyanov - Russian businessman Connor has paid to help him

Connor Chessick - Narrator/cameraman

Cousin Alex - Ilya's cousin from village farm

Emile - Blue beret former military, bodyguard to the 'Turk'

Feodor/Fedya - TV-N staff, social director

Gasha - TV-N staff, reception

Gennadi Illich Milov - Founder/president of TV-N

Grisha - TV-N staff, marketing

Ilya Bilaev - TV-N staff, news reporter

Kalesnikov - KGB/FSB agent

Kolya - TV-N staff, driver, security; Afghan veteran

Mama Luba - Tomsk business woman, reputed head of the '*shapka mafia*'

Marat - TV-N staff, studio director

Lubomira Markova - Translator, head of the English department in *Akademgorodok*

Masha - Boris's assistant in Moscow

Nadia - Pavel's wife (daughters Vika & Katya)

Nastia - TV-N staff, Nikolai's girlfriend

Nikolai - TV-N staff, marketing director

Oleg - TV-N staff, cameraman

Pavel - Boris's associate, drummer in airport band

Sasha - Boris's *krisha*/mafia boss

Sveta Vodopyanov - Boris's wife

The Turk - Mafia guy, Alina's stalker

Vanya - TV-N staff

Victor Israelievitch - TV-N staff, advisor

Wilhelm Fest - Tomsk politician, astronomer

Yanek - Soros advisor to TV-N

SOROKA: Part One

To Your Health, Vodopyanov

Chapter 1

In January 1994 I went to Siberia to make a documentary film about a new independent TV station in the city of Tomsk. That film was never made. The TV station no longer exists.

From a small New England state, I took a commuter prop to a bigger city with a bigger airport. On the runway waiting to board, I exhaled a cloud of vapor that rose, sunlit in the winter cold, and disappeared. Without looking back, I walked up the gangplank stairs. I thought I was cool.

JFK was bogged down with snow. I wheeled my baggage cart between the makeshift camps of travelers and enjoyed the detachment of travel. Three hours later, I boarded again.

A stewardess welcomed passengers with free newspapers. Spotting me in line, she flashed an authentic smile, spoke to me in Finnish, and held out a Helsinki daily.

"I'm American," I said. "Do I look Finnish?"

She snapped at me, "It wouldn't hurt you to learn another language."

Without a newspaper, I went to my seat.

The flight was long, but the final descent came suddenly. With a sense of dread, I touched my money belt, my passport, and then reached down to check the sock where I'd stowed more cash.

The state of the Moscow Sheremetyevo airport was somewhere between renovation and collapse. It was full of concrete dust and nothing worked. The luggage carts were broken or stuck together, the escalators stood frozen like Soviet-art waterfalls. The baggage conveyor worked, but my bags weren't on it.

"Looks like they lost our bags," I said to a passenger I recognized from the flight.

He smiled but didn't seem to understand.

"Our bags," I said in Russian.

"No speak English."

"*Français?*"

"*Nyet,*" he said.

My bags had stayed in Helsinki. I would have to come back to claim them.

It was a Saturday night and getting late. I was supposed to be met, but given the delay, I expected to be on my own. I was wrong, luckily, and a young woman greeted me as I came through customs. "Connor? Hello." She had a pretty round face and a gracious, if weary, smile.

I knew Masha only as Boris's assistant. Boris I knew only from a few phone calls and a recommendation from a friend. I was paying them to help me.

"This is Mama. She waited with me," said Masha gesturing to the woman standing next to her. During the long wait, they had taken off their coats and beneath wore long homemade skirts and white blouses. She and her mother were nearly identical but for the age on their faces and figures.

"I can't believe you stayed so long," I said, meaning to sound apologetic. Masha looked away bashfully.

Mama didn't seem to understand me but smiled and said in halting English, "There is only one bus. We must hurry."

I explained about my bags, and we headed off, descending through the layers of the wrecked airport to the bus stop below. Masha carried my big black coat. She and her mom walked ahead of me, looking anxiously back at me like Mennonites fleeing a tornado.

It was forty-five minutes into the city. On the highway we passed billboards for American cigarettes and German vodka. I watched cars, mostly models unknown to me, drive alongside the bus. Laying my head against the glass, I was bumped by the pitted road. From the seat behind me Masha's mother placed her hand between my head and the window.

"You are very tired, *malchik*," she said soothingly. She laughed as if to a child in her arms. I was tired enough to appreciate the comfort but reflexively sat up.

Wet snow fell as we walked from the bus station to the metro. The sidewalk was covered with a thick layer of dirty ice. Unseasonably warm weather had raised slush pools at street corners that had Masha and Mama hopping over them to keep dry, while I sloshed through in waterproof boots. With a dreamlike feeling of vertigo, I stood with them as we were lowered by escalator into the red-tiled throat of the transit system.

"Stalin built these subways deep underground to double as bomb shelters," said Masha. Then translating for her mother, she added, "Mama says we used to have art shows and exhibits in the metro." Mama nodded and spread her arms to show that they'd been grand. Things had changed, but the platforms and cars were still clean.

"The next station is *Frunzenskaya*," announced the automated female voice of the train.

Back at street level, Masha and Mama brought me to a change kiosk, where a man behind a barred window passed each of my US twenties through a chintzy bill roller. Whirring like a buck sucker on a vending machine, and about as effective, it spit back several bills.

"I just got off a plane from New York. They're all real."

"*Nyet*," he answered, pushing the rejects back to me before changing the others.

We crossed the street to a new German supermarket. A uniformed doorman, who looked like a bouncer at a club, took my coat and bags in trade for a basket. I turned to Masha and her mother to attempt a joke, but in the bright light I saw how tired they were and kept quiet.

They stood at the front, unwelcome in this hard-currency paradise, and waited for me.

I browsed the aisles as dance music thumped over the intercom. At every turn I was assisted by a different powdered and painted young woman wearing a striped apron over a black mini-skirt. Each swayed to the music and motioned to the imported and exorbitantly priced groceries as if to fabulous prizes.

A handful of cans and sliced white bread cost me fifty thousand rubles, nearly fifty American dollars.

"A week ago you would have had to pay in German marks," Masha told me as we left the store, "but Yeltsin made a decree, now only rubles in Russia."

With each of us carrying something, we headed down a side street and into an apartment building with a police station on the ground floor.

"Very safe," said Masha's mother.

"The elevator is not safe," apologized Masha.

We climbed the stairs to the fourth floor and entered a dark hallway. I followed Masha's footsteps and stopped when I heard her keys jingle and peck at a lock.

The two-bedroom apartment was Boris's Moscow office. In one room was a computer and a fax, in the other a TV and a foldout couch. There was a small kitchen with a desk for a table and a loudly rattling mini-fridge.

Masha's mother made the bed for me. I thanked them profusely, though wearily. They left me a key and a phone number.

The bathroom, I found, was steaming hot from a leaking tap and missing the toilet. So my muddled mind thought until I remembered that in Russia the sink and tub are in one room, and the toilet in another.

Still feeling pressurized and propelled by transport, I attacked the hot water knob on the sink but failed to tighten it. I wasn't going to sleep, so I went back out to the kiosk near the metro station for beer. When I returned, I drank standing in the kitchen, practicing saying the name of the brew, *Zhigulevskoe*, every few mouthfuls. It was flat, malty, somewhat sour, and blessedly high in alcohol. I looked out at the dark courtyard and the silhouettes of the playground and the big old trees that reached well past my floor.

I woke in the morning to the ringing of the fax machine. 'Connor, Welcome to Moscow,' I read on the coiled thermal paper. 'I will be there soon. I have some business that I think will be no problem for you –Boris.'

I'd been introduced to Boris by Anton, with whom I'd corresponded since meeting in then-Leningrad when I was a member of an exchange program. For this trip, I'd needed help finding work and a place to live. Boris had organized a number of group exchanges. Anton vouched for him, so I sent him a money order.

Anton had come to Moscow to study medicine, but had dropped out. I gave him a call.

"*Allo,*" answered an old woman.

"*Allo,*" I said. "*Anton Tam?*"

"What?"

"Anton."

"*Nyet.*" She hung up.

Next I called the airline. My bag would be in that evening. I would have to make the trip to the airport to get it. "You have to bring it through customs, sir."

Hanging up the phone, I looked out at the courtyard again and opened the window to listen to the children on the swings. Bundled in coats, muffled by scarves, and while their grannies watched from benches, they shrieked and chattered on the creaky old sets like a monkey's clockwork. I marveled at their rolling Rs but couldn't make out a word.

"*Caww,*" I heard, and realized that the tree in front of me held five or more enormous gray-shouldered crows. Attentively cocking their heads, they hopped from branch to branch toppling snow. On all sides of us—the grannies, the kids, the swings, the crows—were the same monolithic apartment buildings. Each flat had the same two windows and the same little balcony. It began to snow.

I went to see Red Square. Along the way, and almost everywhere, I found Muscovites selling their belongings. Standing along the sidewalk or against the walls in the pedestrian subways, they used boxes as tables or had blankets on the ground. I saw well-dressed middle-aged women, old women, too, who sold tea sets and silverware and even makeup and homemade food.

I bought an éclair from a babushka with rosy cheeks. Smiling at me, she said in bubbling Russian, "Yes, my boy, they are delicious. You're really going to enjoy it. Such a treat."

I set off the metal detector at the Kremlin. The guards, in grand uniforms with broad lapels and brass buttons, closed in on me like the sentries of Oz. I stepped back and felt my pocket bulging with coins. "Maybe it's my money," I stammered.

The first guard laughed. "Yeah, probably it's your dollars."

"Heh, heh, *da*, dollars," chuckled the other. "How long have you been in Moscow?"

"It's my first day."

"What do you think of it?"

"It's very nice."

"You're joking," he scoffed.

"*Da*," I said, unsure now.

"It's expensive."

"*Da*."

He waved me through.

I awoke the next morning to the ringing phone. I laid in bed listening to the foreign tone. "*Reet reet... reet reet.*" An answering machine clicked on.

"Connor, are you awake? It is Anton. Answer the phone, please."

I ran into the other room and picked up.

"Anton?"

"Connor, how was your trip? Did you get your baggage?"

"Yeah, last night."

"I spoke to Masha. She told me it had been lost. Be glad you weren't on Aeroflot, you might have never gotten it back. Masha tells me Boris will be in Moscow tomorrow. You'll finally meet him. Okay, Connor, I have to hurry. Do you have everything you need? I have work to do now, but we will meet tonight. Okay? What are you going to do today?"

"I've got to pick up some food."

"There's a new grocery store near you, a good German one."

"I've been there."

"Okay, Connor, I will see you tonight."

I showered and put on clean clothes, happy to have my stuff. As I locked the padded apartment door behind me, I met Masha coming up the stairs.

"I'm glad you're awake. I was afraid of bothering you," she said.

"Don't worry about that. I'm glad not to have to pay for a hotel."

"You are paying Boris," she noted.

"I was just on my way out to the stores. I'll get to test my skill with numbers."

She smiled. "The Germans speak English, I think."

"I'm going to the real stores."

"I can come help you."

"*Ne nado*, Masha. I need to learn."

She smiled and held her hand over her mouth. She turned to unlock the door then looked back at me. "I'm sorry I haven't had time to help you more, but I am studying for my exams at the university. Boris will be here tomorrow."

"He sent a fax."

"He'll help you with everything," she assured me as she struggled with the key.

"Do you need help with that?" I joked, but she promptly stepped aside with a meek sigh.

"Enjoy our Russian *magaziny*," she said as I held the door open.

It was colder than the day before, and the big fur *shapkas* were out on their scowling Russian heads. No mere rabbit hats, some of these toppers looked like they should be pulling sleds. I grinned to myself, thinking my wool cap was plenty warm.

The store was mobbed. I was up to my armpits in a herd of stumpy old ladies in wool coats, bumping me side to side like scarf-draped bulls. I needed to find a corner to stand in to read the signs and rehearse my orders, but I was swept by the mob and wound up in front of a tall counter with a woman in a smeared lab coat glaring at me. It was the cheese counter. I said stupidly, "Cheese."

"How many kilos?"

I hesitated. I was unfamiliar with the metric system. A woman behind me angled her shoulder into my back. "One," I said, not knowing the word for 'half.' The attendant wrote a number on a scrap of paper and handed it to me. As soon as it was in my hand, the women around me shoved me on my way.

I stood in another line to pay. A steel-toothed, bleach-blond in a pulpit with a cash register rang me up. She told me a number. Suddenly nervous, I asked her to repeat it, but it didn't help. I fished in my pockets for currency.

I had a wad of old rubles my Russian tutor back home had given me, herself a recent immigrant. She had told me that she wasn't sure if they were still good, but not long ago it was quite a lot of money. I showed them to Chopper at the till. She amusedly examined the notes. "*Tualetnaya bumaga*," she said with a metallic sneer. Toilet paper.

I fumbled for new bills. I handed over the largest I had. She raised an eyebrow and made change. Back at the cheese counter, I waited in line again to wave my receipt and pick up my purchase. A kilo is a lot of cheese. Next I stood in line for eggs.

Anton arrived in the evening in a new, fragrant black leather coat. "How do you like my coat?" he said as we shook hands. "This is my business —leather from Turkey."

Taller and broader than me, and with handsome Georgian features, he was striking and well-dressed. When we met as teenagers, he'd been pale and gaunt, just like most of the other Soviet students I'd met on the exchange. Their skin had been thin and bluish. 'Malnourishment,' we Americans had whispered. Now I chuckled in amazement. A lot of good vitamins did me!

"What are you laughing about?" he said.

"You've changed."

"Hmm," he nodded coolly, "everything has changed."

I offered him a beer. He said he didn't drink. I put on water for tea.

"Your English is good."

"Yes. I use English in my business. It's better than learning Turkish."

"What happened to medical school?"

"Connor, you cannot understand the conditions in the universities here. No one has money. Those who do go to school in England or America." He shrugged his shoulders dismissively. Without taking off his coat, he sat down in the kitchen. "The dorms are like prisons, dirty, full of criminals. I couldn't live there anymore. I tried, but I couldn't take it."

"You couldn't stay with your aunt?"

"I didn't want to bother them. Now I don't mind because I am paying. They don't mind either," he laughed sardonically. "I find I only have to explain this decision to my foreign friends, people like you I met in the International Club. Everyone here understands. Nobody asks why you dropped out of university, they only wonder how you stayed there so long." He laughed again with a slight snarl.

"In your letters you were always so excited about it. Right from when we first met you said you wanted to be a doctor. Have you tried to go to school in the States?"

Anton sighed. "What can I do without money?"

"There must be scholarships."

"I've gotten tired of not having money. My whole life, we never had money. Now the opportunity is here. I can go into business and take care of myself and my family. How can I be a doctor and take care of other people if I can't take care of myself? In your country you value doctors, but here they get nothing. We have good doctors, but they're poor. I'm sick of having nothing. Welcome to the new economy," said Anton, sitting back. "Welcome to the new Russia."

It struck me that he'd rehearsed what he said.

"Remember how it was when we met in Leningrad?" he went on. "Everyone said the Cold War was over and everything would be different. We actually thought that we could help each other as friends, each person, each country. Just by being friends we could help. But I remember there was also an arrogant attitude among your group. Not with you, Connor, that was why I liked you. There was so much I wanted to tell you then. I don't know why. Those times are over, Connor. Don't you think? All those promises were like things you say to a girl you only want to sleep with." He smirked.

"Despite what we've written to each other in letters, I wonder if we have anything in common. Now that we're no longer enemies, and the excitement has worn off, maybe we are just two people in the world, two separate people. We can do nothing for each other, and the world will go on, and our lives will go in their own directions. Maybe you wonder why I never said anything like this in a letter. Why should I, though? What purpose would it serve? You wouldn't want to listen to me complain. Now you've come back to Russia. You want to know more about us, so I'm telling you my true feelings.

"You should tell me, too. Maybe it will help me feel differently, or understand more. Tell me your true thoughts about me, about my friends. What was the worst? Don't try to spare me," he laughed royally. "Tell it like it was, like the snobbish American school children that you were, come to gloat over Glasnost."

Annoyed by what I took for smugness, although smiling as if joking, I told him, "We thought you all had weird old clothes, like tweed pants and boots that zipped up the sides, and big ugly eyeglasses. You had greasy hair and dandruff. You smelled like sweat and onions."

Anton chuckled, somehow pleased to hear me say it.

I continued, "We didn't like the food. We were all constipated for the first time in our lives."

"Too much bread and tea."

"See, there's the doctor in you."

"Hmm," he hummed. "We thought you were all super cool, if maybe a bit spoiled. We wanted your clothes, and your shampoo, and your leather jackets, entirely to be American high school students." He sneered. "Maybe that is the most desirable state of existence in all the world."

I was disheartened with where this was going. "Bullshit," I said and attempted to change the subject. "Remember we were at the same table in the Metropol Restaurant when they announced the Berlin Wall was being torn down?"

"I remember," he answered, becoming solemn.

"We didn't know how to act. We weren't sure what it meant, if you and your friends were happy about it, if you thought it was good news or not."

"It was big news. That's all we could tell."

"We were afraid we wouldn't be allowed to go back home."

He scoffed as if our fears were absurd.

"What I remember about you, Anton, was that you weren't afraid to ask questions about things we pretended weren't even there, like national philosophy and religion. It was easy to imagine you as a doctor. You were a philosophical young gentleman, like a character in Chekhov."

Anton smiled absently, as if wrangling with a separate thought.

I continued. "On the night we were leaving, I remember, you and your friend Dmitri walked to the airport through a snowstorm. Everyone made a fuss because you had only thin coats and no gloves. You shrugged it off. You were impossibly good-natured. Nobody I knew would have done that, not for the sake of a gesture."

"You gave us your gloves," said Anton. "So it wasn't just for the gesture."

"Dmitri was a bit over-excited about it, I remember, like we'd given him a college scholarship or something. I think you were embarrassed for him, but you put your arm around him and said to us, 'Dema is a very good friend to me.' Maybe it was defiance you felt, but at the time, it was infinitely more mature than anything my friends and I were capable of. Honestly, it's part of why I wanted to come back."

"Yes," he agreed. "I was more mature than you. I wonder how many other places in the world people get to be children as long as they do in America. Tell me, what do you think, Connor?"

"I'm not sure about that."

"It's no use to reminisce, anyway. What if I told you that I wonder if this trip back to Russia is a further extension of childhood for you? I wonder if you are coming back here because you had an interesting time before and now you want more, and since you have the money, you can do it."

"Don't you think travel has its own benefits, Anton?"

"I do. For the rich it is better than doing nothing. It is better than being idle, better than being bored by your job. After all, your job was not so hard to find and will not be so hard to replace when you go home. If I am wrong, say so," he added dispassionately. "Maybe you think I'm bitter for not having the same opportunities as you."

"I don't know what to think."

"Well, if you did think that, you would be right in many ways. Tell me, Connor, why have you come back? Why are you going to Siberia? Do you think maybe you're going to discover some business and get rich?"

"Not at all. I want to get out in the world. You're right in a way, I was bored at home."

He laughed. "I don't know what you will find. People have no money, so they spend most of their time trying to get it. They are like me. They give up what they want to do to make money. Maybe you think you will find a wife, a nice Russian girl. Someone a little softer than your crass, selfish American women. Is it true?"

"I'm not looking for a wife."

"You couldn't love someone who smells of sweat and onions?" he smirked.

"Anton, you surprise me."

"I am different. Yes, you said. People have had to change. Have you seen the women in the street, the old women, selling their things? My aunt was doing that before I started in business. I don't make a lot of money, but I make enough, and I will make more." With a short cough, he stood up to go. We awkwardly exchanged farewells as I walked him to the door. "It was a beautiful time, back then, Connor, and I hope you have a great adventure now. But I don't think I will be part of it. I hope you're not heartbroken."

I was a bit. "So what are you telling me, Anton, to go fuck myself? Why did you come by? Why did you introduce me to Boris, if you felt so negatively?"

"I'm not sure," he said. "I didn't realize it until I came in the door."

I met Boris a couple of days later.

I'd just gotten out of bed when he arrived. I didn't hear him come in over the rattling fridge. "*Privet*, Connor. Welcome to Russia! Ha, I made you jump." He thumped the rattling fridge as he came into the kitchen. "At last we meet." He took a step forward and shook my hand. "This will be a great adventure for you."

Boris was tall and broad, even more than Anton. He had a buzzed flat-top haircut. His face was pitted, but he was still a sharp-looking guy. He had the easy confidence of someone who'd been a sports star in school or who'd been in the military. He dressed in casual western clothes and could have blended into the crowd in any major city in the world.

He made himself a cup of instant coffee and went to check his faxes. I heard him call Masha. He spoke to her in English. "Are you coming into work? No, he's awake." He switched to Russian, and I couldn't follow.

"Masha is a funny girl," he said, coming back into the kitchen and again thumping the fridge. "She thinks because you are here she can't come to work. She doesn't want to disturb our guest, she says. I tell her, 'He is not our guest. He is our client,' which is much better than a guest." Boris laughed. "Americans know what a client is. Or a customer. Which word is correct? But listen, Connor. Maybe you can help me with something. I have a group of firefighters from Saratov trying to go for training in Virginia, but there's some kind of problem with the visas. We can go down to the American embassy. They respond better to someone with no accent." Boris chuckled, "If you get me these visas, I'll give you back the money you paid me to get yours. We'll call it even, yeah?"

I agreed. On our way via metro, Boris told me a story: "One time I had a group of nineteen American tourists. We first spent a day in Moscow looking all around, Kremlin, Red Square. They were all smiling, excited like happy little birds, but they were very tired, too, and we had to fly to Novosibirsk that evening. I bought them tickets for rubles. It's much cheaper but illegal. That doesn't mean you can't do it, of course. You can do anything, but I was a little bit worried.

"We got to the airport just forty minutes before the plane leaves. I wanted to be in a big rush, so no one would have time to say, 'Hey, why did you buy tickets for foreigners with rubles?'

"So, I am standing in line, and I look at the tickets and see that we're supposed to take off from the other airport. I was, you know, *agghh*! So, I think, what can I do? The other airport is two hours away, and I've got a group of Americans that are, like, 'Oh yeah, we are going to Siberia.' I have no money to put them in a hotel. Then, I had an idea. The only chance.

"I go to the girl at the desk, and I say, 'Okay, we are here. Let's Go!' She says, 'Okay, how many are you?' 'Nineteen.' She says, 'We have only seven seats left.' I say, 'What? Are you sure? I made these reservations months ago. I have a group of *Americans*! It will be a big international scandal. You will lose your job. Come on, do something. Do something!' I say, 'Let me talk to your boss.' I tell her, 'Come on, do something! The plane is going to leave. It will be a scandal.' She says, 'Okay, we have twelve Chinese on board. We can leave them here. They have too many big bags.'" Boris laughed giddily, "So, Connor, they threw the Chinese off the plane.

"Everything worked. I got my Americans to Novosibirsk and no one ever noticed that I bought tickets with rubles for foreigners and was at the wrong airport. That's how it is, Connor. You can do whatever you want." He slapped his leg, laughing, and stood up. We were at our stop.

At the embassy, I did what Boris wanted. I even harried the woman behind the counter. "This is an important exchange. These are firefighters!"

Boris slapped me on the shoulder and laughed, "You're going to be very successful here, I think." After that, we went to the train station where he bought me a ticket to Tomsk at the resident rate. "They can't tell you're not Russian. You're my cousin. Just don't let them see your boots. Stay close to the counter."

Walking away from the station, I asked Boris if all my arrangements in Tomsk had been made. "I'll have somewhere to stay, right?"

"Of course, no problem. Everything will be taken care of when you get there."

We walked on a street lined with upscale Western franchises. "Look at all this," he said, holding out his gloved hands. "This was impossible just three years ago."

"It could be any city in the world," I observed. "Except for the *shapkas*. Do you think Russia could have gone in a different direction?"

"No," he answered decisively. "I know what you think: it's bad that we have these Western chains, McDonald's and so on. And it's more than just stores, there are American and European companies trying to gobble up everything they can all over Russia. This is just a first step for us to get our economy started, I think. It will only be for a few years. They will not do lasting damage. We have many things in this country to be concerned about, but you know something? Our culture will never be one of them. We survived Communism. We will survive Capitalism.

"The people you see selling their belongings on the street, this is too bad. These people are victims of the reforms. I feel obligated to give them money when I see them, but it's not charity.

Do you know why? It is because only by them suffering from the death of the old system that I could have made that money. I know that."

"You've got that paired with things like that crazy German grocery store with attendants in every aisle and ten-dollar cans of ravioli."

Boris snickered. "The German store is ridiculous, of course, and the people that think they are important because they buy expensive imported groceries are fools. But our Russian *magaziny* are crazy, too. Why should you stand in three lines to make a purchase? I go to the German store so I don't have to wait in lines."

By the time we headed back to the apartment, the light was fading and a bitter cold was creeping in. We stopped at a couple kiosks for supplies and turned down our street.

"There are many advantages to having my office above a police station," chuckled Boris as we climbed the stairs. "The officers think I must be legitimate, or I wouldn't dare stay in the same building. My associates think I have a special arrangement for protection. I don't confirm or deny."

"This is your Russian christening," announced Boris, raising a glass of vodka over our meal of sausage, cheese, and bread that he'd arranged on plates. "I am not as my name indicates. Do you know what it means, Vodopyanov?"

"Water drinker."

"Very good."

"To your health, Vodopyanov," I said. We clinked three fingers of vodka, from which I gasped after drinking. Following my host's lead, I picked up a piece of dark rye bread and a slice of a three-dollar tomato. Boris poured us another round of the Swedish vodka he said he preferred to Russian.

I told Boris about my conversation with Anton.

"I'm not surprised that he wanted to be a doctor," he responded thoughtfully. "So now he's bitter. I'm worried about him sometimes. I've heard of him being dangerous in his business, being disrespectful to people he should be afraid of."

"Do you know him well?"

"I bought my coat from him," he chuckled. "We've had some business dealings. We've done this, too, sat and shared some vodka. I feel like I know him. He is the opposite of me. He is like the women selling things. The same changes that allow me to do what I want have made it impossible for him to follow his dream. Just a few years ago, our situations would have been reversed, and I would be the one who is depressed." He drank and sat back.

"But you know what? This is what I want. I love doing business. Something is happening all the time, and one of these days, I'm going to find something really big. It's not just money. I want to be part of what's happening here. I want to take part in this construction, and I am doing it by going into business. There are lots of things we don't have. You will see. It has to start somewhere, right? This is the Wild East. We are going through what America did two hundred years ago. The people who do well —like me, I hope— will give back. They will pay for schools and hospitals and libraries."

"You're making me feel optimistic, Boris," I said, raising my glass. "Even though you sound like a Republican."

He laughed. "You shouldn't worry, Connor. Anton shouldn't worry, either. Everything will be okay!"

The afternoon I left for Tomsk, I arrived at the train station early. I picked an empty compartment that I hoped I'd have to myself. Choosing a top bunk, I stowed my bags in the ceiling compartment. One after another, my cabin-mates arrived. The first man was a soldier. He slid open the door and slammed it shut behind him as if returning from a short time away. Without looking at me, he set down his bikini-girl plastic bag. He had no other luggage.

The soldier took off his greatcoat and hung it from a hook near the window. He took off his shirt and tucked it under the coat. Standing in a striped undershirt, he had a strangely thin waist and the powerful, densely muscled look of an acrobat.

I introduced myself. He looked at me as if he'd never heard a foreign accent before. He nodded and sat down. He took a triangular paper carton of milk from his bag and drank. Before the next passenger arrived, the soldier had laid down and gone to sleep.

The next man struggled to get his bags through the door. He was a Tartar with a tan, an older guy who wore lots of gold jewelry. He had on a shiny purple track suit. His belly protruded over his waistband, and he huffed as he roughly stowed his bags overhead next to mine.

He talked from the moment he entered the compartment, but I understood little of it. When I got a chance to introduce myself, he said immediately, "Where are you from?"

"America."

"Where are you going?"

"Tomsk."

"Why?"

"To work for a television station."

"Why?"

"I work in television."

He cocked his head. Then he looked down at the soldier. "What's this, a sleeping *soldat*?"

I nodded.

"What's his name?"

"He didn't say."

"I won't wake him." He sat next to me, still catching his breath. "I'm just coming back from the U.A.E. Do you know what that is? The United Arab Emirates. Ever been there?"

"No."

He laughed with satisfaction. "I was on vacation. On the beach! It's nothing like here. Beautiful beaches, palm trees. I've got pictures. You go on vacation all the time, I suppose. To Disneyland! I had to save to go on vacation. My bar's doing well. That's what I do. I have a bar in Kurgan."

The final passenger to join us was a student named Sergei. The soldier, when Sergei asked him to sit up so he could sit down, said his name was Igor. As the train got underway, dance music played over the intercom at too slow a speed. The lyrics slurred. I looked out the window and tried to ignore it. I watched the gray blocks of Moscow disperse and disappear as we glided into the countryside. *Dachas* appeared, most boarded up and looking cozily snowed in for the winter.

"It's hotter in here than in Arabia," shouted the Tartar as he came back into the cabin after going for a smoke. He charged at the window and fought with the latch. "Damn things are sealed, *bladt*," he cursed. Stripping off his shirt, he clamored into his bunk with his gold chains tangled in his sweaty chest hair.

Igor sat eating linked sausages one after the other, washing them down with gulps of milk.

The evening sun was low in the sky, hazy, and orange. Snow blew from the front of the train, lashing against the window with barely a whisper. Moscow was well behind us. Purplish bushes grew along the tracks holding puffs of snow in their scrubby brambles. Farther back were rough-barked birches with long and thin weeping branches. Electric lines raced beside us. We came upon fields of tall golden-brown grass with heavy tasseled heads. As the light faded, I watched black and white magpies elegantly plane through the air using their long tails as rudders.

The lights went out at ten o'clock, and the sonic torture of distorted Swedish pop was put to sleep.

The dark compartment quickly became humid and stank of human breath and sweat: cigarettes on the Tartar, sour milk on the soldier. Both men coughed incessantly. I fell asleep concentrating on the white noise of the train as I was tilted head to toe by its swaying. With my feet pointed south, we traversed through the night the long flat geography east of Moscow toward the Ural mountains.

Chapter 2

The cold of Tomsk was welcoming, I thought. Released from the airless train after fifty-six hours, I squinted in the light. I took it in: the frigid air, the endless brilliant sky. I said to myself, "I can handle this." I zipped my coat and fished for my hat. "It's not that cold."

I set myself at the front of the squat, snow-covered station facing the large parking lot. I watched swirling columns of snow dance and sway across the pavement. Boris had said I'd be met by someone, but that he would likely still be in Moscow. Before I could wonder how long I might wait, I heard the man himself. "Connor," he called, waving as he crossed the parking lot. He wore a heavy shearling coat and bellowed in grand rolling Russian, "*Dobro pozhalovat' v Sibir.*"

Following just behind him was a younger man in a blue and green tracksuit. Coatless, he had his hands tucked into his sleeves.

"I didn't expect to see you here."

"It's a surprise for both of us," he said. "I had some unplanned business. There are always details, you know," he laughed.

"Let Alex help you. This is my brother. He will drive us." Alex nodded to me and smiled weakly as he picked up my bag. Weaving through the parking lot to a small Lada, we loaded up the trunk. Alex nodded to me again. I nodded back.

"Connor, you are a lucky man," said Boris as we got into the car. "You are right off the train and already we have a surprise for you. We're going to a wedding. I hope you are hungry."

I hadn't changed my clothes or showered in nearly three days. My hair was greasy, my shirt stained, and my jeans were dirty enough to write on with a thumbnail.

"Don't worry about how you look," said Boris "It's the second day of the party." Then he thumped the dashboard, which was decorated with sports banners, tassels, and mini soccer balls. "Look at this, my foolish little brother," he hollered. "I get him a car to help me with my business, and he makes it look like a harem tent for a footballer." Boris laughed heartily and flicked a small American flag hanging from the rearview mirror. Alex stared ahead as he pulled onto the road. Big brother translated for him and Alex smirked back at me in the mirror. He accelerated roughly, jostling us like eggs in a paper crate. "Nitro," Boris sarcastically read the giant sticker across the top of the windshield. "*Eto shto?*"

The morning sun shone in flashes between buildings as we drove. Interspersed with the Soviet prefab-slab apartment buildings, were old ornately carved wooden gingerbread houses with snow piled on their roofs three feet high.

The wedding party was in a Chinese restaurant, but the food was all Russian. Heaping bowls of creamy diced salads and plates of greasy cutlets lined the long banquet tables. Each of the servers stood with a bottle of vodka at the ready.

"Magic Vodka, yes," chuckled Boris, reading the pink labels on the bottles as he motioned for glasses.

Directing me with a hand on my shoulder, he took me to a rosy-cheeked woman in a puffy gold dress. In an admiring tone, he introduced her, "This is Mama Luba, the mother of the bride. And she, my American friend, is a good person to know!"

Laughing warmly, the woman took my hand and pulled me into the seat beside her.

"Mama Luba is one of the richest women in Tomsk. She is the godmother of *shapkas*," said Boris, and translated for her.

"And many other things, Boris Mikhailovich," laughed Mama Luba. The steel crowns on her incisors glinted. She introduced me around the table and piled food on a plate for me.

"Poor boy, you must be starving after being on the train for so long. Why didn't you fly?" I nodded dumbly for a moment as I mentally translated. "I think he must be exhausted," she announced loudly. She turned accusingly to Boris. "Boris Mikhailovich, why didn't you bring this boy somewhere to rest before coming over here?"

"He got off the train just now," he protested, laughing. "We'd have missed the celebration. He wanted to come. He told me he wanted to see a real Russian wedding celebration."

Turning to me kindly, she said, "You want to see how we ordinary Russians live. Probably you've had your head filled with crazy things about us all the time you were growing up. *Molodets!* He wants to learn for himself. You should meet the bride." She called out, "Tanya, come here, darling. Come meet this nice American boy. He just got off the train." She turned back to me. "I don't know why you didn't fly."

Tanya came over smiling and shook my hand. She was young and slim. Her mousy hair was elegantly sculpted. Her hip bones rippled the smoothness of her tight, silky, white dress. She looked tired. Her mother filled me in: "This is the second day of the celebration. Tanya's darling new husband hasn't arrived yet." She looked knowingly at her daughter. "It's tradition for the newlyweds to serve the guests on the second day of the wedding feast. Probably you don't have that."

The groom and best man arrived shortly thereafter, both visibly hungover. The guests laughed and clapped and called out jokes. The men bowed in good humor and took the abuse along with slow, deliberate breaths.

Mama Luba laughed effusively. She piled a second plate for me with *pelmeni* and sprinkled the meat dumplings with black pepper from a pinch bowl. She gave me a soup-spoon dollop of sour cream and refilled my vodka glass. "Only a dog eats *pelmeni* without vodka," she pronounced as if quoting scripture. She waved to the waiter to leave us a bottle. "And you are not a dog," she laughed and poured herself another round.

Boris smiled and flicked his finger against the side of his throat.

I ate my *pelmeni* and sat back smiling as the old woman filled my plate again. I politely told her I was full. Mama Luba cozily reached over and patted my stomach and said that I would want more later.

After a while, a young woman arrived and pulled up a chair between Boris and me. She kissed him lightly on the cheek.

"This beautiful woman, Connor, is Marina," said Boris.

"I'm glad to meet you, Connor," said Marina in heavily-accented English. She was a magazine-ready, brown-eyed blonde. She wore a miniskirt and a blazer with no blouse or bra. "Pour me a vodka, please," she requested.

Boris talked business with a man across the table. I couldn't follow, so I talked to Marina while trying not to witness her struggle to keep her breasts inside her jacket. She worked in a hospital, she told me. I should teach English, she suggested. The University would be happy to have a native speaker. I told her about my plans to work at the TV station. She shrugged. "I don't see what you're going to be able to do until your Russian improves."

When she got up from the table to visit the bathroom, Boris leaned over, and with vodka-flushed cheeks, poked me in the ribs. "She could be in next month's *Russian Bosoms*, eh? It's a magazine, like *Playboy*."

I laughed. Boris looked around to be sure he was unobserved. He cupped his hands against his chest and added, "Those, my friend, are nothing to laugh about."

The vodka had me feeling warm and sleepy. By the time the bride and groom served dessert and coffee, I could barely keep my eyes open. Mama Luba insisted that Boris bring me home.

Where was *home*? I had meant to ask Boris; I had no idea where I was going to stay.

"We haven't found you an apartment yet," Boris said over his shoulder as we drove away from the celebration. Alex sped through the dark bumpy streets. Tomsk had turned bitter cold and deep blue. "So, until then, you can stay with my associate, Pavel. He will be glad to have you."

I lolled drunkenly in the back seat. "In Moscow I saw a TV show with *Mama Luba,* I mean *Mama Yaga,*" I babbled, referring to a cartoon fairy tale I'd watched featuring a witch living in a magical hut that walked around on chicken legs.

Boris and his brother laughed heartily. "*Mama Yaga*! Ha! You mean *Baba Yaga.* You don't know how funny it is, what you just said," said Boris. "But right now you are too tired, I think, or maybe you have had too much vodka."

We parked outside of one of the town's antique wood houses. The front door hung crooked and unlocked on its jamb. Snow had sifted in through the gaps and drifted into the stairwell, bringing the night-blue cold with it.

Alex spoke to me, maybe something I would have understood normally, but I nodded absently. The stairs creaked as we put footprints in the dusting of snow. On the third and topmost floor, Boris said, as if to fellow sojourners before the lair of a mythical creature, "This is where Pavel lives." He knocked on the door.

I woke the next morning beneath a warm duvet in a room filled with toys and bright light blazing in through frost-covered windows. I heard the door creak and pretended to close my eyes. A little girl appeared in the doorway. Her older sister, Katya, whispered behind her, telling her to get something. Vika, the little one, stood watching me until her sister gave her a shove. She came into the room, almost up to the bed, like a cautious duck approaching a gift of bread. She heard her father's voice in the hall and hurriedly snatched a toy from the floor and scuttled back to the door where Katya scolded her and sent her back into the room to grab a second toy. Pavel appeared in the doorway, whispered to her as he led her gently from the room with his giant hand on her head, and quietly closed the door.

Big and bearded, Pavel was a soft-eyed bear in a flannel shirt. Freckles across his high cheeks compounded his woodsy appeal and appearance of mellow power.

By the time I got out of bed, the girls had gone to school. I met Pavel's wife, Nadia, in the hallway. The night before, she'd been in bed not feeling well. She was pretty to the point of seeming an odd match to her husband, but had dark rings under her eyes and looked fatigued, maybe perpetually so. "*Dobroe utro*," I chirped, "I hope you're feeling better."

She shrugged and frowned casually.

Pavel emerged from the living room where he'd been having a smoke. "Good morning, Connor," he said softly in English. "Welcome, again, to Tomsk and our home." He asked his wife to make me breakfast.

Pavel learned to speak English by watching American movies on videotape, Boris had told me. "And on our dear TV-N, of course."

Nadia served me tea, bread, cheese, and apple slices in the kitchen. Pavel didn't think it was much of a meal and told her so. "It's fine," I said, not wishing to be the cause a tiff. "I never eat much in the morning."

Afterward Pavel took me into the living room and closed the doors. "So, Connor, today, we will try to find you a job," he said calmly. "And then a place to live."

"I thought it was already taken care of," I said.

He smiled lightly and cracked the door to the balcony outside. He lit a cigarette and inhaled it deeply. He shook his head. "No, but don't worry. You want to work at TV-N, I will call them."

He crouched in front of his stereo and put on an ABBA CD. "I love ABBA." He stood and took another lung-filling drag. "I love ABBA and cigarettes. I'll never give either of them up. Here, see what brand I smoke." Pavel reached into his shirt pocket and tossed me the pack.

'Clinton,' said the red-white-and-blue label. 'Filterless 100% American Tobacco.'

"They used to be called 'Bush,'" he smiled. "Yeah. You want to see how much the price has gone up?" He showed me a pad of paper on which he'd recorded the price increases of the brand over the last three years. "It goes up every few days."

"They're still less than half the price they would be in the States," I told him. "Tax."

"I guess I won't be able to move there," he grinned serenely.

"What do you think about TV-N?" I asked him.

"I love it. They show lots of movies.

"Subtitled?"

"No. I'll show you." Pausing ABBA, he turned on the TV. "They almost always have movies on, or music videos." As the set warmed and the picture appeared Pavel cooed, "Oooo, it's *Zorro*. They show this a lot, too. Everywhere in Tomsk you'll find Zs marked in the snow."

On the tube, as the masked avenger spoke, he was translated into Russian by a monotone male voiceover. No matter the character or pace of the scene, the same voice plodded on.

"This is how I learned English. Yeah. The famous voice. Everyone wants to know what he looks like."

"Probably he can't open his mouth without everyone knowing who he is," I suggested.

"'Can't open his mouth,'" pondered Pavel. "I like that." He took out his pad of cigarette prices. "I try to write down new expressions. We're lucky to have TV-N. It was one of the first independent stations in the whole country. But you can't learn to write from TV," he smiled.

"How long has it been around?"

"Two years. At least, two. Gennadi Milov is the guy who started it. He's famous in Tomsk. Everybody loves TV-N. If they had a celebrity gossip show, they'd have to cover their own staff. A friend of mine in Kemerovo, who plays in my band sometimes, says their *Kanal 8* isn't as good. Did Boris tell you I have a band? I play drums. We're called *Chas Pik*. It means Rush Hour. I'm hoping to work out some kind of cultural exchange for us so we can go to America. For that we call the band *Ruskaya Pesnya*, Russian Song. Maybe you can help me write a proposal."

"When can I see you play?"

"I don't know," he sighed. "We play in the airport bar. It isn't safe —full of mafia, black market people. When they find out you're American, they'll rob you. I don't think it's a good idea. Not right away." Finishing his cigarette, he said, "Okay, Let's call TV-N."

After chatting amiably with the station's receptionist, whom he seemed to know, Pavel asked to speak to TV-N's president. He showed me thumbs up as the extension rang. "Hello, Gennadi Ilich? I would like to offer you an American!"

After a short conversation, Pavel hung up and said, "We have a meeting with them at the end of the week."

I gave a surprised laugh. "What did he say when you said you wanted to offer him an American?"

"He said, 'Yes, I'm interested. Go on.' They want a fax of your résumé. We can go down to my office to do it." He called Boris's brother, Alex, and pleaded with him to come pick us up. Pavel said sadly, "We'll have to take the bus. Alex always has a reason not to do his job."

We geared up to go outside.

"We'll get you a real *shapka*," Pavel said, noticing my cap. "A nice rabbit hat. The Siberian is not one to be cold; the Siberian is one to dress warmly."

"What about the ones that look like dog fur?"

"It's dog. Yeah. They're expensive. Do you want a dog hat? Now that you've been drinking with the *shapka* mafia, maybe they'll give you a deal," he chuckled.

We left his flat without a word to his wife. Outside my lungs got a quick shock from the cold. The air was still and dry at minus thirty degrees Fahrenheit. The sky was brilliant blue, just as the day before. The sidewalks were packed thick with snow and slick. I looked up at the drifts leaning dangerously over the eaves above us. Suddenly Pavel grabbed me by the sleeve and pulled me toward him.

"Better to watch out for the manholes," he said gravely. To my left, in the middle of the sidewalk, gaped the hole, steam rising from it as if from a hot spring. The snow around it had melted to form an icy-sided funnel. The lid lay nearby.

"It's the hot water pipes," Pavel told me. "Most of the city is heated by water pumped from a central plant."

"Why is the lid off?"

He sighed, blowing steam through his beard. "Because the workmen are lazy."

"Don't people get hurt?" I asked.

He nodded. "My mother fell down a manhole last year. Vika fell down one, too. She had to get stitches in her chin. Everyone has a story about falling down a manhole. There's a joke: that's why people get drunk, so it won't hurt when they fall down a manhole on the way home."

"Ha."

Pavel nodded with a sadly humored grin. "Even when the lids are on, sometimes if you step on them they can flip up and crack your ankle. That happened to me."

"Why don't they do anything about it?"

"Who?"

"The city, people."

"They do," he said, smiling more broadly. "They tell their friends to watch out for the manholes." Pavel seemed to me a wonder, a giant of calm acceptance and humor —cigarettes and ABBA.

We walked on. I read street signs and tried to commit the names to memory. We stopped at a kiosk for cigarettes on the wide, tree-lined Vershina Street. "See," said Pavel, sliding his money beneath the glass. "They always go up."

As we boarded the bus, Pavel pointed out a Z traced in the grime on the side of the bus. Slicing the air with his hand, "Zzzzzoro," he said.

The small office where Pavel and Boris housed their cultural exchange business was equipped much the same as the Moscow apartment. "Every Russian wants to learn English and go to America," Pavel told me as he turned on the lights. "The new people with money are happy to send their kids to English camp in the States. People know Boris. They trust him," he added. "This is just one of his businesses. He set it up for me, really. We've been friends since we were kids. I work from home when I can. I like my couch better —and my ABBA CDs."

We faxed my résumé. Later Alex came by, and the two men took me to the bazaar to buy a rabbit hat. I could get a dog hat, Pavel told me, if I decided I was going to stay for more than one winter.

That evening the weary-eyed Nadia served cabbage soup, meat, potatoes, and a shredded carrot salad. It was delicious, and with my metabolism tweaked by the cold, I ate even more than Pavel. The girls were playful and chatty. I kept them amused with my bad Russian. Their parents barely spoke and rarely looked at each other.

"Our cat is going to have kittens," shouted Vika as their expectant gray kitty strolled into the room. "Do you know what that is?"

Her sister laughed. "They have kittens in America, silly."

Nadia declined my offer to help with the dishes, though she gazed at me directly for the first time. She seemed to think it was absurd for me to suggest such a thing.

In the living room Pavel came back to life. He tapped a button for ABBA, cracked the balcony door, lit a cigarette, and inhaled deep enough to make me cough. "We had a good day today," he said. "We got you an interview and a rabbit hat. Soon we'll have everything lined up."

In the hallway behind curtained French doors, we could hear the girls whispering. "Girls," Pavel softly scolded them as he exhaled smoke into the draft escaping the room.

"Papa, we want to come in."

"Not just yet, little ones." He smiled at me. "They want you to play with them. I hope you don't mind. I've got to go to the bar soon."

"I won't be able to convince you to take me along?"

"If something happens to you, from the stage I might not see. I won't be able to help you."

"Maybe Alex would like to come along."

"I don't think so, Connor. People there would know he is Boris's brother and give him a hard time. They only don't bother me because I'm in the band."

"I'm sure your physical stature has something to do with it, as well," I chuckled.

He paused. "'Physical stature.' I like that." He stood up to get his pad. "It might," he smiled. Tossing his cigarette stub out into the snow, Pavel closed the balcony door and opened the gate for the girls, who came scuttling in on hands and knees.

The girls played quietly until their father put on his coat and left the flat. They listened as he descended the stairs, then with a glance at me, Katya got up and turned on the TV.

"*Simply Maria*," whispered Vika. The show, a Mexican telenovela, was dubbed by the same monotone voice as *Zorro*.

At the station break, I got my first look at TV-N's logo. An animation rolled: a bird soared on a blue background, diving suddenly and shooting through the station's call letters. "*Eto TV-N.*"

"What does the N stand for?" I asked.

"Don't know," sang Vika.

"I do," said Katya, "It's for *Nezavisimaya.*"

I tried to say the word, and the girls laughed. "What is that?" I asked the girls, pointing at the screen.

"A bird, silly," said Vika coyly.

"Do you know what kind of bird?"

"*Eto Soroka,*" said Katya.

I got up to get my dictionary. "I saw lots of them on the train."

"*Nyyyyet,*" giggled Vika. "There aren't any birds on the train."

"*Dura,*" scolded her sister.

"I saw them from the train."

In drowsy hilarity the little girl laughed and rolled on the floor.

Nezavisimaya, I found, means independent.

TV-N was housed in one of the city's former Pioneer Palaces. The Young Pioneers was a compulsory Soviet program for kids aged nine to fourteen. It ceased operation in 1991. The building was now privately run, and while it rented space out to businesses, the largest part of it was a daycare and youth center called the Hobby House. With Pavel, I waded waist-deep through a yammering tide of children in the lobby to the front doors of the TV station. Inside, the small reception area was crammed with people. Two people spoke loudly on phones at the front desk, one sitting, one standing, hands covering their free ears. Others took turns at a fax machine, and still more people were working from clipboards on their laps on a pair of couches against the wall. There was barely room to stand.

After a bit of confusion with the receptionist, who despite appearing frazzled remained pleasant, we were greeted by the owner of the station.

"I'm Gennadi," said a slight man in a Cosby sweater. He flipped a swoop of blond bangs from his brow and held out his hand. Barely over thirty, his bright instigator's eyes were immediately apparent. Two men stepped up beside him to be introduced and regard me with an air of officious suspicion. Seeing their put-on seriousness, Gennadi smiled as if certain that anything that might happen would be fun. "This is Marat, our studio director," he said.

Marat was a Tartar and had a wide tan face and curly black hair. Despite being a large man, he was wearing a suit that was too big for him. Suddenly changing his demeanor with a giant goofy grin, he joked, "So this is the American you have for sale." He laughed while the rest of us smiled politely. Marat huffed and spit a little and had to wipe his chin.

Turning to the other man, who was much older and wore a red vest beneath his blazer and carried a newspaper under his arm, Gennadi said, "This is our chief advisor, Victor Israelievitch." The old man's face was like one of the city's antique houses, his thick gray brows hanging on the eves of his big ancient nose. "Victor Israelievitch has been in the TV business since before any of us were born," said Gennadi as if making a toast. "Without him, we would never have gotten on the air."

"Politics," croaked the old man.

Gennadi led us back through the youth center and up stairs to the mezzanine and a small café-bar. We sat on stools around raised tables. "Just coffee," said Gennadi to the bartender, who sat watching television.

Pavel and I piled our coats in a vacant spot, our *shapkas* balanced on top.

Before taking his seat, Israelievitch grasped the edge of the table and shuffled slightly as if working up to something. Then, addressing me formally, with Pavel translating, he said, "I'm glad that after all these years, and all that nonsense of the Cold War, a young man such as you can come here and see for yourself what kind of people we Russians are. In my many years of life, you are the first American I have met, and I am pleased to make your acquaintance." With that, he cleared his throat and began again. "You are very lucky to have come to our country at this historic time. It has only been three years since the government allowed independent stations to operate, and TV-N is one of the first. Three years ago, I didn't believe it could happen. I was a manager at the State station for thirty years. TV wasn't a business back then, you understand, it was part of the Revolution. Communication was central to the continuation of the Communist effort, but after time and corruption and degradation, it became the opposite of what it was supposed to be. It did not communicate. It did not speak to people or have any useful part in their lives."

"I was also at the State station," said Gennadi with an easy smile. "We used to joke that governmental TV was the most independent in the world —Independent from the wants of its viewers."

Around the table we chuckled, and Israelievitch nodded solemnly in sad acknowledgment. "People criticize us now for playing music videos and American movies, for filling our citizens' heads with foolishness," he said. "But I say, people work hard; they need diversion, entertainment, something to take them away from their everyday hardships. What's wrong with that?"

Gennadi moved to speak, but the older man held up his hand. "We also provide important services to this city. During last year's *putsch*, for example, when our government was shelling its own parliament building, where was State TV? They played Swan Lake over and over again."

"A sure sign of a *putsch*," sputtered Marat, laughing.

"We were there," croaked the old man grandly. "We had people bringing video tapes back and forth between Moscow and Tomsk. We got information from the outside, from the BBC, CNN. We called our friends and relatives in Moscow and abroad. We got the information out. The people of Tomsk were better informed than anyone in the country. This is how great things begin." He took a breath. "We have received threats, of course. The government has tried to shut us down with backhanded tactics, but we continue on. We are growing. And it is all thanks to this man," he said with a gesture to Gennadi. "This man had the courage and the forethought to make this possible. We will continue with our independent news, and eventually we will have our own Russian programming." The old man sat down, as if drained.

"Bravo, Israelievitch," smiled Gennadi. "I'm sure our American visitor is impressed."

"I thought for a moment we were at the assembly of the old Communist Party," joked Marat.

I attempted a speech in kind but bumbled my language, humiliated myself, and turned to Pavel to translate for me.

Israelievitch kindly smiled and placed his hand on my shoulder. "Don't worry, son. The language will come."

"You'll learn quickly," said Gennadi. "We're not worried about that."

In English, Marat said, "Russian is fucking hard language."

"What'd he say?" grumbled Israelievitch to Gennadi. "Is he cursing?" He looked at Marat with disgust.

"But tell us, Connor," asked Gennadi, "what would you like to do at the station?"

Relying completely on Pavel now to translate, I told them I went to school for film production, and I'd worked professionally in the U.S.

"A trained professional," quipped Marat. "We have an editing deck from the Soros people that no one really knows how to use."

Gennadi ignored him and encouraged me to go on.

I suggested the station could overdub its best reporting in English and try to sell it abroad. Gennadi nodded. I told him I'd like to produce a documentary about the station. "That could be good for us," he said. "Maybe once your language improves, you can have your own show." Gennadi smiled. "Do you like beer, Connor? Beers all around."

It was eleven in the morning, and I had a job. It was settled. We drank to our success. I would start right away. My wage would be two hundred thousand rubles a month, about one hundred and twenty-five dollars.

"That's much more than most people make," Pavel told me on the way out.

We found Alex, who had driven us, waiting in the car outside, reclined in the front seat smoking cigarettes with the window cracked and the stereo on. "*Nu,*" he said, "do they want him?"

A few days later, Boris told me he'd bought me an apartment. "You'll be spoiled," he said loudly, standing in the doorway of Pavel's flat with his coat on. "A whole family would live in a place of this size."

Pavel smiled dubiously.

"It's a new flat in a new building," Boris said on the drive over to check it out. "It's near the Frunze bus line, only a few minutes from your new job, yeh. There are shops nearby, too. You can pay me sixty US dollars a month. That's cheap for you. You can pay me up front for a few months. That'd be best."

The building didn't look new to me. It was ten floors of prefabricated concrete slab. Garbage was piled in the back and littered the entranceway.

"You know about elevators in this country," chuckled Boris as we headed up the stairs. "Luckily, it's only on the second floor."

On the landing we passed a wall of mailboxes, most of which had been pried open. "This is a good area, but there's crime everywhere," said Boris.

The apartment door was fitted with a welded iron door. "This is always a good precaution. You bolt it from inside. You can look through here." He pointed to a peephole, then unlocked the barrier and the apartment door behind it.

The flat would have been better described as unfinished than new. The creaky uneven floor appeared pieced together out of scrap wood. Sloppily painted brown, it was also coated with cement dust, clumps of plaster, and splattered whitewash from the walls. There was no furniture, shelving, or closets.

"Do you know what I studied in school, Connor?" asked Boris, his voice echoing in the low-ceilinged suite. "Mathematics. I thought maybe I could be a teacher. How about that? One thing is for sure, I wouldn't have had much money to count." Talking as I toured the flat, he went on, "Do you know what people do, Connor? They live out the lies they have been told. Always under the Communist system we heard that Capitalism is about robbing people, that it is survivalist, selfish, and is of no overall good. So when our system falls, and we become Capitalists, we rob each other. All we know about Capitalism is what the Communists told us, and that is all the worst parts. But because that is all we know, that is what we do. So Capitalism here is not as you know it in America. It is more like organized crime. People don't know the difference between a fair deal and a robbery. For them it is the same thing. Do you realize how much of your thinking is part of you because of where you grew up?"

After walking through the two empty rooms, kitchen, and small balcony, I stood again with Boris. "Don't look so unhappy," he said. "We'll get some furniture. Lucky for you, my wife never throws anything away."

That evening, while Pavel was out playing drums for the mafia, and after the girls had been put to bed, I sat with Nadia in the kitchen stirring sugar into tea. She'd invited me to join her the last few nights and was warming up to me. Usually she was silent, but tonight she sat sipping her tea tensely as if holding back. Suddenly she said, "Don't believe Boris Mikhailovich about buying that apartment for you." Her dreary eyes showed a spark, and though her tone of voice was dismissive, it held an edge. "He always tries to make things sound grander than they are. I can't tell you the problems we've had because of his exaggerations and false promises. He's been working on buying that place for months. He was going to fix it up and use it as a place for his visiting business investors to stay. His wife and I are old friends. She told me. I'm not saying he's a thief, but at times he acts like one." She paused and sipped her tea and took a piece of buttered bread from the plate between us. At last, as if taking comfort in it, she said wistfully, "His wife and I are old, old friends."

Chapter 3

"Good morning, motherfucker," called Marat in English, grinning as I entered the office. He laughed and took a sip of tea.

I nodded and shook hands with Victor Israelievitch, who was reading his paper on the couch.

Marat said, "Come with me." He led me back out through the main doors and across the hall to the studio. There was a small common room with a couch, a few chairs, a sink, and a samovar. Just as in the lobby across the hall, the seats here were occupied with people working in their laps. The walls were papered with a mural of a tropical beach. An air conditioner rattled in the window despite it being minus thirty degrees outside. The room was stuffy, nonetheless.

"We call this room our Island, and we call this gentleman Nikolai," said Marat, gesturing to a serious-looking man on the couch. "He's our director of advertising, but he likes to hide over here from all his women."

Nikolai was annoyed at being interrupted. He looked up briefly. "I hope we get a chance to work together." He was sharply dressed in a well-tailored suit and wore a blaring yellow tie printed with the English words OVER ACHIEVER.

"Have some coffee, motherfucker," said Marat. "The water is still hot." I stuffed my hat and coat into an already-full wardrobe by the door and rinsed a cup in the sink before making Nescafé.

Marat stood joking with the other men present, a cameraman and a driver, both of whom had looked up from what they were doing just long enough to be introduced and shake my hand.

Just then Gennadi came in to welcome me. "Let's get some time together this week to talk. Marat, take him around, introduce him to everyone."

Marat raised his hands grandly, "What am I, boss? A goat? Don't worry."

"Also, Marat, see about getting him a television for home. He should be able to watch us," Gennadi smiled.

"Of course," said Marat, "I've already made inquiries about it."

Looking back at me as he left the room, Gennadi said, "We'll work things out as we go along. You can see that we're short on space and equipment, but Marat has plenty of work for you."

"*Vot*," said Marat. "We have much work."

As if pleading, Gennadi said to Marat, "Have him work with the editors on the new equipment. Okay, Connor, we'll talk later."

Gennadi left and Marat took me on a tour.

Extending from the studio's common area was a narrow hallway with three doors on the left and two on the right. "This was my office," said Marat, throwing open the entrance of the smallest room, "but we needed the space for our musician, the other Marat."

Startled out of his headphones and looking up from his keyboard, the other Marat, who had a mustache and wore a black turtleneck, nodded meekly.

My tour continued down the hall. "This is where you will spend most of your time," said Marat. He threw open the door like a watchman checking bathroom stalls. "Our editing rooms. Meet Sergei, our chief editor."

"*Vot*," said Sergei in surprise, removing his headphones. He sat before a small editing deck and a stack of VCRs.

"Unfortunately," said Marat, becoming serious, "our equipment is mostly home electronics, and just for that we have to send people to Europe or sometimes to Hong Kong. They can never bring back much at once because of customs, and we never have enough money to get professional stuff." He threw up his hands. "But it's better than what we started with, which was cardboard boxes to sit on and nothing else. It reminds me,

Connor, there's something I think you can help me with today. I'll explain at lunch."

Seeking to get a word in edgewise, Sergei said, "Actually, we have this new editing board from the Soros people, but I only know how to do simple things, and I have to go back to stupid old methods on these stupid things." Sergei flipped his hand at the VCRs.

"Of course, the Soros people," interrupted Marat. He unceremoniously closed the door on Sergei and crossed the hall to show me two small production studios. "This one is for our news broadcast, and the other is for programs like mine and advertisements. *Marketeer* is my show," beamed Marat. "We keep track of consumer products all over the city, who has what and the prices, food, clothes, petrol, everything. We find the deals and tell our viewers to 'say you saw it on *Marketeer.*'"

Most of the programming for the station, I soon learned, consisted of pirated music videos from MTV Europe and American action movies. Marat told me that they had a guy in Moscow with an illegal satellite who taped everything and another guy who did the translation and the renowned dreary voiceover.

"Now I've told you our dirty secrets," he said. "So if you're a spy for American movie companies, we'll have to send you out on the *taiga* in your underpants." Marat laughed and repeated the joke to Sergei and the other Marat, making both of them once again remove their headphones to listen.

The final room in the studio was the control room. "This is where everything is sequenced and made ready to go on the air," said Marat, choosing not to interrupt the man at the controls. "*Eto* Anatoliy."

Pavel and Alex had driven me to work that morning and wished me luck. I'd stayed with Pavel for ten days. "We've got you a job and a place to live," he'd said, "everything you need but a nice Russian girl. Then you'll really learn Russian."

The day before he and Alex had helped me move into Boris's apartment. I'd climbed the dirty stairwell with a feeling of gloom at losing the warmth and fun of Pavel's family.

Inside, however, I was happy to find that some basic furniture had appeared, a bed and a wardrobe in one room, both pink. There was a mirror on the wall. In the other room was a desk and rocking chair with a side table. The kitchen was outfitted with a card table with stools and a few basic utensils, plates, pots, and pans.

"The furniture is a bit crazy," said Pavel, "but it's better than nothing, right? You can use it until you decide what you're going to do. If you meet some young lady and want to stay here in Siberia, then you can buy your own furniture."

"A real bachelor pad," said Alex.

On the wall I noticed a speaker in plastic housing. It was for the State radio station. Every apartment in Russia was hardwired for it, Pavel told me. The only dial was for volume.

"How do I get a phone?" I'd asked.

Pavel sighed. "You can wait for a long time, pay bribes... or you can use the phone at your job."

That night I sat in my rocking chair listening to talk on the radio, although I understood little of it.

"There is only one bad thing about working in the studio I have to tell you about, Connor," said Marat as he continued to show me around the station. "There are no women in the studio. All the beautiful girls are in the marketing office. Nikolai has them all." He led me to a room off the main lobby crammed with six desks and four computers. At least ten people were in the room taking turns with machines and desk space.

"Welcome to the *Zholty Dom*," said Marat. "This is our advertising firm." A chorus of greetings and jeers rose as we entered.

"*Vot*, the Americans are coming."

"At last we are conquered."

"Hide the pirate videos."

"Hide the single women."

"For the Americans, we're all single."

Marat laughed as a ringleader among his clowns. He raised his arms. "Yes. We have truly succeeded, my friends. We now have Americans coming to work for us." Turning to me, he said, "You see, this station is already full of crazy people. You're not the first."

I shook hands and was introduced around and nodded as if understanding what people said to me.

Chief among the hecklers were a woman named Yana with short bleached hair and a tall gaunt man with a long wispy mustache. "This is Uncle Sam," said Marat. Sam saluted. "Sam and Yana do a comedy show called *Zholty Galstuk,* 'Yellow Tie.'"

"That's slang for crazy," explained Yana.

"Like Nikolai's tie," I joked and all erupted in laughter.

"*Tochno,* like Nikolai's *Amerikanskiy* 'Power Tie,'" breathlessly exclaimed Yana. She put her hand on my shoulder, leaning for support as she laughed.

Wiping his chin with the back of his hand, Marat announced, "Our American has a sense of humor."

"*Slava Bogu,*" said Yana, starting to cough. "He'll need it."

As Marat had indicated, there were several attractive young women in the marketing department. "This is Nastia," Marat said saccharinely. "This is Yulia, and this is Alina."

"What's your problem, Marat?" sniped the last of the women. "Are you introducing us as children or as prostitutes?"

This got a fresh round of laughs.

"The American arrives and already I'm having the best day of my life," said Yana, coughing and still holding onto my shoulder. "Wait a minute, why didn't I get an introduction like that? I'm single. Am I too old? Too ugly?"

"There, there," said Sam, consolingly taking her in his arms.

"Watch out for Alina," said Marat. "She's beautiful, but poisonous."

"Hello, *Konnere*," said Nastia, mockingly cloy. She held out her hand and curtsied. She and Yulia were dressed in light blouses and tight mini skirts, both heavily made up. Alina, by contrast, was dressed in jeans and a rosy button-up shirt.

"Good morning my American comrade," Alina said sarcastically with a sly smile. Despite the humor, she was still clearly angered or embarrassed by Marat's introduction. "Don't listen to anything he says. He's a notorious liar." She turned back to the computer where she'd been working.

"I guess you're off to a bad start with her," Marat laughed. "Let's go see the newsroom."

The door to the newsroom, he told me, was kept closed to discourage distraction. Yet Marat did not hesitate to throw it open and announce, "These are the horses that pull the cannons." He sputtered his laugh, but was caught short, spotting something as strange to him as it was to me. Tucked beneath a table at someone's feet were two giant stock pots filled with bloody red meat. Barely able to speak through his laughing , Marat shouted, "Ilya Bilaev, what is happening with all this meat? Are you going to make *Pelmeni* for all of Tomsk?"

Heedless of our interruption, the newsroom worked with besieged determination, heads down and deadline driven. The room wasn't as packed and cluttered as the ad room, but there were still more people than desks.

A young man with short blond hair stood and picked up a pack of cigarettes from his desk. "Feodor's turned our newsroom into a butcher shop, *bladt*," he swore.

"Gentlemen, please, there are ladies present," said a woman in a fashionable brown business suit.

"Only you, Tatyana, but you're a seasoned journalist. You're accustomed to such brutishness."

Drawn by the commotion, Gennadi popped in from his small office next door that he shared with the station's accountant who was also his aunt. She was known in the office as Baba Raisa. "We like to keep them well-fed," he joked. "Where's Fedya? He can't just leave that out all day. Has this meat been tested?" He glanced at me as if he'd caught himself saying something he shouldn't.

"Look at our working conditions, boss," said Ilya with his unlit cigarette bobbing in his lip. "How are we supposed to produce a news show from an abattoir?"

Gennadi chuckled and shook his head. "Connor, you see? We have all these mouths to feed, but the baby birds are never happy.

"Marat," said Gennadi. "Take Connor to lunch downstairs. I wanted to join you, but I can't. Find somebody else to go as well."

Ilya brushed past to go outside to smoke. "Ilya, go to lunch with them."

"*Nyet.*"

"Who needs to go to a restaurant? We can start a fire and have *shashlik.*"

Coming out of the newsroom, we ran into Alina, who scowled at us. "Don't be mad. Come to lunch with us," offered Marat. "Alina is our top salesgirl. I didn't want to say so in front of the others and make them jealous. We're going to the restaurant downstairs."

"Me, Marat? But I'm just a little slut in marketing."

"*Vot,* oh my God, the mouth on her. Gennadi told me to bring him to lunch, but everyone is too busy to come with us."

"So you pick me as your last resort?"

"*Da,* but you are a most beautiful last ditch."

Unlike the bar on the second floor with its blacked-out windows that gave it a cozy, pub-like ambiance, the restaurant in the basement of the building was alarmingly bright, as if lit by an unfading flare. Decorated with white marble and Greek columns, it was a polished Parthenon with every corner lit for film.

Marat popped the collar of his suit jacket as if arriving now into the luxury he deserved. We ordered *pelmeni*, which were served in broad white bowls sprinkled with parsley and ground black pepper. The rich pork-and-garlic fragrance of the broth encircled us.

"Connor, is this the first time you've had our Siberian *pelmeni*?" asked Marat, slurping broth. After I told him about the wedding and Mama Luba, he exclaimed, "Mama Luba? I see Vodopyanov is introducing you to our underworld."

"What do you know about him?"

"Nothing, nothing," he said in mock alarm. "He's a successful businessman. Everyone knows him."

I noticed that every time I spoke Russian, Alina pursed her lips and wrinkled her nose as if holding back laughter.

"Who's Feodor?" I asked.

Marat answered, "Our social director."

"What does the meat get tested for?"

Marat paused, then shrugged.

I grappled with a slippery *pelmeni*, much to Alina's amusement.

"Radioactivity," she said. "Don't you have radioactive meat in America?"

"Not that they tell us about," I answered, scoring a grin.

"Since the accident at the chemical combine last year, they test everything for contamination. Do you know about the accident?"

I nodded and recalled the articles I'd read a year before about the radioactive cloud released from the plant at Tomsk 7, a restricted nuclear city. I'd considered not coming to Tomsk, but the cloud had reportedly blown away from the city.

"Connor, you mentioned in your interview that you want to produce a documentary," said Marat waving his spoon. "What about something on Tomsk 7? I have a visa to go there myself this weekend," he bragged. "I've been several times. Maybe I could arrange something."

"Why are you going to *Pochtoviy*, Marat?" Alina asked brightly.

He laughed as if at an inside joke.

"Ilya might be upset if you're doing any reporting from there."

"No, no, Alina. I'm not going there to do any reporting."

"I didn't think so," she smirked.

"It's called *Pochtovi*, Connor, because the only way to communicate with people inside, unless they come out, of course, which they can do as they wish, is to send a letter through a single mailbox, a *pochtovi yashik*, at the front gate. I think I'll be able to get you and me into Tomsk 7, and we'll bring a camera as well."

"Are you making a promise, Marat?"

"We should have this beautiful young woman working for us as a journalist. She asks so many questions."

Marat paid for lunch, dropping bills on the table like a gangster and turning his back in nonchalance. We followed Alina up the stairs.

"Remember I said there was something you could help me with?" asked Marat. "I have an important meeting this afternoon I'd like you to attend. You'll be our advisor."

A short time later, a driver named Kolya was waiting for us in the parking lot.

"First some background," Marat told me as we got in the car. "You know banks for private businesses are completely new."

"None of them know what they're doing," raucously interrupted Kolya, blowing cigarette smoke against the windshield. "But they all pretend like they're the heirs to the czars, *bladt*."

Marat didn't laugh. "This is an important meeting for the station. If everything works out, we'll get a loan to buy equipment for the studio. Gennadi has already met with them several times. Now it's my turn to tell them how better equipment will help us improve our broadcast and attract more advertisers, and of course, pay them back."

Kolya laughed sardonically. "Which one of your eggs will you give them, Marat?"

Ignoring the driver, Marat added, "It's a pity you don't have a suit."

At the bank, which was merely an office in a government building with a paper sign on the door, we were met by four men in starkly angular suits. The boss wore a black double-breasted pinstripe. I was in black jeans and a gray army sweater.

"This is our American advisor," Marat said seriously. "He has extensive experience in American television studios and will be able to assure you of our success in purchasing professional quality equipment."

The boss raised an eyebrow. "You have worked for American television stations?"

"*Da.*"

He nodded solemnly.

The talks commenced. I understood barely a word but remained attentive. Marat turned to me occasionally to say, "You agree, of course." or "We've discussed this and our American specialist concurs."

As we returned to the car Marat declared the meeting a success. "If we're lucky we'll only have to pay one hundred percent interest, and they'll give us twelve months." Seeing my reaction, he laughed and said, "You think that's bad, you should have seen the terms on the last loan. At least this time we can use the station's assets as collateral instead of all of our personal belongings."

That afternoon I sat in an editing room with Sergei and read the English manual to the editing board while he worked. Sergei was a tall, lanky guy with overgrown wavy hair and a prominent Adam's apple. Almost every day, I would observe, he wore the same black cardigan sweater over a button-up shirt, also usually black. He was reserved with me at first, but as we worked out a common vocabulary, he loosened up.

"Let's have some music," he said, popping a cassette into a boombox balanced on a stack of video tapes. "Nazareth," he growled, waving devil horns. "They rock," he said in English. "Hair of the Dog. Love Rusts. *Facking* cool, man."

Later Marat popped in to say goodnight. "First day on the job and our American is already working late. I'll tell Gennadi we've made a good investment."

"What's Marat's background?" I asked once he'd left. "How did he get to be the director of the studio?"

Sergei raised an eyebrow and shrugged. "He's been here since the beginning. He used to have Nikolai's job, but they moved him over here."

"How's he doing?"

Sergei shrugged again. "He hasn't been here for long. I'm not sure what he does, really. All I know is that he insists on editing his show *Marketeer* himself. He keeps me out of the editing room, and then I have to stay half the night to fix his mistakes." He looked at me over the top of his bulky Soviet glasses.

"*Yasno*," I said, using a new word.

Sergei and I spent a couple hours going through the editing board functions. He caught on quickly. He was an engineer by training, he told me.

"Am I keeping you from your family?" I asked, suddenly realizing the time.

"*Nyyyyyet*," he yawned, stretching his shoulders. "You know what I like best about being an editor? You get locked up in this room by yourself." He gestured around at our container. "Maybe it smells bad in here, but nobody else gets to be alone around here, not even Gennadi. Ever! Even at home we don't get to be alone. Wife, kids, mother-in-law. Bah! Only here."

"Do people know we're still in here?" I asked. "We won't get locked in the building?"

He looked at me strangely. "Everyone is still here," he said. "Not everybody, but a lot of people work late. Sometimes I sleep here, especially if I'm fighting with my wife. Anatoliy, too. He has fights with his uncle. Although now he has been cut back to part-time. Let's go have a beer in the marketing room."

The ad agency was even more raucous at night than it had been in the afternoon. Dedicated marketers hunched over keyboards with computer mice at one hand and bottles of beer at the other.

"Connor!" I was hailed like a regular in a bar.

"Sam," shouted Sergei, "We've been listening to Nazareth." Sam had a bottle of vodka as well as a beer on his desk.

"Nazareth," he bellowed back, his voice booming and throaty. "Connor, *pivo piyosh?*" Sam picked up a beer from a case beneath his desk. "Watch this."

"*Nyet,*" protested Yana. "He'll think we're a bunch of savages."

Holding the bottle up to his face, Sam opened it in his eye socket with an excruciated grimace. He held it out to me.

"Watch out, you'll catch his *SIDA*," said Misha, who sat beneath a map of Israel.

"Connor, Connor, have you ever worked in such a crazy house?" asked Yana.

"Never."

"Ha. We love it. This is when we get the most work done."

"Be quiet. You're ruining it," complained Misha, who I found out later worked almost entirely at night.

"Don't you have families to go home to?" I joked.

Yana laughed. "That's why we stay here."

"Not me," said Sergei. "I've got to go."

"Oh *da*," Yana teased. "The one with the long ride back to *Pochtoviy.*"

"Connor, ask her where she sleeps," Sergei returned.

"Do you sleep here too?" I asked.

Yana frowned. "What, in this dump? I wouldn't dare with all these drunken molesters around."

"Come sit with your Uncle Sam, *devochka*," put in Sam barely looking up from his screen.

Becoming somewhat serious Yana explained, "My old grandfather moved in with us, so I gave him my bed. I sleep on the kitchen floor. But that's not why I'm here, Sergei, *durak.*"

I wanted to hang out, but my Russian had dried up. I tried to tell them as much but garbled it. Everyone stared at me. Misha chuckled.

"You're tired, *malchik*," Yana said sympathetically. "*Ty durak*, Misha. Why don't you try speaking English all day."

"Hey, yeah, another totally awesome video," mocked Misha in imitation of an MTV veejay.

I pulled on my coat, a child headed for bed, unable to keep up with the grown ups. As I walked down the hall through the dark and deserted Hobby House toward the iced-over front doors, Yana called after me. "Connor, don't forget your *myaso.*" Catching up with me, she handed me a clear plastic bag containing a bright cut of room temperature meat.

"Connor, you're still coming back," laughed Israelievitch as I entered the station one morning later in the week. "*Tak*," he croaked as he held his hand out to me. "We haven't scared you off yet. I understand Sergei is pleased with the training you've provided." Giving my hand a grandfatherly squeeze, he asked, "Are you going to the banya with us?"

"So this is the young American I keep hearing about," said a woman behind me in English. I turned to see an older woman with a great gray bun of hair on her head coming out of Gennadi's office.

"*Vot*," called Israelievitch. "This is Lubomira Markova, the head of the English department at our *Akademgorodok*."

"The academic city," said the woman in nearly unaccented English. She shifted her many bags to shake my hand.

"Lubomira Markova was translating for me," said Gennadi, stepping out of his office behind her. "Documents from the Soros people."

"Nice to meet you," I said.

"You may call me Marion when we are speaking English," she told me. "You must come to one of our parties to speak English with my students." She took my notebook from me, and wrote down a date, time, and directions on the bus. "I will translate for you when you need help," she said, "and you will tutor students for me. We have a deal, yes?" She handed me back the notebook and reclaimed her bags from where she'd piled them on the floor. "I'll see you then. I know you won't disappoint me. I can tell by looking at you what kind of person you are." She bustled off.

I looked at Gennadi and Israelievitch, who waited for her to be out of sight before smiling and patting me on the shoulder. "You didn't know you had a Siberian *babushka* here waiting for you," chuckled Gennadi.

"That woman is a commotion," said Israelievitch. "Commotion is the word for her!"

"Connor, I'd like to speak to you about something," said Gennadi. "Let's go up to the bar." I eagerly followed him up the stairs. The desire to please this man was palpable among everyone at the station, and I'd already been influenced. "Is it too early for a beer? Almost *nyet*. So, I want to talk to you about the Soros people. You know them, *da*?"

"The Soros Foundation? *Da*, that's what gave me the idea to come here. I read an article about their work."

"Do you know anyone there?"

"I sent them my résumé and had a phone interview, but they didn't hire me. There was a woman I was talking to."

"We've gotten money from them through general funds," said Gennadi, looking at me intensely, "but I'd like to deal with them directly. What do you think?"

I nodded, taking a drink of my beer.

"I'd like you to write to them about us. Tell them your ideas about doing stories in English. A station in Kemorova got a grant from them, and they don't even have a newscast. We're better. It could be big for us if we get some of that money."

I agreed to write to them. "Would it be alright if I started putting together clips for a documentary while we wait to hear from them?"

Gennadi looked at his watch. "Fantastic idea. Speak to Marat about lining up equipment and time in the studio."

I suggested I start by interviewing Gennadi himself. That way I could work out a direction and identify what I needed to cover.

"Yes, no problem," he said. "Let's try for next week."

"I'll try to work up a draft script."

"Very professional." Gennadi finished his beer and clapped it down on the table, ready to get up. "Connor, your Russian is already getting better. Are you going to the *banya* with us? All the men go on Fridays. I can't, unfortunately, but that way everyone has an opportunity to complain about me." He winked and headed down the stairs at nearly a trot.

On Friday I went to the bathhouse. I arrived a bit later than the rest of the men, having gone back to my apartment for a towel. I rang a bell on a wooden door at the back of a squat brick building. Grisha answered, naked but for a hand towel held loosely over his groin. I wasn't sure what Grisha did at the station, but I knew I was in the right place. "Everyone's inside," he told me. He dropped the towel and bustled through a second door, ass shaking flaccidly.

I stripped in a tiny hallway between a few rusty lockers overflowing with my colleagues' garments and shoes. I found a space for my stuff and hid my keys in my shoes. I'd left my wallet in my apartment, locked behind the metal door.

I entered the next room with my towel around my waist. "*Privet, Konnere,*" called Sam, the first to spot me. The men raised their chipped teacups to me from a worn wooden table, around which they sat cheek-to-cheek on benches, one and all wet and naked. I recognized the cups from the station. Three bottles of vodka stood on the table between them. Just present in the air was the smell of something sour, something aged, verging on rancid.

"I tried all week to get the women to join us, Connor," said Sam. It was true. No fewer than ten times I'd heard him announce, 'I'm only going to the *banya* if the women can come too. I stand for equal rights.'

"There's no justice, Connor," he said.

"Only in America," added Kolya, who sat across from him.

"The sauna's through there," Feodor instructed, pointing me on my way. I entered a large tiled room with a wall of showers on the right and a small murky pool on the left. Leaves floated on the surface of the water. The cedar door to the sauna was at the far end. Suddenly a naked man burst from it and slipped on the tiles. He yelped and cartoonishly threw out his arms, balls flopping, to catch his balance. Bits of leaves clung to his shining glazed skin. With a roar he charged into the pool and yelped again as he came to the slimy surface. It was Sergei. "*Oy, bladt,* that's cold. Are you going to go in? Go in!"

I went into the sauna, and the men inside squealed at the heat loss. I quickly clapped the door shut behind me. My skin prickled from the heat. On three levels of risers before me, glistening in the dim light, men from the station stood with leafy branches in their hands, thrashing themselves and those around them. The branches whistled and smacked wet against skin. Stones hissed on the heater at the back.

Marat danced and sang, "Ach, cha, cha, cha." Smiling broadly, he stood like a Sumo wrestler and held his nuts up to whip the insides of his thighs amidst hoots and laughs. I saw a man named Vanya squinting his eyes and pursing his lips as he batted himself in the face with a whisk of branches.

Marat stepped down from his perch, dunked his branches into a bucket of water and flipped it back and forth over the hot rocks. He stooped to pick up a smeared jar containing a yellowish fluid. "It's honey and butter," he said. "It's good for your skin." He laughed and poured the runny, viscous mixture into my hands. "*Davai*, let's go." He whipped me lightly at first, while he explained, "The *beriozki* bring the *microbi* to the surface. Then you shock them by jumping in the pool." He turned to the other men and shouted, "Look at me, I'm beating an American. This is for McDonald's, and this is for MTV. This is for chewing gum, and this is for pizza. What else should I flog him for?"

I stepped up onto the risers and into increased heat. I sat on my towel and watched the sweat drip from my eyebrows and the tip of my nose. Someone threw water on the stones, sending up a fresh, sizzling cloud of steam. Too hot for me.

"Don't forget to jump in the pool. Kill the *microbi*," called Marat as I left the sauna.

Like Sergei, I slipped on the tiles but caught myself. I flung myself into the cold water and gasped when I emerged, exhilarated.

Kolya was right behind me and cannon-balled into the pool. "It's good, *da?*" he said with a wide grin. We pulled ourselves out of the pool and stepped into the showers. "Connor, are you Jewish?" he asked me, jerking his chin downward.

"No," I said, pausing for a moment, my mind snappy from the excitement, "but all our American doctors, they're Jewish."

In the other room Kolya promptly related my joke and got a good laugh.

"Are all Americans circumcised?" Feodor earnestly asked as he unpacked bottles of beer onto the table from a bikini girl bag. "Why?"

"Health, they tell us," I said, taking a beer.

"That's why you Americans are so aggressive," called Ilya as he came from the shower. "You have early childhood memories of pain."

"You're Jewish aren't you, Ilya," said Kolya mockingly. "That's how you got your position. You're part of the family."

"*Da, poshel ty, Kolya, bladt.*"

"This is where I learn to speak the real Russian."

Feodor brought another bag in from the hall and emptied it in the middle of the table. Whole dried salted fish tumbled from it like relics dug up in a swamp. The men reached for them ravenously. Each had his own method of eviscerating his snack.

"Our techniques are as varied as the cocks that swing between our legs," hollered Kolya, teaching me a new word.

"Swing or merely point out like a small nose," piped Ilya. He then carefully plucked the fins off his fish and peeled the skin back as if pulling tape from a roll.

Feodor awkwardly tried to tear his fish in half but couldn't quite manage it. He stood twisting it back and forth like a stubborn green branch. Finally, he wrenched off the head but was still no closer to the meat. Marat arrived at the table and opened the belly of his fish with an index finger as if opening a letter.

Using his fish as a puppet, Marat squeaked, "Tell us why all you Americans are snipped. Snip, snip."

Picking up a fish of my own, I mimicked back in English, "What's Russian for smegma?"

"Connor, here's to your first week." Marat raised his beer and said to the others, "Have you seen what he did with the titles?"

Sergei nodded in agreement. "It's a good trick."

Marat drank. "Just wait until he gets us new equipment from the Soros people."

We drank and talked. The offal pile in the center of the table grew, and the number of empty beer and vodka bottles multiplied.

"You drink and then sweat it out," said Ilya, heading back to the sauna. I followed.

The heat made me nauseous from the booze and fish. Ilya felt the same. "*Bladt,* I don't know why I eat that fish. It always makes me sick, but it's good with beer" He threw water on the stones and sent steam boiling up around us. I took slow scalding breaths as sweat beaded on my skin.

"Tell me something," said Ilya. "I'm working on a story idea. What do you think about Bosnia?"

I stood, likely with my mouth open, thinking of what to say and how to say it. "The world sits and watches," I said carefully.

Nodding at my meager response, he said, "I want to go there and see for myself. Right now we don't have the money, but Gennadi assures me in a couple years we'll be able to do such things. Maybe if we get money from the Soros people, d*a?* You and I can go find out what the hell is going on in Bosnia."

Just then the door to the sauna opened and through the steam, I recognized the blunt torpedo shape of Kolya. "*Vot,* Here is a veteran of our illustrious war in Afghanistan," called Ilya. "Kolya, what do you think about Bosnia?"

"*Bladt,*" said Kolya, " I don't know, and I don't want to know. I've got enough horrible shit in my head from Afghanistan. There's no more room, *bladt,* or else I'm going to lose my mind." He threw water on the stones, sending up a plume of searing steam.

Ilya and I left the sauna and plopped into the pool.

"Could I go out with the news team, just to observe?" I asked as we treaded water.

He shrugged, "Sure. I'll just have to make sure Oleg doesn't think you're after his job."

As I sat back down at the picnic table in the other room, Marat called out, "Connor, I have an idea for Marketeer. You can tell us all what you think of our shops and tell us what it's like in America. What do you think?" Marat smiled and pushed a shred of salt fish though his puffy lips. He tilted himself and farted, then told me the Russian word for it.

"There's something very disgusting about a naked man farting, *bladt,*" grimaced Ilya.

Kolya emerged from the shower, his hair matted to his round head. Standing in the doorway drying himself, he shouted, "For Russians, there are three lines to wait in to get into heaven. For Americans, there is only one. And it is the Express Lane!"

"Connor," shouted Marat drunkenly. "You are only drinking beer. Why not have some vodka? You are in Russia."

"Marat," I shouted back at him. "I may be in Russia, but we Americans are all circumcised beer drinkers."

"And you don't smoke either."

When the laughter died down, Feodor asked me, "What are you going to do over the weekend?"

"I hadn't thought about it. Go shopping. Do laundry."

The men laughed. "I hope you know how to cook."

"Oi, *bladt,* you've got to get a nice Russian *devushka* to do all that for you."

"Get busy and start chasing our women," hollered bleary-eyed Sam.

I said my goodbyes, shook warm, wet, fishy hands. "Connor, I will come to your flat and take you to the bazaar this weekend," said Marat.

"Now I have something to look forward to, motherfucker."

"Ahh, motherfucker," he repeated, hearing his favorite English word. I left the *banya* warmed and soused.

Over the weekend I had three visitors, but Marat was not one of them.

Chapter 4

Victor Israelievitch was the first to greet me on Monday morning, as he was for nearly every day of my short career at TV-N. While we shook hands and attempted small talk about the day's news, Alina passed us in a tight pink dress. I hadn't particularly noticed her figure before that, but now I saw she was curvy and lean and had beautiful long legs. A sleek horse in high heels, our eyes followed her.

"*Tak*," cawed Israelievitch. "I guess she has a client meeting today."

I'd thought about her over the weekend, I realized. Not a lot. I'd only wondered. On Saturday I'd woken relaxed and rested after the *banya*. She'd been my first thought. It turned out to be an odd morning, but not because of that.

I'd gotten up and boiled eggs and water for tea. I plugged in the little State radio for noise. I drew water for laundry in the claw foot tub, which was the single decorative element in the apartment. I wondered if the Soviets had always made claw-footed tubs. Maybe the original casts came from Czarist times but the Communists hadn't bothered to redesign them, claw feet not having been quite too bourgeois.

I had a big bar of foul-smelling brown soap stamped "65%." Sixty-five percent of what? I couldn't tell, but I'd seen Pavel's wife use it for washing clothes and had picked some up for myself.

Kneeling on my towel, I'd scrubbed until the water turned black with dye. With no line to hang laundry on, I'd draped my clothes over anything I could, the doors of the wardrobe, the radiators, windowsills. As I scuttled about my flat leaving drizzled trails along my grubby floors, I'd been interrupted by pounding at my great gong of a metal front door. I thought it was Marat and opened up, but instead of my spittle-chinned boss, I found a little old woman.

"What the devil have you done?" she bellowed at me. Without waiting for a reply, she pushed past me. "There's water coming down through our ceiling!"

"I was doing laundry," I stuttered. Detecting my accent, she cast me a sharp scowl. She turned and saw the hanging clothes.

"Devil take you, it's more water than that." She bustled into the bathroom and got on her hands and knees to look under the tub. "You're going to pay for the damage." She flung open the door to the toilet for inspection. "You've ruined my husband's books. I hope you're happy." She stomped into the kitchen to examine the plumbing in there. "I should call the police." Turning the taps on and off, she huffed furiously. I stood back.

"Maybe a pipe burst somewhere."

"A pipe?" she'd screamed in outrage, but at just that moment, both our sets of eyes spotted a rusty wet streak in the corner of the ceiling. "Look at that! It's the floor above." She took a breath. The contempt and rage drained away from her face as the hex lifted. "Where is your family, young man?"

"Far away," I answered, feeling more secure.

She looked at me softly. "Who cooks for you? Who does the shopping?" She took my hand and patted it. Suddenly, she was my grandmother. "If you need anything, you can knock on my door. We're right below you."

"That's very kind of you."

The old woman covered her mouth as she smiled and bashfully swatted the air with her soft old paw.

She left my place and headed up the stairs. I imagined her rage returning with each step she ascended the steps until she was ready to eviscerate whoever answered the door above me. I listened but heard nothing through the concrete.

My second visitor for the weekend came on Sunday night. This time when I heard the knock at the door, I'd looked through the peephole. I saw no one and wondered if my *babushka* had returned but was too short to see. "*Kto tam?*" I demanded.

There was a pause. "We're here to fix the electricity." The voice came from the side of the door. Whoever said it was deliberately standing where I couldn't see him.

"There's nothing wrong with the electricity." There was no reply. I waited to see if I would catch a glimpse of whoever it was when he turned back to the stairwell. I heard a foot scuff. He waited likewise. I closed and bolted the inside door.

After working all morning with me in an editing stall, Sergei dropped his headphones on the control board and said, "*Nu*, Connor, it's time for lunch. Let's go to the *stolovaya*." We put on our coats and set off out the front doors.

By now the cold had revealed to me that its magnitude was constant. It wasn't bad at first, not for a few minutes at a time; you dressed warmly. But its everlasting presence gradually took effect. You were always fighting to get warm, drinking tea, rubbing hands. After a couple of weeks, my metabolism had geared up, and I was eating more than I ever had before.

"I love this place," said Sergei as we cut through a park, the snow crunching beneath our feet. "It's one of the best cafeterias in town. We're lucky."

Sergei, I'd come to know, loved two things more than anything else: seventies hard rock and food of any kind, but particularly from the cafeteria we visited nearly every day for lunch.

We stepped into the eatery and into a cloud of fragrant greasy steam. The windows were obscured by ice, giving the place a dim, igloo light. The draft from the door kept the floor cold enough to maintain a snow trail well into the room. At the back, behind a glass counter, the day's menu items were displayed on individual plates and in bowls. I was starving and ordered just about everything. They had fresh cucumbers and tomatoes with sour cream. There were potatoes, of course, but also meat with oyster mushrooms.

"Where do they get the fresh vegetables?" I asked Sergei as we sat at a table.

"They have a greenhouse. If you ask at the counter sometimes they'll sell them to you." Sergei smiled and raised an eyebrow towards the servers, each born into the ferocious caste of shop women. "You'll want to ask nicely."

Alina came in the door as we began eating our salty, greasy, delicious soup. She wore a dressy wool coat with a wide fur collar and a fur bonnet. She could have passed for Anna Karenina stepping down from her horse-drawn trap.

"Well, Yankee, it's our second date already," she said when she sat down with a tray of food equal to my own. "*Privet*, Sergei. How do you like your new American?" Sergei raised his eyebrows again as she shed her coat and made a pleased sound as he chewed his lunch.

"So what do you think of our little hobby station so far?" asked Alina, gazing at me with her clear, mischievous eyes. Her nose wrinkled when she smiled.

"He's having trouble with Marat," answered Sergei. "He wants to make a film, but Marat just wants him to sit on the beach and look Occidental."

That morning I'd asked Marat how I could schedule the use of one of the station's cameras, and he'd given me the run around.

"Is Marat breaking his promises? Big surprise. I'll speak to him."

"Look at who really runs the station," I attempted.

"Sergei," she continued, talking past me, "have you noticed that everyone talks to Connor like he's a child or an imbecile?" Sergei nodded but was more involved with his lunch than the conversation. "Don't be so cautious about speaking," she said to me. "You don't sound that bad. You'll get better. You and I can have some *praktika*, maybe. I should brush up on my English."

I watched her eat. She had long fingers with neatly glossed fingernails. I was stunned by her appetite. Catching me watching her, she smirked.

"Tell me, Connor, what did you think of our *banya*? It must have been strange to you."

"A little." I smiled at her, delighted to have her there. "By the number of people who asked me if I was going to go, I was beginning to suspect a trap."

"No, Connor," she said seriously. "They were afraid you wouldn't like it." She paused and glanced at Sergei, who stayed focused on his lunch. She smiled again and said, "I bet our dear men taught you some interesting new words."

"I learned the word for 'circumcised,'" I said triumphantly.

She blushed and scolded me, "*Foo!*" Sergei laughed so hard he nearly choked and fell into a fit of coughing. More embarrassed than offended, Alina gave me a wink.

"Breaking news," said Ilya excitedly as Sergei and I returned to the studio. "One of the University dormitories has collapsed. Do you still want to ride with the news team?"

Excited now myself, I followed Ilya outside to a waiting car. I sat in the back with Oleg, the cameraman. Cigarette smoke swirled in jets of frozen air let in through slit windows as we were jostled and bounced at high speed though the streets of Tomsk.

"The government has abandoned the universities," Ilya told me, turning around from the front. "They don't have money to pay the teachers, no money to maintain the buildings. It was only a matter of time before something like this happened. We've heard from the police that no one was hurt that they know of, but they don't know if anyone was buried."

We arrived at the scene and gazed in amazement. It was hard to believe no one had been killed. An entire vertical corner of the five-story building, top to bottom, had collapsed, leaving it looking like a layer cake minus a greedy slice. The rooms revealed inside displayed toppled furniture, scattered clothes and books, wrenched spurting pipes, mangled rebar, and hanging electrical wires.

Notebook in hand, Ilya questioned onlookers. Oleg unpacked the camera and began filming. I walked to the parameter of the ruble, the snow around it covered with gray dust. Ice had begun to form around ruptured pipes, engulfing debris. I saw a sink, a toilet seat, and a samovar crushed by a tub whose claw feet held their ice-coated orbs crookedly into the cold air.

I found chunks of concrete that were chalky and brittle like packed dust, no doubt degraded by years of leaks and freezing temperatures. I looked up at the building. I noticed walls painted a salmon color and half expected to see the rosy, wind-burned face of a forgotten child. I dreaded spotting a corpse but kept a close watch as I circled the wreckage past where the footprints in the snow had stopped. The plug to a sink, shards of a mirror, the contents of a medicine cabinet in brown bottles —I found a dead cat powdered gray with the dust. I waved to Oleg.

"*Tak*," he purred after trotting to me through the knee-deep snow. He filmed the cat as it was and then pulled it from the pile and posed it with other articles in the rubble, taking shots from every angle.

Ilya picked his way over to us in his dress shoes. "Faculty live here. The building was condemned over two years ago." He looked at Oleg on his knees getting creative with the dead animal. "I've got a whole group of families over there to interview, and you're wasting tape and battery time on a dead cat, *bladt*."

"It's a symbol," objected Oleg.

"A fucking cat, *bladt*. The fucking symbol, *bladt*, is the people with nowhere to live!" Ilya stormed back towards the car and the people waiting for him there.

The families were in shock. "We knew it would happen," said a woman with only a shawl over her clothes. "When I heard the noise I knew to get out. Thank God the children were in school." The others nodded mutely.

"They don't have much more to say than the cat," grumbled Oleg.

We heard yelling and spotted a man arguing with police officers. "I wish I had been killed," he called shrilly as we approached. He was tall and gaunt and wore a brown overcoat. His eyes were watery and red with the cold and emotion. "If someone was killed, maybe they'd take us seriously! We've been living in a condemned building, waiting like chickens for the ax. They were supposed to put us in better housing years ago. It's in our contracts. We're supposed to have flats, not dormitories. We've lived like refugees. Now what? Are we going to live like gypsies in tents? I'm going right back in that building. Where else am I going to live? How am I going to keep my daughter warm? You pick the drunks up off the streets at night, but we'll freeze in our own homes. This is a nightmare!" The cops stood without an answer. The man walked back toward the building while Oleg filmed his departing back.

"This isn't the only building like this," said another man at Ilya's side. "I live in a place just like it. Come with me, I'll show you." We followed him up the street. He was short and round and wore a wool suit. He looked like a professor. "Years of leaking plumbing and leaking roofs. They say they don't have the money to fix it, but who will have the money to bury us all?" His effort to joke appeared to strain him. He was exhausted, beyond weary.

He led us to one of the city's ancient wood buildings. It lurched to one side, rot evident. The man tore a chunk of wood away with his hand to demonstrate. He pointed out that one of the top corners of the building, roof and wall, was caved in. "There are ten families living here," he said. "We're all employees of the Poly-Technical Institute or else retirees from there on a pension. Some have lived here for a decade."

About a dozen people, mostly women, came out of the house to meet us. They were ordinary, well-dressed citizens. You wouldn't expect them to live in such a hovel by looking at them. Oleg switched on the floodlight.

"Come inside and see how we live," invited an old woman with a pleasant pudgy face framed by a bright flowered scarf tied under her chin. Wearing a worn black coat, a brown skirt that hung to her ankles where heavy black stockings and wool socks were stuffed into old leather shoes, she led the way. She warned us, "Watch your step, the floor is rotted."

Following the small crowd and the light from the camera, I entered the house. It was warm inside and smelled of cooking potatoes. A little old man with a cane doddered beside me while the old woman took us on a tour. His face was expressionless, as if he'd suffered a stroke. A hammer-and-sickle pin was affixed to his lapel.

We walked through a makeshift kitchen equipped with a pair of electric hot plates. The rotten floor bowed beneath us, despite a hundred years of patches. The ceiling and walls were pockmarked and scared where plaster had fallen away. Nevertheless, the inhabitants had obviously made an effort to keep it clean.

On the second floor, as we'd seen from outside, part of the roof had fallen in, leaving a tub-sized hole. The old man, whom I'd helped up the stairs, tugged my coat sleeve and pointed. I nodded, and he slowly shook his head.

"Look at our toilets," said our guide. She opened a door at the end of the hall, revealing the source of a stink I'd noticed since climbing the stairs. Oleg's spotlight shone over piles of feces and crumpled newspaper. Water dripped from the ceiling. Black mold grew on the walls. Oleg puffed out his cheeks as he held his breath, and the skinny old man next to me let out a startling cackle.

"They send us eviction notices as if we want to stay here," said a young woman. "It's them that put us here. Where are we supposed to go?"

"They want to put us in another rotting dormitory, but we won't go," said another woman. "We're supposed to have proper apartments. They say the police will come and throw us out on the eighteenth."

The woman who had stoically led us through the house began to sob, making a deep moaning sound. She used the corners of her scarf to wipe the tears from her deep wrinkles. Others in the group began to weep; the old man patted each of their hands as if consoling fussing babies. The old woman walked back to the stairs with a limp I hadn't noticed before.

"I don't know if it will help," said Ilya, "but your story will be on our broadcast."

Outside Ilya stood in front of the house to film an intro to the segment. Up pulled one of the old white Volgas usually belonging to State officials. The inhabitants recognized the car and came storming from the house. Ilya motioned to Oleg, who swung around with the camera.

A man in a mangy-looking, brown mink shapka got out and introduced himself. "My name is Privkin. I am the housing director for the university." He had dark, deep-set eyes and a dour face. "These people live in this condemned building by choice. The university has made an alternative dwelling available to them, but they refuse to leave. We have no option but to remove them forcibly for their own protection. I can show you the documents." He dispassionately swung his briefcase onto the hood of the car and opened it.

"You rascal," cried the woman with the flowered kerchief, her tears running anew as she stomped down the icy path from the door. She and the other inhabitants gathered around the car.

The younger women shouted, "They want to put us in another rundown dormitory that'll end up collapsing just like that one today. They have to get us apartments. That's what's in our contracts."

"Those are old contracts that are no longer valid," said Privkin coldly. "You need to sign the new contracts."

"The new contracts are an outrage," shouted the inhabitants. "They think they can change the terms whenever it suits them."

"We'll sign the contracts and move into the dorm if you specify when we'll get proper apartments," said the young woman, thrusting her finger at Privkin.

"That's impossible," he said.

"You cold-hearted bureaucrat," bawled the old woman, wiping her eyes.

"The university has the right to fire those who do not sign the contract," he pointed out. "We have not done that." The inhabitants roared and cursed, each person gesticulating angrily.

The Volga driver, upset by the mob pressing against the car, got out and stood next to his boss.

Speaking to Ilya, still dispassionately, though a bit louder to be heard over the howling crowd, Privkin said, "They act as if nothing has changed in this country. It is a war situation. There are things we simply have to endure. When they signed their contracts, it was feasible for them to get apartments of their own. Now it is not. The university is funded by Moscow, and Moscow isn't sending enough money. Neither I nor the university has the slightest control over it. I am sorry that they live in these conditions, but the only thing I can do is move them to a better dormitory. It is the only option we have."

The fight raged on. After a few moments, Ilya motioned to Oleg to stop filming. We left the inhabitants of the condemned house hollering impotently at Privkin across the hood of the Volga. The driver stood aside smoking a cigarette, immune.

"I need a beer," said Ilya when we arrived back at the station. As we sat in the mezzanine bar, he sighed, "Tell me something that doesn't have to do with pensioners living in a sewer."

I told him about the supposed electricity repairman that had showed up at my apartment on Sunday night.

"They didn't waste any time getting to you. It's good you didn't open the door. You'll have to be careful, Connor, there are many scams like that. Usually people are so happy that any kind of repairman came to their flat that they let them right in. I've heard they make people sign over ownership of their apartments at gunpoint. You know," he continued, taking a drink once the barman brought our beers, "if they recognized your American accent, they might come back." He leaned forward and said, "I've got something for you, a little extra protection. 'American style,'" he added in English. "It's in my car."

After draining the beers, we went to edit the dorm piece.

"Connor, motherfucker," blared Marat as we came down the stairs. "My American thinks he can run off and do whatever he wants, even when I have given him a job to do."

Ilya was still in bad humor and snapped at him on my behalf, "Listen to you, *bladt*. You old party boss! I asked him to come with us, now he's going to edit with me."

Thinking Ilya was joking with him, Marat laughed.

"I thought I heard your name," said Lubomira Markova, the translator, coming out of the station lobby.

"You heard his bad Russian," said Marat.

"I haven't said anything."

"I heard some very unpleasant English words," she admonished Marat and then to me said sternly, "I need to talk to you."

"I'll see you in there," grumbled Ilya, unwilling to defend me further.

"You haven't gotten back to me about the English party tonight."

"Now you have the academics mad at you," laughed Marat as he headed upstairs to the bar.

"I don't have a phone at my apartment. I was going to call you today, but I've been out with the news team."

"I'd assumed you would come. I just need to make sure. It's not a simple thing to set up, you know. I expect you'll arrive around seven. I wrote out directions and left them with the receptionist."

"*Konnere, Konnere,*" called Gasha, the receptionist, from the lobby door. "You have a telephone call."

I told Lubomira I would see her later and went to take the call. It was Boris inviting me to play tennis. "Okay, Connor, no problem. I don't want you to get in trouble with Lubomira. She's a good person to know. Maybe not as good as Mama Luba, but good. Okay, Connor, I'll come pick you up next Tuesday for my next lesson. I have a big meeting in the US in a couple weeks, and they want to know if I play tennis. I tell them, of course I play tennis. So now I take lessons."

"Was that Boris Mikhailovich?" Gasha asked breathlessly. "Connor, you know all the big wigs in town."

"All the Mafia," joked Kolya as he came through the lobby.

Ilya and I put the dorm piece together quickly and were happy with the outcome. Said Ilya, "This is better than our usual work, but you've had training. We complain about the old status quo, but then everyone gets threatened when somebody comes along who knows how to do something they don't. Sometimes it's just bad taste that holds us back. People are used to seeing things a certain way, both the audience and the producers, and they like it to stay the same, even when something better comes along."

Emerging from the editing room with the evening's main story, Ilya met with the other journalists and Gennadi to assemble the newscast. It was recorded at five and went on the air at six o'clock.

"Good work on the collapse piece," Gennadi mumbled to me as if in confidence, "but I don't want you to get too busy with editing work and forget about the letters to the Soros people. I know Ilya is going to want you to do more work with him, but you're the only person we have that can help with the Soros people." With urgency in his hushed voice, he continued, "We're not really going to be able to improve without better equipment and training. We need to do the newscast live. Even State TV does that. Connor, you understand me, *da*?"

I had to rush to get to the English party in time. I began the strangely lonesome routine of gearing up for the walk out to the Frunze bus stop. Big boots, big coat, big hat, outside the wind would still be painful. I had Lubomira's directions in my pocket.

Just then, Alina emerged from an editing room laughing, her back to me. Sitting inside the narrow room, the usually sober Anatoliy was smiling back at her. He caught sight of me and hid his crooked teeth.

"Connor," she laughed as she turned around, "you look like one of our Chukchi. We just finished a new commercial —why don't you come have a drink with Anatoliy and me?"

"*Ne mogu*," mumbled Anatoliy, "I've got work."

"Well, just with me then," she said.

I accepted. In the bar I draped my coat over a vacant stool. "Today has been a good day," said Alina cheerfully. "Look what I got." She slid a business card across the table. "I've been waiting for these for more than a year. I kept calling the printers, but it was only after months of asking that they told me the station owed them money. How do they expect to get paid if they don't tell anybody? Believe it or not, these cards can get you places. People think because you have a business card you're someone special. It's ridiculous, of course, but that's the way it always was. The party officials went everywhere showing their cards."

We sat silently for a moment, drinking our beers. I knew I was going to be late and tried to drink quickly.

Alina ran a finger over the embossed logo on one of her new business cards. "Do you know what it is, the bird, our mascot?" she asked.

"*Soroka*," I said.

"I'm impressed. I love that design. Uncle Sam did it, can you believe that?"

"The guy who opens bottles with his eye socket?"

"Ha, a natural artist! I wanted to work for the station as soon as I saw that design," she said wistfully. "Connor, tell me how you decided to come here. Not many people come to Siberia who are not made to."

"I just came," answered accurately. I told her about Anton and how he'd introduced me to Boris. "It strangely fell into place. It was a series of steps, and after each one I wasn't sure if I would take the next. But then I quit my job, and I had to do it."

"Why leave?"

"It was dull where I was. Everyone was the same."

"Everyone here wants to go there, but for you it was boring so you came here."

I shrugged. "I didn't make the world that way." This got a genuine laugh.

"It's good that you came to Russia and not some other country." Noticing my beer was gone she said, "I hope I'm not keeping you from anything." She smiled, believing the answer was surely no and that she was saving me from a lonely evening, which usually would be true. I told her about the English club.

"Oh, that's what Marat was talking about."

"Marat?"

"He was just telling me something," she said. "You must be looking forward to speaking your mother tongue. You had better go. You're late."

"I can wait until you're done."

"So polite," she smirked. "Go."

At the stairs I turned back and waved. Snickering, she shook her head as if embarrassed for me.

I stuffed my gloves in my pockets, and as I walked to the bus stop, I read Lubomira's instructions written in precise capital letters on flimsy gray notepaper. The sun had long since set, and there was little lighting. A car pulled up alongside me. It was Ilya in a sporty new Lada.

"You're going to freeze your eggs off, *bladt*. Get in. I've lived here my whole life, and I never get used to the cold. You're on your way to *Akademgorodok, da*? I'd give you a lift, but I'm late for something. Listen, remember I told you I had something for you? It's in the glove box."

I sat in the passenger's seat and opened the glove box. Folded in a newspaper, like a movie prop, was a handgun.

"It's not as deadly as it looks," he said. Taking it from me, he pulled out the clip. "*Bolonchiks*," he said, showing me the red-capped cartridges. "The bullets are plastic capsules full of tear gas. There's a hook inside the barrel that splits them open, so the gas sprays everywhere." He shoved the clip back into the gun with a satisfying clap. "But you have to be careful. I've heard of people being killed with the plastic part at close range." Handing it back to me, he added, "You're supposed to have a permit for this, so don't get caught with it."

Ilya let me out at the bus stop, and I continued to my tea party.

I found the Academic City English Club in a nondescript institutional building at the end of a cold, dim, unadorned corridor. I could see light beneath the door and hear music and people laughing. I went unnoticed as I took off my coat and boots. The club was in a suite of rooms decorated in a way that reminded me of kindergarten. Everything was plaid. Wallpaper, tablecloths, upholstery, all were dizzyingly mismatched plaids.

"Connor, Welcome," called Lubomira in her British-inflected English. She stood in the doorway of one of the rooms holding a knife she'd been using to cut a cake. "Come meet everyone." Even she, in a heavy wool jumper, was dressed in plaid. "Now I must explain," she said, taking me by the hand and leading me into the room like a teacher with a shy boy on the first day of school. "Everyone has an English name here. This is so we don't have to be self-conscious about speaking poorly at first. I am Marion."

I'd assumed wrongly that the students would be student-aged. All of Lubomira's students were adults.

"Good day, no, evening. My name is Betty Boop," said one woman extending her hand. Marion nodded approvingly and pushed me forward.

"I am Steve McQueen," said a middle-aged man proudly.

I noticed Marat sitting at one of the tables and made my way towards him.

"Yes, you see, even your boss has joined us," said Marion.

"What are you doing here?" I asked him in Russian.

"No, no," he said, "English only."

"What's your English name, Badass Motherfucker?"

He sputtered his laugh but was embarrassed. "Connor, shh, such language," he said looking down.

I laughed, and said in English, "Are you afraid the teacher will make you stay after school?"

"Oh, he's saucy when he can speak his own language," delighted Marion. She then went on to explain to the group of about twelve what saucy could mean other than 'covered in sauce.'

I had a couple glasses of sour, extra-bubbly champagne, a piece of a gelatinous pudding cake, and chopped liver salad. I stood with Marat and observed the group attempt silly made-up conversations while Marion and her instructors corrected them along the way. I felt like I was at a cast party where everyone was playing theater games and comedy sports.

"You wouldn't know it, but most of these people are scientists, some very respected in their fields," said Marat defensively. "She teaches them English so that they can present their work at international conferences."

"Why are you here?"

"She asked me to come. I live in *Akademgorodok* because my wife's parents are researchers."

"Excuse me," said a woman who introduced herself as Melanie Tormé, "My son wants to know what does it mean, '2 legit 2 quit?'"

"I've got to go," Marat whispered as the focus of the room turned towards me. "Come over to my flat for beers sometime."

"Pardon me, pardon me," called another woman, "I would like to tell you something. I am a journalist like you, but I was trained as a mathematician and not as a psychiatrist." She laughed giddily. Such was the overall goofiness of the party. Like the *banya*, the English Club was an oasis from the heaviness of the everyday.

As Marat left, Marion again took me by my hand. "Let me introduce you to our youngest and most beautiful instructor, Lena. She is also my niece. What is your English name today, dear? Lena likes to change her name."

"Today I am Cindi Lauper," she said, and she actually bore a resemblance.

"Oh, but you should have put dye in your hair," objected one of the other students.

"What do you think of the German language?" interrupted another student, a small man in his thirties wearing a bulky green sweater.

"I never thought about it. I'm not crazy about it, I guess."

"I am of the Volga Germans," he said, offended. "Do you know what I thought the first time I heard a man speaking

English? I thought he had a hot little potato in his mouth." Making a face he imitated: "Muh, muh, muh, muh."

"Fascinating," I said. "What do you think about the current Russian Nationalists?"

"We won't have to worry about them," said the Volga German vehemently. He then made a joke in Russian about Jews that I didn't understand. He went on laughing by himself.

Lena, who'd been listening, leaned over and said in a stage whisper, "Stalin sent the Volga Germans to Siberia because he thought they would side with the Nazis in the war. Perhaps he was correct."

Shocked out of his mirth, the Volga German said, "I don't see how that could possibly be funny, Lena."

Cindi Lauper shrugged. "My family was sent to Siberia because of a barrel of pickles, and I think it's funny," she said. "Just ask my Auntie."

Having caught some of what Lena had said, though she was across the room, Marion called, "Let us not spoil our good evening by talking about politics."

"Unless it is the politics of 'A, E, I, O, U,'" cackled Betty Boop next to her, who was by now nearly delirious with glee.

As the evening wound down and those remaining helped clean up, Marion called me over to her. "I have a welcoming gift for you." Out of a plastic bag with a kitten on it, she pulled a gallon jar of pickles. "It's ironic that I have this gift for you. I heard Cindi say something about the pickles." With both seriousness and humor she said, "It may seem like a funny thing, but it's true that I am in Siberia because of pickles. Would you like to hear the story?"

"I only wish I had a camera."

"When I was a little girl in Ukraine, we lived in a house with another family. We shared the basement but divided it for storing food in winter. One time our neighbor moved a barrel of pickles over to our side. My father said to him, 'hey, move that barrel. It's on my side.' They got into a big fight and yelled at each other until finally the neighbor moved his barrel. But after that, he went to the KGB and told them that my father had anti-Socialist views, that he was an enemy of the people because he wouldn't share his storage space. They arrested my father, and we were told that he would be taken to Siberia. We had to follow, of course, but my mother had little money. We ended up, ourselves, going to Siberia in the open jail cars. All the way to Siberia in winter with other women and their children, we rode in jail cars with a bucket for a toilet. I remember my sister, Lena's mother, crying because her hands were so cold. We had nowhere to live when we got here, so we stayed in the jail along with all the other women. Eventually they gave us a cold concrete flat. My sister was always crying because she was so cold."

I left the English club with the pickles in the kitty bag and Ilya's pistol in my pocket.

Chapter 5

It was a warm day for Siberia. Chickadees with yellow-dashed breasts darted across the path I was on. It hadn't snowed more than a few inches since I'd been in Tomsk. The bulk of it comes in December, Alina had told me in one of our increasing number of chats. Nevertheless, while the streets and sidewalks were enameled with hard-packed dirty ice, the yards and lots between buildings were layered deep with snow as clean and white as the day it had fallen. Only paths such as this, like jittery pencil lines, marred the surface of the otherwise blank spaces. In these back areas, Tomsk was transformed into a village. Kids bundled in coats, *shapkas*, and *valenki* played in the snow, sliding down the dips and mounds along the path on pieces of cardboard. Women trundled with bags of groceries.

After working for TV-N for a few weeks now, I'd finally been lent one of the cameras for the weekend. I was out looking for everyday scenes.

I'd spent much of my time at the station working on the letters to the 'Soros people.' I'd write the letter, have Lubomira translate it for Gennadi to approve, and then spend hours and hours trying to get faxes through to Moscow and California. On Friday, I'd run them through the machine dozens of times while Gasha watched amusedly.

Coming into the lobby, Marat shouted, as if bidding me a casual hello, "Connor, fuck you. You've got Alina after me about letting you use the cameras."

"*Foo*, Marat," said Alina, walking behind him, "don't talk to him like that."

"What?" he said. "Don't you watch the movies? That's how they all talk over there. Connor, do you know what we call your actors? We call them fucktors because they say fuck, fuck, fuck."

"Only you say that, Marat, *durak*."

"Okay, come edit *Marketeer* with me," he went on, ignoring her. He then took on a fatherly tone and put his hand on my shoulder. "How long have you been trying to send that fax, motherfucker?"

"He's been here all afternoon," said Gasha.

Marat laughed and imitated me running the pages through the machine. "*Zoop, zoop, zoop,* all day," he giggled with wet lips. "Why do you do this? Vanya has email. You can send them like this," he snapped his fingers.

Annoyed beyond restraint, I snapped back at him, "How am I supposed to know that, Marat, if nobody tells me?" My face burned red. Alina smirked and looked away. "If you've seen me standing here, *zoop, zoop,* with the fax all afternoon, why did you wait until now to tell me? I think I could help out with a lot of things around here, but I just need a little help getting started. Is that too much to ask?"

The bustling office had gone silent. Gennadi stood in his office door.

"Connor," Marat replied with genuine surprise. "Your Russian was perfect just then! We should make you angry more often." With that he slapped me on the back and walked away laughing. "Speak to Ilya about the cameras." Likewise, Alina went away with her hand over her mouth.

Gennadi said something to Marat as he passed. "*Ladno,*" he said, half turning back to me. "I'll speak to Ilya."

A little later, Ilya came to find me in the editing room. "Just tell me when you need a cameraman, and I'll schedule it."

Explaining that I'd rather do the filming myself, I joked, "You trust me with guns but not with cameras?"

He laughed but looked around nervously and quietly shushed me. "The thing is, each cameraman is responsible for his own equipment. They take it home with them, so it won't get stolen. It's not safe here, even locked in the closet. Too many people have keys. But seeing how I have armed you, let me talk to Oleg."

Oleg was less than happy to make arrangements with me, but we agreed that if he needed the camera, he'd come by my apartment. If I went out somewhere, I'd leave a note on the door.

"You shouldn't take the camera out on your own," he warned. "Someone might steal it from you."

"The camera mafia," I kidded, "I'll be ready for them."

He'd shook his head seriously and said, "*Bladt*, if that camera ends up missing..."

After scanning for Mafiosi, I pulled the camera from my duffel bag. Ilya's pistol was nestled in my downy pocket. I lifted the camcorder to my shoulder just in time to witness a quarrel among the children playing along the path. There was a tussle, a whitewash or two. The children allied against a girl who stood jeering at them, musically defiant, as she picked melting snow out of her collar. Cursing like the men at the *banya*, she went on and on and had to gasp for breath between strands of obscenities. She would take them all on, she said.

Then the kids noticed me filming, and the girl suddenly stopped her lambasting. They stood silently for a moment before sulking away, as if reprimanded. I panned across the path to a tiny old wood house buried in snow. I followed the edge of a nearby building up to a balcony where I zoomed in on laundry frozen on the line, flapping stiffly in the breeze like sheets of molded tin. I panned down and found a couple boys on the roof of a shed jumping up to swing on drooping power lines. I thought I was about to capture a terrible accident when I heard the unconcerned voice of someone near me say, "Oh, look, he's taking pictures." Two passing women stopped and smiled at me with rosy cheeks.

I smiled back at them and motioned to the boys, expecting them to holler at the hoodlums, but instead they nodded, smiled on, and continued walking. If the *babushki* weren't worried, I thought, neither was I.

I packed up the camera and walked down to *Lenina Prospect* and then to the river.

On the banks of the Tom, I shot the flat grayness of the panorama, the meandering trace of the iced-over river, the bristling taiga beyond it. I swept the lens upriver and found ice melted where warmer liquid flowed in, steaming slightly. I recognized the smell of sewage. I followed the contour of the far shore downstream and saw a cluster of wood houses, then something like an oil refinery.

Packing up again I headed back to the street, but before I reached the sidewalk a man with a long white beard in a black wool overcoat approached me.

"Good afternoon," he said. "It's a beautiful view from the river bank over there. I saw you were filming."

I tried to explain myself, suddenly nervous.

"Oh, yes," he said amiably. "I heard about you from an acquaintance at M-Bank. It's none of my business, of course. I'm not KGB, if that's what you were thinking. I was only curious. I should have learned my lesson by now," he chuckled. "If you're doing a documentary about Tomsk, you'll want to talk to exiles, people persecuted under the Soviet system. And you'll probably want to speak to a government official, *da*? Also, it would be good to find someone whose life has been turned around by the collapse of Communism." Smiling through the yellowed whiskers around his mouth, he said, "I think I can help you because I am all of those things. Get your camera out, *malchik*.

"I saw you from my office, up there." He pointed to a huge white-block structure that could only be a government building. "I'm a member of the regional Duma." He chuckled, "I've never been married, so I'm always working."

I lifted the camera to my shoulder and looked into the viewfinder. Immediately, the man faced the lens and began to testify.

"My name is Werner Fest," he said. "I am of fifth generation German descent. My family are Mennonites who first migrated to western Prussia, now the Ukraine, for religious reasons. In 1938 my father and grandfather were arrested and exiled. They were not told of their crime, but we know now that it was simply because they were German. Stalin was afraid German migrants would help Hitler, so he exiled them. In 1941 the rest of our family was deported to Kazakhstan. When I was six years old my mother was drafted into the Workers Army and sent off. My father was in a work camp in the Urals at the time. For a while I lived among the invalids and infants at the camp. Everyone else was gone. People around me died of starvation, and I would have as well, except I was put into a school that provided one meal a day. That kept me alive. Later on, my mother deserted the army and came to save me. We went to Tartaria and lived there for three years. My mother worked as a lumberjack. I dug ditches to lay pipes for oil wells."

He stopped for a moment. "I don't know if you think this is strange, for me to tell you all this, but I think these stories need to be told. So, I'll continue. In 1945, my father was released from the labor camp (my grandfather had died there) and was exiled to Novosibirsk. We applied for permission to join him there. After four years, we got it.

"We traveled as prisoners in jail cars packed with people and were locked up in prisons along the way, sleeping on shelves like in concentration camps, and with a barrel for a toilet. When we arrived in Novosibirsk, we each had to sign an agreement saying that we would never leave. Our entire bloodline was to live in exile.

"We lived in camps surrounded by intellectuals. I learned a great deal from them. One of my neighbors spoke sixteen languages, and one man I knew, who always claimed to be Armenian, turned out to be the Iranian ambassador. Stalin had exiled him, too. Eventually the British helped him escape.

"After Stalin died, the laws were eased a bit. I was allowed to enter the university in Tomsk in 1954. Under Khrushchev life was easier, but people were still arrested for so-called subversive activities. I once had a roommate, for instance, who was arrested for an essay he wrote for a contest. The subject was 'what I would like my Komsomol to be like.'" Lost in his remembrance, the old man chuckled, unaware that the cold was turning his nose and what showed of his cheeks crimson. "The young man's suggestions for the Komsomol were more than enough to get him arrested.

"I wished to study astronomy, but my father was against it. 'We have no use for astrologers in the camps,' he said. 'Just look at our neighbor, the lawyer. He is forced to repair shoes to make a living.' Electrical engineering would be a better choice, he thought. All the camps need electricians. I went my own way, which didn't do me much good at first, but I have since become known for my work in astronomy."

I breathed as lightly as possible, directing my steam away from the camera to avoid fogging the lens. I felt my toes numbing through my boots and inadvertently shuffled.

"Would you like to come inside to my office, young documentarian?" suggested Fest. "It's much warmer there."

"I would," I admitted, "but the camera will get fogged up from the temperature change."

"Very well, we'll continue in the cold. After graduation, I worked as a researcher in the university, but I was stripped of the job after I was arrested for an 'immoral endeavor,' section two hundred and fifty-four, article one of the criminal code. I circulated *samizdat* and was known also as a religious man who refuted Soviet atheist propaganda. They told me I was known to have 'bad friends.'

"Like the lawyer-turned-shoemaker, I had to make do. I became a star-gazing beekeeper, and it was while doing this that I contracted encephalitis. I was laid up and unemployed for quite some time." He took a breath and shuffled himself. It was easy to imagine him as a beekeeper.

"After that, my only option for work was to sweep the streets, and it turned out to be my greatest blessing, if you can believe it. I was delivered from my position as the lowest of the low by a fireball from heaven. Yes, literally my friend! On February twenty-sixth, 1984, a huge meteor lit up the Siberian dawn like the sun at noon. I had just started my sweeping, and I was nearly blinded. When it hit the ground, seismic stations throughout the oblast registered an earthquake. There was a great number of electro-magnetic phenomena as well." Fest chuckled, puffing steam through his beard. "Immediately I began to investigate. My family did my sweeping for me, and I traveled around the region collecting eyewitness accounts of the event. After a year of self-funded work, my findings caught the attention of the Moscow Academy of Sciences, and for the next three years they funded my research. Such a windfall for a street sweeper, *da*? But the story doesn't end there, young man, even though I can see you're getting cold from standing still.

"I interviewed fifteen hundred people and learned about much more than the fireball. I came to realize the extent of government repressions in this area. The magnitude was astounding, even for someone who was an exile himself. Of the million people living in the Tomsk oblast, one hundred and three thousand are on record as exiles. Considering the family that accompanied them and children born during the exile, I estimate more than half a million people were involved.

"I wished to find a way to help all those who had suffered. And that is why I decided to get involved in politics when the opportunity arose, when a fireball of another kind called me to it.

"I think we're both getting cold now," he clapped his lapels amusedly, "and the sun is disappearing into Moscow. Did you understand everything?"

I nodded. "What I didn't understand, I got on tape."

"I will only add this small bit," he said, reaching out to stop me from taking down the camera. "The results of my research on the meteor were published, and I spoke at an international conference. The director of the university was forced to cancel the order of my firing, and I retired the broom and went back to the astronomy department. I know one thing for certain: if I had been anything but a street sweeper, I would not have been able to do that research." Smiling broadly, he took off his glove and grasped my hand. "If any of what I've said interests you, perhaps you will come back for the rest of the story. I'll tell you what I'm trying to do in the Duma."

"I'd like that."

"We can talk inside next time. Be careful with that camera," he said as he turned to walk back the way he came. "The city is full of thieves."

Just then I noticed a man in a parked car watching me. Hurriedly, I packed up the camera, the battery nearly dead, and headed toward the busier side of the street.

When I got back to my apartment, I found Oleg waiting for me in his car. He shook his head at me, but seemed amused. "It'll be my head," he said. I took the tape out and handed over the camera.

At the end of a particularly long and frustrating day, Ilya stopped by the editing room to say, "Connor, Let's go drink. You're welcome to come, too, Sergei, but I know you won't." Sergei waved him off.

"What a shit week I've had, *bladt*, a month, a year, *bladt*," Ilya complained as we climbed the stairs to the mezzanine. "I'm fighting with Gennadi, fighting with my father, and breaking up with my girlfriend. I'm taking tomorrow off, except to come in to read the news, so a few friends of mine are coming by, and we're going to do some drinking. There's some kind of jazz club night that we're going to. It's not a real jazz club. It's a business. They rented out a café in *Akademgorodok*. They put on a disco here at the Hobby House every couple of months. They do a good job. Anyway, the jazz is supposed to be good. You can come, but you won't make it to work tomorrow if you do."

We walked into the bar, and Ilya called to the bartender, "*Vot*, let's have the real stuff. I know you've got it."

The bartender shook his head. "We only serve beer and wine. Those are the rules of the center."

"Wine, *bladt*," laughed Ilya. "When was the last time you had any wine in this place? I know you've got a little *voda* back there, *davai*."

The bartender sighed and put a bottle of vodka on the counter. "Four thousand."

"*Davai, davai, davai*," said Ilya motioning for the barman to pop the cap. We took a seat at a table, and Ilya poured. "Our health, *bladt*." He raised a glass.

Ilya's friends arrived shortly, saving me from having to keep up with him shot for shot.

"*Eto* Leto. Watch out for him, he's entirely crazy," Ilya introduced a burly, thick-necked guy in a black military sweater.

"This is my cousin, Alex. He's in for a visit from a village. Did you have a good day in the big city, eh, *bladt*?"

Alex was the same age as Ilya, and the family resemblance was apparent. He was cagey, maybe shy, and looked down when he talked. "I've been taping TV all day," he admitted. "We have shit in the village."

"Ha," laughed Ilya, "what about your wife, *bladt*, hasn't she given you a shopping list?"

Smiling weakly, Alex sat down. "Tomorrow I'll shop. She'll be happy to have something to watch."

Ilya poured the vodka, hollered at the barman for more, and griped about the price. "Can you believe this guy charging me four thousand rubles for what he bought at the kiosk for less than half that?"

"I'm not even supposed to serve it," objected the barman. "I only have it around because you and Sam pester me."

"Sam! We should go get vodka from him. He's always got a bottle in his desk."

"I could get fired for your vodka."

"Congratulations, you're participating in our black economy. Everybody is doing something they're not supposed to do! Otherwise we would all starve."

"Or worse," shouted Leto, flicking a finger against his neck, "We'd have nothing to drink."

Ilya turned back to the table. "Speaking of black economies, Leto, what's your latest scam?"

"Heh," wheezed Leto between shots. "I just bought a truck full of frozen oranges. Two fuckwit Arabs drove it here from Egypt but didn't take the cold into account. They arrived in Moscow to find their cargo frozen solid." He laughed meanly and lit a cigarette. "They thought they'd lost everything. People in Moscow won't buy frozen oranges; why would they when they can get fresh? *Sibirskie* people, on the other hand, we'll buy anything frozen. *Chort*, we buy milk frozen in the shape of bowls. So I buy everything from them cheap, including the truck, and buy them tickets back to their pyramids and orange groves. I shipped the truck on the train. I pick it up tomorrow, and my brother and I will be selling oranges in the bazaar on Saturday."

Ilya laughed and shook his head, "I'll be there with a news crew. Lead story: What are people going to do with frozen oranges?"

"Just let them thaw, *bladt*. They'll be good as fresh."

"They'll be mush, *bladt*," laughed Ilya, deliberately aggravating his friend.

Threateningly, Leto bellowed back, "Then you'll squeeze them for juice, *bladt*. We lack vitamin C out here." The rest of us erupted into laughter. Feigning rage, Leto slammed the table. "My God, that's why we're so pale and sick-looking, there's no vitamin C in vodka."

"*Ne nado,*" mumbled the barman.

The red fading from his face, Leto sat back. "Can you imagine driving a load of fruit through Russia in February and not thinking about the cold? Fucking *Khachiks* are so stupid, *bladt.*"

"What's *Khachiks?*" I asked.

Alex laughed and rolled his eyes.

"*Boje moy,* don't teach him that," said Ilya. "It's a racist term."

"People from the south," said Alex. "Georgians. Uzbeks."

"It's like your word for blacks," said Leto. "Stalin was a *Khachik,*" he added thoughtfully.

Shaking his head as Alex and I laughed, Ilya got up and paid for our drinks. "I'm getting my coat."

Out on Frunze, Ilya led us into a café with no tables or chairs. The patrons, most of them haggard, drunken, and smoking wet-looking cigarettes, stood at chest-high counters while they slurped broth and ate greasy cutlets with battered tin cutlery.

"My favorite place," said Ilya loudly, turning a few heads, "a classy joint." He mumbled to us, "If anyone wants to fight, you guys have my back, *da?*"

"You and your big mouth are on your own," chuckled Leto. "You get me in too much trouble."

We stood in line before a small window in the back wall. A male attendant sat by the money box while a woman in a stained lab coat dished out food. We ordered, paid for, and received bowls of pelmeni. The staff eyed us suspiciously.

"Look at these bowls," sneered Ilya as we found a spot to eat. "I think they wash them in grease instead of water. And look, they're all different, like they stole just one from each flat in the neighborhood. They'd make a set with all the cracked tea cups at the office, eh, Connor?"

I nodded, straightened my spoon, and tested the cloudy grayish broth. Finding it sufficiently infused with pork grease and salt, I gobbled the dumplings and drank the remaining broth from the bowl.

"It might not look like much, but it's not bad," allowed Ilya. "Not as good as the *stalovaya*, but still good. Sometimes I end up eating here several times a week."

We all went back for seconds.

Back out in the cold, the warmth of the broth in our throats had us huffing great clouds of steam. Ilya stepped to the curb and hailed a car. Most anyone would play taxi for a few extra rubles. Ilya slid into the passenger seat and greeted the driver, who wore a *shapka* that looked like an old cat.

"We'll find someone to drive us back," said Ilya as the rest of us climbed in the back. "If not, we'll wake Marat."

"Tell me what you know about jazz, Connor," said Leto as we got under way. I did my best, but noticed the driver looking at me strangely in the rear view.

"What's wrong with him?" he asked Ilya. "Why can't he talk right?"

"*Shto?*" grumbled Ilya. "Nothing's wrong with him, he's American."

"Why do you speak so badly," he called to me.

"He's just learning," said Ilya.

"Learning to speak?" the man said incredulously.

Annoyed, but making a joke of it, Ilya said, "Have you not heard, comrade? There is a whole world of people who neither live in Russia nor speak our lovely mother tongue. In order for them to speak it well, as you seem reasonably able, they have to learn it first."

"Of all the people to pull over to give us a ride, we had to get the stupidest man in all of Tomsk," roared Leto. Laughing, he pounded me on the shoulder, then menacingly punched the back of the driver's seat. Cat-head remained quiet for the rest of the trip.

"*A vot i mafia,*" exclaimed Alex as we arrived, pointing at a row of new Mercedes outside the makeshift club.

"They don't belong to the scientists, *bladt,*" Leto concurred.

Ilya scoffed at the cover charge but paid for us all. "This is our new moneyed class, *bladt.* They want to be exclusive. That's the only reason they charge so much. "

"We should have stopped to buy our own vodka," added Leto.

We descended into the club and towards the music. The institutional setting lent itself to the feeling that we were heading into a church basement for coffee and doughnuts, but I was soothed by the familiar sounds.

"Look at this guy," laughed Leto. "They're speaking his language."

The band was set up on a small stage, standing rigidly as they played. But they sounded good! A number of women were dancing with each other. The men, almost all of them in dark suits, sat at tables with bottles of vodka and smoldering, overflowing ashtrays.

"Look at this," declared Ilya, although more quietly than he might otherwise. "The elite of Tomsk all dressed up in their foreign clothes, perfumed, and drinking imported vodka."

I looked down at my clothes. "Don't worry, Connor," laughed Ilya. "Cousin Alex looks more like a peasant than you. And Leto, he looks like somebody's bodyguard."

In solidarity of our shabbiness, Ilya threw his suit jacket over the back of a chair and rolled up his sleeves. "Let's get drinking."

I bought the first round from a swarthy youth with Groucho-Marx eyebrows at a table in a corner. His imported offerings were lined up on a window sill behind him.

"Look who's here," said Ilya as I returned to the table, pointing out Nikolai and Nastia.

"Power tie."

"Now it's his crazy dancing tie. Look at him go."

Nastia wore a thin black dress with a white belt. Her long brown hair, which she usually wore primly tied up, swung midway down her back as she danced. She had a doll's face and danced somewhat childishly, but she was young and lovely. Nikolai was forty, but remained fit and was striking in his seriousness and confidence.

"That's not the same girl I saw him with before," commented Leto.

"When?" asked Ilya.

"I don't know. It was a while ago."

"No, not the same girl," said Ilya.

"What happened to her? Is she still at the station?"

"Who?"

"Alina," said Leto. "Wasn't he going to leave his wife for her?"

"What are we, *bladt*, gossiping women, *bladt*?"

"What kind of journalist are you?" joked Leto. "We want to know."

"It's a pity, then, Tatyana does entertainment news."

"What's this girl do?"

"Marketing."

The band stopped for a break, and Nastia spotted us. She pulled Nikolai over to our table. Ilya invited them to sit and have a drink. Declining vodka, Nastia chirped, "I'm thirsty."

"*Pivo?*" I offered with a gesture to an open bottle.

She pursed her lips and squinted her eyes in exaggerated offense. "May I have a glass please?" I went to the bar to get her a glass and inadvertently bowed as I put it down. Alex, whom she made uncomfortable with her blatant flirting, turned away to chuckle.

Nikolai leaned across the table to admonish Ilya. "You should have told Connor that he needed to wear nicer clothes for this."

"That's alright," I interrupted cheerfully. "I don't have any nicer clothes." Nikolai turned away as if he hadn't heard me.

"They want their American to be pretty," grumbled Ilya.

The band retook the stage and eased into something slow. Nastia, who had sat girlishly sipping her beer, asked me to dance. "I haven't slow danced since high school," I said. And had it not been for the vodka I'd drunk, it would have been as awkward. I put my arms around her taut waist. She was warm and damp with sweat, though the skin of her arms had just started to cool as she'd rested. Nikolai, I saw, was watching us. Nastia pushed her hips into mine.

"Nikolai is upset that you're not dressed better," she said close into my ear. "He thinks that you should better represent TV-N."

"Nobody told me I was a mascot," I said in English.

"Connor, do you understand me when I talk to you?"

"*Da*, mostly."

"You know you talk like a baby, so it's hard not to treat you like one." Nastia laughed softly and nestled her face against my neck intimately.

After the dance, Nikolai and Nastia left us. He talked to her sternly as they walked away.

Before I could have a drink or take my ribbing from Ilya and Leto, another woman, a stranger, asked me to dance. She was in her thirties, but looked worse for the wear. She spoke to me slowly as she led the way to the floor. I couldn't hear what she said, but I nodded. She danced as if to an entirely different genre of music, swaying and throwing her long dry hair from side to side. There was no matching her, but I kept myself moving.

As if conspiring to entrap me, the band returned to a slow number. The woman threw her arms around my shoulders and exclaimed into my ear, "We don't need language. We can communicate with our dance."

I laughed rudely, pulled away from her, and headed for the bar (as it was). Whatever was still on the table wouldn't be enough. Halfway there, I was caught by the arm. It was Boris looking royal in a black suit.

"Connor, look at this. They're taking you everywhere, banks and clubs, and soon you'll be walking down the halls of our Duma." He thumped me on the shoulder. "But all the while you'll dress like an American college student."

"I came straight from work."

"You should dress better for work," he advised.

"Fuckin' eh, I'm sick of hearing about my clothes," I griped in English. "Besides," I joked, "you brought me to a wedding dressed exactly the same."

He laughed. "What is 'fuck-an-A?' You can tell me later. You should try to impress TV-N. You could end up with your own show. 'Connor Chessick, Live, from Siberia!'"

"I work behind the camera, remember."

"You know, you just missed Mama Luba. She was here. She's been asking about you. She said she was impressed by how much vodka you could drink. I see you're building up your strength some more tonight. Come over here, there's some people I want you to meet." Boris turned me towards his table where a group of seven people watched us expectantly.

I looked over my shoulder to Ilya, who plainly recognized my escort. "Ilya Bilaev, our famous newsman," said Boris. "I know his father. But Connor, these are some of my friends." Continuing to speak in English, he introduced them. "This is Donat. He used to be a university professor, but now he is a successful businessman.

I guess his studies paid off for him." The friends chuckled, and in turn, Boris presented each of the men as 'businessmen.'

I drunkenly mumbled, "Oh, yes, my father is a businessman, too. I am also a businessman whenever I am doing my business." The wives smiled.

"Have a drink," said Boris. His wife, Sveta, easily the prettiest, waved me over to her. She was not the woman he'd introduced me to at the wedding, and it took a moment for me to understand.

"I've been wanting to meet you," said Sveta in halting English. She poured me a glass and switched to Russian. "We play tennis on Tuesdays. Would you like to join us?"

Boris roared in Russian, "Look, he's already making plans with my wife. When they say 'Russian Brides,' Connor, they don't mean women that are already married." He sat and said to her softly in Russian. "I invited him already. I told you that."

The conversation at the table quickly turned to business, and I had a hard time keeping up. Sveta was uninterested, and a bit more drunk than even me. "This woman," she whispered to me about one of the others, swaying slightly near my ear, "watch how she looks toward the coat check by the front door. She's afraid someone is going to steal her new fur coat." She covered her mouth and laughed quietly.

After what I deemed a polite interlude, I excused myself and headed back to the other table. My eyes met Ilya's, and he gave me a gesture of warning. Before I could look around, I was intercepted by the crazy dancer.

"Please dance with me," she begged. The band played an easy listening version of a pop song. She pulled me up to the edge of the stage. "I'm not usually like this," she said into my ear as she embraced me. "Something very bad has happened to me. I know who you are, so I am going to tell you. There was an accident at the nuclear facility. I was exposed. I don't know how long I have left. You should believe me, and you shouldn't drink the water."

She held me tightly, though it was not a particularly slow song.

"What kind of accident?" I asked.

She tucked her chin against my chest and sobbed.

"Okay, well, you take care of yourself," I said in English. It stunned her somehow. She looked at me expectantly, but I again left her there and walked away.

"That woman has mistaken you for her husband," chuckled Leto when I returned to the table. "She has to sleep with you before she can pester you like that."

I sat down and told them what she'd said.

"She's drunk," Leto laughed.

"*Bladt,* it wouldn't be the first time, *bladt,*" spat Alex who had gotten sloppy since I last saw him. "I already have to test all of my fucking cows."

"We would have heard about it," said Ilya as if he didn't want to be bothered. "I'll have someone look into it, but I can hear the plant spokesman now, 'Is that what you call a source, a drunk woman on the dance floor?'"

"If she bothers you again, I'll slap her," said Leto, relishing the idea.

"Who are you going to slap?" asked Nastia as she staggered up to sit with us.

"No one," mumbled Leto.

"You'd better not let any of your mafia friends start a fight here, Ilya," she slurred.

"Who's mafia?" said Leto, insulted.

"This is a place for the successful people in town," she went on haughtily. Turning to me, she said, "Connor, tell me something." She smiled, her catty mouth full of fangs. "You and Alina seem to be becoming friends. Do you like her?"

"For that, Nastia, you'll have to go dig in the snow," I said, trying to be clever. No one understood.

"My God, we're back in school," chuckled Ilya, covering for me.

"I like her," exclaimed Leto. "Tell her I like her."

She scowled at him. "I don't know why you're here. *Poshol ti.*"

"I love you, *devushka*," he said through pursed lips, and we all laughed at her.

Suddenly Nikolai was at her side apologizing for her. "Come on now, Nastia, don't be unpleasant." Taking her by the arm, he gently pulled her to her feet. Looking at me, he said softly, "I'm so sorry. She's had a bit too much to drink."

"Why are you apologizing?" said Nastia. "I didn't say anything. I didn't tell him anything."

"*Ne nado. Ne nado,*" Nikolai hushed her softly.

"Wait," she said as he started to lead her away. "I want to dance with Connor again. Connor, you want to dance with me, *da?*"

Attempting to be conciliatory, I repeated Nikolai's words. "*Ne nado. Ne nado.*"

"Ridiculous, *bladt,*" growled Ilya once the pair was out of earshot.

I got up to go to the bathroom. Standing before the urinal, I wondered if Yeltsin had to hold his nose at the pissoir in the Kremlin. I worked on translating the question but was interrupted by the guy next to me.

"Those people you were talking to aren't good people," he said gruffly.

"I work with them."

"Not those people. Vodopyanov's people," he said. He stood behind me as I washed my hands. I watched him in the mirror. He was drunk and scruffy-faced. He wore the ubiquitous hoodlum's athletic suit. A bodyguard, maybe.

"Boris is an associate," I remarked, using a term I'd picked up that evening.

"Maybe he's alright, but not those others," he conceded as if not wishing to offend me. "I'm Emile. You're the American. Why don't you come to my table for a drink? There's something I want to show you."

I followed him out of the bathroom, through the café, to the entrance to the kitchen. He held the door and flipped his head for me to go in. I looked to see if Ilya or Boris were keeping an eye on me, but they were lost to me in the dark and cigarette smoke.

Around a table that had been pulled into the middle of the small kitchen sat three black-coated mafia types. On the table sat a large bottle of vodka and a plate of what had been nicely sliced and arranged pieces of apples, sausage, and bread.

"These two are Sergei," said Emile, gesturing to the larger two men. "They call him the Turk," he said of the third. He fit the description. "But you should call him Mr. Turk," chuckled Emile.

"Never Comrade Turk," joked one of the Sergei's, slurring his words.

"He's the one that set this all up tonight," Emile went on. "It's him raking in the profits tonight. But he doesn't want to play host. He is one of the most successful businessmen in all of Tomsk, all of Siberia. Maybe he misses his desert, but he is doing well in our dunes of snow."

The Turk scowled. "This is the VIP section," he said humorlessly. "Sit and have a drink."

Emile poured me a hefty shot. "Have a snack. Not even a dog drinks vodka without a snack." The other men nodded: *Pravda.*

"Out there is the kennel," I joked. No one laughed. Maybe I had the wrong word.

"He was talking with Vodopyanov's people," said Emile as if issuing a statement to superiors.

"Yuppies," said the Turk in English and smiled coolly.

"*Da,* but they also introduce themselves as businessmen," I drunkenly replied to scowls around the table.

"Go ahead and eat," said Emile. "Put something in your mouth. I think you've had too much to drink. You're not used to this, eh?" he smiled.

"You work for TV-N," said the Turk. "You're lucky to work there, lots of beautiful women."

"The women were all over him on the dance floor," reported Emile dutifully.

"I'd like to get to know some of those women at TV-N myself," the Turk intoned lewdly.

"Are you a businessman, too, Emile?" I asked.

"No. Look at this." He pulled up his sleeve, revealing a tattoo. "See this emblem? I am a Blue Beret." He turned solemn. "I was stationed near Gorno Altaisk. It's near Mongolia." He shook his head sorrowfully. "There I had to shoot criminal people. It was necessary, but still it is a pity."

"Rambo," said one Sergei, who was barely conscious.

"You have Green Berets," said the other. "Do you know about Russian martial arts? Show him, Emile," he laughed shrilly. "Emile can break your neck with one finger. He could kill you with your credit card."

"I do a pretty good job of killing myself with my credit card," I said in English. Sergei shut his yap. The Turk coughed a short laugh.

"Come with me," said Emile, getting to his feet. I smiled at him, unsure. He looked as though he was disappointed in my behavior. He pinched the shoulder of my shirt in his woody fingers and pulled. "I want to talk to you in private. Don't worry."

Leading me back into the bathroom, he turned and declared, "I like you. I won't let anything happen to you tonight. You can feel free. This is my gift. The Turk is easily offended, but I won't let anything happen to you. There's something I want to tell you that I couldn't say at the table." He crossed his arms over his chest and looked at me with a furrowed brow. "I have become aware that I am a dissident. I've always known it in my heart, even when

I was in the military. I see that everything is in the wrong direction."

I nodded as attentively as I could manage. I put my hands in my pockets and concentrated on not swaying. "The people in this club, the Turk, they are the agents of wrong thinking." He went on, but it was lost on me. After a few minutes, the Turk came into the bathroom.

"What are you talking about?" he demanded. He held one hand straight down at his side as if concealing a knife. Emile took a step forward, but at that moment the door again swung open. Boris stood holding it. The other men stiffened.

"Connor, my friend, we have an interview to do," he said casually with barely a look at the other two.

I gave the Blue Beret a quick wave as I followed Boris back into the club. He gestured back seriously with thumbs up.

The band was taking a break. Boris turned back to me and said, "You know, Connor, in a place like this, you have to be careful who you associate with. Everyone will want to know you, but you have to remember that they may also want something from you." I nodded drunkenly.

Boris laughed. "I guess he's not so much of a Mohammedan as they say, since he seems to have had quite a bit of vodka."

"Are we really doing an interview? I'm drunk."

Continuing his chuckle, he said, "You seem alright to me. Your Russian is better when you are drinking. Come, it will only take a couple minutes. The TV-N people will be glad for the publicity."

"And you, too."

"Of course, me too. You know me —I am a businessman."

"I don't think I know what that means here."

"Then I can tell you, Connor. To people here, Capitalism is all the same thing. You are selling things. You are making deals, taking advantage of the other guy. These are the things you do to be a businessman, right? What does it matter what you sell? So we call everyone a businessman, no matter what he sells. I know it's not true to you, but this is how Russians think. Westerners laugh about the idea of a Russian businessman, like we don't know what it is. They think that the Russian businessman is the same as the mafia, and in some ways it's true. But who is an outlaw when there are no laws? You had your robber barons in America. Do you understand me? Maybe you are too drunk to do an interview," he laughed.

We sat down at a table with a jittery little man in a pinstripe suit with a meager mustache and a large tape recorder slung over his shoulder.

"I am from the state radio station," he said apologetically.

"It is the only radio station in town, after all," laughed Boris. "Until maybe TV-N goes into radio."

The man laughed nervously, "Heh, maybe we should get started, Boris Mikhailovich, before the band comes back." He turned on his recorder and put on his radio voice. "We are here at the opening of one of Tomsk's newest cultural locations." He went on to introduce Boris, "one of our city's most knowledgeable and successful businessmen," and me, "TV-N's American advisor." Boris got a chance to pitch his exchange business with Pavel and gave out a phone number. He then moved on to me.

"We thank Boris Mikhailovich for this rare opportunity to discuss cultural affairs with an American friend. First off, can you tell me, is it common in America to find people wearing suits and those dressed as you are, in jeans, at the same party?"

"*Da*," I said. "It's very common."

"Jazz is very casual in the United States," put in Boris. "After all, it is not some kind of music created by the wealthy. It's the music of smoky bars and clubs, not of opera houses."

"Bill Clinton plays sax, not George Bush," I said. The interviewer nodded eagerly and peppered me with several other inane questions, to which I gave equally incoherent answers. The state reporter said, "As one final question, we understand that smoking has become very unpopular in America. Is that true?"

"*Da,*" I answered, "Even a dog doesn't smoke."

Boris laughed so hard he started to cough. The band was going back on, and the interview was over.

Chapter 6

I was puny-chested in the mirror. I was drunk out of my mind. I posed with Ilya's gun. I cocked it, put a *bolonchik* in the chamber. Marat and Ilya had brought me home a few minutes prior.

By the end of the night at the jazz club, I'd passed out on the bathroom floor. Emile, the Blue Beret, had found me. Clicking his tongue like an old woman, he'd thrown me over his shoulder.

"I can walk," I burbled as he carried me through the club and outside into the parking lot.

I heard Ilya. "There he is, *bladt*. Alex has gotten plastered and has disappeared. We thought we'd lost you, too." He instructed Emile to put me in the backseat of a waiting car.

"I can walk," I protested. I started to shiver as he carried me across the frigid lot. He rolled me off his shoulder and onto the ice-cold vinyl of the seat. I heard Marat's spluttering laugh.

"Connor, you are drunk, motherfucker."

"Is that your other friend?" asked Emile. I sat up. At the edge of the lot was a man attacking a tree, punching the trunk with full force.

"Look at that idiot," laughed Marat. "This was worth getting woken up for now."

Alex was coatless, his pants soaked up to the knees. There was blood in the snow around him. "*Eob tvayu mat,*" groaned Ilya.

They had to wrestle Alex into the car. Leto held him down, but he still managed to hit me once. I still had the blood from his mangled fists on my face.

I put down the gun and watched myself take swigs of orange pop from a plastic bottle. It was supposed to be mango-flavored but tasted strangely medicinal. I'd been making a big deal about not drinking the water and had made Marat stop at a kiosk.

"This is all fine," I told myself. "I'm out in the world." With that, I picked up the gun, switched off the safety, and headed for the balcony. In my long johns and bare feet, I stepped outside, finger on the trigger. I took a deep cold breath and fired the gun. The open door sucked the smoke and cold air back at me. I felt the mist of gas. I closed my eyes, but it was too late. My lungs seized. I couldn't cough. My eyes burned, my nose and throat, my sinuses. I ran inside and threw myself into the tub. Panicking, I turned on the water. I couldn't breathe. I threw up. The drain clogged. I wretched but no breaths came. I passed out.

I came to moments later, choking on the water that was filling the tub. My sudden movement broke the clog and the orange-tinted slop receded. I scrubbed off and went shivering to bed.

The next day I laid sick in bed. I had no phone, so I couldn't call the station. As much as I needed it, I didn't drink water. The day after was Saturday, and around noon I heard a knock at the door. Rushing to put on clothes, I answered expecting to find Marat smiling and ready to joke about my condition.

It was Alina. "So you're alive. I thought I'd make sure," she smiled. "I brought you some orange juice. I hear you're not drinking our water these days." She stepped inside. "I'm sorry, I shouldn't make fun. I'm terrible. How are you feeling, *malchik*?"

I croaked a dry-mouthed response and left her to take off her coat while I went to brush my teeth and wash my face.

"*Foo*," she called, "it smells like a drunk tank in here. It's coming out of your pores. Marat's been going on and on about how drunk you were, that someone had to carry you to the car."

"I didn't have to be carried," I grumbled. "The guy wouldn't put me down. Did Ilya make it in for the news yesterday?"

"*Da*, only he didn't look too good. His cousin hit him, and we had to put makeup on him." She laughed lightly. "All the old ladies were calling in to find out what happened to their nice little news man. Ilya's only fans are people that don't know him, of course." She paused. I heard her looking around. "I'm mad at

Ilya," she said from the kitchen. "He should have known better than to let you drink so much. I'm sure they were egging you on."

"I lost track."

I heard her walk into the middle room. "*Boje Moy*, Connor, what are you doing with this?" I'd left the pistol on the windowsill.

I explained.

"Giving guns to drunk Americans," she joked. "Ilya must be crazy."

"I don't think I'll be drinking vodka for a while," I said, coming out of the bathroom. Alina had thrown her coat over my rocking chair and was wearing a loose-knit purple sweater and jeans.

"Are you going to sip compote with the ladies?" she smiled mockingly.

"Beer only."

"*Molodets.* Why don't you go have a big glass of German orange juice first?" she said, pointing to the kitchen where she'd placed a liter box on the table. "Citrus grows rampant all over Bavaria, we're to understand," she smirked. "My goodness, your eyes are red," she said when I came towards her. "Why don't you get dressed, and I'll take you out for some air?"

She pulled me into a beautiful, crystalline day. My head swam in the brightness. "Come this way. We'll go over to Kirova Street."

Two steps behind her and taking measured breaths, I concentrated on remaining upright on the icy path. She looked back at me. "When I left my apartment this morning I wasn't sure if I would come see you. Marat told me where you live, but I figured we all knew why you were out. It was no mystery. But then I saw what kind of day it was, and while I was out shopping I thought about how you were all alone and not feeling well." She turned and continued walking. "I thought about how when I was out sick from work a couple of months ago, no one bothered to come check on me. I've known most of the people at TV-N since we were children. They know I live alone, that my family isn't close. Anything could have happened to me, but no one came to see. So while I'm shopping for kasha and chicken this morning, I suddenly felt sad." She paused before turning back again with a smile. "So it's a mission of pity. I've saved you from depression. Some days make you do things."

A few steps further on, she said, "I was thinking. You've come all this way. It must be for something. Here you are in our little city in Siberia. We don't know what you want, but we hope you find it." She turned, smiling bashfully. "Have you eaten? You seem weak. Connor, you have to eat," she chided, evidently getting a kick out of mothering me.

She led me on a shortcut between two buildings, and we came to a lively wide boulevard. Bundled and careful on the ice, people shuffled haltingly. A stiff rumbling tram arrived, slicing up the middle of the street beneath its hovering wires. Vendors were set up around the tram stops at the intersections. Their breath hung still in the air around them and their boxes and bags.

"Let's get some ice cream," called Alina happily. Crossing to the tracks, we walked up to an old woman with an old cooler at her feet. "Two, please, *babushka*."

"*Morodjenoye*," I attempted as we unwrapped the rock-hard ice cream bars. Alina laughed at my bad pronunciation.

"*MorRRR-RRRodjenoye*," she rolled her tongue at me playfully. "You must think it's crazy to have ice cream in the middle of winter, but you're not yet thinking like a Soviet. Consider the practicality! Do you think that in the summer heat the *babushki* can lug around freezers?" she joked. "We're used to having it in the winter. I don't even think about it in summer. Mexicans eat peppers in the heat; in Siberia we have ice cream for the cold."

We walked as far as Lenina Street and then came back up Kirova on the sunny side. The cold air and the boost to my sugar level had livened me up. Alina and I slipped easily into conversation as we did most days at work.

"*Vot*, here is my chicken," said Alina suddenly as she spotted a vendor with a stack of suitcase-sized boxes. The top one was cut open to display a jumble of frozen chicken legs. Each box was marked with red, white, and blue stickers reading 'USA Food Aid. Not for sale.'

"Look how enormous your American chickens are! We hear it's because they're full of antibiotics. Some people won't eat it, but I'm not afraid." She turned and smiled at me. "You seem to be alright." The vendor placed four fat legs in a bag for her.

"We survive because we only eat the white meat."

"Ha, the dark meat is healthier. Do you know what we call these? *Nogi Busha*. Bush Legs!" Both of us and the vendor laughed, puffing up a great cloud of frozen vapor.

Seeing us, an old woman sitting nearby on an downturned pail called, "What a nice-looking couple. Why don't you buy some pine nuts? They're good for the man and the woman."

"*Babushka*, we're not yet a couple," said Alina, pretending to be offended, and with dramatic haughtiness she added, "For your assumption we'll walk on."

"Don't punish me, *devushka*," pleaded the granny. "I only saw you two laughing together."

Smiling, Alina told me, "Connor, buy some pine nuts from this nice *babushka*." Now grimacing as if she was being made fun of, the old woman pulled off her thick knitted mittens and scooped me a newspaper cone of the smooth brown kernels from a sack she held propped between her knees.

Standing in the sun, Alina demonstrated how to crack the seeds. "Here, like this." Her cheeks were flushed, and I watched her soft beautiful lips form around the tips of her fingers as she cracked the tough shell with her front teeth and worked the seed out of its casing.

"This is the nicest street in Tomsk," I said.

"Of course it is," she laughed, "I live here. Look, my building is right across the street. I wasn't going to tell you that I live so close to you. I didn't want you expecting me to do your shopping for you. But seeing how we've had such a nice little walk, why don't we go back to my place for tea, or maybe some beers?"

"I don't know if I feel up to beers."

"Sometimes the kiosks over here have American and European beer. I don't drink beer often, but I love it. It might make you feel better. Whenever we're on the big company *pyanka* all the men keep a bottle of beer under their beds for first thing in the morning. Come on, Connor, we'll buy a couple. First we can have tea to warm up. Here, I'll buy a chocolate bar to have with tea." She zipped over to a line of kiosks. "Do you know this one, Molson? Let's get two. No, let's get four. Two each."

We scuffed up the stairs of Alina's apartment building. She told me that she and her neighbor had invested in a barred door to go over their end of the hall. With a flourish of prison sounds, she unlocked it and slammed it behind us.

"Are you ready to meet my jealous boyfriend? I have to go make sure he's not in a bad mood. Wait right here. Don't be scared, poor boy."

The dog was locked in the bathroom when she let me in. She'd have to chain him to the door knob for introductions, she said.

The apartment was tiny, half the size of mine. There was a small kitchen, an all-in-one bathroom, and a single room not nearly big enough for all it contained. Rising up from patterned rugs on the floor were two tall bookcases, neatly arranged but completely loaded. There was a large wardrobe with boxes stacked on top of it. There was a small desk, two chairs, and a foldout couch draped with embroidered cloth. The room was decorated with pictures and photos and lacquerware. Still, it wasn't cluttered. Everything had its place.

"It's like a warehouse, *da*? My mother and my sister went to Belarus to live with my aunt, so I got all the family belongings. Someone has to keep them, the photos and books and memorabilia. This is everything. It's a little bit sad. I try not to think about it. I can be such a silly girl. But you know, it's unusual for a woman my age to have her own apartment. I'm lucky to work at TV-N." Alina started for the kitchen. "I'll put water on, then we can introduce you to Otto."

Otto was a Giant Schnauzer. She led him out of the bathroom with her hand over his eyes and wrapped his lead around the door knob. "It's been a while since we had a visitor, *da*, Otto? I have to tie him because I can't hold him back. He hates it, but sometimes he'll take a dislike to a man and go right after him. Look at him, he's jealous. Let's get this over with."

Otto gave my hand a single brusque sniff and looked me in the eye. "He's an arrogant dog," she said delightedly. "He seems alright with you, not threatened, I guess," she said ironically. "Is it alright if I let him go?" Otto stood stiffly at her side even once unhitched.

"Have you visited a proper Russian household yet, Connor?" I told her about Pavel and his ABBA CDs. "I'm a more traditional person. I'll show you how it's done. First, while I'm making tea, you can have a look at my bookshelf. I think you'll be surprised by all the American authors I have."

Otto stood guard as I perused the library. I tried to pat him, but he moved back and continued staring, daring me to meet his eyes. "What are you, some kind of macho poodle?" I muttered.

"Otto, stop it. Go to your bed," Alina commanded when she returned with a tea tray. Dutifully, Otto sat on a pillow in the corner. "What do you think of my flat? It's cozy, I think. Otto keeps me company."

"Have you read all those?" I asked as we sat together on the couch.

"Naturally," she said. "Now for the photo album. I don't usually show it to anyone, but since you've come so far..." Her albums were beneath the couch, and for a flash as she crouched and fished them out, she appeared childish, vulnerable. "I won't bore you with everything. Here are some of my family, my mama, my sister. They just sent me this one. That's my aunt. My mama and her sister are very close. I hope my sister and I will be like that someday, but for now we barely speak. She's six years younger than me. I always thought of her as a baby, but she's a young woman now. Unfortunately she's got my mother's nose," she joked, but then said seriously, "and she wears what everyone else wears. I can't blame her, she's still young. You can see here how much bigger our old flat was."

"There are no pictures of you."

"No. I've taken them out. These are the ones I like to look at. Here's some pictures of my friends on a hiking trip we went on. I won't bore you with any more of these. What I wanted to show you was this." She traded the binder in her lap for a much older one. "I've only had this for a year. I never knew about it before." She opened the book. The pages were yellowed and brittle, but the photos were carefully laid out and held in place with paper corners. "Don't tell anyone about this," she said suddenly, having a second thought, "especially at the station, okay?" The first photo, an old cracked black and white, was of a group of finely dressed people posing in front of a horse and carriage.

"It looks like the last photo of the Romanovs," I said.

"Not quite, but it turns out my great-grandfather was a count. After the revolution he was thrown in jail. Everything was confiscated." Slowly flipping through the pages of old gray photographs, she continued, "The whole family was sent to Siberia. My grandfather was in jail for a while, too. He walked with a limp because of beatings by the police. He was killed by a train when my father was little. They called it an accident, but the police had done it. My father grew up mostly in institutions. He almost never got to see his mother. They wouldn't let her take him out.

"All of this was hidden from my sister and me. I remember my mother being upset with me for always asking questions. She was afraid people would find out about us, that we were aristocracy. It was something they could use against us. She was terrified of the police and the KGB. I asked her why she didn't tell me after the collapse and she said, '*Nu*, you never know what's going to happen. They might start it all over again.'" Alina laughed and said slyly, "But it does mean that I am a *princessa*." She put her hand over her heart and batted her eyes at me. "I don't really feel anything for it. It's a bit of trivia, that's all. Still, it's interesting. Think of all they lost. We never thought of that, you know, when we were Young Pioneers.

"It explains a lot about my father. You hear about orphans now and how terrible it is for them not to have love from a parent, that it does something to them and part of them dies. They become incapable of loving. It's what happened to my father, I think. I can see him like that. He never loved me, I know that. I knew it even when I was a little girl. I told a neighbor that once, and she slapped me. 'You shouldn't think such things,' she said. 'It's impossible for parents not to love their children.' But it's not, and the unloved child knows it from the start. It's like food, *da*? You can't pretend to feed someone. That same neighbor was upset because her own sister, who lived with her, used to say that she didn't love her son. She would say it out loud right in front of him when she was drunk. She'd say she didn't understand it herself, but she just never loved him. That was the first boy I went to bed with." She looked up at me. I raised my eyebrows, and she blushed. "Actually, that's not true. I never did. Although I always thought I would, since we had something in common. I was just making sure that you understand me. I don't want to be saying all this and have you not understand. Or maybe it would be better if you didn't," she said coyly.

"Where's your father now?"

"He still lives in Tomsk, but we rarely see each other. Once I passed him on the street and pretended not to recognize him. He saw me, too, but didn't say anything. We were giving each other a test, and we both failed. He wasn't bad to us. He wasn't an alcoholic. He rarely drinks. I've only seen him really drunk once or twice, and he never did anything. He just smiled at us in his way and went to bed. He has this certain kind of smile... Enough of that," she said. "It's depressing. Ha, just like most Russian traditions." She clapped shut the album and dropped it on the floor next to her. Otto jumped up from his pillow in alarm. "I don't know why I told you all that. Are you ready for a beer?" She went into the kitchen to fetch the drinks and glasses. "This is Canadian beer. Have you ever had it?" We poured and clinked glasses. "It's bubblier than our beer. I like it better."

"I suppose Marat told everybody at the station about the other night?" I asked.

"Don't worry about him," she said, taking a sip. "Nobody takes him seriously. He makes stupid jokes, but Marat is a good guy."

"He did drive us home. And Alex bled all over his car."

"*Da*, we heard all about it."

"Did they tell you why I didn't want to drink the water?"

"Yes, I heard all about the woman you danced with. Ilya wants to go out to the *combinat* with a geiger counter, but he can't find the one we had at the station. Marat claims Alex stole it because it went missing at the same time he had to begin testing his cattle. Ilya is so angry at this cousin for hitting him, he says he's going to go out to the village and beat a confession out of him himself. So you can see, it was an eventful day around TV-N, despite that you weren't around for me to talk to."

"Well at least it's not us being gossiped about," I hazarded.

"Not so. I don't know what you said to Nastia, but she's continuing to spread rumors. What did you tell her? What did she tell you about me? You know we don't get along. She's the office slut. She's slept with nearly everyone. Please excuse my language," she joked, holding her fingers over her lips. "She's with Nikolai now just to try to get more money and a better position. What bothers me is that it's working. I should talk to Gennadi about it. That bitch is my sworn enemy. Nikolai and I used to be close friends, but now she's got her hooks in him." She stopped and smiled. "Now that I've sworn in front of you, you know what kind of bad woman I am."

"What did Nastia tell people?"

Pausing, Alina answered, "She says she asked you if you like me and you said *da*."

"*Da*."

By the time we finished the beers, it was getting dark. "Otto wants his chicken kasha," she said. "Do you remember the way home?"

At the door, she asked me, "Tell me, Connor, what is your impression of me?"

Without time to compose and translate, I stuttered in phrasebook Russian, "You are a very *sympatichnaya devushka*." She was unsatisfied. Her look said 'don't disappoint me.' Taking an awkward moment in the doorway to come up with a more Russian answer, I told her, "You are a romantic, but..." I halted, unsure if my words, "but a fatalistic one."

She sighed now and smiled. "I guess you are getting to understand me, even if your Russian is bad." She came out to lock the cell door behind me. "*Poka*."

Early in the week, Boris picked me up after work to play tennis with him and his wife. I had a lot of work to do but declining didn't appear to be an option. He showed up in a new Lada 4X4.

"Fitness," cried Sveta as I got into the car. "Tennis."

"*Da*, fitness. Okay, Tennis."

She laughed, "*Otlichnaya*."

"How do you like my new car, Connor?" called Boris "Only it isn't new. Not quite. It's re-imported. Do you know what it means? It's my new business."

"It's a Czech Lada," giggled Sveta as we pulled away.

"I can buy any Russian-made car in the republics or Eastern Bloc states and bring it back into Russia without paying tax. The Russian plants can't keep up with demand, but the tax on imported cars is very high. So I can make a good profit. You see? Re-importing and re-selling," he chuckled.

"We go to the *Sportzal*," chirped his wife in English.

"Speak Russian with him, Svet."

We pulled up to a large gymnasium complex that was at once impressive, and like most things in Tomsk at that time, dismally run down.

"This used to belong to the town, but now it's private," Boris told me proudly.

"Who owns it now?" I asked as we got out of the car.

"A rich factory," said Boris dismissively. Catching sight of my boots, he said, "I guess you will play in your *valenki*." Both he and Sveta wore new running shoes and tracksuits beneath their coats.

The security guard at the front desk recognized Boris and waved us through. The place was nearly empty. We entered a small court with painted wood floors where a small man in his forties dressed in a worn tracksuit bearing CCCP across the front was waiting for us.

"Connor, I am pleased to introduce you to the tennis champion of Tomsk, Vasily Ivanovich."

His smile revealing a steel crown or two, the man energetically shook my hand. "Are you a tennis fan? We'll have a good session today. We can play doubles, *da*? Boris Mikhailovich and his lovely wife against you and me. We'll have an excellent session."

It was chilly in the gym, but Boris and his wife stripped off their tracksuits down to coordinated shorts and polo shirts. I took off my boots and socks. Sveta stretched. Boris whistled.

We played badminton, not tennis. Valsily Ivanovich took turns with us on the court to warm up. He merrily and immaculately popped the birdie from one side of the court to the other, making us run while shouting encouragement as if coaching Olympic hopefuls. "Wonderful, perfect, you're really improving, Boris Mikhailovich. Excellent form, Svetlana Vodopyanova."

"Birdie!" shouted Sveta as she dove for it.

"Ha, ha, *molodets*," Ivanovich shouted at me as I pounded my heels across the gym. "Be careful, there's a large crack in the floor. Here, let's switch sides."

"Ha, ha, fitness!" cawed Sveta.

We took sides to play doubles. Boris narrowed his eyes and rocked back and forth. Sveta pounded her racket with her hand and bounced on the balls of her feet.

"Look at this, Connor," shouted Vasily Ivanovich with a wide grin. "They think they can beat us." He clenched his racket in his fist and shook it at the ceiling. "But we're unstoppable."

"Birdie," squealed Sveta.

Vasily Ivanovich was indeed unstoppable. With precision unimaginable with a floating plastic doohickey, he conducted Boris and Sveta's workout around the court like a maestro. And despite him occasionally allowing me to mess things up, he politely trounced them.

"He's the only Russian I've seen smile as much as an American," said Boris as we got in the car after the match. "He has reason to smile. I pay him well. And he likes to beat me," he laughed. "So, Connor, Sveta and I would like to invite you to our home for something to eat. What do you think?"

When we arrived at their flat, Boris swung his Lada into an armored garage. Likewise, the entrance to his stairway was fortified with welded sheets of iron. As we climbed the stairs we heard an ominous howling above.

"*Eto*, Kirby," grinned Sveta. Kirby was a Great Dane and was very excited to see his family home. He wasn't as thrilled about me, however, and took my hand and most of my forearm into his mouth when we were introduced.

"He's pleased to meet you," chirped Sveta.

"He needs to chew you a bit," chortled Boris. "If he decides he likes you, he'll give you back your arm."

Grinning nervously, I wriggled free and wiped drool on my pants.

The apartment was furnished contemporaneously, with much leather, and had a TV and VCR in every room. The flat was on the fourth floor but the windows were barred and wired with alarms nonetheless. "What makes people think thieves don't know how to use ladders?" said Boris as he gave me a tour.

"This is Sveta's room," he said in the kitchen and opened the fridge.

"*Foo*," scolded Sveta, waving him away.

"Now it's time we undo some of that fitness with beer," Boris announced, heading for the living room. With a huff he dropped himself onto a big soft couch and Kirby joined him. "Yes, Kirby, oochie woochie." He leaned forward and snatched the remote from the coffee table. "Nosie wosie," he said, avoiding the dog's reaching mouth. "I buy all these things, and the dog wants to chew them. He's not impressed. So tell me something new, Connor. What interesting things have you been up to at the station?"

I told him about my meeting with Fest.

Boris nodded silently for a moment. Sveta arrived with a tray of beer and snacks for us, then returned to the kitchen. "Golden Rooster," said Boris, taking a drink. "I imported this from Czechoslovakia along with my Lada four-ex-four. Nobody else has it." He flipped the channels. "Here's your TV-N. But about Fest," he said. "I don't know if he is a scientist or a lucky street sweeper who saw a falling star." He chuckled, crunching peanuts, but he was obviously displeased. "He certainly hasn't noticed our falling economy, our rising prices. People have to do what they can to make money. They can't sit on their hands and do nothing and shiver and starve while the niceties of our new economy are worked out here in Tomsk. It's crazy, of course. That's not how it's going to happen. He can pass ridiculous laws. Why not? We already have thousands of them, but there is no way to enforce these laws, so they have no use. He doesn't see the big picture. Fest is not fast; he is slow." Boris laughed. "As you can see, the man boils my blood a little bit."

He sat back and watched the TV until Sveta came in with plates of food and laid them out on the coffee table.

"You know what a client of mine said to me?" asked Boris, smiling again and nodding for me to help myself to snacks. "His wife didn't want to send their boys to camp in America because they wouldn't be used to the food. 'They won't get our good Russian food,' she said. 'I won't have them eating pizza and white bread, they'll come back flabby and covered with zits.'"

"*Zitki?*" asked Sveta, then laughed.

"Go and talk to Fest, Connor. I understand his appeal for you, but understand something, the man doesn't understand how things really are. He lives in a dream, no, an ideology, but an uninformed one. It's strange, don't you think, that a person who was harmed by our previous ideology is so quick to try to replace it with a new one? I understand he wants to make a difference, but he goes about it in all the wrong ways. The guy thinks of himself as a prophet or something. Maybe that's why you like him, Connor," Boris chuckled. "He reminds you of another prophet. He looks like Marx but talks like Christ. You Americans are too religious for your own good. What he says sounds good to those that don't know, but it's not reality. Of course, you don't really know what's happening here, either.

"I'm more on his side than I am on the side of the mafia, but you have to understand that the mafia has its place in all this. It always has. The truth is that the old black market system is closer to where we need to go than is our existing legal system or business laws. Capitalism is a natural structure, yes? The systems of the black market are still black, of course, but the obstacles to success that are there are related to the market. In our legal system, the obstacles are everywhere and exist for no reason other than they are still related to a dead ideology. Do you understand me?"

I told Boris that I'd only discussed Fest's past with him so far. "Then I've given you a primer on him." He laughed then took a long drink. "These are the things he's going to talk to you about, reforming the reforming and so forth. The man is a hero for what he's done to help exiles, but he should stick to that. You'll need an experience to offset what you'll hear for him. Maybe I'll think of something."

Just then the door rang, and Kirby bristled to attack.

"Who's there, Kirby? Who's there?" Sveta sang.

"It's your uncle Donat, Kirby," Boris chimed in.

Sveta got up to throw the multitude of bolts on the door. "That mutt barks like heavy artillery," said a man in the hall.

"Let's have your coat," said Sveta cheerfully. "Have you had dinner?"

"Donat," Boris hailed the visitor from the couch.

"Borya," he hollered back, "call off your dog and your wife."

Laughing, Boris stood to welcome his guest. Donat was a big man with a small round head that was evenly carpeted with bristling salt and pepper hair. He had a wide jack-o'-lantern grin and devilishly arched eyebrows, although his protruding belly softened the effect.

"Look here," said Boris, taking Donat's leather coat from his wife, who was about to hang it in a closet. "It's another one of your friend Anton's coats. I bought it for him. He had me looking everywhere for a brown coat."

"Mafia wear black coats," Donat zipped back, smiling. "I wear brown, so you know I'm a good guy."

"A good guy and one of the most successful businessmen in Tomsk," Boris put in. "Speaking of which, we have some things to talk about, but it will only take a few minutes." With that the two men disappeared into Boris's office.

Sveta brought me another beer and sat with me on the couch. "You can't understand him, can you?" she smiled. "Donat. He talks too fast. I can't understand him half the time, either. He used to be a professor at the university. Can you imagine his students trying to take notes?" Sveta giggled and clinked glasses with me. "He taught veterinary medicine. Do you know why he stopped?" she asked, sounding like her husband, "because they stopped paying him. None of the teachers get paid. I know a woman in the market who sells carrot salad —she's part Korean, I think— nobody knows what's in it, but it's delicious, it's a family secret, but guess what she teaches. Brain surgery! She's practicing too! A brain surgeon, but she doesn't get paid. She has to sell carrot salad. If you ever see her, buy the salad, it's like nothing else you'll ever taste. Unless maybe you plan to go to Korea when you're done with Russia. Ha, ha, why not? You're already halfway around the world.

"Boris's father was also a veterinarian. That's how he met Donat. They work together on deals and such now, business deals. Probably you think Kirby is the biggest animal in this family, but he's not. Have you ever ridden a horse? Boris and Donat keep horses in a village. I don't like going to villages. It depresses me." Sveta made a face. We heard Boris and Donat laughing, then they opened the door to rejoin us.

"Stay and have a beer with us," said Boris with his hand on Donat's shoulder.

"*Ne mogu.* I can't stay, Borya," he protested, but sat down on the arm of the couch.

"I was just telling Connor about your horses," said Sveta.

"*Da,* I was going to mention that," said Boris. "Maybe you'd like to come out to the village for a ride."

"Let him ride, Mikhail. We have a horse named after Gorbachev, except only his ass is named after him," blazed Donat. "The rest of him has seceded and is nameless. It's all the Republic of Obstinate Goddamn Horse. You can ride him. Americans love Gorbachev. They gave him the Nobel prize. Only the Swedes did that; they got too much of a whiff of Chernobyl; it went to their heads. You can ride him. Only don't let him get near pigs. He hates pigs."

Sveta laughed hysterically. It was nearly impossible for me to follow what Donat was saying. "Pigs, pigs," she repeated and snorted as she laughed.

"Svet, you're turning into one yourself. Why don't you get Donat a beer? Okay, Connor, another adventure," Boris went on. "I won't even charge you, but you'll have to take the bus. I'll give you directions before you go. Donat, when are the Olgas there? How's Thursday? Okay, no problem. Only try to get there early, Connor."

"Maybe if our young friend becomes proficient on horseback he can come with us on our annual trip, eh, Borya? Maybe he's got some Mongol blood in him."

"They go on incredible trips," called Sveta from the kitchen. She returned with Donat's beer in a glass and a plate for me. "Here's some of the carrot salad I told you about. See what you think." It was the first thing I'd eaten in Russia with any spice to it. It was also sweet and sour and tasted of sesame oil.

"It's hot, *da?*"

"I think there's cilantro in it," I said, unsure of the word for the herb.

"What's that, the brain surgeon's salad?" asked Donat. "Better watch out, you don't know what she puts in there. What are those?"

"Cashews."

"Cashews? Looks like gray matter to me, neurological material."

"Donat, *foo*," Sveta whined, looking genuinely distressed.

"I'm not criticizing, Svet," he teased, "you have to make do with what you have."

"*Foo*, stop."

"Last year we rode out on the steppe for ten days," said Boris, getting back to what we were talking about.

"You have to condition your rear end for that," said Donat, interrupting him. "I'll take care of the horses' asses, but not yours."

"We rode out to an abandoned gulag. There are no roads to it. They've all been covered up. The railroad tracks were torn up as well."

"Covered up," echoed Donat. "That's what they want to do with that particular piece of our history. Bury it."

"It was unbelievable, like a ghost town, everything left to rot."

"Maybe you could bring a camera," said Sveta. "That would be a documentary for you."

"If I could go with you, it'd be fantastic," I begged.

"We'll see. It's a hard trip," said Boris. Then to Donat, he said, "Tell him about the other trip you went on, about the river. Donat knows your Fest first hand."

"Fest? *Da*, well, that was a somber affair, not something for light conversation," said Donat, looking down at his drink in his hand.

Boris charged ahead. "He wants to know everything, go ahead and tell him."

"I'm not listening to this," said Sveta and got up. "I'll clear the food. Only speak slowly so he can understand, Donat."

"It was a few years ago, now," started Donat, rubbing his eyes. "It was the first trip I took after I got the horses. What year was that? Not that long ago. It was before I owned the horses, they still belonged to the university then. I was out with a colleague. We were about two hundred kilometers north of Tomsk, along a tributary of the Ob. Suddenly we saw that the river bank up ahead had crumbled with the thaw in the spring and that there were bodies in the sand, dozens of them, men, women, and children. Each had a bullet hole in the back of their heads, some two." He looked at me directly, speaking slowly. "The bodies were so well preserved that you could have recognized them if you knew them. It was as if they had just died.

"We tried to cover the bodies, but there were too many. It was the saddest thing I've ever done, kicking sand over those ghosts. We marked the site and came back to Tomsk. The first thing I did was call Fest." Donat shook his head. "He orchestrated proper burials. He collected name tags from the bodies himself. He had a whole bag of them. The work he does for exiles is important."

"Horrible," said Sveta, who had stood and listened despite getting up to leave. She picked up the plates. She reached out for the orange-grease-smeared saucer I'd been holding since eating the carrots.

"I felt that we have lost our souls," said Donat. "That's why we're able to live undisturbed on top of these mass graves. They're off in the woods; they're under the streets. On our way back I made my mind up about leaving the university. I wasn't abandoning my students, I decided, or my university or my profession so much as I was abandoning the government that did these things. The people in charge are still the same. The KGB has changed its name, but they're waiting for their chance."

Boris nodded as if to say, 'you see?'

"Whose fault is it that I had to remember these things?" said Donat, "Yours?" He jokingly pointed at me with his beer in his hand. "Well, don't remind old Mikhail Sergeevich —the horse. He won't like it. *Vot,* I've got to get going, Borya."

"I should go as well," I said.

"I'll give you a ride." Donat stood and buttoned his coat.

Chapter 7

"Tell me about a bad day you've had," said Alina one noontime in the steaming *stolovaya*. We sat lunching with our coats thrown over the backs of our chairs and our boots thawing together in puddles under the table. I crunched a plate of sliced cucumbers, dipping each slice in a dollop of sour cream. This was how our conversations often went: one of us asked a random question, and we took it from there.

I spoke without hesitation since Alina generally understood my bad Russian. "The other day one of the drivers told me that being an American is enough to get me out of anything. If the police harass me, I should wave my passport and say loudly, '*Ya Amerikanets!*' It irritated me at the time, but later I started thinking about how funny it would be if I believed it. To hell with 'cultural sensitivity!' If Russians are so convinced that everything Russian is bad and everything American is good, why shouldn't I benefit, *da?* Show me hospitality! Everything for the guest!"

A tiny smile wiggled across her lips.

"I was thinking this while I was taking out the garbage from my flat, and while I was out there, a man came up to me and asked who had given me permission to dump trash in 'his bins?' I was never sure which bin belongs with my building and which are for the buildings around us, but I said, 'My landlord, Vodopyanov!'"

Alina gave a quick laugh and covered her mouth.

"The guy stood there shaking his head and looking at me like he expected payment. I thought, 'What the hell is this, the garbage mafia?"

"Mafia *Musura*," said Alina, parting her fingers to speak.

"But then, I thought, I could say those magical words. I would empty my trash on his shoes and say, 'Go fuck yourself, *Ya Amerikanets!*'

Alina shushed my cursing and looked around to see if I was overheard. Nonetheless, she was pleased by it. "You didn't say it, did you?"

"*Nyet*, I turned around and went back inside."

"But still, you left him standing in the potato peels," she joked. "I don't think Oleg's advice would have worked for you."

"*Nyet*," I agreed. "I told him about how the police came to my door precisely because I am an American and are going to start chasing me for a blood test. But I didn't explain it well, so now Oleg thinks I have AIDS." This made her laugh. "You have a dark sense of humor, *devushka*," I said.

"*Nu*, you already knew that," she shrugged. "But you still haven't told me about a bad day."

"I can't think of one in particular. It's small things that frustrate me, mostly my bad Russian and shopping. I've been going crazy trying to find rice and salt."

"Poor *malchik*," she kidded. "We'll have to find you some Uncle Bens."

"What about salt?"

"Everybody has salt," she said, her ironic smile swinging side to side under her little upturned nose.

I worked in the editing room that afternoon with Sergei. We were interrupted by Marat. "Connor," he shouted as he threw open the door. "What's this I hear about you wanting tomorrow off to go horseback riding?" Most of the staff treated the editing rooms as sacrosanct, expressly 'do not disturb' zones, but Marat thought nothing of it, even if he spoiled an overdub. The only exception being if Ilya was around. Marat was afraid of him.

"Is this summer camp, motherfucker? Your friend Vodopyanov sends rich Russian kids to camp in America, but I thought he brought you here to work." Marat sputtered at his jokes. "First you're out with a hangover and now you want to go on vacation," he laughed. "Motherfucker!"

"Everything will get done," said Sergei next to me. "Please close the door so we can get back to work."

"You're telling me to close the door? Wait, Connor, here comes Gennadi. He wants to talk to you."

"Sorry, Sergei," I said and got up to go outside.

Gennadi stopped me in the doorway. "Remember what we talked about the other day, the Soros people, going to Moscow?"

"*Da*," I said, trying to usher them into the hall so Sergei could work.

"What? Moscow?" peeped Marat.

"I called them, and they said you'd promised to send them a tape."

"A tape?" questioned Marat more loudly, "what's this about a tape? I didn't see any tape. You sent a tape without showing it to me? Did you see it?" he asked Gennadi.

"*Nyet.*"

"We had to do it in a hurry," I protested.

"When was this?"

"Last week. I sent it with Boris Mikhailovich."

"Vodopyanov?" shouted Marat, slapping his forehead.

"He was going to Moscow on business. He said he'd drop it off."

"What now?" shouted Marat to Gennadi, nearly panicking. "Do they think Vodopyanov is associated with us?"

"*Nyet, nyet,*" said Gennadi, brushing Marat aside. "I don't care about that."

"He did us a favor," I said.

"He probably made them pay for it. He probably tried to sell them something," Marat laughed edgily.

"Marat, *ne nado*," said Gennadi. "Connor, what was on the tape?"

"News segments, and I did a little English voiceover as an introduction."

"It was good work," muttered Sergei, still waiting to be left alone.

"No one else saw it?" Marat stammered.

"Ilya saw it. He picked the segments." Ilya and I had spent a late night putting it together and then he drove over to Boris's in the morning before he left for the airport.

Marat huffed dramatically.

"I'm not upset," said Gennadi to Marat's surprise. "They agreed to meet with me next week."

Robbed of a chance to be a disciplinarian, Marat stuffed his hands in his pockets and pouted. Gennadi put his hand on my shoulder. "Listen, I know I mentioned that perhaps you should come to Moscow with me, but after talking with them, they seem to speak Russian quite well."

"Connor," hollered Ilya as he burst through the studio door with a tape in his hand. "We've got to get this ready for tonight." He stopped when he saw Gennadi. "Are you meeting?" he asked.

"*Nyet*, we're just finished," answered Gennadi and with a flash of a smile went out through the still-swinging door.

"Duma debate," announced Ilya.

"You're going to Moscow?" Marat asked me enviously.

"*Nyet*."

"Moscow?" said Ilya.

Marat then turned to him and demanded, "Why didn't you tell me about the tape? You could have called me at home. I'm the studio director, and I should review things like that."

"What's he talking about? The Soros tape, *bladt*? It was nothing. We've got work to do," he said, and pushed past Marat. "Let's go," he called as he sat down next to Sergei. "We've got some good footage of your friend Fest calling for hearings on corruption."

"That reminds me," I said to Marat. "I have an interview set up with Fest for next Tuesday. Oleg agreed to come and tape it for me."

"Oleg? He'll be busy."

"It's all taken care of," said Ilya.

"What about *Marketeer*?" Marat protested.

"Everything will be finished," called Sergei.

"This is how America maintains economics at the top," proclaimed Marat, smiling despite his irritation. "People always look after their own interests!" He turned his back, and at last we were able to close the door.

"*Bladt*," sighed Ilya, "*Takoy durak.*"

The next morning I took a bus forty minutes through the snowy landscape north of Tomsk. My cue to get off the bus would be a pine nut oil plant. I kept watch for the landmark through a small square in the window where I'd cleared of frost with my thumbnail.

"How will I know a pine nut oil plant?" I'd asked Boris.

"The sign, Connor, has big pictures of pine cones," he'd answered over the phone, amused at my skittishness. I easily spotted the plant on the long straight road. I stepped down from the bus and unfolded the rest of the directions he'd dictated to me.

"Just ask anyone in the village if you get lost, they'll know where it is. They all keep a close eye on us," he'd chuckled.

The oil plant was a long corrugated-steel shed. It showed no sign of being in operation. I saw no one on the road but saw smoke rising from the squat brown cabins alongside it. Electric lines loped between the ramshackle dwellings. The odd tractor appeared fifty-years-old or more. It was hard to imagine much else had changed in the village for two hundred years. I thought of the bodies Donat had found uncovered by the river, pickled in the swampy acidic soil.

'End of the road, go right, end of the road, on the left,' said the note. I found the stable and a little cabin built of fresh new wood. The place was looked after by a pair of women, both named Olga. "The Olgas," Boris had laughed suggestively. "But as you will see, one is Olga and one is Olya. You'll be able to tell which one is which."

A knock on the rough wood door raised a chorus of barking dogs inside. Olga let me in. She was middle-aged, had a gap-toothed grin, and wore her graying hair tied in a braid. I could hear the younger woman behind her shushing the dogs, but it was too dark inside to see her. Greeting me quickly, Olga ushered me in and sealed the door, which was rimmed with thick felt to ensure a tight fit.

The place was hot and airless. There was a pungent funk of dog and horse and the sweat of the women. I gulped for breath as I shed my layers and wrenched off my boots. The Olgas stood smiling at me, holding off the animals as I blinked to adjust my eyes in the darkness.

"You're blinded by the snow," chuckled the older woman. Both wore old barnyard jeans and had stripped down in the overheated hovel to their turtlenecks. Olga red and Olya white. Only Olya was braless and had an achingly beautiful figure. She held out her hand to me, and as I reached for it, the three skinny dogs that had crowded around her thighs came forward. The sight of them made me jump back. The women laughed. Dogs with no ears! They had gaping cartilaginous gorges in their heads.

"It's so the horses can't grab them," explained Olya and introduced each one by name. I held out my hand to be sniffed, and the mutilated curs wobbled their knuckle-stub tails.

"I guess they don't like being out in the rain," I joked once I'd recovered.

"They lay down and cover their ears with their paws," smiled Olya, and cutely imitated them with her hands up over her head.

A horse blanket covered the cabin's one window. The only light came from a soot-dampened oil lamp on a kitchen table. "We'll let you warm up with a cup of tea before sending you out again," said Olga, inviting me to sit.

I looked around. The cabin was packed with stuff. There were two big cats on patrol, weaving between the legs of chairs and those of the dogs, climbing up onto things, constantly in motion. A brick-sided wood stove took up a large part of the room. To one side jutted a short counter where the tea kettle was set on a horseshoe, next to that an open can of sweetened condensed milk and a box of sugar cubes. An old enamel wash basin held the morning's teacups and crumb speckled plates. On the floor nearby sat a jerry can of water. Nearly a half of the cabin was filled with saddles, piles of horse blankets, and shaggy gray pelts that the dogs went to lay on once they'd calmed down.

The Olgas loved the animals, loved the den. They were at home smelling like the animals, being constantly touched and rubbed and sniffed. We sat for a bit, chatting pleasantly and sipping tea at the table until Olga said with a big sudden grin, "*Nu*, I guess I'll leave you two alone. I've got errands to run. Make sure he doesn't freeze out there. Keep him warm, won't you, *devushka?*"

Olya's cheeks pinked. "Would you like some more tea before we go outside, *malchik?*" she asked playfully. "*Tatya* Olga is worried you might catch a cold." She stuck out her tongue.

"Ah, you wild thing," scolded her elder, and mimed slapping her face. "Don't mind us," she told me, "we're only teasing each other."

Smiling affectionately, Olya put in, "She'll be across the road having tea. She doesn't think I know she's sitting there watching me do all the work. She'll come back with a bit of cheese or bread she's borrowed and act as though she's trekked all the way to Tomsk for it."

"You mind your manners," said Olga, now pulling on her *valenki*. "I have to get meat for the dogs." Hearing this, the dogs came to their feet as if yanked up by strings and danced anxiously around us.

"*Vot*, you'll have to take them now," teased Olya.

"Don't let them follow me. Wait a couple minutes before you go out."

"Dogs want meat?" sang Olya smiling, whipping the dogs into a whining frenzy. "Dogs want to go with *Tatya* Olga to get their meat?"

"Arrroooo," wailed one of the mutts, and both women laughed.

"Stop it now, Olya, they're going to pee." Olga put on her coat, and with Olya holding the wheezing, pop-eyed dogs, left the cabin.

As the door swung, I gulped a gush of cold clean air and hastened to put on my boots.

"Those won't fit in the stirrups," said Olya, placing a saddle down beside me. She moved effortlessly through the dim clutter of the room, even with the dogs pestering her, panting, and eagerly looking up at her. She showed not the slightest annoyance. "Here's a pair of *valenki.*"

We hauled the saddles across the frozen yard. "V*alenki* in the village, right out of Tolstoy," I joked. Through the pliable wool boots, I felt every lump of frozen dung and nearly turned an ankle in every sunken hoof print in the barnyard.

Olya laughed at me tripping along. "They take some getting used to, *da*? It's like walking in bare feet." She'd put on a heavy canvas coat with a broad collar, which she wore up around her pale cheeks. She wore her rabbit *shapka* with the earflaps down, framing her pretty grinning face. As steam flowed from her bowed pink lips, I thought inadvertently that her breath would taste of sweet milky tea.

The long, low-ceilinged stable was sealed up tight like the cabin and without electric light. Olya threw open the double doors so we could see. The livestock stamped and shuffled in their stalls. There were ten stalls, but only six animals: four horses and two cows.

"*Moloko*," explained Olya, indicating the cows. "Olga thinks I'll milk them since she's pretended to have forgotten, but I won't," she smiled. The cows looked on blankly chewing cud. Olya laughed at them fondly and chased away the dogs, which were sniffing around their udders.

"Can you tell the difference between these horses and other breeds, your mustangs for instance?" asked Olya brightly. "These are Altai horses. They're longer and shorter, heavier. See how thick their coats are? They don't really require much care," she said with a shrug, "just feed them." As if concurring, the horse nearest her bobbed its head and blew steam.

"*Eto, Mikhail Gorbachev*," she laughed. "Donat says we're to put you on him. Have you ever ridden before? Watch out, he bites. Don't be afraid to slap him on the nose." As the other horses munched on the frosty hay in their troughs, Olya harnessed Mikhail, tossing a worn leather bridle over his head. He twitched his ears and half-heartedly tried to fling it away with a languid toss of his head, but Olya already had hold of it underneath his jaw.

"They grow very slowly," she went on. "A European horse takes only four years to mature, but the Altai take seven. They're adapted to our climate. People use these horses all the way up in the arctic circle."

"The Chukchi?"

"*Da*. You know about our Chukchi?"

"I saw a documentary."

"I don't know about them, but the Yakuts use the Altai horses. They even make a drink out of fermented milk called *kumis*."

"Horse vodka," I said, so she knew I understood her.

"*Da*, yuck." She made a face. Mikhail suddenly turned and nipped her through her coat. "Oh, you scoundrel," she yelped, and whopped him solidly. "Are you in one of your moods? I'll fix you." Grumbling and rubbing the spot near her armpit where he'd bitten her, she finished saddling him. He remained still, and she fed him a knotty little apple from her pocket when she was done. "Here, you give him one," she said, holding the crabby fruit out to me. "Make peace. Hold your hand open when you feed him. Fingers together."

She led the horse into the yard. "Do you know how to mount him? Go ahead," she said. "I'll hold the lead. Let's see how he's going to behave."

Excited and feeling nimble in my valenki, I hooked my left foot into the stirrup and sprang up onto the saddle. Mikhail remained calm. "*Ladno*," said Olya and began walking us around the corral, steadily letting out more rope as she instructed me on how to move up and down, bracing my knees, with the horse's trot. Once she was satisfied that the horse had resigned himself to obedience, she untied the lead and threw me the reins. Immediately old Mikhail kicked up his heels and raced around the corral. "*Stoy, stoy*," called Olya. "Pull in his reins!" I pulled. He bucked. I clung to the saddle like a cartoon cat. Again with a flourish of heels, Mikhail galloped for the awning over the front of the stable.

I looked to Olya for help and saw helpless mortification. The guillotine edge of the corrugated metal roof flew toward me. At the last second, without conscious thought, I laid back flat against Mikhail's churning haunches.

"*Molodets!*" shrieked Olya rapturously. "Oh, thank God!"

Having failed to execute me, the horse consented to being reined in. Olya ran up beside us. "Now you've won his confidence," she laughed nervously. "Let me saddle the other horse, and we'll go for a ride."

Mikhail waited patiently until Olya opened the fence. He then bolted and threw me, ass over rabbit hat, into the deep snow. Laughing hysterically now, Olya made sure I was alright and then went after him.

I stood dusting off as she rode back victoriously rosy cheeked astride her horse holding Mikhail's reins at arms length. "You are

Sibirski cowboy," she said in English as she hopped down. "Mikhail's not behaving himself today, but I know how to teach him." She led the horses back to the stable where she harnessed Mikhail to a sleigh. "You don't like this, do you," she laughed at him. He huffed and fluttered his lips. "*Da*, that's right, you; we're going to hit you with the whip. He loves to gallop, but hates to work, hates to pull anything."

Minutes later, Mikhail pulled us through snowy fields, Olya and I bundled up together beneath sheep skins and a canvas tarp. We squinted at the blaring white landscape, at the crystal sky. "Go on and gallop now," she shouted, smiling and giving the horse a switch. We flew through the snow. Birch and cedar raced in a wooly blur at the edges of the field. Upon hitting a drift of snow we smashed through like a boat through a wave and were encircled for a flash by a phosphorescent plume of icy dust. Laughing, we squinted against the tiny stings, then brushed ourselves off.

Olya pulled back on the reins; we slowed. "I don't want to make him too tired," she cried. The snow shushed as we took frozen breaths and smiled mutely with watery eyes.

"Was it worth coming all the way out to the village?" she asked me as we headed home. "Not disappointed?"

"*Absolutno nyet*," I said exuberantly, and asked, "What do you do when you're not racing horses?"

She grinned and sniffled and told me she was studying forestry at the university. "I work out here a couple times a week. Do you know Olga is my professor? Are you surprised? Did you think I was a village girl?" She brushed snow from a wavy tuft of yellow hair that had worked its way from under her hat. She gave her nose a quick wipe with the back of her mitt. "Do you have a wife back in America?"

"*Nyet*," I said, "but if I did, I'm sure she'd be jealous of this beautiful sleigh ride we're having."

Olya gasped but then laughed as I smiled at her. She flipped a rein across the horse's back, and Mikhail cut a wide arch across the field. As we neared the village, the old horse slowed. The afternoon light was fading, and the low houses in the distance were discernible only as shapes and shadows.

"We've worn him out," said Olya. "The drifts were big. I pushed him too hard. *Nu vso ravno*, he won't tell on me." She smiled lightly, her face bright pink. "Olga won't be back at the cabin. She's gone back to town by now. If you can wait while I shut everything up, we can take the bus back to town together. Do you mind? There's a drunk in the village that comes out to pester me if he sees me at the bus stop. One of these days I'm afraid he's going to pull me into his disgusting little house where his wife sits with two black eyes." She shuddered.

"You should mention it to Boris," I suggested.

"I don't dare. There's no need, really. He's just an old drunk."

The little cabin cast a long shadow across the barnyard. We unharnessed and watered Mikhail and closed up the stable. Inside the cabin, the dogs, sedated by their dinner, barely rose to greet us. They stretched and yawned with meat on their breath.

"Look at this," said Olya. "Olga has cut up bread and sausage for us, an apple, even some chocolate." She picked up a note left with the food and smiled shyly. "It's silly," she said, turning away from me. "She's teasing me like always." We pulled off our coats and boots, and Olya stoked the fire and put on the kettle.

As we ate and had our tea, Olya reached up under her shirt and gently surveyed the mark left by Mikhail's bite. She winced as she touched it. "Scoundrel," she growled. "I don't think I can show you without exposing myself," she joked flirtatiously. "Maybe like this." She leaned toward me and pulled her gathered collar across her chest.

"Libertines!" roared Boris, suddenly bursting through the door. Startled and accused, Olya and I sat up straight. Boris laughed and laughed until he had to hold his knees and catch his breath. "Ha, did I sneak up on you? I had Alex drop me at the turn and sent him to get spring water. I never drink the water in Tomsk if I don't have to. I came up here to check on some work. I paid a workman to put lights in the stable. I find he's only put up one single light. I'll feed him to the dogs. But, Connor, I'm glad you came out. I can see by your cheeks that you've been out riding. Unless you've been up to something else." He laughed again. "What do you think of our village? I can tell you that villages are not my favorite places. In fact, I would say the Russian village is a terrible place. It is the stronghold of Soviet thinking. The people don't work because they don't know how to. And they are suspicious of everything and they spy on each other. People like this have nothing to do but die. Physically, they will die off, and the new generation will work at rebuilding our country." He took a slice of sausage from Olga's plate. "This is a nice little snack. There's some beer in that crate over there. Help yourself. I'll give you both a ride home if you don't mind having the water jugs at your feet."

I had my second interview with Werner Fest several days later. I'd asked Lubomira to translate. "I've brought you something," she said when she came to the station to meet me. She handed me a bag of salt and another of rice. "A little bird told me you weren't able to find these things."

"Little birds deliver," I thanked her.

"We are very hospitable people, Connor," she answered with stern humor. "Do you know our word *cvoy*? It means 'one's own.' People are hard on the outside here, but once you crack their shells, once you become *cvoy*, you will find them very warm indeed. It's a beautiful term. Maybe you are becoming *cvoy*," she chuckled, "at least with someone."

I hid my new supplies in the editing room. "Guard this with your life," I said to Sergei.

Oleg was waiting for us in the parking lot. "Have you heard about our rock 'n' roll member of parliament?" he asked me as we sped away from the station. "This one guy always wears a rock shirt to the sessions of the Duma; one time it's Megadeth; then it's John Lennon, then Velvet Underground."

"That man is an embarrassment," said Lubomira from the backseat where she appeared uncomfortable with Oleg's driving.

"We love to put him on TV," laughed Oleg. "It should be harder for you to be embarrassed, Lubomira Markova." With barely a pause in his mirth, Oleg swerved suddenly to avoid a pothole.

Lubomira was jostled onto her side. "Oleg Sergeivich, please slow down," she admonished him as she recovered herself.

Oleg went on driving fast and talking around his cigarette. "He quotes lyrics in his speeches, too. I don't think anyone knows what he's talking about, but we like him. Some others proposed a law that would require wearing a suit to sessions of the Duma. He claimed that prices have gone up so much, he couldn't afford a suit. Ha, ha, how do you like that? He'll be re-elected for sure."

We parked alongside a collapsing building beneath the sweep of the outstretched arm of a massive statue of Lenin. The legislative building next door was an imposingly immense altar of concrete, although it, too, was crumbling, and as we crossed the threshold, paint chips and concrete grit crunched beneath our feet.

"With Fest, you don't so much get an interview as a lecture like you're one of his students," mumbled Oleg.

Fest appeared almost instantly after the receptionist dialed him, walking briskly from his office in a poorly fitting gray suit. Still, with his gray mane bobbing along with him, he had an air of eccentric dignity.

"Your work is well-known to me, Mr. Fest," said Lubomira with a slight bow. "I often translate for our astronomers."

"Wonderful," he grinned, bright eyed in the midst of his whiskers. "I have heard much about your English tea parties, Lubomira Markova. I have considered joining your classes myself."

"You'd be most welcome," she answered, flattered.

Fest held out his hand to Oleg, "And you are here three times a week."

Oleg nodded, now chewing gum.

We followed Fest to a small meeting room. "My office is much too much of a mess. You'd never know I'd once been a street sweeper or a cleaner of any kind," he joked. "Where shall we begin?"

"On Tuesday you called for hearings into corruption," I started in English.

"Of course!" he declared while Lubomira was still translating.

I continued, "What sort of corruption? How would you go about it?"

"*Tak*, where do I begin?" Fest tugged at the yellow-tinged whiskers at the corner of his mouth. He sat back, crossed his legs, and folded his hands over one knee. He sighed. "We have corruption at all levels of our society. This we inherited from the Communists, but we're now taking it with us into our new society. We are starting our democracy with one of the worst traits of the previous regime, a trait that could prevent a lasting democracy from taking shape. My fear is that if we do nothing to stop it now, we may lose our ability to choose. The networks of corruption will become the master of our society, not us, not the people. It's already happening.

"I propose there are two primary sorts of corruption, though not always entirely distinct. There is old corruption, and there is new corruption. The old is related, almost entirely, to that massive pageant of theft we called privatization. Redistribution of wealth, indeed. Under Communism, influence within the party was power. With Capitalism, money is power. So what happened, simply, was that those who were influential within the party cashed in their influence for capital.

"My hypothesis (now there's a word you're glad you have the lovely Lubomira Markova to translate for you) is that it was not 'mismanagement' as people say, but a deliberate lack of management, a cover-up in effect, so that those with influence could take what they wanted, so that they could easily distribute the resources of this country among themselves. The farce of distributing vouchers, for instance —these were scraps thrown to the dog while the master had his feast at the table. Ordinary people were never going to have any influence.

"Much of the crime is complete. The money has disappeared. It's been taken abroad or otherwise hidden. All the same, the people responsible for these economic atrocities must be investigated." Fest paused. I looked back at Oleg, who winked at me from behind the camera.

"I was against Communism," Fest began again after taking a deep breath and running his fingers over his beard. "I lived much of my life under its heel. It crushed the lives of my entire family. So goes the course of history. The majority of people, however, worked within that system in good faith. They spent their lives working, and they built a superpower. They are entitled to a full accounting in the same way the victims of exile deserved disclosure. There must be reparations," he said passionately.

"And what of the New Corruption, as I've called it? You're a young man, you want to know about new things. Am I against the businessmen? No. I know there are few laws to protect them or guide them. There is no infrastructure to support them. The people I wish to pursue are those who are deliberately taking advantage of our weakened situation to the detriment of the public. These are people who are committing crimes and pretending it is a business. I think there is a clear line between someone doing the best he can within an imperfect system, even a corrupt system, and someone taking advantage of it. *Tak*, they are looters.

"Let me give you an example, although your employer may not like it," he chuckled and glanced up at Oleg. "Let's look at the company MMN. They advertise more than any other on your TV-N. They must be your biggest contributor. In one commercial I saw a middle-aged woman, someone about the age where she is unlikely to benefit from our new economy, someone worried about having money to take care of herself as she gets older. This woman walks into an MMN office, puts down a few rubles, and gets a certificate of some kind. After an undisclosed amount of time, she comes back, turns in her certificate, and is given a stack of money. As simple as that!" Fest slaps his knee and pauses for effect.

Oleg joked lamely, "That's just inflation she's been keeping up with."

Fest continued, "They promise a thousand times return, but is that possible? Is there a bank anywhere in the world that has such returns? I can't say for certain that it is a fraud, but shouldn't we look into these things? At the very least we could give a recommendation to people, to suggest if this is something to risk your money on.

"Many people say we have to wait for new laws and reforms from Moscow, but I have been elected a law-maker here in this oblast. Why should I hesitate to make laws where they are needed? Yes, as a nation, we are building new systems, new laws, a new judiciary. But the networks of corruption are also building. They are constructing their oligarchy. What do we expect should happen? When we finish with our reforms, these criminals, who in the absence of law have taken over our society, will kindly step aside and give back the money they have plundered? I don't think so. If we allow an outlaw society to continue to take root, it will continue to grow. We need to fight corruption or it will be what defines our future. What I'm saying is that we are in danger of having corruption itself govern us, not just now or for the time being as if it were merely a rough spot, a growing pain, but going forward and for the rest of our lives. What we will have is just as before, but instead of Communists, Capitalists."

We sat for a moment. Lubomira caught up with the translation. Fest chuckled, "In the Duma, I am rarely allowed to finish what I have started to say. I appreciate the opportunity.

"People call me an idealist, but that says more about them than it does about me. I am a realist. If you have a fire in your kitchen, you cannot wait for the fire brigade. If all you have to fight the fire is a bucket, you will fill the bucket. There is a joke that goes like this: the pessimist says, 'life is terrible. It can't get any worse.' The optimist says, '*da*, it will get worse.' Do you see? I am the optimist saying 'it will get worse.' If we do nothing, it will get worse." Fest smiled. "What I am not is a fatalist, one who sits back and says there is nothing he can do.

"How can we wait for Moscow? I say, 'look at what happened with Communism while we were waiting.' The Revolution was always going on, they told us, but that was only a way to tell people to wait. Wait while we slaughter these people; wait while we imprison these others. It will be better. This is only temporary. As if Stalin could do the dirty work of being a butcher, and then it would be done with!" he scoffed. "That is what people thought. It is all dirty work, my friends. The dirty work never ends, so it is how you solve your dirtiest problems that define your society.

"I arrive at this judgment not by choice but by necessity. You know about my life, so you understand why. The people in power at one time thought that German Mennonites would side with the Nazis in the war. They had no evidence to fuel their paranoia, but they had all the power, and we had none, so we were dispatched much like insects. Now my problem, as a person given some kind of power by the ballots of others, is to not be like my former oppressors. I must have compassion for the victims of corruption and endurance in addressing the problem."

Fest paused and shifted in his seat. Behind us Oleg's knees cracked as he squatted to check the battery pack.

"Do you see?" exclaimed Fest, still as energetic as when we began. "All this has happened, and we go on missing the point! One grows old and sees the same things over and over again! Isn't it true, Lubomira Markova?"

"It's true," she said in English.

To me, Fest said in English, "You are understanding me?" I nodded. "Lubomira Markova is a very good translator," he continued, and she suddenly shook her finger at him.

"Tut, tut," she scolded, "When we are speaking English, you must call me Marion, please."

Fest laughed as did I. Then, reverting to Russian, he put in, "Lubomira Markova is the best translator in Tomsk. Everyone knows her by reputation."

"Ah, well," blushed Lubomira, "I most often translate for scientists. Compared to that, a politician is not so difficult, even one as eloquent as you, Deputy Fest."

"Am I so simple?"

"It's not nuclear physics," she flirted.

"Next time you'll have to interview me about astronomy. But for now let us move on before I forget where I've left off. I am an old man, you know. *Tak*, about corruption, what do I plan to do? I propose public hearings in which we will take testimony from former party officials and bosses in the KGB who have mysteriously done so well for themselves. The ones that are building palaces for themselves and importing Mercedes. We want to know how it is so. We will ask the officers of MMN to tell us how they can guarantee a one thousand percent return, to show us that this is not merely a scheme. These will be public hearings. We can air them on your TV-N and give the public a rest from music videos and American action movies, *da*?

"These are not criminal trials, simply hearings. I would also like to hear the testimony of businessmen who are making an honest attempt at enterprise, your Gennadi Ilich for example."

"Excuse me, Mr. Fest," Lubomira interrupted. "What would you hope to achieve with these hearings? It might be very difficult to get anyone to tell you much. The criminals surely will not admit to their crimes. The legitimate businessmen cannot expose criminal activity because outside of your chambers, they are at its mercy."

Fest appeared slightly put off, but quickly answered, "An excellent point, Lubomira Markova. Perhaps, at times, we will need to arrange for secret testimony. If there are further actions to be taken because of some individual's testimony, personal security for instance, we will deal with it case by case. The way I look at it, no matter what happens, it will be worth the effort. Perhaps you are worried that someone's testimony, if it is open and honest, may get them killed. This could happen. But people are already getting killed for nothing.

"If we ask ourselves, 'What kind of society do we want?' If we say, 'yes, we are in a period of change, but we cannot resign ourselves to it being lawless,' we must make the effort. People may choose not to speak to us. That will be their right, but others may, and it could help us make a difference. Most importantly, it could stall the systems of corruption, the criminal elements, from surpassing everything else as we're trying to accomplish. People want something done. That is why they elected me. So I am trying to do something."

Fest's passion made it difficult to question him. I knew, of course, what Vodopyanov would say.

"Come now, I see you're mulling something over," Fest said to me.

"I'm trying to imagine how entrepreneurs might look at this. To them it might look like a witch hunt," I said, and explained the term.

"Scapegoat," answered Lubomira, nodding, "it's from the Bible."

I furthered my question, "Also, do you think some would see this as a kind of vengeance, the street sweeper at the head of an inquiry targeting former communist party members and the rich?"

Without hesitating, Lubomira translated. Fest frowned, and I quickly added, "What I mean is, it might be important how you position the hearings, make sure people understand why you're doing it."

Fest laughed. "Talk to an American, and he will teach you marketing." Everyone laughed. "Yes, you are right. It is important how we communicate. In fact, my friend, you should keep in mind that I have said things to you perhaps a little more frankly than I would to your colleagues on the news program." He winked at Oleg. "I am expressing the reality of what is going on here so that, perhaps, people in the West may see our struggle and do more to help. Chicken legs will only take us so far."

We chuckled. After thinking for a moment, Fest continued, "As to the question of this being a personal vendetta, I must say that those we call to testify do not leave their pasts behind them, and neither do I. When I ran for this office, I told people that I would do something about corruption, and that is what I am attempting to do. Whatever other appearances one may imagine, that is the truth."

Fest smiled. "I can see we are all getting a bit fatigued by such serious matters. And I imagine that your cameraman is ready for his cigarette." Oleg nodded in appreciation. "I will say just one more thing: people ask me why don't I simply mind my own business. This would be like willing myself to relive everything I've gone through in life, to willingly choose those same conditions that were thrust upon me by history."

Outside, after lighting his cigarette, Oleg joked, "I think he means to steal you from your husband, Lubomira Markova."

"He's a very charming man," she answered with a slight smile. "Maybe if he shaved his beard."

"How is your husband? I remember hearing he was quite ill," said Oleg, blowing smoke into the frigid air.

"*Da*, he's been ill for a long time. Shortly after we were married the doctors told us he would not live past forty, but he's here still. He's not able to do much for himself, but we carry on."

Unfazed, Oleg replied, "Well then I guess he won't be able to fight off even the wiry Mr. Fest." Lubomira laughed as if paid a compliment.

We got in the car, and Oleg asked me, "What do you think your friend Vodopyanov makes of our Deputy Fest?"

"I already..." I started, then choosing caution, finished. "I don't know."

Oleg laughed. "Fest is a brave man, but he's making a lot of enemies: mafia, corrupt officials, the police, the KGB. Fest has risen as far as they're going to let him go. They'll get rid of him, if he gets too loud."

Lubomira gasped sharply, "Oleg Sergeivich, curse your mouth," but appeared scarcely surprised by what he'd said.

Chapter 8

Alina knocked at the door of the editing room. It was after eight p.m. I was alone. "*Privet*, workaholic," she said, slipping into the chair beside me with a flicker of a smile. "I hope you're not here late doing some silly thing for Marat."

"It's my own stuff." I smiled back. I'd been working on the voiceover of the translation for the Fest interview.

"Show me," she said.

"It's just talking; I'll show you something else." I switched tapes. "These are various scenes I've been collecting when I manage to borrow a camera." I rewound to a point on the counter I'd marked down and turned on the speakers. The picture bounced with my walking on the uneven icy path behind my block of apartments. A light layer of snow creaked beneath my feet. You could hear my breathing.

I glanced at Alina to see her eyes light up with interest.

In the video, it was late afternoon. The light was fading and the snow looked blue, everything looked blue. There was a frozen haze in the air. Up ahead on the path was a woman standing still. Her back was to me; one of her heels was crooked to one side in the stance of a little girl daydreaming. My boots continued to creak as I approached her. She wore a scarf over her head, as the older women often do, but her pose was utterly childlike. I was witnessing her outside of herself. I stopped quite close to her. My breath was visible before the lens. She was frozen there, awestruck, transfixed, in reverie or sorrow.

As I started to move around her, she turned around suddenly and looked directly into the camera.

Alina jumped back in her chair.

The woman had sharp features, high cheeks. She was not old. Her face was rouged with the cold. I stepped out of her way, and she passed me the way I had come.

"Like a ghost," said Alina, the blue afternoon light from the monitor reflecting in her pupils. I watched her for a moment, her face illuminated as a mask of flickering light.

"There's more," I said. The camera moved on without looking back at the departing woman. A few steps on was a boy standing almost exactly as the woman had been. He looked down at a piece of cardboard he'd been using as a sled. In the blue light, with the white surface, and in his great bulk of clothes, he looked like a little cosmonaut on the surface of the moon. He was disoriented, somehow stunned or deprived of oxygen. It was as if he and the woman had just emerged from the wreck of their spacecraft. At his feet was a wheel from a toy truck. I walked past him. He didn't look up.

I head home towards my building, which loomed now, darkened in its own shadow, like a giant door away from this haunted afternoon.

"What was that about?" asked Alina, grinning but puzzled.

"It was a strange day."

"The woman was heartbroken," she said. "You might as well have pointed a camera through the keyhole into her bedroom. Do you have any more like that?"

"*Da*," I said, "destitute Siberians keep falling into my path."

She laughed. "*Eta problema.*"

"I'll show you one I haven't looked at since I filmed it. I feel a bit bad about it." Alina was curious. "Remember you asked me about a bad day? This one might have topped the list." I took a tape from my duffel bag.

First there was the confusion of the camera being turned on and hefted into position, the microphone picking up the movement of air, brushing against my coat. I fumbled to turn on the light. As the lens adjusted, we saw at my feet a man collapsed in a doorway. Curled into a sloppy fetal position, he wore a high-collared sheepskin coat. His *shapka* was knocked down over his face.

"This is my apartment building," I said onscreen in English. "This man is drunk or dead. I can't tell which, but it's very cold out, and I don't know how long he's been here. Unfortunately for him, he's passed out just far enough from the door that I can step over him and get through it, which is what I'm going to do. Why am I not going to help this man? Because I have just bought a chicken, and I'm hungry. I had a shitty day; Russia can take care of its own drunks." I reached out and opened the door to the stairwell until it bumped the unconscious man in the middle of his back. No movement. I stepped over him and clomped up the stairs. My hand put the key into my metal door before the screen went blank.

"Terrible, Connor," said Alina with a quick laugh.

Lines etched the screen as the camera was turned back on. I was in my kitchen seated at the small table. The camera was on a tripod in front of me. "The chicken is in the oven," I said. "I've rubbed it with salt and pepper and stuffed it with apple slices. It smells delicious. I've got some good bread, a cucumber to slice up. This will be a good meal. The man in the doorway? Maybe he will freeze. Maybe other tenants will find him and drag him into their apartments for some strong tea. I'm a ghost here," I said, looking into the camera. "If I had a phone, I'd call the police." I reached forward and switched off.

"You were drunk yourself," scoffed Alina. "It's strange to see you speak English. You're a different person."

"Could you understand?"

"*Da.* Enough."

"What would you have done?"

"I'm a woman, Connor. I don't go prodding drunk men when I'm alone at night. Someone else would have found him."

"See! You didn't have any more sympathy for him than I did."

"I didn't say I had sympathy for him," she answered. "I'm just surprised that you didn't."

"That was the most Russian I've felt since I got here," I joked.

"*Poshol ti*! America is full of Samaritans, I suppose," she mocked. "All believing in God and looking out for each other. What a heaven on Earth!" Taking a half-heartedly scolding tone, she added, "Connor, you should have woken him. He could have frozen to death." She sighed. "You've ruined my good mood."

"I'm working on a short film about borscht," I told her. "That should be more cheerful."

"It better be. I came here to tell you about a party. Gennadi has talked the Soros people into giving us money. He called today from Moscow to tell Fedya to set up a party next week for when he gets back."

My borscht video premiered at the Soros party. As I set up the VCR, I heard Gennadi say to someone, "He's got all these things going on around him. History. And he makes a film about borscht. *Nu, ladno.*"

<u>What went into my Borscht: A film by Connor Chessick</u>

Day 1

"Where did these beets come from, Babushka?" I asked from behind the camera. An old woman stood on the sidewalk in front of a closed-down shop, bundled up with her hands in a fur muffler. At her feet, laid on a plastic bag, were two bunches of beets and a gallon jar of dill pickles.
"What?" she reflexively growled.
"I'm sorry to bother you, but I am doing a film about making borscht."
"These beets will make excellent borscht, *malchik*."
"Where are they from," I repeated.
"My datcha, of course. I've had them in the cellar so they are still very fresh and firm."
"Thank you. I'll buy them and the jar of pickles as well."
She smiled and asked for five thousand rubles.

"*Vot!* She's taking you for a ride, Connor," called Yana from the audience. "She knows a dizzy foreigner when she sees one."

"I would have gladly paid fifty dollars for those pickles," I called back to laughter. We'd all already had a few drinks back at the station. We were now in the banquet room of a Chinese restaurant, much like the one where I'd met Mama Luba.

> "What else do I need to make borscht?" I asked the old woman on the sidewalk.
>
> "Didn't she give you a list?"
>
> "Who?"
>
> "Your wife."
>
> "*Nyet, babushka,* I don't have a wife. I'm going to make borscht for myself."
>
> "Well I hope you aren't planning to put the pickles in your borscht," she said, and laughed despite herself. Warming up a bit, she said, "Poor man, making borscht for himself." She then counted on her pudgy fingers, "you need cabbage, potatoes, meat, onions, garlic, and sour cream to top it off. It's a pity I didn't bring any potatoes with me. Maybe if you come back tomorrow."

Day 2

> "You're lucky you came when you did," said the babushka from the same spot on the sidewalk. "People have been pestering me all afternoon for these potatoes." She opened a plastic bag to show me a dozen clean-scrubbed potatoes. "*Da,* and look, I brought you something extra. Horseradish. Put some of this in the sour cream, very tasty. Two thousand," she said hurriedly, as if making an illicit deal.

"Aooo," howled Yana.

"Oi, Connor, we have to send you shopping with my wife," said Feodor. "She'll teach you how to barter."

"How do you afford to live on what we pay you?" called Gennadi.

"I don't," I shot back to a frown from my boss and laughter from the rest.

The next sequence was a montage showing me going to all my neighborhood stores and kiosks in search of the remaining ingredients. I bought onions; I passed over some slimy gray meat. In another store I found sour cream; in another I bought bread.

"You've got to go to the bazaar," called one of the receptionists, and as if on cue, the next scene began.

Day 3

> It was Saturday in the city bazaar, and the place was bustling. I walked past a phalanx of old women shuffling in the cold with the projected surplus of their root cellars for sale at their feet. Most had potatoes and onions, a couple had apples that were themselves bundled in scarves wrapped around their containers against the cold. Others, still, had milk frozen into the domed shape of bowls. I found a cabbage and paid eight hundred rubles. The old woman looked suspiciously into the camera.
> "I'm making borscht," I told her cheerily.
> She frowned. "Since when do you need a video camera to make borscht?"
> I asked her in formal Russian to direct me to the meat market. She jutted her chin towards the center of the bazaar. "*Tam*," she said dismissively.

Ilya called out, "Over to the left you'll find crazy Leto and his hijacked Egyptian oranges."

> I passed a bright yellow kiosk blaring Russian pop, a sinuous, syrupy mix of Euro dance music and traditional Russian instrumentation. A woman burst from the latrine-sized shelter and nearly collided with me. Manic or drunken, she screamed at someone behind her. Waving her hands frantically as if drowning, she started to run. A man sprung assassin-like from the booth, clamped her in a choke hold, covered her mouth, and dragged her backwards, kicking, into the kiosk. He slammed the door and slid the bolt. With darkly comic timing, the booth shook and the music skipped as they fought inside.

151

"Because the most important ingredient in borscht is love," called out Yana to the already hysterically laughing room.

No one in the bazaar found the commotion in the music booth alarming. I continued on to the meat market. The woman at the counter wore a faded flowered apron over her winter coat. Her large round face held up a heavy nose, looking like a potato on a pancake. Her thick brown hair was held back with a gold ribbon. On the counter in front of her sat hunks of frozen meat, clear and bright in color. The head of the cow was on the floor behind her.

I lifted the camera to get the shot. The woman looked me over. "Excuse me, *Xenshina*, what is the best meat to use in borscht?"

"*Shto?*" she said, displaying a steel tooth. "The best meat is the best meat." She pointed to a nice light piece. "But you don't need the best meat for borscht." She pointed to a darker, less marbled piece.

"All this meat is tested for radiation, is that right?" I asked.

"Are you a journalist?"

"A filmmaker."

"You'll have to speak to my husband." She called behind her, "Dmitri."

Incongruous amongst the scowling shoppers, other vendors, and even his own wife, Dmitri turned around with a smile. His face was as square as hers was round, each of his teeth a small bright pixel. He wore no apron, had dark stains on his shirt, and blood on his hands.

"What can I do for you?" he said merrily. I asked him my question. "Of course," he answered immediately, "we perform all the tests required of us." To his wife he said, still smiling, "You know that."

"He has the camera," she responded under her breath.

"*Da*, I can see that," he laughed and put his big arm around her. "Smile, you're on television. We have the best meat in the oblast, booth number thirty-seven in the pavilion."

I purchased the cheaper meat indicated by Dmitri's wife and asked him if he had any recommendations for making borscht. "Don't ruin it by putting potatoes in it," he laughed, and looked at his wife. "I hate potatoes."

As if having a scripted line between them, she chided him shyly, "What kind of Russian man doesn't love potatoes?"

"Look at this guy," laughed Gennadi. "A foreigner with a video camera shows up at his booth asking about radiation, and he laughs it off. Not a care in the world! I'm going into farming."

"Only if the cows take charge one day, will he be in trouble," put in Uncle Sam.

"*Tochno.*"

In the last scene, I prepared the soup. My colleagues laughed as I diced with a Swiss Army knife and attempted to crush peppercorns under the bottom of a vodka bottle. When I nicked my finger slicing garlic and exclaimed, "*Bladt!*" they roared with laughter. The borscht complete and ladled into a bowl, I spooned on a dollop of horseradish sour cream with beet-stained fingers.

"Bravo, Connor," called my colleagues, clapping. Gennadi stood to address the company and said grandly, "It is my suggestion that you rename this film 'Candide's Borscht.'"

"And I will tell you the proper way to brown meat," called Baba Raisa, our accountant and Gennadi's aunt.

"I think we can see from this film some of what our friend Connor is capable of. He also shares some of the success of our meeting with the Soros people. Dan told me that he was impressed with him on the phone."

"Dan," laughed Yana, pronouncing it as Gennadi had, *Duh'an.*

"*Nu, shto,* Yana?" chuckled Gennadi at her interruption. "Connor, is that how you say it, Dan?"

"*Tochno.*"

"*Duh'an,*" giggled Yana.

"*Tak,* back to what I was saying," said Gennadi amicably, trying to regain the attention of people drifting towards the table of drinks and food. "Dan says it is precisely because of projects like TV-N that the Soros people are in Russia. They are going to send us a consultant to work out what kind of equipment and training we need. I don't want this to get around town," he added, "but they've given us a small budget for immediate needs."

"*Vot*," Sam had shouted, raising his arms to indicate the whole of the gathering, "our immediate needs."

"*Absolutno nyet*," answered Gennadi emphatically. "The party is strictly on me."

"*Bravoh*," answered the staff, clapping and rolling their Rs in unison.

After he'd sat back down, I went over to Gennadi and asked him, "What did they think of the tape?" I asked.

"*Tak*," he said, expecting the question, "it's strange, Connor, he said he never got it. Things get lost. But like I said, he learned a lot from you on the phone."

Disappointed and wondering if Boris had lied to me, I made my way to the beverage table. Feodor presided with obvious pleasure. "I've got beer for you, Connor." He smiled through his mustache and grabbed three bottles between his fingers from a crate beneath the table. "And in case you want a little vodka..." he mischievously tapped a bottle with a fingernail.

"I'm off vodka."

"*Da*, since the jazz club, you said. But Connor, I saw you drinking vodka at the banya last week."

"I only appeared to be drinking vodka, Feodor," I smiled back. "What I really was doing was spitting it back into my *kompot*."

He laughed, and then told me, "I couldn't find the good *Altaiski pivo* for you, only *Zhiguliovskoe*." He placed the bottles before me. "I'll leave the rest under the table, or else the others will drink them all." He winked.

"Any ice?" I asked, touching a warm bottle.

"Ice, what for? You can put it outside for a few minutes if you want it cold. You don't put ice in beer, do you?" he asked with alarm.

"*Nyyyet*," I crowed.

Feodor laughed, "I heard that Americans like to put ice in everything, even in vodka. Is it true? For a Siberian the idea of putting ice in your drink is crazy. We get enough ice."

I stuck the beers in the snow outside. I looked up and down the sidewalk for Alina, who had yet to arrive, before returning to the food table to fill a plate. I sat at a table by myself and noticed Nikolai staring at me. He was already quite drunk. He spoke to the people around him and jerked his head toward me, encouraging them to join me. I waved. I saluted. I gave a thumbs up. I got up to get a beer out of the snow.

When I returned, Nikolai joined me. "Connor, I wanted to say I enjoyed your film. And I want to say on behalf of all the staff that we are very pleased you are here with us." He nodded as he spoke, his eyelids heavy, slurring his words. "On a personal level, however, I wanted to ask you if you're doing alright, if you're happy in your position here?"

As he finished this last sentence, Alina entered the room, and both of our eyes went to her. She'd gone home to change. She shed her coat and changed her shoes in the foyer. She came into the main room wearing a tight black dress woven through with sparkling silver thread. She had done up her hair and makeup. She was beautiful. Nikolai put a hand on my shoulder as if seeking solace, needing support, or else in silent encouragement. Or as a warning. I couldn't tell. She passed us with a glance and continued to Gennadi's table where she was greeted with cheers for going all out.

Nikolai looked back at Nastia and found her scowling at him. Cut off and not remembering what he'd been saying, he returned to his table.

Alina didn't give me another look. She sat with others from the marketing department. Nikolai, I saw, stole an occasional glance at her.

All week Alina had been talking about how she was looking forward to the party because she was going to drink Dubonnet with Bogdan. I didn't know him. "Bogdan is an old friend, Connor," she'd said haughtily. "He and I started at the station on the same day. You don't see him in the office because he films his show late at night. He comes in with his friends and turns the whole place into a party. It's called the Blue Door. It's one of the most popular shows. He shows videos and movies. Bogdan has lots of fans. He's very popular."

"As popular as Zorro?" I joked.

"Little boys like Zorro," she answered, annoyed with me. "Bogdan is always at parties, the kind that last all night. We don't see each other often, but we're very close. That's why we have our tradition with the Dubonnet, to catch up. Anyway, Connor, you might not see me much on Friday."

I'd met Bogdan at the station later in the week. He had a shaggy brown mane, a formidable beak, and wore tight pants and a snug little jean jacket.

"Oh, *mmm*, ha, ha," Bogdan hummed and giggled as he limply shook my hand.

He and Alina shared a bemused sideways glance. "Connor doesn't think you're as popular as Zorro," she said to him, scrunching her nose mischievously.

"*Nnnn*, ah ha, *mmmmnn*," went Bogdan, shifting his weight back and forth on his hips.

"Bogdan and I don't fit in with other people at the station," Alina had told me. "I don't know what it is, we stand apart."

I went up to the food table for more. "Don't eat too much," said Feodor. "There's going to be *pelmeni*." Back at my seat I watched Sergei across the room fumbling with RCA cords and his lighter to set up a stereo in the darkened room.

"*Nu*," said Alina, coming over to me with a smile, but as if approaching a younger brother. "Nikolai says I shouldn't leave you sitting over here by yourself. He says you look sullen." She pulled out a chair and sat down.

"Me? He should worry about himself and his jealous girlfriend. Nastia goes crazy every time he looks at you."

"There could be a reason for that," she smirked. "What about you, not feeling social?"

"Just not drinking vodka."

"Might as well build up your tolerance."

"I'm debating that," I sulked.

She shrugged. "I'm going to drink..."

"...Dubonnet with Bogdan," I said with her. "I know."

"How's your special *pivo*?"

I shrugged.

"You are sullen, *malchik*."

"You look nice this evening," I said, trying to turn myself around.

She smiled. "That's better. If you're nice to me, I'll save you a dance or two. It's impossible to find nice dresses in Tomsk. I'm about due for a shopping trip to Moscow."

"Sergei," called Sam at the back of the room, "aren't you supposed to be an engineer?"

"Sergei," echoed Yana. "We're drinking your portion of vodka."

Sergei grumbled, "I can't see anything."

"Someone turn on the lights for Sergei so we can dance."

"In the meantime, let's have a game, children."

"*Gorka! Gorka!*"

"What's *Gorka, gorka*?" I asked Alina.

"You'll see."

"Yana, you first."

"*Nyyyet*, Sam, you first."

"*Gorka! Gorka!*"

"We're first," exclaimed Sam and suddenly embraced and kissed Yana.

"*Vot*, I'm in love with a frog."

"Who's next?"

Recalling where I'd first seen this, I leaned over to Alina. "Isn't this a game for weddings?"

She shrugged. "Doesn't matter. Do you have anything like this in America?"

I laughed in disbelief. "In the States this game is called 'workplace sexual harassment.'" She looked at me puzzled, and I explained as another pair of co-workers were chosen to smooch.

Alina bristled. "Here it's just a joke for people."

Across the room Yana shouted, "Gennadi, oh yes, I think you should give a big kiss to poor Gasha who answers your phone calls all day."

"*Gorka! Gorka!*" demanded the crowd.

To me Alina said, "You'll notice no one has their wives or boyfriends with them. It's more fun that way. No need to worry about jealous husbands and wives. They're not invited."

"Otherwise everyone would be like Nikolai and Nastia."

"Shhh," she said, putting her finger to her lips and glancing in their direction. "That's different."

After a half dozen or so of the most unlikely couples were picked out to awkwardly press lips, the pelmeni was served, and Sergei got the music working.

"Here's Bogdan," said Alina, announcing his arrival. "This is our tradition at these things. In a way, I feel Bogdan is the male version of me."

"You think you'd be gay?"

"What?" Nervously she looked around, then whispered to me. "Connor, don't say that. That's a joke that could be taken the wrong way." She looked up at Bogdan who stood in a doorway at the edge of the room waving from his wrist.

I laughed. "It wasn't a joke."

Plainly she was embarrassed. "I'm upset with you for saying that."

"I didn't mean it as an insult."

She slapped me lightly on the arm and left me, looking once back over her shoulder.

After a few ecstatic euro dance tunes, the slow dancing began. My colleagues eagerly swayed in one another's arms. Not to be taken for a pity dance, I wandered over to Gennadi's table. As I sat down, I was promptly poured a large glass of vodka and supervised in drinking it by Baba Raisa, who also told me the proper way to brown meat. Gennadi was flushed and smiling, animatedly telling stories. Clearly he'd had a great weight lifted from him with the success with the Soros people.

Misha, who was a mathematician who created computer animations for commercials, turned to me across the table. "Connor, maybe you can settle a bet for us. Is Soros a Jew?" Typically Misha was a curmudgeon, but tonight he was tipsy and beaming. "Soros must be a Jew."

"Soros is a person?" shouted the receptionist Gasha in disbelief. She'd sat with Gennadi since their kiss. She had a pretty round face and long straight hair. She smiled and showed the glint of a steel front tooth.

"Of course!" Misha shouted back. "A rich American! He wants to save our poor society from itself."

"He supports a free press," added Gennadi.

"*Hoora* for Soros!" called Misha raising his glass. Laughing, he asked me, "Connor, did you know that every Jew in Tomsk works at TV-N? We're all Jews!" he said grandly. "Exiled by Stalin! Gennadi's family, mine, Isrealievich, of course, Sam, who else?"

"Not mine," said Gasha as if insulted.

"No, not yours. Your people were exiled for being too blonde," Misha shot back. Gasha began to explain her origins, but Misha said over top of her, "Lots of people don't even know they're Jewish. Their families don't talk about it." Gasha turned away, and Misha stopped yelling. "The parents think it's better for the kids not to know. I know people who grew up getting into fights because people said they looked Jewish." He smiled. "You know what that's like, *da*, Connor, telling people you're not Jewish? At the *banya*, maybe?"

Gasha turned back around. "What? Why? You don't look Jewish to me, Connor."

We laughed, and Misha continued, "Most of my family has left and gone to Israel. I'll probably go as well, but if I can make money and be rich, then maybe I can have some influence on things. I don't like the way things are looking here."

"Do you mean Zhironovsky?" I asked.

"*Tochno!* The nationalists. I'm afraid they'll come to power when Yeltsin steps aside."

"Pardon us, Comrades," said Yana, who clicked her heels at attention beside me. "I know you all are busy shirking your duties, but Uncle Sam and I have only work on our minds, and we need to speak to Connor."

"*Da*, please, work!" joked Gennadi.

Pulling up chairs, Sam and Yana sat down. "Simply put," began Yana, "we liked your film, and we want you to work with us on a commercial."

"*Da*," croaked Sam, who was drunk.

"Comic timing," hollered Yana suddenly. "It's all about comic timing. That's what you had," she hiccuped, "comic timing."

"*Da.*"

"We need to do a promo, something funny. You know about Leto's Egyptian Oranges, *da?* He's had so much success with the frozen ones, he says he's going to ship them fresh now from Greece."

"*Etot durak*, we'll believe it when we see it," growled Sam.

Gennadi, overhearing, leaned forward and shushed. "Don't insult Leto. He's going to help us buy some equipment from Moscow and ship it back with his oranges."

Sam saluted.

"Come dance with me, Yankee," said Yana. With a slow song playing and her in my arms, Yana asked me, "What do you think of all this, Connor?" Her tone was familiar and friendly. She appeared more sober than I'd thought.

"The dancing?"

"Everything."

"I don't think I've slow danced since high school," I said, repeating a line I'd worked up somewhere before.

"*Da*, it's like in school. Probably you think it's strange. Maybe we do this because it's what we remember as most pleasant from when we were younger. We haven't aged so much in years, but everything has changed, the country has aged. *Da*, Connor, you understand me? We can take comfort in dancing slowly with the people we've known through all this. It's like crying to a friend." Yana mimed tears against my shoulder. "But we have too much to cry about, so we need to slow dance with everyone we know," she laughed.

I nodded, squeezed her.

The music changed to something faster and Yana mimed the dancing girls from the video, which TV-N aired relentlessly. She had to stop and cough and catch her breath after a couple maneuvers. I stood back and laughed.

Nastia approached confidently and said humorlessly, "Seeing how your girlfriend smokes too much to dance on MTV, maybe you'd like to dance with me."

Yana made a face. "*Figgha!*"

Nastia pulled me by the wrist a few steps away before turning back to me to dance. She wore a tight silky black dress and danced seductively, her fingers pulling lightly at her hem. The song changed again to a slow one, and Nastia came to me as if it was what we'd both been waiting for. She pressed herself close against me.

"I enjoyed dancing with you at the jazz club," she murmured, her lips brushing my ear. I put my arms around her slender waist. As we danced I let gravity and the frictionless material of her dress pull my hands further over her hips. "I had to borrow this dress from a friend, so you wouldn't see me in the same one twice."

"You look very lovely," I said, attempting not to tremble.

"As nice as Alina, do you think?"

"You both look very nice."

"Some people at the station think you and Alina should get together," she said with a look of childish seriousness, "but not everyone thinks so."

"Sssh," I attempted with humor and added, "I'm tired of speaking Russian, now."

"Poor boy," she cooed. "Come sit down with Nikolai and me and I will translate for you. I got good grades in English at school." She led me to the table where Nikolai sat looking thoroughly sauced and on the verge of either rage or tears. His bottom lip was wet and protruded as if it had gone numb. Even his power tie was askew. He looked up at Nastia like a pet, and she obligingly stroked his head, happy with his suckling devotion.

"Connor," he slurred, "You are a very good dancer."

"Nikolai needs a translator just to speak Russian." Nastia gave his ear a twist as she sat. "Connor is tired of speaking Russian, Nikolai. I'm going to translate for him."

"You need to drink more, Connor," answered Nikolai. "Your Russian is always better when you drink." Then, as if getting ready to confide in me, Nikolai leaned forward, looking me in the eye, and sighed with boozy breath. "I'm glad to finally have a chance to talk to you, Connor."

"Nikolai says he is..." began Nastia in thickly accented English.

"I understood, thank you, Nastia."

Clasping his hands together, Nikolai said, "There's something I need to tell you."

Nastia kicked him under the table. Without a wince, he leaned over to her and whispered. "*Nyet,*" she snapped.

"Tell him in English," she pleaded. He raised his hands to her. She crossed her arms and glowered.

"Okay, *ladno,*" he conceded before turning back to me. "Connor, I am going to ask you something that means a great deal to me. It will be very..." he paused, hiccuped, "significant to me." Nastia maintained her glare, foot cocked under the table. "I would like you to come over to my flat and meet my family. It would be a great honor. My two children. My wife."

"Ex-wife," interjected Nastia.

He paused and swayed, his eyes heavy-lidded. He looked to Nastia, and then back to me. "Tonight."

Nastia struck, delivering a sharp kick with her pointed shoes.

"Tonight after the party," he went on desperately. "Both you and Alina. You can sleep over with us."

"Where will they sleep, Nikolai? With the children? With us?" Nastia hissed. She got up and pulled me up from my chair. "Let's dance some more, Connor. I can't bear to see poor Nikolai like this." She gave him a look. "Making a fool out of himself."

Registering the song that was coming on, Nastia was transported. Appearing to easily shake off the strange and disturbing conversation of a moment before, she looked around to see if everyone else heard what she heard. And indeed the tune, a slow one naturally, had stirred a move to the floor.

"I love this song," Nastia cooed. She looked around again, searching for someone. She put her hand on my neck and slid up close to me. She purred as we danced, and I moved my hand in a circle in the small of her back. "Alina loves this song, too. I bet she's upset that you're dancing with me." Nastia scooched forward, pushing the softness of her mons against me. "I don't feel like talking, either," she said. "Movements like this are much better."

I looked up to see Alina sitting at a table in the corner looking anxious. I pulled my hands away from Nastia's rear. She snickered. Nikolai, too, was watching us, looking dejected and drained. At the end of the song, I excused myself, straining momentarily against Nastia's firm grasp on my hand, and went to sit with Alina.

"*Nu*, Yankee, what's happening?" said Alina with little red stains at the corners of her lips and a looseness in her voice.

"Everyone calls me Yankee when they're drunk."

"And everyone's getting drunk," she answered. "Everyone but you, I suppose. You are sitting back observing. You are wishing that you had your video camera so you could make a movie, *da*?" She paused. "I'm sorry. I don't mean to be rude. I've been drinking, too. It's silly, but I came back in here to dance with you to that song."

"Do you want to dance now?"

"Let's wait for a slow song." Another pause. "Bogdan was getting on my nerves. Maybe you're right about him being a blue boy, after all."

"Nikolai said something strange," I said. "He wanted you and me to go back to his flat after the party."

Alina covered her mouth. I couldn't tell if she was laughing or something else. "Did he say anything else to you?"

"Not really. I didn't know he had a family."

"Ssshhh," she put her finger over her mouth and secretly looked in his direction. "He and his wife don't sleep together, but he still lives with her and their children." Then she smiled wickedly and said, "Nikolai would like to watch, I bet you. Watch and cry." She snickered. "His wife is worse than he is. She flaunts it to him about the other men she sleeps with." She paused and again covered her mouth. "I shouldn't have said that. How crass. I'm not drinking anymore. He's a sad man, really, but I've had enough of him. I'm sorry, I can't believe he said that to you. He must be very drunk."

Alina got up to ask Sergei to stick to slow songs. Sergei, I could see, was also much more animated than his usual dutiful self, and he protested with wide gesticulations. Nastia also strode up to the table and held out a cassette for him to play. The women stood side by side. Alina was taller and curvy. Nastia had hardly any hips, but had an athletic little bum. Alina was softer, more feminine. Alina took the tape, looked at it, made a joke that made Nastia frown, and handed it to Sergei.

We slow danced. For the first time I put my arms around Alina. The fabric of her dress looked soft but was not, and the plastic tinsel woven through it did not lend itself to the same kind of manual drift as Nastia's had. I would not have attempted it. Her sides, her torso, her hips were soft, tensile, youthful. My hands rested on the curve of her hips, my fingers reached towards the small of her back where I imagined two shallow dimples.

"I hate to admit it, but Nastia and I share taste in music," she said casually. "I should have shared the Dubonnet with you, since I had promised you red wine. Next time. But I'm not going to drink anymore tonight."

"No?"

"Not tonight."

"Why not?"

"Why not, you're asking me, *malchik*?

In between songs, Alina and I occasionally sat down only to get up again and dance. Others noticed but weren't surprised. We received kindly smiles from Gennadi and even Bogdan. I felt pleasantly exposed.

The night went on. The alcohol began to run out. Sergei flipped the tape and played it again. At one point we were alone on the dance floor, and everyone was watching us, several squinting through drunkenness. Yana laughed and made a comment to those around her. The air was utterly poisonous with cigarette smoke. Someone had opened a window and the icy draft ushered people to find their coats and make their way home. It was our last dance. Alina told me she would be back in a moment and left the room. I decided to have a drink after all.

"This is the *pyanka* of all *pyankas, da?*" said Feodor, still manning the drinks table. For some reason I noticed just then that Marat wasn't there. And neither was Ilya.

"Connor, Connor," Sam called to me. He pulled me into a corner of the room, and held me close to him. Laughing and slapping his knee, he cried, "Connor, Connor, you can screw her. Take her home with you, and you can screw her. She's beautiful. You should do it. Something to remember us by." He jammed his fists onto his hips and thrust. "You can do it. She wants you to. Everybody knows it. Take her home with you." Pump, pump, went Sam with his wobbling hips. I looked to see if Alina was witnessing this. He laughed so hard he could hardly stand up. I slapped him on the shoulder and said alright, I would do it for him. "Yes, yes, bite her for me. Take her home for me, and you can tell me on Monday."

Then it was Sergei: "*Nyet,* Connor, don't do it! I will rescue you from her." I led him to a table and sat down with him. He waved his finger drunkenly. "She will ruin your life. I have seen it. She's the Siren of TV-N. You know the Sirens, *da?* Calypso, it is she! A nymph, a nympho! *Nu stho,* not afraid of Greeks? *Vot,* Russian people are much worse! Don't go home with her." Alina, we both saw, was crossing the room towards us. She had her coat and mine. Sergei ended his tirade in English, "I tell you: NO GO!"

"What's he saying?" she asked me quietly as I stood up.

Sergei followed us into the foyer and then to the door. "A Snow Nymph, *tak!*" he ejected as he stood teetering. He waved his finger and said in English, "Danger... her."

Alina addressed him calmly, "Seriosha, why are you doing this? I'm very sad that you would say such things."

Glassy eyed, he looked at her as if not recognizing her. "You can sleep at my house. Don't go with her."

I waved to him dismissively and took her arm and set us toward the sidewalk. "I'm really sorry," I said. "I must have done something wrong."

"*Nyet,*" she said sadly. "That's just how it is."

The buses had stopped. There were few cars. I stumbled over words. "A bad ending, maybe, but a nice night in all."

"I think we were waiting," she said. "We knew we wanted to see each other outside the office again, at night, at a party." She looked over to me meaningfully. I met her gaze, nodded.

The air was frigid and still. The moon was out, and the sky was clear. The smell of cigarette smoke on our clothes, the events of the evening, everything else, froze and sloughed off behind us. We left invisible crystals and a vapor trail. Alina hummed a song, and I softly sang her the words in English.

"You can sing?" she said, surprised. "It's like finding out your dog can talk." She laughed. "We only hear you struggling with Russian, but here you are singing like you know how." She turned to me excitedly with a smile. "I'll teach you Russian songs."

"This is where we took our walk, Kirova Street," I said as we turned onto her street.

"*Tak,* and here is my apartment, remember?"

"I remember."

"Come inside the doorway, there's a little light."

We opened the door and stood in the dim stairwell. She pulled back her hood and shook her hair. "*Nu,* I'm home. Thank you for walking with me and being nice. I don't know what was wrong with Sergei."

I took her mittened hands and kissed her. She kissed back before gently, hesitantly, parting us. She held me at arm's length, as during our first dance. "*Nyet,*" she said shyly. She took three quick steps up the stairway then turned and waved goodnight.

Chapter 9

"*Tak*," croaked Victor Israelievitch as I walked into the office Monday morning. Lowering his paper and looking over his glasses, he said, "You had a nice time at the party on Friday?" I said I had. "Good, good, everyone had a good time." With that he got back to his reading. "My dog," he said behind his newspaper, "is still not smoking, even when I give him a snack." He was still chuckling to himself when I came back through the lobby a few minutes later.

I swung through the studio doors and found Marat with a video camera filming someone stirring Nescafé into a teacup by the Samovar. He turned the Cyclops' eye to me. "Here he is, Connor Chessick. Another day at work in Siberia. We are waiting for you. All work has stopped." He laughed, wetting his puffy lower lip. "I am making a documentary, Connor, just like you. Say something!" Marat never tired of this joke about making a documentary, and whenever he got hold of a camera, he roamed the station pestering people while they worked. That didn't mean some of the footage wasn't good. I'd made copies, unbeknownst to him, and they were now part of my growing collection.

I walked past Marat into the editing room. Sergei greeted me apprehensively. Marat stood behind me in the doorway with the camera. "Wait, Connor. What are you grumpy about? I heard you had a nice time on Friday, *da*?"

Sergei blushed and then hardened. He growled, "And what about you Marat, where were you on Friday?" Falling out of his laugh, Marat lowered the camera, looked over his shoulder, and shushed Sergei.

"I was there," he protested in a warning whisper. The joke was over. "Listen, we've got to get Leto's oranges on the air today. I made them shoot it over the weekend," he said, puffing up. "Our clients need to be supported."

"He needs to sell his oranges before they freeze again," said Sergei.

"*Tochno*," grinned Marat, never serious for long. "Yana wants you to edit it."

"Comic timing!" I beamed.

"We need this done quickly, or we'll all be eating mushy oranges until spring." Marat turned away, laughing heartily, and immediately repeated his joke to someone in the hall.

The commercial was a joy. Yana starred as a woman who has no idea what to do with a fresh orange. She tries plopping it into a pot, pushing it into a meat grinder, and cracking it on the edge of a pan before being instructed by a strange, gangly man in black. He dances and sings of the joys of oranges from Greece while juggling the citrus before a wall of boxes bulging with fruit.

"This guy," said Sergei as we watched, "used to be a big star as a kid on State TV. He hosted a kids' show. He's an amazing *garmushka* player. He was a cute kid, but he's a weird looking goat now, *da?*" We rewound and fast forwarded the tape, making our cuts, and sent the performer bouncing at high speed among the oranges, the pouncing spider to Yana's Ms. Moffet.

We finished the edits, synched the vocals and music, and were done. Sam and Yana brought Leto in to see the finished product after lunch.

"*Vot*, Connor," leched Uncle Sam.

"Sam," Yana warned him under her breath.

Leto loved the commercial. "I'll give you all a kilo of oranges," he laughed as he clapped each of us on the back. He left saying he was going to find Gennadi and buy him a drink.

"The commercial is good," said Sam as soon as Leto was gone, "But tell me, how was Alina?" Yana shook her fist beneath his nose and pulled him out of the room.

Not long after that, Alina came by, gave me a quick wink, and asked Sergei if she could talk to him for a minute. My heart leapt when I saw her. I hadn't seen her again over the weekend. As

Sergei, the guilty prisoner, rose and passed her in the doorway, she made a face at me. Sergei returned twenty minutes later grumbling and unable to look at me. I didn't see Alina for the rest of the day.

Later in the afternoon word went around that Ilya had been beaten up over the weekend and was too banged up to do the newscast. "Mushkin's doing it," said Sergei. "Ilya's up in the bar drinking with Leto."

I went up to see him. He laughed when he saw me and pulled deeply on his cigarette. Exhaling over the table as he spoke, he said, "How do you like my new fashion statement?" He had a dark black eye and a couple stitches in his lip. His nose was swollen, and he had bruises around his neck.

"I'm telling you," Leto was saying. "You took this beating for their blessed station, you should ask Gennadi for money."

"You think like mafia yourself, *bladt*," cursed Ilya shaking his head.

I sat, had a beer, and Ilya told me what happened. He'd been the last one to leave the station on Friday before going to the party. As he was locking up, a couple of mafia types approached and mistook him for Gennadi. "You've got money," they'd said. "Give us some."

"Idiots," shouted Leto. "How could they mistake you for Gennadi?"

Ilya had lain unconscious on the steps of the *Hobby Dom* in the cold. He didn't know for how long. "I came in on Saturday and found my frozen blood trampled under boots," he said. No one had taken his absence at the party as unusual since he often skipped such events.

"But you know what this means, *bladt*," said Ilya. "The word was already out about the Soros money before Gennadi even announced it to the station."

"He must have told a few people," I said.

"He told me and a few others."

"I've got to use the phone," said Leto, standing to go down to the lobby. "I've had my sister minding the phone at my parents' flat since the commercial ran this afternoon. We'll see if it's worth the money."

"Is that the money you haven't gotten around to paying us yet?" coughed Ilya.

Leto laughed, "My word is as good as that of all the others who haven't paid you yet. It's as good as MMN's, *chort.*"

As Leto departed Ilya growled, "It was probably him, *bladt.* There's a New Russian for you."

When Leto returned a few minutes later he was smiling broadly. "Everyone wants oranges. Who would have thought Siberians could eat so many oranges?" He ordered us another round of drinks. "I've got someone that wants to ship them to Omsk and Novosibirsk as well."

"Don't get too busy to help us with the equipment," said Ilya, whose mood was worsening as he drank.

"Of course, I'll do it. I'll be going to Moscow in a couple of weeks." Leto, Ilya explained, was going to help TV-N obtain new equipment with the Soros money. While the Soros people were willing to import equipment from the U.S., Gennadi hoped to get more for his money by buying stuff through a contact of Leto's.

"It's probably stolen from Bosnia," said Ilya.

"*Da,*" laughed Leto, "Probably it is."

Moments later Artur Losha burst through the doors and loudly announced to the bartender that he would buy the next round and to bring out the vodka. "And don't tell me you don't have it!"

Ilya looked at me and rolled his battered eyes. Losha had attained local-legend status as a dissident journalist during Communism and made no secret of his opinion that he, not Ilya, should be heading up the news department. Losha was a large lanky man of sixty or more with a grayed handlebar mustache and a booming gravelly voice. He dressed like a prospector or a hunter or a retired pirate. Looking at him, you'd expect his hands to be calloused bear paws.

He swaggered to our table and let fall one of his meathooks with a thud, making our bottles jump. "*Nu,*" he spat, gassing us with the vodka on his breath, "you missed your broadcast."

Ilya scoffed. "I didn't miss it, *bladt,* I was too ugly to go on." He took a drink and chuckled. "Alina even tried putting makeup on me, but it only made me look like a sex change disaster."

Leto and I laughed. Losha remained ticked off. "I have suffered beatings many times, but I have never missed a deadline."

"But you're not as pretty as our boy Ilya here," cackled Leto. "In fact, you're probably no more ugly beat up than you are normally."

Losha's irritation bloomed and his eyes grew wide. He held his noxious breath and then let it burst in our faces as he listed the times he'd been beaten by thugs and police, gangsters, and the KGB. This was a contest Leto could jump right into, and within seconds they were rolling up their sleeves and pant legs to show off scars. Then Losha unveiled his ultimate wound. "You won't beat this, you ungrateful brat," he growled and wrestled his knotty sweater over his head. "*Vot!*" He pointed to just above his left nipple. "I was stabbed in the chest. It came only millimeters from my heart."

Conceding defeat, Leto straightened his clothes. Ilya sat shaking his head.

I'd come up with a joke, but by the time I translated it in my head, Losha had revealed his near-death blow, and it was no longer appropriate. I said it anyway: "It looks like you both have a scar for every time you've been drunk." Leto laughed and pounded the table, but Losha was insulted, and after putting on his sweater, left the bar in disgust. Leto laughed all the harder, but Ilya tried to apologize on my behalf.

"It's no good," he said, "we should pay him the respect he deserves."

I stayed for another couple drinks before going downstairs to get my coat. I found an apple in my pocket. Smiling to myself, I decided to walk home rather than wait for the bus. It was warmer than usual. Maybe winter would end before too long, after all. I indulged the thought as I headed off down the sidewalk. I took off my glove so I could feel the apple. I was tipsy. "Don't be swallowed by a manhole," I warned myself, and stepped around one of the gaping mantraps. The steam rising from it tasted like dust as I inhaled.

It wasn't late. There were other people out, though not many. Frunzenskaya Avenue was deeply rutted, and chunks of ice and pavement laid along its sides like slag at a quarry. Still, the little Ladas, the kalashnikov of cars, charged over the potholes with sounds akin to a dumpster being hit with an aluminum bat. Inside the cars, I knew, the ride was as uncomfortable as it sounded.

It was a longer walk than I'd thought and not so warm. I quickened pace and concentrated on the rhythm of my boot clomps and the swishing of my coat. At intersections I barely looked up, not even bothering to scavenge at the kiosks.

Suddenly I was upon two women. One was an old *babushka*, tiny and hunched, walking slowly on the icy sidewalk with a cane. Between us was a big woman in a heavy coat. The frail granny called out to her, "Do you know how far it is to Komsomolski Prospect?"

"What? Komsomolski?" the woman snapped angrily, but then in an instant answered with empathy, "Oh, *babushka*, it's a long way." The old woman gave a slight cry. "What are you doing out so late?" asked the woman. "*Babushka*, how did you get so far from home?"

"I'm not ignoring you," Alina told me one day that week with a wink. "I'm busy. We'll talk soon."

I hoped she'd come over to my flat that evening, and in anticipation I scrubbed the floor on my hands and knees with a t-shirt sacrificed for a rag. It barely took off a layer of dust. I did the dishes. Those that had sat in the sink had gained a layer of rust and calcium from the dripping faucet. They, too, were stained for all time. Preparing for the best, I spliced two sets of headphones to one plug. We'd talked about music, maybe we could listen to something together. Just as I finished wrapping the wires in tape, she knocked lightly on the door.

She stepped in, pulling a cool current of air from outside, and smiled at me softly. She put down a shopping bag and handed me her coat, which I hung in the wobbling wardrobe by the door.

"I have something for you and something for us to share," she said coyly. First was a knife and a small cutting board. "I was told you needed these." She smiled. "I had extras." Second were a few cans of beer she'd picked up. "It's Danish, I think."

She slipped off her boots. "You should have slippers for guests."

"I just washed the floors," I said as I went into the kitchen in my sock feet. "I could give you some wool socks."

"Did you clean because you thought I was coming over?" she asked as she followed me. "Are all American men so domestic? Do you clean with a smile, just as you do everything with a smile?" she teased.

I used my new utensils to cut up sausage and bread and the apple she'd left me.

"That's a lovely *Yabloka*, young man," she lilted playfully.

We popped our cans and drank.

"When I was in high school," I told her. "I worked in a grocery store, and I wore a little red vest and a button that said 'Ask Me, I'm Here To Help.' I had to smile all day."

"Just like the ladies in our shops," she joked.

I nodded, taking a gulp of the tinny, overly carbonated beer. "I used to have metal teeth as well," I answered, and we laughed.

"Did you have braces?" she said motioning across her teeth so I would understand the Russian word.

I nodded and displayed the payoff of orthodontics. "I had donkey teeth before."

"Now you can smile like a good Yankee," she said. "I'm lucky I didn't need them. I couldn't have gotten them."

"You could have gotten your teeth done now, like Grisha," I kidded and she shook her head solemnly, as if at something tragic. Grisha was a wiry-haired man in the office who'd been going through the slow torture of having his smile renovated by a local, although reputedly western-trained, dentist. Western Poland, maybe. They'd filed all his teeth down to jagged white points, and for several days he had to go around looking like a man morphing into a monster. His mouth appeared so wide and empty, save for the stubs, and his eyes so pained and humiliated, that he looked like some sad deep-sea fish evolved in deprivation. You had to look away; it was that bad. Finally, when they set the caps, he looked almost as frightening. It was as if the teeth they'd given him were one size too big, and he was transformed into a different kind of animal entirely.

"My God, Grisha," shouted Uncle Sam as his co-worker entered the room smiling proudly. "You look like a piranha."

Alina was embarrassed by my making fun of him. Attempting to make up for it, I said, "You have a beautiful smile."

She blushed and sipped from her can. "I've done some modeling."

"What kind of modeling?"

She shrugged. "Normal things, clothes, sometimes a bathing suit. I didn't do it for long. I'm a more serious person than that. I wanted to be in business. It was silly standing around for people, having your picture taken. I want to accomplish something. I don't think looking pretty is much to accomplish." After a pause in which I bobbed my head attentively, she asked, "It's a surprise for you that I was a model?"

"No. You're beautiful."

She looked down as if embarrassed for me. "I meant because I dress so badly."

"I'm no judge."

"Yes," she agreed, "maybe you're like me. But tell me, why do you have only old clothes?"

"I'm a cameraman. There's not usually a dress code."

"Have you noticed that I dress differently? The other women all wear the same things, always a black skirt and a blouse. I can't wear that. Even Nastia, she dresses too old. I just can't look like that," she said, her voice giving away that it was a matter of importance to her. "All I can get here are those kinds of clothes, so I just wear jeans."

"You've got the pink dress," I proffered and made her smile.

"Do you like that one? I wear that when I have a meeting with a client, otherwise I don't bother. Look what I'm wearing now," she said, sweeping her hand down the front of her faded purple sweater. "I look like a university student."

"You're not far out of university."

"Once you're out, you should be out. No pretending that you are young forever."

"We're still young."

"Maybe we have different ideas about what is young, *malchik*. Women have things they have to think about."

"Children?"

"Not now, but you know, it's better to have them before you are thirty."

"I thought it was thirty-five."

"Am I making you nervous, talking about children?" she grinned. "I wouldn't have children here, not now. Things need to get a lot better, and I don't see anything changing fast. It's the instability of things that worries me. What will happen next year, or after that? Nobody knows. Of course, it was worse before. In 1990 it was hard to find food, even bread. Everyone was taking buses out to the country to grow vegetables in the fields. You had to have dollars. If you didn't, you had to find a way of getting dollars."

"What did you do?"

"I was living with my mother and sister then, so I wasn't completely on my own like I am now. They paid me in dollars for the modeling. It's sad to remember those times. You know, I was going to say, when we were talking about cleaning, next time I come over maybe I'll bring you some good soap, some Tide for your laundry. Tell me the things you need," she said. "I like hunting for them."

"I can't do that," I told her and tried unsuccessfully to translate the phrase, 'you're not my maid.'

"I want to be like your Lubomira and bring people things when they need them," she said.

We talked next about Ilya. "Nobody wondered where he was because he often doesn't come to those kinds of things," Alina explained. "I've heard him say he only likes to go to parties he's not invited to. Our indefatigable journalist! Probably that's how he gets beaten up so often," she laughed. "But you know, Connor, it's actually very serious. Someone told those mafia guys about the Soros money. No one was supposed to know. We have a rat at the station," she said ominously but with a grin. "Our dear leader, Gennadi, has decreed that a male member of the staff must stay in the station all night to keep watch."

"What's he worried about? They have metal doors, bars on the windows, alarms."

Alina smiled. "Our clever mafia can get past all those things. And the alarms don't actually work. The people that installed them weren't happy with the commercial we made them in trade, so they didn't finish the job. It's a fire he's worried about, that someone could throw a bomb in between the bars on the windows."

We popped the second pair of tallboy beers, which I'd hung in a bag out the kitchen window to get cold. Everywhere in Tomsk you saw food hanging outside kitchen windows in plastic bags. Appearing the slightest bit tipsy, Alina told me, "I have some more gossip, but you have to promise to tell no one."

I nodded eagerly.

"Marat is an old friend of mine," she began, sweeping her hair back, "and I don't want to talk badly of him, but did you notice he wasn't at the party? He went to visit his mistress. Such drama." Grinning, she shook her head and took a drink. "Do you care one way or another if someone is married?" she asked. "Do you think if someone is married you should stay away from them even if they are unhappy and looking for someone?"

"Are you thinking about having an affair with a married man?"

"You're so literal, *malchik.* It's just a theoretical question."

"Are you talking about something you've already done?"

She sighed, becoming frustrated. "Forget it. It was just a topic for conversation."

"I want to make sure I understand what we are talking about."

She fumed, appearing to struggle to keep her pleasant mood.

"Okay, conversation," I smiled. "It's not your job to keep someone else's marriage together. I've never been in that situation, exactly. You'd have to know what you wanted to happen. Do you want that person to leave the marriage for you? Or do you just want something temporary?"

"Do you always think of things in these kinds of terms, Connor?" Alina responded, maybe offended, maybe amused. "Do you always know what you want and make a plan?"

"When I can, I do."

With a wry smile, she said, "You've never fallen in love?"

"*Nyet.*"

"Maybe you'll see then that you can't always plan things so clearly."

I shrugged. "I don't know if I will. The idea that I'm going to meet someone and suddenly be willing to do things that I don't want to do seems unlikely. But what was that question about?"

"I'll tell you another time. I don't give away my secrets for free."

"Can I guess?"

"No. Let's talk about something else."

"Were you talking about Nikolai and Nastia, or were you talking about Nikolai and you?"

Her eyes opened wide. "Who told you that?"

"No one told me."

"Sergei?"

"No one."

Alina blushed. "Well, everyone else at the station knows, so why not you? I told you that he still lives with his wife, but only because of money. He told me they were getting divorced, but it wasn't true. He just kept saying it and saying it, until I got tired and broke it off. Now he must tell Nastia the same thing. But she doesn't care, the whore. She only thinks about how it will help her at the station. She's been through half the men there." Vexed, she finished, "*Nu*, there it is, a simple thing. It was more than a year ago." She pretended to spit on the ground beside her.

We were finished with our beers, so I suggested, "Let's listen to music." I got up and fetched the hacked headphones and tape player from the other room. Amusedly, Alina unraveled them.

"When did you do this?" she smiled.

"Just now."

"So this is your plan?"

"You said you wanted to hear my tapes."

"Connor, I want to apologize. I shouldn't have talked like that, even about Nastia. I know you don't care, but women aren't supposed to talk that way."

"Fuck it," I said in English. She tittered and repeated the same in a half whisper.

I'd recorded a number of tapes from CDs before I'd left home. The tape in the player, I told her, was of an African musician who had moved to London. He was half German and had tried living in Berlin, but he'd been beaten by skinheads, nearly killed, and decided to leave. He was discovered by a big western musician who wanted a little third-world flavor on his latest record. He was so impressed with the African that he funded and produced an album for him.

"I've had bad experiences with Germans, too," frowned Alina. "But I've already told you too much tonight."

"Tell me."

"It isn't very comfortable sitting here at a kitchen table. Maybe there's somewhere else we can go to listen to the African sing, *Da?*" With her lips pursed in a repressed grin, she sauntered to the bedroom. "Just to sit," she said. "Just to listen to music." She laid on the bed crosswise with her knees bent over the side. It was warm and dark. "Leave the light off," she instructed. I put the headphones over her ears and laid beside her.

As the music played, I stole a glance at her profile; her eyes were closed, her lips relaxed instead of smirking. I could feel her tapping her finger on the sheet beside me. I put my hand over hers. I traced the line of her arm to her cheek and kissed her. With the headphones playing to us in separate worlds, we kissed and caressed each other. We hung there, wrapped in cords, and smiling as we made out. Then we stopped kissing and started talking again as if nothing had happened, as if our bodies had decided to get together but our minds weren't yet aware.

"I'm glad he doesn't sing in German," she said, sitting up and sweeping the light headphones back through her mussed hair. "I want to be like the African. I'll get away from here, and when I get homesick, I can sing a Russian song."

"Tell me about Germany," I said.

"Connor, you have to be careful what you ask me," she said firmly.

I leaned forward to kiss her again. Now she kissed me harder than before. Her mouth was sweet and soft, and the air in my lungs was her warm breath. She pushed me back on the bed and laid on top of me. I slid my hands under her sweater and against her skin, gliding along the arc of her sides from one finger beneath her jeans to the edge of her bra. She responded with breathy soft sounds and catlike writhing at my touch. My hands met at the small of her back and sailed up the seam of her spine. She leaned back against my arms and pushed her hips into mine.

"You're shaking," she observed.

"*Da.*"

"I better leave now or else we'll get ourselves in trouble, *da?*"

We had another similar evening early the next week. We were careful not to leave the office together.

Boris reached across the passenger seat of his Niva Cossack, another of his re-imported cars, and shoved the door open for me. "Now that Sveta knows I can take you, she doesn't feel like playing so much," he said as I got into the car. I was his stand-in partner. Every couple of weeks, he'd call me at work and tell me that he was going to pick me up.

I rarely got phone calls at the station, and it was even more infrequent that I was notified of them or given a message. Boris was the exception. With a look of urgency, if not panic, the receptionist would search me out. Today she'd caught me coming back from the *stolovaya* with Ilya and a small crowd from the news department. "Fucking badminton," I'd groaned to my laughing colleagues. I was too busy, I'd said. Within moments of returning to the studio, Gennadi came by and took me aside. "Sergei can finish the work," he'd said. "It's better that you go with Vodopyanov."

Said Boris, "I tell her she's going to get fat sitting around the house. I don't want to be married to a *babushka.*" He laughed as we pulled away from TV-N.

As was the routine, after our game we went back to Boris's flat where Sveta served us dinner and Kirby demonstrated his willingness to maim me, tonight by resting his muzzle in my crotch while daring me to make eye contact.

"So Connor," said Boris after we'd had a couple drinks. "How would you like to see Siberian gangsters in action?"

Clapping my bottle of Czech beer on the coaster in front of me, I responded enthusiastically, "I'd love to as long as we don't get shot! And I can bring a camera."

"No camera," he chuckled. "You can have a chance to see what your friend Fest can't understand. Maybe you will tell him about it."

A couple evenings later I was again in Vodopyanov's Niva. We drove to a place just off Prospect Lenina, next to the tram tracks. The sickly greenish neon sign read, 'Grill*Bar.' Three guys in leather coats were waiting for us. Immediately one of them stood and demanded, "What the hell did you bring him for?"

"*Ni nado, ni nado,*" Boris calmed him. "This is my American guest..."

"I know who he is, Borya," interrupted the other, sitting back down.

"This is my representative, Igor. He takes my business affairs very seriously," chuckled Boris calmly, easily overriding him. The man seated next to Igor, who looked like a college football player in a pinstripe suit and leather coat, chuckled as well. His name was Sergei. Igor reminded me of Anton in Moscow. He was slim and tall and appeared of Georgian descent.

The 'Grill*Bar' was cold, dark, low-ceilinged, and smoky. We sat in flimsy plastic patio chairs at matching wobbly tables. A song came on the TV, probably TV-N, and the barman turned it up. Boris called into my ear, "This group is called Yanksters Gangsters."

Igor smiled and shook his head amusedly. Gesturing around us, he said, "Chicago in the 1930s."

Another guy joined us momentarily. He was short and broad, had a buzz cut and dark, deep-set eyes. His name was Sasha, and the reverence with which the other men welcomed him made it clear that he was the boss tonight. He observed me with apparent indifference.

"We are lucky to have Sasha here," Boris told me. "He works as a bodyguard and has a special permit to carry a revolver." Vodopyanov laughed, "Tonight he is my bodyguard and my lawyer, too." He turned back to Sasha. "Let's go find them, I'm tired of waiting.

"While we're gone," Boris told me as he got up. "Tell Igor what you were telling me about Chapter Eleven bankruptcy in America. He'll be interested."

Boris returned almost an hour later. Excited, he told me, "Connor, this is a bit more serious than I expected. If you want to go home, I can have someone drive you."

"That's a good idea," said Igor, who had indeed been interested in U.S. business law and in the intervening time had gotten me to tell him everything I knew. "To do business in these times in Russia," Igor had told me shaking his head, "you can't be too ethical of a man." He'd also predicted that this dispute would become more of an issue than Boris anticipated. As if complaining about a boisterous younger brother, he'd said, "Always Vodopyanov says, 'no problem,' like he is from Texas, like he can have anything he wants." He now said eagerly, "I can drive him."

"I'm not sending you away, Connor," said Boris, "You can still come, of course. It's no problem."

Not able to hide a smile from Igor, I said, "I still want to come." I could see Boris was pleased. Sasha, Igor, Sergei, and I climbed into the Niva with Vodopyanov and drove fast through town.

The other night after badminton, Boris had said, "So let me explain the situation. You know about my business re-importing cars. And you understand that we don't have real banks the way you have them. I can't go to the bank and get a loan without a great deal of difficulty. Even if I do get a loan, it is very expensive and short term. I have to pay it back within a year, usually, and the interest is one hundred percent. This is on top of the fluctuation of the currency. You see our difficulty. So for these reasons, it is common to exchange goods that have a resale value. We trade instead of buy.

"In this case, I agreed to trade a number of cars for some other goods. I delivered the cars, but this other businessman has decided to try to steal from me. He says we never had a deal."

"What were the goods?"

"It doesn't matter, Connor. He is a businessman, simply. We were to trade some goods, merchandise. He is a Russian businessman, Connor, he sells everything, ice cream and automobiles. You sell what you have, and you buy what you can sell.

"He paid me for some of the cars, but then suddenly he forgets that he still owes me eight thousand dollars. I have proof. He is simply lying, but what can I do? To you, I should bring him to court. They will hear both of our sides and look at our evidence and make a reasonable decision, right? But that is not how it works here. We have no business law. If you go to court it's just a matter of who will pay the bigger bribe. So we don't go to court. We don't hire lawyers, Connor. We hire mafia. Every businessman must have connections, *cvyazi*, within a mafia. Do you know *cvyazi*? The mafia I hire will represent me in this case. They are my legal team, and they're well armed," he'd laughed.

In the Niva we arrived at a rundown university dormitory, looming, bluish, like a tenement made of chalk. Sasha, Sergei, and Igor got out to check the scene.

"Why the change of location?" I asked Boris.

He sighed as if bored of dealing with stupid people. "They said the bar was on our territory. Now we're in their territory."

Igor came out of the dorm and waved us in. We stepped into a dusty foyer where a watcher woman sat behind a rectangular window on a gray cot in a small room. The light from her cell spilled into the entryway, casting her as an exhibit in a sad post-Soviet human zoo. She propped herself up on one arm and scowled like a lizard in a cold cage.

Without acknowledging her, we headed down a hallway. Sasha swung in behind Boris, so he couldn't see, and pulled me aside. Holding my arm solidly, but without hurting me, he said calmly, "Borya wants you here, *da*. I do not. You make things more dangerous for us. Do you understand my Russian? Take off your *shapka* and keep your mouth shut." I noticed his pointed and broken teeth. I nodded fearfully.

We entered a smoky meeting room, where the other gang awaited us, and sat around one side of a table. They were all southerners. The darkest guy sat facing Sasha across the corner of the table. His name was Iosif. He was their man in charge. Behind him sat an arrogant-looking guy with a green down coat and a white scarf. He was the businessman. In a back corner sat two young guys looking bored, like Dobermanns at rest. They reminded me of the *soldat* on the train from Moscow. A fat, unshaven, sickly, and possibly drunk guy named Armand paced back and forth.

We were outnumbered but were certainly the cooler looking gang. Boris and I sat behind Sasha. Boris handed him several long fax sheets, and Sasha began to speak. His voice was rich and resounding. I could feel it pulsing through his back. As he read the litany of evidence, his tone veered back and forth from imploringly reasonable to sneering intimidation. The whole while Iosif listened calmly and occasionally smiled, nodded. His pleasant grin even made Sasha cool off once or twice. He blinked his eyes slowly like a sleepy lion, sending a message of confidence, an assurance that he could get nasty, too.

Sasha spread the faxes on the table and bumped them with his finger. There were two packs of cigarettes on the table, one for each gang. Both made from American tobacco, but ours was a name brand while theirs was generic. The hosts had provided a case of orange juice for the meeting, and several one-liter juice boxes were scattered around the table. Sergei drank the most juice, but frequently spilled from the troublesome containers that required that a corner be torn away. He kept himself busy throughout the hour-long meeting by preventing the tail end of the fax sheets from sliding into the orange juice he had spilled.

The two sides debated what had actually happened, who had agreed to what, and who faxed whom. They went in circles. Armand paced, stopping only to hack and spit weakly into an empty juice box.

Sasha directed his growl at the man in the green coat. "The only evidence here is this fax. Everything we need to know is right here. It is from you to Vodopyanov. It says exactly what the deal is to be. We have a receipt from you for the delivery of the cars from Vodopyanov. So the only thing left is for you to deliver the specified merchandise."

"It is delivered," said the man dully.

Boris picked up a duffel bag from the floor and unzipped it. "You sent me this shit," he said and emptied the contents onto the table.

Sergei chuckled, "Women's pants." He held up a flimsy bright red bit of fabric.

"They're tights, *bladt*," said Sasha and flipped a pair at Iosif. "Six fucking boxes of red tights in exchange for three cars, *bladt*."

Sergei caught my eye and smiled as he wiped his sticky juice hands on a pair of tights.

Sasha appeared ready to come out of his seat. The man in green looked at him blankly.

"*Ni nado, ni nado,*" said Iosif. "I am inclined to agree with Vodopyanov in this case."

Armand nodded. "The trade wasn't fair."

"Golden words, golden words," said Sasha sitting back.

"Will you accept a trade of more substantial merchandise," asked Iosif dispassionately, "or are you only willing to deal in cash now?"

The man in green looked down his nose at the proceedings, but was plainly agitated that his own representatives had sided against him.

Boris borrowed Igor's pocket calculator and started figuring. After a moment, he announced his number.

"This is impossible," huffed the green coat.

"I have figured in compensation," said Boris.

Green coat offered a lower number. Sasha laughed maliciously. "Listen to this, *bladt,* we're at the bazaar."

"*Oi, yoi, yoi.*" Boris refused. They argued some more, but not long. The green coat gave in at the behest of his mafia. Boris wanted everything in writing, so most of us got up to stretch our legs while they worked out the details.

Sergei winked at me as he stood up. I sidled up to Sasha and cautiously offered my compliments. "Thank you," he said with a surprising grin and gave me his hand to shake. "So this doesn't look like a crime to you, after all, *da?* It's a relief. This is the only way anything gets done. We're lucky the Armenian is reasonable."

"How often do meetings like this happen?" I asked.

"All the time."

"What happens if the two sides can't reach an agreement?"

He shrugged. "Then there's a fight."

"How often does that happen?"

Sasha shook his head and said with a smirk, "You need to work on your Russian, I can't understand what you're saying. Why don't you go out to the car and practice your verbs."

Boris emerged from the meeting room victorious. The two gangs shook hands. "I don't know anything about the mafia," joked one of the Dobermanns, "I'm from the Pioneer Palace."

"It's not a lot of money," Boris told me in English as we departed, "but worth the effort." The watcher woman glared from her exhibit. Igor, Boris, and I piled into the Niva. In his joy, and concern that his wife would think he'd been killed, Boris drove fast. "This car, she moves," he said. We arrived back at Boris's place knowing that dinner and a bottle of vodka was waiting for us.

SOROKA: Part Two

The Progress of Exclusion

Chapter 10

Alina peeked through the door of the editing room. I was alone. "Young man, my American friend, I would like to invite you for dinner at my apartment on Saturday night. I will make you real *pelmeni*."

By now we'd had a number of music sessions at each other's apartments. Our coy pretext each time had been that one of us had found a new beer to try while kiosk hunting.

"I've found a beer from your Milwaukee," she'd say.

"And I've found a beer from your Germany. So we'll have to have two meetings after work."

"*Da*, we're having many meetings after work, aren't we, Connor?"

On Saturday afternoon, I picked out clothes that might somehow be different from what I wore to work everyday. I shaved looking in the mirror and noticed my hands were shaking. I'd already stashed a condom in my coat pocket. The last time we'd met, we'd almost taken it through the night. I was kissing her standing, and she'd turned around in my arms, my lips first against her cheek, then on the back of her neck. She'd leaned into me and pushed my hands beneath her waistband and held them there as she rolled her hips into me. I rubbed her until she was slick between my fingers. But we'd stopped. We pulled ourselves apart. We kissed once more. Her eyes were glazed and her cheeks flushed.

I walked to her flat taking the shortcuts she'd shown me, one through a schoolyard with a junked playground, another set of overflowing dumpsters.

Instead of entering her building at the back as I usually did, I went around to Kirova and bought chocolate at a kiosk. I fumbled the coins as I paid. I looked around for a bottle of wine, Dubonnet maybe, but there was none.

I knocked on the security door in the hall and heard the scuffle of her locking Otto in the bathroom. She opened the door for me wearing her mother's apron and with flour on the tops of her hands and wrists. We hugged each other, something we'd never done before as a greeting. She might have told me, 'You're shaking already and my clothes are still on.' But she spared me her wit this once. She smiled, and I ventured to kiss her. "*Fu,*" she said and looked down the hall to see if any of her neighbors were out before kissing me back.

The apartment was fragrant with the smell of uncooked meat and garlic. Her small kitchen was full of equipment and the windows were steamed up, which made it look even tinier and more crammed. In what cabinets she stored all these things, I had no idea. There was a towering multi-tiered steamer that stood at least two feet high from the stovetop. She had a meat grinder bolted to her small table. In one big mixing bowl there was a mound of ground meat mixed with garlic, onion, and herbs. In another bowl she was mixing flour and water for dough.

"I'm making you pelmeni, remember?" she said sweetly over her shoulder. "I'm going to let Otto out. You boys are going to have to get used to each other." She opened the door, and the dog charged me. Alina caught and scolded him, after which he stood glaring as I presented him my hand to smell.

Alina flipped her dog some meat. He snatched out of the air with an impressive snap of teeth.

"Why does everyone in Russia have a dog? You don't have room in your flats for them. You don't even have dog food."

"Connor," said Alina with a comic glint in her eye. "If you want cat people, you'll have to go to England."

Expertly this young woman, beautiful even in the dowdy apron, neatly folded scoops of meat into squares of rolled dough. I sat and watched her fingers flick through the assembly line, shaping her dumplings and setting them on the stacked grates in the steamer. "Every family has their own recipe," she said. "This is my mama's, of course. It's the best, you'll see. It's in the blend of meats. We use beef, pork, and lamb. It's hard to find lamb, so I always try to have some in the freezer. You can make it without the lamb, of course, but it's not the same. If there's no lamb, you need more onions."

Alina made tea, opened the chocolate. "You should have filmed me making *pelmeni* for your documentary."

"I should be filming all kinds of things," I droned. "It's turning out to be a waste."

"A waste?"

"Maybe more valuable as life experience than a professional one."

"You're sure there's a difference?"

"I'm glad to be useful at the station, but I'm just doing basic stuff. That's all anybody wants me to do. If I can't get out and do more than edit Marat's weekly epic on egg prices, I'm not going to have a film."

"Epic, that's a good word," she complimented my Russian.

"I got it from Sergei. What I've got to do is put together some kind of work that I might get into film festivals. Something that will get noticed."

"I'm sure we'll give it to you sooner or later," she smiled. "Gennadi knows the value of it. A documentary about the station, in English especially, will help him get more funding. You know things at the station are unstable now. It's all he can do to pay us. And you're a great help, Connor. Everyone says you're going to be a great success. It'd be better for you not to be so pessimistic, *malchik.* "

"I'm just trying to gauge what I can accomplish. I appreciate everyone's confidence in me, but I went to school for video production. My skills are the same as everyone else who graduated."

"*Vot*, pessimism," she chided cheerily. "Do you know this joke? When the pessimist says, '*Oi*, it can't get any worse' what does the optimist say? 'Oh, *da*, it can.'"

"I know that one."

At last Alina positioned the final rack of pelmeni in the steamer. "Now we have to find some way to entertain ourselves while our dinner goes to the banya," she said with a wink. We opened beers and went into the living room.

"Do you play an instrument?" I asked her.

"A little guitar. I took lessons when I was a little girl." Alina sat with her legs folded next to her on the little couch and flipped through a fashion magazine.

"Americans take pride in not being able to do anything," I griped sycophantically. "Especially women."

"Probably your sister would slap you for saying that."

"She would. I mean things like cooking or playing an instrument."

"So, at least, American women can stand up for themselves, even if they cannot cook or play an instrument." She smirked dryly.

"You stand up for yourself. You make your own decisions."

"It's different for me. I'm alone. Nobody tells me what to do."

"There's one good thing about the situation at TV-N," I said. "I won't hesitate to leave. I'd like to do some traveling in the summer. But that's a secret."

"*Bolshoi secrete*! Where do you want to go?"

"Baikal. Ilya mentioned maybe driving there. Boris has also talked about going on horseback to an old gulag out on the steppe."

She nodded, glanced downward.

"Ilya would be a good person to travel with, I think."

"Probably he would be. Now come have *pelmeni.*" She scratched a match and lit a candle. She filled our bowls with dumplings and broth, Otto too. The *pelmeni* were delicious.

"The cook doesn't clean," I insisted after dinner. She dried and put things away. "I want to see what magic cupboard you store that giant steamer in."

"*Nyet,* I borrowed it from my father. I took a bus and carried it. I'll have to take it back soon," she said, appearing tired now. "He always gets nervous about me taking things."

"I feel bad you've gone through so much effort. I could help you bring it back."

"It's aluminum, it's not heavy. I wouldn't take you to meet my father anyway. He'd get the wrong idea. He's a bastard. I've never brought anyone to see him," she said sternly. We washed and dried for a few moments in silence. "Tell me, Connor, you must find my life very boring. This little apartment. My silly pelmeni."

"*Nyet,*" I answered as emphatically as I could without sounding condescending. "Don't put yourself down. Your life is more interesting than anyone I know."

She looked dubious.

"*Pravda,* you're a professional woman making good money. TV-N is doing exciting things. You've got a future there."

She sighed, "I don't belong here. I want to go to Europe, or America, maybe England. I'd fit in better there."

I laughed cautiously. "Why? Everything is in movement here, history. In the west, it's stagnant. Here you contribute, there you participate."

She shrugged.

I took a breath. "I was thinking the other night that maybe people can sometimes accomplish things without even trying when they are in the right place at the right time. Conditions motivate them to act, and in whatever direction they turn, there is a vacuum. So a talented person will almost always succeed. That's how things are here. Anything you do will be moving towards something better. You almost don't need to try. You just need to be here and not turn away."

Alina stood deciphering my bad Russian. She shook her head, "You always have to try, but that aside, Connor, you don't know what it is to want stillness. I'm tired of struggling. I want to relax. What we want more than anything is for things to be easy. Not everyone can fight all the time. There are more kinds of talent than that." She sighed. "Do you think I should stay here for my own good? Or for the good of my country? If you tell me I have opportunities here, maybe I want those opportunities and am willing to pay the price for them, but maybe I am not. Maybe you are willing to pay the price for them, but I don't think so." All this she said calmly, good naturedly.

"Whatever the bad things about Communism," she went on, "there was a time, around the time I was born, maybe, when you didn't have to worry about much. It was a slow decline, but it was comfortable for children at least, like spending time with an idealistic, maybe temperamental, grandparent. You hear a lot now about how people should stay in Russia to build a new country. We assume that we all have connections to each other as Russians and that individuals should be willing to suffer in order to help. That's still Communism, isn't it? I'm not one of those people. I don't think I like Russian people any more or less than I would like people anywhere else. Just because I was born here, doesn't mean I automatically have a special affection for things. Maybe the opposite. What I want is a better life in a place where people are at least no worse than they are here. Maybe it's even an American idea, *da*? Isn't America populated by people who decided to give up on their so-called own? So maybe it's ironic for one little Yankee boy to tell someone else to stay in her own miserable country to help it succeed when she could go somewhere else where she might have more opportunity, where her talents might be more profitable." She gave me a victorious feline smirk.

I tried to keep up with her. "I didn't tell you that. It just seems to me that here, right now, anything is possible."

Unwavering, she looked at me and laughed. "I take back what I said about you being a pessimist. You are either pathetically optimistic or horribly misinformed."

We both laughed.

"I think now we can find nicer things to talk about."

We went into the living room, and Alina folded out the couch. She tossed a sheer scarf over the light. We kissed, and after a while, she undressed, and there were the sounds and tiny breezes, nearly silent, of her clothing hushing as she slid it over her skin.

"This is a nice blanket," she whispered, pulling it over her mostly nude body. "Feel it, it's very soft, *da*? I don't know what it's made of, something from China, but it's not *fuflo.* I like this blanket."

"Can I come underneath there with you?" I asked as I undressed.

"Of course, I'm waiting for you."

"Under the blanket."

"All warm and full of *pelmeni.*"

"Thank you for the *pelmeni.*"

"*Ni za shto.*"

"And for the blanket."

"Well, come under."

"Do you want to do sex?" I asked her, mixing up my verbs. She smiled, her lips shining.

"Do I want to *do* sex? Poor boy, didn't they even teach you to ask a girl to sleep with you?"

"Only to order beer and ask for the bathroom."

"Shh, don't make jokes. We should never laugh in bed, Connor," she instructed seriously.

I kissed her. I kissed her breasts and stomach. I kissed around the stitching of her panties before she lifted her hips for me to remove them. I ran my tongue through her sprightly dark pubic hair and gently parted her lips. She had the taste of melon and seawater. She moaned softly and held her breasts.

I picked my pants up off the floor and felt for the condom I'd transferred from my coat. I went into the bathroom to put it on and wiped Nonoxynol on my thigh.

Otto laid quietly on the floor.

Alina held me by the hips and slowly guided me into her. She closed her eyes, and we moved slowly. Her mouth was open slightly. Her cheeks were flush. Her breasts pressed against my ribs, and our hips were linked. I trembled and came quickly.

She smiled sympathetically and put her hand on my burning face. "I don't think you're such an experienced *chelovek*."

I smiled abashedly and laid back. "*Nyet.*"

"I'll give you lots of practice." She wrinkled her nose at me. We laid side by side, naked on the narrow couch, our clothes on the floor, the scent of us haunting and uncomfortably strong. After a moment I got up to discard the condom. She came into the bathroom behind me, her body so beautiful, her sparse pubic hair matted. I ached even more. I touched her. I kissed her. I stole a glance in the mirror of her in my arms.

"Let's take a bath, and I'll teach you Russian songs." She stooped over the deep claw-foot tub to test the water before climbing in. She sat back beneath the high tap and let the water spill over her shoulders and chest, gasping at the heat. She smiled and invited me in.

"This is a song I will sing when I am homesick, when I'm far away from here." She began a mournful song in a soft voice. "*Oi moroz, moroz. Ni moroz mnya.*" After going on for a while as the tub filled around us, she stopped and said, "But that's not how it's sung. It's a song for open-voiced throat singing. Do you want to hear me do it?" she asked. "I don't know if I can right now. I'm too relaxed. She took a deep breath and then belted out the verses in an unearthly near-wail, changing the melancholy song into a desperate one. "To hell with my neighbors," she laughed. "I'll sing in the tub if I want to." She taught me the words, and we sang it together until the bath water was cold.

As we dried, she saw I was hard again and smiled. "You want to try to do sex again, Yankee?"

"I only brought one condom."

She shrugged mischievously. "You didn't want to jinx it by bringing more, *da?*" she grinned. "Well I certainly don't have any. I'm not that kind of woman, you know."

We stood kissing in the steamy bathroom. When we emerged, we found that Otto had chewed up my clothes. With a gasp and maybe a giggle, Alina snatched them away and chased the dog into the corner, hollering, naked, kicking at him.

"That stupid jealous dog," she shouted as she retrieved our damp towels to cover us.

I put on my long johns. My underwear was chewed. He'd chewed up the front of my shirt and the crotch of my jeans.

"I can sew them," she said with a sorry smile. "Maybe he doesn't like you, or maybe he wants to make sure you stay the night."

I pulled on the tattered jeans and Alina laughed. "You look like you've exploded down there. You can't go out like that."

"It's alright, my coat will cover everything."

"You can stay."

"You won't have to hurry to fix them this way," I said, trying not to appear put out. "Besides," I added, my Russian becoming poorer, "it's better to walk home in the dark with torn clothes than in the morning."

"Leave me the shirt, I'll sew that tomorrow. Come back tomorrow evening with your jeans, and I'll fix those."

I nodded.

"He's never done this before. Well, one time, but I'd forgotten. You see, Otto, you've spoiled his mood."

I assured her that I had a wonderful evening and kissed her goodnight. I walked home, crotchless, laughing to myself. My hair was still wet, and I had a chill. I closed my eyes and remembered the smell of her. I could feel her tight around me, soft, warm, the slickness on the other side of the condom. I pondered: Otto had given me an excuse both to stay and to leave, and I chose to leave.

Alina knocked on my door late in the afternoon the next day with my shirt stitched, washed, ironed, and folded.

"I had to use the pocket to patch the hole." She shook out the garment to show me. She'd done a fantastic job, matching up the pattern on the shirt and the patch. The repair was nearly invisible. "Let's have the jeans. I think I have some fabric that will match reasonably well. But Connor, listen, I wouldn't have asked you to stay over, normally, but since my dog ate your clothes, and it was late. *Ladno?* Do we understand each other?"

"*Ladno.*"

She smiled now. "I don't think I can fix your undies. If you want to tell me what size, I'll see if I can buy some at the market."

"Do you want to come in? I have some tea."

"*Nyet.* I don't think I do. I'll try to have these fixed tomorrow."

We didn't see much of each other for a few days. She brought my jeans to work, as expertly stitched as the shirt. She slipped them into my duffel bag when no one was around.

One day that week we ended up at the *stolovaya* alone together after everyone else had left. I asked her if everything was alright. She smiled noncommittally. "*Da,* Connor, but I think we should give ourselves some time to consider things."

I nodded, attempted to look understanding, but told her I couldn't wait to be with her again.

On Friday she got a strange haircut, long in the front and nearly shaved at the back. It made her head look small and her neck elongated. The bangs swung to below her jaw line and both hid her eyes and made them look too big. The tips of the bangs clung to her lips, to the somewhat garish red lipstick she wore that day.

"Look, friends," bellowed Marat as she walked into the lobby where I was sitting, "we have a supermodel working here."

"Whoa," shouted everyone in approval and surprise. She beamed and just perceptibly pursed her lips as if looking in a mirror.

"Are you having a meeting with a client?" grinned Marat. "It's his lucky day!"

"I can tell you don't like it," she told me later when she found me at the bar. She pouted, half-seriously. "Do you like me less because of a haircut?"

She got up quickly and left when Yana and Sam approached with their switched-on comic swagger. Yana made a face at her departing back, then with exaggerated seriousness and thumping my shoulder said, "I have a proposition to discuss with you, Mister Connor. My associate and I are interested in your comedic attributes. Actually, we want you to make an ass of yourself on television." With a glance at Uncle Sam, she couldn't hold the gag, and started to laugh and then to cough.

"Someone get my associate a glass of vodka," cried Sam.

"And a cigarette," gasped Yana with eyes watering. "So, Connor, what do you say?"

"I'll do it."

The proposition: a promo for Marat's show *Marketeer*. I would mimic the amped-up exuberance of an MTV Europe VJ, the pirated broadcasts of which were a staple of TV-N's programming. To the people of Tomsk, said Yana, it was an immediately recognizable mascot of the West. "*Maya Mama* sits and watches MTV while she's peeling potatoes," she laughed, then quickly went into an imitation. "*Devushka,* tell me why must they always shout? What are they so excited about?"

Yana and Sam had the studio reserved, so we went downstairs to get started.

"You know who else we could get to do this, Connor? Alina, with her new high-fashion hairdo. I saw a Dutch girl on MTV with that same cut." She melodramatically swept imagined bangs back from her face. "Or maybe she was German," she sniggered. "It's too bad she doesn't speak English, *da?*"

"*Devushka,*" warned Sam.

"*Da, Da*, Sam. It's good that we keep each other in check."

"We are our very own Communist Party," he quipped.

Chuckling and coughing intermittently, Yana gathered props and dictated the script to me. The final result had me superimposed over a whirling kaleidoscopic backdrop dressed up in mixed Siberian kitsch.

"Hey, what is Tomsk?" I bellowed in hyper-spirited English. "Tomsk is *Shapka Ushonka* (doffing the ear flaps of my hat), *Fufika*, (tugging the collar of my trapper's coat), and *Balalaika* (holding aloft a tiny triangular mandolin-like musical instrument)." Then in cascading orgiastic summation, I cheered, "Tomsk is TV-N! And TV-N is Marketeer! And You are watching Marketeer!" At the end, like a bad boy in a cable-access spot, I looked over the top of my sunglasses and nodded lecherously.

The night crew at the station were treated to the premiere, but the real laughs came from the outtakes and flubs I had punctuated with '*bladt*' and other native curses.

"My Goodness, Connor," hollered Marat. "Who taught you such language?"

"*Kovo?*" I responded, "Your mother."

"*Vot!* Like a Cossack!"

Alina and I adhered to a self-imposed waiting period over the weekend. We met at my place on Monday night, having left the station separately. We drank our scavenger-hunted beers and listened to music on the double-dragon headphones. I had a dub album that made Alina want to dance. "But not the kind of dance I could do with anyone watching," she said slyly. I promised not to watch and held the tape player at arm's length from the rocking chair so the cord would reach her as she swayed and caressed herself in the doorway of my main room.

I enjoyed the sounds and what I could see in my peripheral vision for a while, then I got up, stood by her, and took off her clothes as she continued to sway.

"At home I would do this in front of a mirror," she said. "You have a mirror in your bedroom, *da?*" We took it to the bedroom and faced the mirror swaying.

"Such a beautiful *princessa,*" I said, removing the headphones.

"*Fu,* don't make fun of me," she said, turning around and hiding herself against me. "*Amerikanskiy durak.*"

"I'm not making fun of you," I murmured. "Only someone as beautiful as you could really be a *princessa.*"

"Is this the kind of nonsense you say to American girls?"

"We don't have *princessas,* not real ones, not like you, a stolen *princessa.*"

"You'll make me sad," she said laying on the bed.

"So the rules in bed are no laughing and no being sad?"

"*Pravda.*" She giggled, "You made a wet spot on my bum."

I went into the hall to put a condom on. Still smirking when I returned, she asked, "Why do you go into the hall?"

"Not very sexy," I flushed. I laughed with her. "I need the light to figure out which way is up."

Throwing her arms up, sending her pale nipples bobbing on her breasts, she smiled, "Do you have only the one box of condoms? I guess you weren't so confident in yourself. We're going to need a lot more than that."

"I can write to my sister." I knelt on the mattress and crawled toward her.

"You're going to ask your sister to send you *prezervativy?*"

"She'll be honored."

"You should tell me more about your sister." She closed her eyes. "Don't push into me too quickly, a woman needs time."

Later, as we laid beneath my spread-open sleeping bag, she said, "Are you going to say anything about my haircut? My friend Tatyana did it for me."

"Did you see it in a magazine?"

"*Da*, of course, in one of my fashion magazines."

"Are you taking steps toward finding your sense of fashion?"

"Maybe one. Or maybe I feel different, and I wanted to look different. I started thinking about it while I was fixing your clothes, since I had all that time to think." Then she said cheerfully, "Anyway, spring is coming."

I saw no signs of spring. Again we let a week pass before seeing each other. We met at her place on a Sunday to take Otto for a walk. It was a brilliant, bright cold day.

"I don't want you to think badly of my dog because of your clothes. He's important to me," she told me earnestly.

"It's alright with me if he doesn't like me."

"He's jealous. He's just being a dog."

"He wants to bite me now, look at him," I joked.

"Maybe I should let him."

"You like him to be jealous."

"Otto, attack!" Otto glanced upward at us both and continued sniffing the ground and pulling toward the dumpsters. We walked down Kirova Street to take him to a park near the river. As we crossed an icy square of a gesturing hero, Alina pointed out a young woman pushing a baby stroller.

"She's known all over Tomsk," she whispered. "She has a negro baby."

"What's her story?"

"Shhh, look when we go by."

As we passed her, the young mother looked me in the eyes. I looked back at her, then down into her stroller. There I saw a little brown face bundled in a red hood and blue scarf. As I looked up, I caught the woman's scorn.

Once we were a few steps away, I asked again, "So, what's her story?"

"I've only heard rumors, and they're all different. Who knows what's true. Want to hear the worst one I've heard? Bogdan told me she was an exchange student in Cleveland, USA. It's a real place, *da?* She was coming home from the library one night, and she was attacked and raped, and the guy cut his named into her back with a razor. A nightmare, *da?* But I've also heard that she just had an African lover in Moscow. I've also heard that it's not really a black child but simply a skin condition. That's probably what her mother tells people," She laughed, "So maybe it's nothing so terrible as being raped in Cleveland."

I turned and looked back at the young woman shuffling her legs over the ice, jostling pram over the rough ground.

"Imagine what it's going to be like for him in school," Alina said with a chuckle.

Without thinking, I said, "If Lubomira is what happens to people who have generous souls, and the hags in the shops are what happens when you don't, where are you headed, I wonder?"

I expected her to be upset, but she laughed it off lightly saying, "Connor, please, I'm just pragmatic. Even your precious Siberian grandmother must sometimes wish everyone would go to hell. Where do you think you're headed, *malchik?*'

We walked into birch woods. Alina took the dog off his lead and kept him close by whistling, "hoot, hoot," puckering her lips like a child who had just learned. "Don't laugh, I can't whistle." Laughing, she threw herself into the snow, and Otto rolled beside her. I jumped in, too, but he snarled at me. I found a stick to toss for him and played happily for a while. When he tore my glove, I said I didn't mind.

"What's he rolling in?" she shouted and tromped hip-deep through snow to chase him away from whatever he had.

"Something dead."

We walked on and looked out at the river *Tom*, the snow blown on the ice into pitching dunes in places, opal veins of exposed ice in others. There were patches where the black current welled up through the crust. "It's starting to melt," insisted Alina, and we stood silently watching for a while, exhaling steam.

"Connor, do you know what someone at work said? It was Tatyana, the receptionist. She asked if we were still friends. 'You used to spend more time together,' she said. Funny, *da*? I told her we're still friends. Ha! What if they knew? What would they think? We're not keeping it secret. There's just no reason to make an announcement." She paused again before going on. "How old were you when you first had sex, Connor? I know you want to know that of me, so I will tell you. I was seventeen. I won't tell you who with, because you may know him. You never know, he may work at the station. But I wouldn't want you to be jealous."

"Seventeen is a good age."

"You were seventeen?"

"No, older."

She looked surprised. "Really? I've heard Americans are prudes about sex."

I laughed defensively.

"What? It isn't true?"

"Alina, I think there's something wrong with your dog," I said suddenly with genuine alarm. I pointed out that Otto had splattered the snow nearby us with deep red diarrhea.

"*Nyet*," she said breezily, "We just had borscht."

"*Bozhe moy.*"

With rosy cheeks and Otto limping from the snow between his toes, we left the park and headed back to Kirova. "Now that he's tired, I can leave him off the leash."

We spotted a kiosk that had stuff nobody else had and stopped to have a look.

"Look, Connor, Uncle Ben's," Alina teased.

"Oooh, I didn't know they made tomato sauce," I brightened.

"Are you going to buy yourself some comfort food?"

"Do they have spaghetti, too? I'm going to make you dinner. Do you have chicken?"

"I have Bush Legs in the freezer."

"I'm going to make you chicken cacciatore in payment for the *pelmeni*...and everything else."

She smiled and took a shopping bag out of her coat pocket.

"This should be something you've never had before, Italian food."

"I've had Italian," she said as if challenged.

"What, that Russianized pizza place Marat goes to?" I laughed. "Mayonnaise and *tushonka* isn't even close to being pizza. That'd be like me filling *pelmeni* with peanut butter."

"*Ladno*, Connor," she said, put down.

"I don't suppose there's anywhere I can get mushrooms around here? Or, heavens, a green pepper!"

"Mushrooms are only at the *stolovaya*, remember? We only have peppers in the summer."

We then heard a voice behind us. "Connor, *privet*." It was Pavel. I found myself particularly glad to see him, as if meeting an old friend.

"Out keeping tabs on the price of cigarettes?" I joked.

"Ah, your Russian is improving."

I introduced Alina as my friend from the station and Pavel nodded knowingly, overtly so.

"You are Vodopyanov's bodyguard," she said slyly as retribution.

"*Nyet*, I'm his business associate," Pavel chuckled, unaware. "I'm glad I've seen you, Connor. I was going to call the station. It's Vika's birthday on Wednesday, and she wants you to come."

"Connor!" Alina screamed suddenly. "Otto, Otto."

I turned just in time to see the doors of a tram that had rattled up the center of the street close and continue on.

"My dog's gotten on the tram," she shrieked.

Both Pavel and I burst out laughing.

"I hope he has a ticket," I said and Pavel began to cough with laughter.

"Very good. You can joke in Russian."

"Connor," cried Alina, her voice quivering as she began to run.

"What do you want me to do? He's your dog." I told Pavel I'd see him on Wednesday and went after her.

She was crying fully when I got to her. I realized how scared she was. I sprinted after the train, which by now was more than a block ahead of us. At the first stop, I paused and looked around, catching my breath, cursing in English. "C'mon Otto, where are you? Otto, Otto." I tried calling with the right accent. I kept running. Up ahead, the tram stopped at a second light, and I caught up a bit. At the next stop, the dog came bounding out the doors and began to circle. Alina had stopped running and was well behind us, too far to see us in the dim evening light.

"Otto," I called. He paused to look at me. I tried to catch him, but he easily eluded me and resumed circling, expanding his search into the street and into doorways, down side streets.

I spoke to him in Russian, "*Eti suda*, Otto. Follow me back to Alina." It occurred to me to mimic her whistle. I puckered my lips, "hoot, hoot." That did it. His ears shot up, and he stopped in his tracks. I whistled and jogged back down the street. Confused, he followed, orbiting me. "Hoot, hoot," I went until I ran out of breath. Alina was close enough to call to him by that time, but she had her head down. She trudged forward, her shoulders heaving as she sobbed.

Otto was on the road again. "Call him," I shouted gruffly in English. She looked up, tears on her face; she cried for her dog, and he went to her.

Even when we got back to her apartment, she was inconsolable. She seemed in shock.

"People steal dogs," she said numbly. "Do you know what they do?"

"Make *shapkas*," I said. "But I doubt they look for them on streetcars very often." It sounded mean, I realized, and she ignored me.

"I've been very alone, Connor. He's been all I've had. How can you hate him? You don't understand."

"I don't hate him. I chased him down for you, didn't I? You just gave up."

She looked up at me, stung.

"How long were you alone? You talk as if it's been years since you've had contact with another human being, but how long were you really alone?"

"What do you mean?" she asked.

"When was the last time you had sex before me?"

"That's not what I mean."

"When?"

"December."

"It's been a lot longer for me. So don't think you're the only person in the world that hasn't had sex in a while."

"That wasn't what I meant, and you know it! You should go home."

Chapter 11

On a cold, dark, late-winter evening, I trundled off to Pavel's house after work. I rode in a packed tram with the bundled Tomskers, jostling like mattresses stacked upright in a truck. I stood with my elbows out, guarding the daffodils I held against my chest for his daughter Vika. I'd wanted to get her something nice, by way of thanks to her father, but the department stores in Tomsk had nothing. I'd spent an afternoon searching the bazaar, where I'd seen goats and car parts and an old woman selling a stuffed eagle, but found nothing suitable for a six-year-old girl. A kiosk near the TV station sold daffodils, the only fresh flowers I'd seen since Moscow. Flowers for spring, or the hope of spring, I'd thought. Maybe it would be more a gift for her mother, something bright to cheer up the gloomy Nadia. There's probably only one greenhouse that grows them in the whole oblast, I daydreamed. By the look of them, the flowers had gotten everything they needed. They were perfect yellow blossoms, stalks bundled snuggly with a brown string. I was proud of them.

In the stairwell of Pavel's house, I found the front door still broken and hanging crooked in the jamb. The wind blew as if through an empty barn, disguising the warmth I knew to be at the top of the stairs and through a single insulated door. I was tired, and uneasy about Alina, but I was looking forward to being around Pavel and his family. Things weren't perfect with his wife, maybe, but Pavel's imperviousness and the joyous energy of his girls made up for it.

Vika, the birthday girl herself, opened the door, smiling in the glow and heat of her home. There was commotion inside, tumbling shadows, and the smell of food. I wished her well and handed her the flowers. "He can almost talk now," she announced over her shoulder. Her mother stepped up beside her as I came in. Vika turned and passed her the flowers. I bent down to take off my boots, but looked up to smile at her. Nadia looked horrified and immediately headed toward the kitchen, carrying the flowers sideways as if she intended to drop them straight into the trash. There was a sudden hush in the flat, and two other women followed her. Ignoring whatever was wrong with the women, Vika smiled on and touched my hand. Pavel likewise welcomed me kindly, and I was immediately comfortable. I spoke to him in English and was ready for as much ABBA as he wanted to play.

With his heavy, warm hand on my shoulder, Pavel introduced me to those still at the table, Nadia's mother and a few women friends. The old woman poured me a big glass of vodka and coached me as I drank it. "*Malodets!*" She served me a slice of cake and then another glass of vodka.

"Not playing with the band tonight?" I asked Pavel after taking in a quick breath from the drink.

"Oh, no," he said in his big, deep, soft voice. "I couldn't work tonight." He put his paw on his little daughter's shoulder and gave her a squeeze; she leaned comfortably into his leg.

Nadia came back to the table looking comically forlorn, the other women followed her like mourners. Pavel said to her softly, "Come on now, don't make a scene over nothing."

"He should know better."

"*Ne nado,*" he rumbled, earth-like.

"Pardon me?" I said.

She sat at the table and took on a scolding motherly tone. "You must never give someone an odd number of flowers. They are for the grave."

"Except thirteen," chimed in one of the other women. "Did you buy them on Frunze? Right outside your TV-N? That's where people get the bus to the cemetery."

Nadia shook her head solemnly. "It's very bad luck."

Grandma dished me up a plate of food, poured me more vodka, and coaxed me to throw it back. "I'm sorry," I said as my eyes watered. "I hope you'll still be my friend, Vika."

"See how much better his Russian is?" Vika smiled, standing at the edge of the table.

"He didn't know, Nadia. It's nothing," murmured Pavel.

"It's not nothing," she whispered as if to herself and covered her mouth.

Unaffected, Vika went to lay down in front of the TV with her sister, Katya, and a couple other girls.

"Oh, look, it's Rostan," said one of the women at the table, noticing what was on. "He's moved to California now." We turned toward the TV to watch the émigré singer lead a camera crew around his opulently decorated house. His silk robe flapped over bare legs as he walked. He led his visitors into the bathroom, and as a special treat for those of us at home, he shaved his mustache before the camera.

The grandmother turned to me and said with a sad smile, "I have nothing against America, but it has turned this man into an asshole."

"Hush, *mama*, the kids."

The old woman chuckled to herself.

After a while, Nadia cleared the table and the other women collected their children and coats to leave.

"So, Connor," Pavel smiled boyishly behind his big beard. "Why don't you come out on the balcony with me for a smoke. After all that vodka, I think you could use some cold air, yeah? Spring almost," he said as we stood outside in our coats and boots. "You can feel it's just a little less cold."

"Just a very little."

Pavel chuckled and drew deeply on his cigarette. "Tell me, Connor, did you catch the young lady's *cabako* or has it gone off to Mama Luba's hat factory?"

"*Da*, I caught him."

"She must be very pleased with you."

"I'm not sure about that."

He paused, studied me for a moment before lighting another cigarette and asking, "how are things at the station, making progress on your documentary?"

"Not much progress, no. Actually it's been an unpleasant couple weeks at the station. Everyone's been having bad things happen to them. You know, Marat? He was in a car accident and broke his wrist. He said he went around a corner, hit some ice, and flipped the car. There were five people inside, but he was the only one hurt."

Pavel flicked his throat and raised an eyebrow questioningly.

"That's what I thought, but he insists no one had been drinking, even though it was on the holiday. Ilya's gotten beaten up again. Some mafia guys thought he was Gennadi and tried to extort money from him. Ilya, of course, told them to go fuck their mothers."

"He's not a big guy, he should watch who he says that to," advised Pavel.

"The guy covering the newscast for Ilya while his face heals showed up with a black eye the other day, so we have two battered news anchors."

"Do you have a television yet?" he asked.

"Marat told me they got me one but that somebody stole it right out of the station. I find it pretty hard to believe that a stranger could waltz right in there and steal something like that. But nobody cares, you know, why should they?

"Sounds like bad luck. Have you given 'flowers for the grave' to anyone else?" Pavel chuckled lightly and touched my shoulder.

I sighed and continued on my tear, rolling now that I could speak in English. "I've come to realize that I will never understand what goes on at that place. I don't know if it's because they're hiding things from me, or because there's bad communication all around. I think Gennadi is worried there's a rat in the place. Do you know that expression?"

Pavel stepped inside to get his notebook.

"The mafia found out that we got grant money from the U.S., and like I said, they're trying to extort us. They've threatened the station and even Gennadi's kids."

Pavel sympathetically hummed in tremolo as he exhaled. I told him how two male members of the staff are on guard every night. "I've said I want to stay, but they won't let me. Ilya says I can stay when it's his turn, and we'll get good and drunk and patrol with our *balonchik* pistols." Pavel continued to slowly shake his head.

"If it makes you feel better, the other American in town, Graham, isn't having a good time, either," he offered. "He's in a fight with his landlord and is getting very angry about it. He has a temper, yeah? He wants to move, but the landlord won't give him back his two hundred dollars that he paid ahead. I'm worried about him. He's doing dangerous things like going to this guy's house and yelling at his wife. You can't do that, yeah. He says he's going to the police, but I'm afraid he'll only get himself in trouble, since he paid rent in dollars, which is illegal. Also we don't want the police to start looking at his paperwork because they can always find something wrong, something that you'll have to pay a bribe for. He should just find another apartment and be glad that he didn't lose more."

Suddenly Pavel remembered something and perked up. "Connor, listen, I've got a story for you. Do you know what a *garmushka* is? It's a small accordion. Yeah? So let me tell you about the *garmushka* player in my band. A couple weeks ago, we couldn't find him. He didn't come to shows. I went to his flat, but he wasn't there. His neighbor told me that he'd been arrested. They say he killed his wife. Yeah! I don't want to have anything to do with the police, so I don't go to the station, but one of the other guys in the band has a brother-in-law who's a police officer and went down and talked to Ivan in jail. He said they'd been torturing him, beating him up, and he'd confessed.

"He told them that one night a couple weeks ago he and his wife got really drunk and got in a fight. I've never seen him drunk or get in a fight. He's a nice quiet guy. He's a music teacher at a school. He told them that he hit his wife, and she fell backward and hit her head on the radiator. He thought she was only passed out, and he passed out himself. When he woke up, he found his wife dead on the floor." Pavel finished his cigarette and flicked it into the street. "It's cold. Let's go back inside," he said, exhaling smoke.

Before continuing the story, he bid goodnight to his wife and daughters and closed the living room doors. "So Ivan the *garmushka* player didn't know what to do. He doesn't go to the police; they'd put him in jail whether it was an accident or not. He left her there for a day or two. He went to work, taught children to play the *garmushka,* yeah? He tried to keep everything normal. He came to our shows, smiled, and played while his wife's body was probably starting to smell in his flat." Pavel crinkled his nose. "Then one of his neighbors said to him, 'I heard you and Irina had another fight. Where is she?' He told her that she'd left him. 'Left without saying goodbye?' the neighbor said, "You must have really beat her this time.' So the neighbor lady is already suspicious, and he panics. He can't keep the body in the flat anymore. This is what he told the police. Yeah! It's a crazy story. I don't know if it's true, since they beat him." Pavel stopped briefly and shook his head in disbelief. He smiled slightly, enjoying the story, though still empathetic in the telling of it. "He told them that he cut his wife into pieces and baked them in the oven. He wanted to burn them up so there'd be nothing left, but the smoke attracted attention. The neighbor said to him, 'Poor Ivan, your wife leaves you and you burn your dinner.'" We both laughed the gallows.

"So now the cooked pieces don't smell, and he goes out at night to throw them away. He tried throwing pieces into the river but couldn't always hit the holes in the ice. Parts landed on the ice so he had to crawl out on his belly to push them in. He tried to bury the pieces in parks, but the ground was frozen, and he said that after the first few nights he could tell dogs were digging them up."

"No way," I gasped and told him about Otto in the park on Sunday.

Pavel nodded solemnly. "Maybe that was the *garmushka* player's wife."

The next day I found Alina in no mood to hear about how her dog may have eaten human flesh.

"Do you want to come over tonight?" I asked.

"Not tonight, Connor. You don't want me tonight."

"No? Maybe just a drink at the bar. What's wrong?"

"Nothing that concerns you," she said grimly. "It would only make you as unhappy as I am."

"If it doesn't concern me, why would it make me unhappy?" I kidded her, pleased to be able to put the sentence together.

"Because it's something sad, Connor. Please don't ask me any more about it."

Nevertheless, she met me at the bar after work. "Aren't you getting clever with your Russian," she snickered, 'If it doesn't concern me, why would it make me unhappy?'" We ordered little bottles of imported beer. "I decided to tell you what's on my mind, Connor. You are my close friend now, *da*? Remember you told me about the Turk, the gangster, you met at the jazz party? I've had my own experience with him. This was a few months ago, before you arrived. I went to a discotheque with my girlfriends. We were dressed very sexy." She smiled slyly. "It's not unusual for some men to behave like pigs," she went on, "but your Turk grabbed me by the arm and pulled me down into his lap. He was very drunk, naturally. I told him to fuck off and tried to pull away. He sat there stunned for a minute. As you know, young ladies are not supposed to use such language. He was hurting my arm. He pulled me down close to him, so I could smell his stinking breath, and said he wasn't going to let anyone get away with saying that to him, that he was going to beat me. 'You're going to wish you hadn't said that, *devushka,*'" she growled, imitating him, "'I'm going to beat you bloody. I'm going to break your pretty little face, and you can have a nice long time in the hospital to think about how you should speak to men.'

"I was very scared then, Connor, and I am not an easily frightened woman, but I could see he was serious. So I sat there on his lap and smiled at him. I reached over to his table and poured him a glass of vodka. I was nice to him and talked him out of it. I made him promise that he wasn't going to try anything. It made me sick, and I felt terrible for days, as if I'd gone to bed with him or done something dirty. But I was scared. I knew he would do as he said. Most men are all talk, or else they're just crazy from drinking, but he was neither. He knew what he was saying and knew that he would do it. I'm sure he's beaten women before. I was sure of it, Connor. It took me a long time to make him promise.

"You know what my girlfriends did? Nothing. They went on dancing as if I was trying to flirt with this man, as if I wanted to sit on his disgusting lap all night and smile at him."

She paused and took a drink. "I thought I might pee on him, I was so nervous." She spoke in a low voice leaning forward slightly over the tabletop. "Then he started saying he was in love with me. That he could tell as soon as he saw me I was the only woman who could put him in his place. 'You will make an honest man of me,' he said. He said all kinds of ridiculous things, clichés out of American movies.

"I wouldn't tell him my name. Even when he threatened me again, I wouldn't tell. I wouldn't say where I worked or where I lived. I wasn't going to lie, I told him, but I wasn't going to tell him. He said he would take back his promise, but I reminded him that Muslim men were supposed to keep their word, and he agreed that it was true and that it was the only way to be honorable. A little later I saw my chance and slipped away. I left the disco right away, just in case he got drunker still and decided to come after me.

"So," she said, raising her eyebrows, "guess who called the station this morning to talk to me? 'I've found you,' he said. 'I've been searching for months and now I've found you. I must see you. I know I frightened you that time, but I was only drunk. I would never do such a thing, and I must see you.' So now, I suppose, I have to meet with him to avoid making him angry. He'll be angry to hear that I'm seeing someone else. This is a man who is angry either way."

"Has he come to the station?" I asked.

"Not yet."

"You'll let me know?"

"It's not a good idea, Connor."

"I could talk to Boris."

"I don't think there's anything you can do. I'll simply have to tell him that I don't want to see him and that I'm sorry for the trouble he's gone through to find me, the love of his life." She smiled and winked. "I feel better after my confession. I thought I would. I am a Catholic, like you, *da?*"

Two days later Alina planned to meet the Turk in a café near the station at six p.m. I came out of the editing room at five-thirty to find her.

"*Ni nada,*" she told me. "What are you going to do? He's mafia, understand?"

She paced in the hall. I sat on a sofa. "I have some notes I have to work on," I told her. She wouldn't look at me. I had the *bolonchik* pistol in my backpack. At ten minutes to six, she put her coat on and motioned for me to follow her outside.

I asked, "You won't get in a car with this guy, *da?*"

"I've changed my mind. I don't want to see him. Why should I? I don't owe him anything. Why should I see him? I don't care if he's mad. I'll borrow your gun. I've had a bad day, and I don't feel like it."

"He may be out in the parking lot."

"Connor, please walk me to the bus stop."

I got my coat, and we circled around the outside of the parking lot and headed toward the *stalovaya* before cutting over to Frunze. I stood with her until the bus came and then headed back to the station. I saw no sign of him.

"I want to reward you for your bravery, *malchik*," she told me later in my room. She undressed and danced for me. She laid down on the bed. I kissed her and guided her hands. She smiled and rubbed herself. She slid her fingers up and down, inside and around her moistening labia. I went into the hall to put on a condom. She continued with her fingertips, and I bent to kiss her there. She bucked her hips and swept her hands over her stomach and breasts. Her wetness came thick and silken. I rose, and she stopped me gently. "Take this off," she said, touching me, holding me back. "Take it off." I shook my head slightly. I kissed her once more, and she guided me into her. She closed her eyes and sunk away inside herself.

"Open your eyes," I whispered, but she would not acknowledge me.

When I laid down beside her, flushed and spent, she reawakened and beckoned me, "Come with me, Connor." She led me into the bathroom and turned on the water. She lathered her hands with soap and reached out to me. She washed me.

"What are you doing?"

"You're still hard, *malchik*, I am still very wet."

I shook my head.

"You've already finished. Don't be afraid, poor boy, don't you want to feel what it's really like? It's so much better." She held me dripping in her hand. She put her leg up on the tub and pulled me toward her.

"Alina," I protested softly.

"Let me worry about the things women need to worry about. You don't need to worry."

Gently I removed her hand.

She sighed and went back into the bedroom.

"Do you have anything comfortable I can wear?" she asked as I stepped into a pair of shorts. I went to my drawer and held up a green silk undershirt.

"What are you doing with a silk shirt?"

"My sister gave it to me. It's supposed to be warm."

She put it on. It hung just over her hips like a very short sheer dress. "This is mine," she said. "I'm going to wear it whenever I come over." She raised her eyebrows and nodded downward at my tented boxers, "Looks like you're going to have that for a while. It's too bad I'm not in the mood anymore." She laughed and flopped down on the bed. "Do you have any pictures of your sister?"

"*Nyet.*"

"Connor," she scolded. "How can you come so far away and not have any pictures of your family with you?"

I laid down beside her. "I wanted to feel far away."

"From them?"

"From everything."

"And will you then want to be far away from everything here?"

"I don't know."

"Connor, stand up and let me have a look at you. Come on, I put on a show for you."

I stood on the bed for her.

"*Davai,* take those off. I like the circumcision. It looks nicer, I think. You're a little *tolstoi* around the middle, though."

"We call them 'love handles' in English."

"*Nyet,* it's not good. You seem a bit underdeveloped in the chest."

I laid back down. "I'll try doing pushups," I said in English.

"It's not polite to say things I can't understand."

"Ha."

"Don't get upset, Connor. It's just that you remind me of a little boy."

"I guess all the other men you've been with have been much better looking."

"Still in English! You shouldn't do that. I'll find out what you've said, and then you'll be sorry. Besides, I'm only joking with you. Connor, have you ever wondered if the KGB is watching you? A few years ago they would have been. Maybe you should get better curtains than just that sheet in the window. It doesn't cover it all. They could be watching us, taking pictures."

"Making filthy videos."

"Filthy," she laughed. "It's too bad you can't get the camera more often. Maybe we could make our own videos."

"Would you do that?"

"I don't know. Probably everyone will soon be videotaping themselves having sex, and we'll all get very tired of it."

"If we had a fight I might show it to Ilya and Sergei."

"I don't care about them."

"We could make copies and pass them around town," I joked.

"And everyone would say 'why is that beautiful woman fucking that fat weakling?'" she chortled.

"And then they'll say, 'probably for a visa,'" I shot back. We mocked and scolded each other, and agreed we were even.

"You said you wanted to travel, Connor. Have you made any plans?"

"Ilya has talked about driving to Baikal. He says we've got to have several cars to go. It's not safe otherwise. Boris says that if I learn to ride horseback well enough, he'll bring me out to an abandoned gulag."

She pouted. "You'll make me jealous with that little stable girl."

"*Da*, Olya," I leered. "She's a wild little barn *devuchka*, but I promise to only kiss the horse."

"You can't go on a trip with any of those people," said Alina resolutely. "You're going to go with me. Why do you want to go see a gulag? Read Solzhenitsyn if you want to know all about it. It upsets me a little, Connor, that you're making plans for travel without me. I thought we could do something together."

"I don't really have any plans yet, I've just talked about things. Nothing is definite."

"Ilya won't really take you on a trip; you'll see. Still you haven't talked to me about traveling. I'm not angry, just a little upset. My father has a car and has said that I can use it if I take lessons. Maybe we can have travels of our own. I'll start the lessons."

We laid quietly as the light outside faded. She held her arms up toward the ceiling, casting shadows in the dim yellow-orange wash of the bedside lamp. "Connor, remember I told you about the discotheque? They hold it right in the *Hobby Dom* ballroom. They decorate it and put up lights. Everyone gets dressed up. I was thinking we should go together. Forget about everyone at TV-N. I don't care what they think. I don't want to pretend we're not together anymore. *Tak*, what do you say, will you go with me?"

More and more I had come to appreciate Lubomira's parties. I'd gone for Valentine's Day and exchanged paper hearts with the scientists. On Saint Patrick's, I led them in a spiritedly discordant version of "Galway Bay." I let it all go, just as they had. I was no longer standoffish. The playland atmosphere of the English club induced me to shrug off some of the oppressive stress that I had come to share, just a bit, with my Siberian fellows. Nevertheless, it was an active shrugging, a struggle, like forcing yourself to smile, that required willful twisting, dancing, silliness, singing. I'd surprised myself, and they appreciated the effort.

"Our friend Connor is here," cheered one of the scientists on this occasion just before the emergence of spring. "Now we can speak real American English. I have found *Martskoye* Beer for us. Have you tried it? It will be the best you've had. Come over to us, let's drink." This jolly beer drinking scientist was glad to see me, and I couldn't have felt more welcomed by it. I couldn't have been more relieved and even healed of the frustration that had been growing in me, momentarily though it was. He had a pleasantly goofy laugh and was all shining doughy spheres and straight lines. He had a jowly face, a bowl cut, and straight white teeth in a fixed broad smile, probably the work of one of the new dentistry clinics.

I turned my shoulder to angle through the small crowd, but was stopped by Lubomira. She held my elbow in her cool soft hand, her touch like a grandmother's, awakened a distant visceral memory of love once received. Her moon face was uncritical, always capable of casting a maternal spell. If she sought to teach morals, the lessons were almost invisible.

"We have a special guest this evening, Connor, who I think you will be surprised to see," she told me.

"Oh?" I questioned brightly. I was sure it would be the other American, Graham.

"Yes, he should be here anytime. You'll see."

I walked to the refreshment table, shaking hands along the way. Ostensibly, we were gathered in the plaid room for a student performance. In the meantime, I toasted my rubicund drinking buddy and many others over the laminated tartan tablecloth, our beer sloshing over the sides of teacups and jars. Here, we drank with easy moderation. The smiles convincingly came from glimpses of joy. Upon request, I interpreted a few slang phrases from movies before Dame Marion called to us.

"Class, may I have your attention please," she requested in the upper register of her voice. "I would like to introduce a new member to our club. This is Warner Fest, our very own People's Deputy for Tomsk in the Oblast Duma. He is also a respected astronomer, as I'm sure many of you know. As a scientist, of course, he may join our club."

Fest stood smiling behind his beard in his trademark black suit, which looked a bit dingy beneath the classroom's fluorescent lights. "Thank you, my friends," he said haltingly. "My English is not good, but I can try."

Smiling, I went to shake his hand. Fest wanted only to speak English, so I soon left him to the junior members of the class.

Marion called again as Mother Superior, "We now have a special performance by some of our advanced students."

"It is Rock Opera!" declared one enthusiastic participant.

Under our teachers' instructions, we moved tables and chairs into a semicircle and rolled standing chalkboards into place as the wings of the stage. The players entered the room with a great many bundles, and beneath the chalked-in backdrops, we could see their feet hurrying into costumes.

Dr. Django (his non-Russian moniker), who we all knew as an impressive musician from our set on St. Paddy's Day, sat to one side of the stage on a stool with his classical guitar. He called us to attention with a flourish of notes, and then began the show with 'Flight of the BumbleBee.'

"*Vot, nash* Rimsky-Korsakov. There's the opera part," whispered my drinking buddy next to me, inadvertently mixing his Russian and English. "He composed this song, you must know. Did you know Stravinsky was his student?" Before I could confess that I didn't know any of it, Marion's niece, Lena, appeared in a home-sewn bee suit. In black tights and a bee's butt of pillow stuffing, she fluttered around the room while the English club laughed uproariously. She smiled but otherwise kept her composure.

A chorus in robes then stepped from behind the chalkboards. They swayed, clapped and sang to us in an approximate rhyming verse that this was the story of Buzzy Wuzzy Busy Fly. Here we find Buzzy set out on his daily chores. Buzzy was a virtuous and hard working fly, but he consistently comes up short in his nectar collecting because he always stops to help others, no matter who they are. On this day in the flower patch he discovers a fellow fly stuck in a spider's web and is sure to be devoured. He swoops in to help.

Galina, a large woman with gigantic breasts and gold teeth, pounced forth dressed in black as the spider. The room shook as she hit the floor, and the class erupted into more laughter at her costume of sunglasses and a mink shapka. Dr. Django chunked out doom and gloom with power chords, and after a partly choreographed struggle, Buzzy and his friend escaped.

"That busy fly does irritate," growled the spider to Dr. Django's metal riffs. "Buzzy Wuzzy I shall eviscerate."

"Wonderful vocabulary," cheered Marion, laughing and clapping her fleshy hands.

In thanks for Buzzy's bravery and compassion, the other bee takes him to meet his friend the beetle, whom he promises will help with his nectar shortage. The beetle, of course, is dressed as Beatle in a gray suit with his hair brushed forward over his ears.

"Wonderful play on words," applauded Marion, bouncing in her seat. Dr. Django hits 'Back in the USSR,' and the Beatle beetle offers Buzzy a job in the mafia selling nectar on the black market. Always one to pay his taxes as is due, Buzzy refuses and flies away.

"It's bad for business, mate," the beetle tells the other fly. "I feel bad for the chap, but Buzzy Wuzzy has become a pest, and so Buzzy Wuzzy must be put to rest."

And so the beetle, the betraying bee, and the spider gang up on Buzzy. Dancing in horrible glee, they sing, "Buzzy Wuzzy set to kill. Buzzy Wuzzy's blood to spill." Complete with red yarn thrown into the audience, the evildoers lure Buzzy into the web and see him flayed. The cast then bowed and handed out printed copies of the lyrics for the class to review.

"You could do a show on TV-N with things like this," called a member of the audience. "An English language rock opera show."

"What do you think, Connor?"

I laughed imagining how Yana and Sam would laugh, how they would beg to tape it and air it on their comedy show.

"I don't think any of the participants want to be on television," chuckled Marion. "This is for our club members only."

"I'm not sure if it was a rock opera or a passion play," I said. Marion quickly explained the reference.

"It was a passion play for a fly."

"I would have thought that a bunch of scientists would know the difference between a fly and a bee," I added.

"Yes, we have no entomologists."

"But many bananas."

"We must start a new religion based on the life of our savior Buzzy Wuzzy. People are so eager to find religion, there must be good money in it."

"It's all in the marketing," I said. "The only problem is that in the end, Buzzy is consumed, not a speck of fly left to resurrect."

Fest, though he must have only caught the most basic drift of our conversation, appeared uncomfortable.

"Terribly sorry to be blasphemous, but you see, we are scientists."

"Are We Not Scientists? That should be the title of our next rock opera!"

Lubomira asked me to stay after the party to talk to her and Fest. She had an idea she wanted to discuss.

"Lubomira Markova, I want to congratulate you on the atmosphere you have created here," Fest opened grandly, switching to Russian with relief. "It is a miraculous place, a sanctuary."

Lubomira beamed at his praise and bowed slightly before speaking. "I was thinking, gentlemen, since we had such an interesting conversation the last time we spoke, that we might do a project together. As you know, Deputy Fest, our friend Connor is working on a documentary film about our time in history, such as it is. Perhaps we could help him, and maybe even interest TV-N, by filming you interviewing prominent exiles here in Tomsk about current events. I know nothing about television, of course, but this seems like something that may be of interest to people in this Oblast and perhaps beyond. Connor and I could translate the interviews into English, for example."

I nodded cautiously. "I think TV-N might be interested."

Fest stroked his beard. "It must be true that worthy minds think as one. I've been considering something similar, Lubomira Markova. Going a bit further on your concept, I ask, 'what does this information do for people?' It is history, of course. But could we also create a dialogue that helps us see with our souls as we make our way through this new time?"

I nodded blankly, looking to Lubomira for a lead, but she did the same.

Fest took a breath, scratched under his chin pensively. "In my travels and work with exiles, I've discovered the power of these peoples' stories, a power I thought I could only feel for my own past. All of our stories are individually affecting, but collectively, they are much more. There is horror in it all, but in the end, I think there is much that can nourish us as a country. That it could have happened to anyone, that it did, to have your bloodline sent to exile, and only now are these families emerging from the ruins of it, we can see our oneness in it. We can see our resilience."

Lubomira was captivated. She nearly bobbed in her seat as she had for her students. Fest, in return, spoke exclusively to her. They were two great flirtatious wizards, powerfully matched. I had never met Lubomira's husband, but I imagined that his long illness weighed on her, a long, unresolved sorrow. I imagined she and Fest comforting each other in their old age.

"So yes, Lubomira Markova," continued Fest, "I am interested in this project."

"Marvelous!" she said in English. After a bit more discussion Lubomira suggested that I write a proposal for TV-N that she would translate and Fest could review. "Now that we've hatched this wonderful idea, I have a little present for you both; for you, Mr. Fest, since it is your first visit to our club, and for you, Connor, because you need someone to take care of you." With a chuckle she fished from one of her plethora of shopping bags stashed in a corner, two jars of homemade preserves.

"There is a story behind this jam, gentlemen. Although I'm not sure it is the kind that helps us to see with our souls. I collected all the berries myself, as my husband is too ill to do such things with me, and my niece was too busy to help me. It was an excellent year for berries. They were as big as the top of my thumb, and I happened to choose just the right time of August to take the bus into the countryside. I wasn't alone, of course, there were many others there as well. At that time of year, Connor, the buses make special stops so that people may gather berries and mushrooms. I hope you'll come with me this year, Connor. It's everyone's favorite time."

"*Da*," agreed Fest. "That is when you feel you are truly Russian. I see it as a painting, women in headscarves with their fingers stained and baskets filled with berries."

"That is how it was, Deputy Fest, something Tolstoy might have described. We were in the woods, like happy peasants, searching out berries, and the bushes were full. We went on filling up our buckets, and then wrapping up more berries in our scarves and aprons. My hands were purple to my wrists. The bees were buzzing around but not stinging. The children there were gorging themselves and had smudged purple lips, and you could hear them laughing wherever you went. It was a beautiful day. So different than when you are just walking down the street in the city, if you understand me. We were out there together as people enjoying our native home.

"You can imagine, gentlemen, I lost track of time. I was thinking of all the pies I would bake and the jam I could give away. The next thing I knew, I heard the sound of the bus. I had to quickly gather up my buckets and bundles and hurry along. I was worried about smashing up all the berries but moved as fast as I could. It was a hot day, and I was more tired than I'd supposed. I found myself losing my breath and others easily passing me by. I climbed the bank to the road and fell just as I got to the top. All the berries spilled out before me on the hot road."

Fest and I gasped and gripped the jars in our hands.

"Still, people passed me," Lubomira continued. "No one helped. One child stopped to stomp on my berries until his mother grabbed him by the ear and hurried him onto the bus. It's not him I blame. Soon everyone was on the bus, but I was still on my knees in the road trying to scoop up my berries. The bus sat there rumbling, and I thought that if the driver put it in gear and started to roll away, I would throw myself under it." Lubomira looked at me meaningfully, but without tears or need for re-composure. "So I hope you will forgive me, if you find any grit in the jam."

"If I do, Lubomira Markova," said Fest pulling himself forward, "I shall happily grind it in my teeth."

Chapter 12

On the night of the disco, Alina wore a strapless blue dress. "*Nu,* what do you think?" she asked me breezily as she led me into her apartment. She turned, and the fabric rustled like Easter grass.

"You are beautiful," I said to her bare shoulders.

"How do you like the color?"

"Moonlight on the snow."

"Now you're poetical in Russian!"

We took a taxi, a one-time indulgence. Arriving at the *Xobby Dom,* we found it transformed into a swank club, complete with velvet ropes and flashing lights. Everyone was in gowns and suits, and the dance music thumped through the walls. Alina and I walked in together. We were coming out, we'd decided. After tonight, we'd no longer make a show of leaving the station separately.

We went into TV-N to leave our coats and found a good many of our colleagues there getting the party started with vodka and beer. We merrily greeted everyone as if it had been much longer than since yesterday afternoon that we'd seen them.

Nastia was there. She smiled at me devilishly and whispered, "Just because you've come with Alina doesn't mean you can't still dance with me." Nikolai gave me a nod of acknowledgement. We stayed and had a drink or two. I met Sergei's wife for the first time and Marat's mistress, Zhana. "Connor, you will have to do all the dancing with these women," Marat hollered with the heavily made up brunette on his arm.

"We didn't get dressed up to stand around in the office," announced Alina. "We can talk to you people anytime."

"Out there you'll have to pay for drinks," protested Sam wetly.

"Uncultured peasants," declared Marat with spoofed grandiosity. "Why don't you stay at home if all you want is a *pyanka?*"

"Connor likes to drink," countered Sam. "*Davai*, have some more vodka with me."

Alina took my hand and led me out the door. Likewise, Nastia and Zhana escorted their males. We got a table together at the edge of the disco lights. The DJ spun a mix of exuberantly tacky Euro dance music, treble-charged Russian pop, and gluey slow songs that got the whole room on the floor. At one point a dance troupe in skimpy sequined outfits took the floor to show us their synchronized maneuvers.

We men took turns buying rounds and drank to dissolve the tension that had come to the table with us. It was no use, it was a bad pairing of couples. After several drinks and rounds of dancing and trading partners, Alina and Nastia began baiting and insulting each other. Additionally, Alina glared at Marat the whole time and made an obvious point of ignoring Zhana. Nastia, meanwhile, tried to catch me for every slow dance and employ her favorite pelvic maneuver against my leg.

"Did she leave a smear on your jeans that time?" remarked Alina, once when I sat back down.

"On the inside or the outside?" I joked, but their rivalry reached well beyond the absurd, well beyond taking a joke. Alina got up and walked across the dance floor, shouldering people out of her way. I followed her to a table on the other side, and then coaxed her to dance to the next slow song.

"No more dancing with anyone else," I said in her ear. "No joking in bed." Having fought and drank and danced, Alina was flushed and glistened lightly with sweat. I brushed away the bangs that clung to the corners of her lips.

"I can tell you, Connor," Alina said vindictively on my shoulder, "Nastia doesn't look so great with her clothes off. I've seen her at the banya. She has cellulite on her ass. I've seen it. It's awful." I chuckled, and she leaned heavily against me. "Admit it," she said after a little while, "you were jealous to see how Nikolai and I danced."

"Why?"

"We danced as old lovers; we know exactly how the other moves."

"You are old lovers. I already knew that." I sighed and then baited her back, "Whereas Nastia and I have yet to be lovers."

"He misses me, I know," she said. "I could make you jealous, Connor," she assured me. "You've been acting a little strange since we started sleeping together. Maybe we should back up a bit, *da*? Go a little more slowly? Get to know one another a little more."

I kissed her neck and whispered, "Not tonight."

We came off the floor and sat at our table alone. Alina smiled and looked at me intently as if trying to put something into my head. Finally, she leaned forward and said, "I had a thought while we were out there on the dance floor, trying to make each other jealous about Nikolai and Nastia. Do you know what it is, Connor? I don't think that we're entirely good people, you and me, and we know it. We know that we're at odds with the rest of the world and that we have to be on the lookout for our own interests. Maybe when two such people meet, they are meant to help each other be better. Maybe they belong together."

I didn't respond with anything more than a deep breath and a diversion of my eyes to the dancers before us. Alina sat brooding for a few moments before she told me that there was someone she had to see. "Wait for me, I'll come back," she said, then added sardonically, "Maybe." I watched her saunter across the dance floor through the strobes and colored lights. She parted a few couples before disappearing into a crowd. She came back into my sight as she climbed the stairs at the other side of the dancehall. She looked fantastic in that dress, smooth and blue. I couldn't wait to take it off her. She stopped on the stairs and looked back at me. She smiled and shook her finger.

It wasn't long before Yana and Sam joined me and poured us all vodka. Boisterous and drunken, they mimicked the people dancing around us.

"Look at him!"

"A robot!"

"I think he may have sat on his vodka bottle."

"*Nu shto*," demanded the offended dancer. "What's your problem?"

"We're just doing our job," said Sam.

"We work for the organizers," followed Yana, stepping into their routine.

"The Organizing Organization."

"We work for *Them*."

"Our official status at this event is as Comic Relief."

"Clowns."

Embarrassed by the stir, the man led his partner off the floor.

"Look, Connor, he's huffed off just like Alina did," cried Yana. "What was her problem? She always gets what she wants, but she's always upset about something. You'd think that someone with her looks could be happy with what she has, but she's always unsatisfied. She's gone through all the men at the station, all of the good ones. Any of them I would be happy with, but they are always not good enough for her."

"*Devushka*, what you're saying is very rude," castigated Sam.

"I'm drunk! I don't care," she slurred. "No, actually," she began again, taking on an even more contemptuous tone. "What? Are you with Alina? Oh, my God! Me and my mouth have done it again. Connor, I'm terribly, terribly sorry! Please, please, please forgive me!"

"It's nothing to me," I said, using slang that sent her into coughing, hip-slapping, hysterics.

"Now let's change the subject," said Sam. "Have you heard about Ilya and the hemophiliac?"

"You tell it, Sam," said Yana, taking another drink and wiping her mouth.

Sam related that late in the previous week a man had come to the studio and demanded that the news team feature him on the program. He was a hemophiliac and needed blood donations. He repeatedly asked people in the studio what their blood types were, and threatened to come after Ilya personally if he didn't do the story. Ilya told the desperate man, 'You've ruined your own chances of having the story done. We can't be threatened into doing something.' The man, who was not much older than Ilya himself, fell to his knees. 'What am I to do?'

"Ilya told him, 'Go bleed to death. I'm sure your mother will be sorry for you.' Sam and Yana laughed riotously. "Then," continued Sam, "the hemophiliac said that it would be Ilya who bled to death and that he would see him again soon."

I shook my head, feeling nauseous. I realized that quite a lot of time had passed and went looking for Alina. I found her on the mezzanine with the Turk. My heart bolted to a near panic. Leto sat at the table, as well as the Blue Beret, Emile, who recognized me and had me sit down next to him. They were all very drunk. Alina appeared glum but gave me a quick smile. The Turk looked me over through glassy eyes.

"Connor, listen, I have a joke for you," called Leto, "One man says to another, 'You are a *mudak*. You are such a *mudak* that if there was a championship match to see who was the biggest *mudak*, you would come in second.' The other man asks, 'Why only second?'" Leto jabbed his finger into my chest, "'Because you are a *mudak*!'" Even the Turk laughed, his broken teeth jagged shadows in the dim light.

"You're Vodopyanov's *Americanets*," he said to me in the darkness between songs. "He's not here tonight, *da*?" he asked the others at the table, though he got no answer. "Let me see your travel papers," he growled, grinning again. "Knowing old Borya, he prints them up himself." He put his hand out over the table to receive my *documentiy*. The others looked away, made uncomfortable by his inhospitality or at the prospect of crossing Vodopyanov. "Let me see them, or I'll have the KGB after you." He looked to Alina, let his hand drop, and then turned his attention elsewhere.

"*Nu*, Leto," I said after a few moments of trying to catch Alina's eye. "How's the market for oranges?"

"A big shipment coming in," he grumbled and looked around as if concerned about being overheard. "I don't want to talk about it now, Connor. *Ladno?*"

There were several women at the table with us having a rowdy conversation of their own. They had long fingernails, dark lipstick. They were southerners and wore a different uniform than the girls in Tomsk. Instead of solid blacks and whites, the theme in their dress and accessories tended more toward black with white vertical stripes. And a pack of skunks they were. They smoked and drank, cursed loudly, laughed coarsely, and cackled. Alina, I could see, regarded them with contempt. They ignored her.

Emile poured me a glass of vodka and coaxed me into drinking with a toast to our two countries. He said, "Did I tell you that I was a frogman in the military? Those were intense days, *nash* Cold War. We are still enemies, you know. The West is too wealthy, and we've lost too much. How can we be allies as long as we are so unequal?"

Suddenly changing the subject, Emile said, "Look at these women here. They're mafia. A pack of dogs. I despise women like these. Can you imagine any one of them having a child? They'd eat it as soon as they saw it. If one of those *pizdy* comes near me, I'm going to stab her in the eye."

He put his arm around me and pulled me close to him. "I can't explain it, but I have a feeling that tonight is some kind of important turning point for me. I need to get away from this Turk. Maybe you will have something to do with it. I work for him, but I feel like a slave. I'm scared to try to leave. It's crazy. Why should I be scared? I could kill him like nothing. It would be nothing for me. Even if he tried to kill me, I could escape him. I can't sleep at night because I lay thinking about what will happen. I have to get away.

"I understand a person can emigrate to America if he has a sponsor. Maybe after tonight, you and I will be friends, and you will want to sponsor me, *da*?"

Nodding vaguely, I attempted to shift myself closer to Leto. I asked him if he'd seen Ilya. "He doesn't like to dance," he replied. I told him about the hemophiliac, and he laughed as if hoping for the worst.

Emile turned his attention to one of the mafia girls, whom he did not stab in the eye but instead flirted with awkwardly.

"Leto," I tried again, in a low voice. "I'm worried about Alina and this Turk. He threatened her once before."

"*Da*?" he said, his attention piqued by the possibility of a fight. "He's dangerous," he admitted drunkenly, "but I can sneak up on him. It's alright. I'll mess him up if he tries anything."

I started feeling woozy, time to go. The Turk got up to go to the toilet. I got up and sat next to Alina. "Are you alright? Let's get out of here."

"I can't go," she said, as if resigned to misery. "My Turk is here."

"Leto says he'll help us if he tries anything. The Blue Beret guy likes me, too. Let's just get up and go."

She sighed. "I don't trust them. There's nothing you can do, Connor," she said wearily. "Besides, sometimes he is nice."

"Nice?" I choked, inadvertently loud. "Are you forgetting that he threatened to beat you? What do you want me to do?"

"*Nichevo*. You can't help, Connor." Alina angled her gaze to look at me from the tops of her large eyes. Her bangs clung to her lips. Her hair was shaken out of how she'd done it and damp with perspiration. She sat slumped in her lovely dress.

"*Ladno*," I said, bitterly superfluous.

"Hey, Yankee," called one of the mafia women, the one Emile had been speaking to. "There's an Irishman here at the disco who says he hates Americans."

"Is that right?" I said loudly in English. "I guess I'll go look for him." I got up and walked off. "Maybe I'll find him and punch him in his smug fucking face." I ridiculously patrolled the party looking for freckles and red hair. The bastard. The pretend club was now thickly shrouded in cigarette smoke and was hot as a house fire.

Some time later Alina found me sitting alone, staring at the whirling lights on the now empty dance floor. "*Nu,* here you are, *mudak.* What happened to your Irishman?"

"What happened to your Turk?"

"He wanted me to go with him somewhere. I said, 'No, I'm going home.' He asked me if I was going home alone, and I told him, 'No, not alone.' He said he'd call me again, that he knows where I work." She stood and shook her head as if gravely disappointed in me. "Have you sobered up a bit, *mudak?* Let's go. I want to go back to your place."

There was dampness in the cold, early morning air as we hailed a ride on Frunze Street. We sat silently in the car. The tension between us of disappointment, irritation, and desire was unabated.

As we entered my flat, I turned on a light. Alina immediately turned it off. Before I could undress her, she reached behind her back and unzipped her dress. She stepped out of it, leaving it on the floor. "Let's go." She unhooked her bra as she walked. Reaching the bed, she took off her panties. Moments later, she whispered to me savagely, "*Cilno! Boystro!*" I held myself above her, arms straight. I braced my knees for the hinge of my hips. "*Cilno! Boystro!*" I went harder. I went faster. I made fists against the mattress and thought of myself as a machine. She laid with her arms above her head. Her mouth was open; her breasts whipped up and down. She winced suddenly and pushed me back. She curled up on her side, clutching her belly. She cried, "That's much too hard. You should know better!" She began to sob like a storm, and I envisioned the steer's head of her organ. I touched her shoulder and fell beside her.

I woke abruptly at dawn. Alina, next to me, was breathing heavily, awake. Her aura was hot and swollen. My blood raged on her command. We'd not gotten what we'd set out for. There was more. She put her hand on me and pulled me until I nudged through her thatch of hair. I deflected her gently and reached for the box of condoms on the floor. She sighed, waited. When I laid back down, she straddled me, plunged me into her. One. Two. Three. Four. Five. She pulled me out of her and pinched the tip of the condom between her fingers. "Take this off," she pleaded and pulled on it as if to pick a flower. I held the base of it and shook my head. We were throbbing, the both of us, our thighs smeared. She took me into her again and rutted me to a count of ten. Then, with a frustrated groan, she threw herself down on the bed. "To me this isn't real sex! When are you going to have sex with me?" Again she curled up and started to cry. I lay still, feeling distant, but aching.

"What are you afraid of?" she said.

My simple Russian was blunt. "A baby."

"I'm the woman! Let me worry about that!" she cried. "I happen to like you, but you don't trust me. I don't know what you think of me. I don't know what I'm doing. If I'm never going to find anyone to care about me, I don't even want to wake up tomorrow."

I touched her, but she shrugged me away. "Get away from me if you think I'm after something. What do you know about my expectations?" She sat up and pulled herself to the edge of the bed. With shaky sighs and sniffles, she began to dress. I watched her breasts swing as she picked up her panties from the floor, as she pulled on the green silk shirt of mine she'd claimed.

Calmly she said, "It's a pity you are such an idiot, Connor."

Feeble blue light seeped through the gaps in the sheeted window, illumination enough to make the room look as it felt to me, deep under water and of crushing weight. I heard Alina in the kitchen fill the kettle.

I was prepared for this. I had already looked up words in the dictionary. I was going to pull the trigger. I dressed wearily. On my way to the kitchen, I stopped to look at my notebook.

Alina sat at the table, a cup of tea steaming before her disconsolate face. I sat and poured tea. "I don't want to presume anything," I began. "I don't want to be insulting. I've never said anything like this to a woman, but given our differences in language and culture, I want us to have a clear understanding about a couple of things. I want to be sure I'm not misleading you."

Whether astonished by my practiced phrases or simply marching on through the newest phase of this endless night, she nodded without a word.

"I'm happy about us," I said. The words began to churn my stomach. "We have a great time together, and you're the most beautiful and *classnaya zhenshchina* I've ever been with. I know that you and I are at the age when people here get married." I said it. I wouldn't say it again. "I know there are expectations around us. Everyone says I came here looking for a wife. I want you to know for certain that I do not have that expectation. I'm going to leave here alone."

Her expression changed. For a potent moment she sat slowly nodding. "Connor," she said, languorously rolling the 'r' in my name, "It's a pity you are such an idiot." She looked into my eyes. "It truly is."

This seemed to me a statement of acceptance. I felt unburdened, relieved, even as she seemed to be adrift in her own thoughts and emotions. We sat and drank tea. The building was silent. Outside the dawn had grown pale, but it was not yet morning.

"Do you want me to go?" she asked finally.

"*Nyet.*"

"Wouldn't you rather be alone?" She struggled to control her voice.

"*Nyet.*"

"But when you go back to America you want to be alone."

"Alina..." I started, but she stopped me.

"I understand you," she said. "I want to go." She got up and went into the bedroom to dress. I followed, intending to walk her home. She had nothing to wear but the blue dress. The indignity of it choked her. It choked me. "Don't look at me," she whispered. She put on her coat before her shoes.

Without another word to each other, we went out the door. She waited as I locked up. We walked down the filthy stairs and out into the cold and empty back lot and then around to the front. "Stop," she said and took my arm and turned me to face her. I watched as a terrible weight came down inside her. "You have no idea how much you've hurt me, Connor," she gasped. She was crushed. Her sobbing wracked her. She threw her shoulders as if in sickness. Angrily, she fought for control.

I squeezed her hand, told her I was sorry.

"So you were right, Connor. Are you pleased? I am thinking much more of this than you. I was protecting myself from these thoughts, but now you've made me go right through it. For what purpose, I don't know. It's not that you want to stop seeing me right now, is it? You don't want to be alone while you're here, do you? You simply want me to take everything, all the weight. You want me to take you to bed and tell you that it's alright, that I will be sad, but that it's what you have to do. So you have told me, it's what you are going to do regardless. What do you think? Maybe I'll have enough of this at some point. I will feel that no one will love me. I will feel that you could have loved me, if you allowed it within yourself. Maybe I will have enough of it. I don't see the point."

Still working within my rehearsed lines, I told her, "I thought we could enrich each other's lives. I thought we already had, but I wanted to be completely honest with you. I realized by telling you this, I was in danger of hurting you, but imagine if we were having this conversation several months from now."

"Hurting me, but not you, *da?* You cannot be hurt by this, Connor?"

"More gained than lost."

"How disgusting! And you make fun of the Germans. *Ti idiot.* I wish you weren't so sure about everything. I wish there was some room in your life for something unexpected, unplanned. Do you know what that could be? You've already made up your mind about everything. You leave nothing to chance. So our relationship is confined. What if we could have had something together?

"For some people, Connor, the search for someone to love you is a horrible, constant torment and heartbreak. Every time is a failure. It takes so much out of me, and I just want it to end. So you say you are not that way. I had a wall to prevent myself from thinking such things, but it was a lie. Sometimes I think I will be alone for all my life, and I wonder if I shouldn't end it."

"Wait!" I said angrily and made her repeat what she'd said, causing her to cry again all the harder.

"I don't need you to walk me home. Leave me alone." She pulled her coat tight around her and walked away, along the gray and pink-lit roadside.

Sunday passed in silence. I was silent even to myself. I wrung out my laundry and hung it from the tops of my doors.

On Monday, Sergei and I got right to work. There'd been a couple noteworthy events over the weekend, and Oleg, with his typical gruesome flare, had got powerful shots: a house fire with a charred body; a thin-ice drowning with a wailing mother.

"*Tak*, the fishermen must clean the fish," sighed Sergei as we reviewed the footage.

"Is that a Russian proverb?"

"*Nyet*, I just made it up." Sergei sipped his Nescafé without taking his eyes from the screens.

All morning I listened for the sound of Alina's footsteps in the hall. I considered taking a break to see if I could spot her.

Ilya joined us shortly after eleven in the morning to review footage and start the voiceover. While Sergei had headphones on, he leaned over to me and said quietly, "Have you seen Alina today? Something's wrong. Probably you should go talk to her. She's upstairs at the bar."

I thought I'd check the office before going upstairs. I felt the eyes of my colleagues on me as I walked through the lobby.

"Connor..." started Gasha as if holding onto a bit of juicy gossip in her steel teeth.

"*Da*, I know."

I'd first been relieved to hear of her presence; now as I climbed the stairs to the mezzanine, I dreaded what I'd see. I half expected to find her facedown on a bar table weltering in wrist blood. Instead I found her with a can of beer and a glass. Her eyelids, smeared with wetted makeup, hung half open. She stared dully ahead as if unable to focus.

She was there as a beacon for me, I thought. She wasn't hiding in the bar, crying her pain away. She was out on the mezzanine, wailing for me to come to her, announcing to all passersby that we had some problem that could not be contained.

Maybe she's pregnant, they think; they've had a fight, broken up; he's refused to marry her. 'I don't want this,' I thought angrily. 'It's not worth it.'

She did not look at me when I sat down. I prepared to speak, to say something that would make it worse. The very words, 'I don't want this,' were in translation on the tip of my tongue, but something struck me that turned my anger to alarm. She was distraught, possibly drunk, but there was something else.

"Are you alright?"

"Did Marat tell you I was up here?"

"No, Ilya did."

"Then I'm mad at them both." She took a drink. "I'm a hysteric, Connor. *Tak,* so now you know. Don't think this is all for you," she slurred. "It's not. There are many things that have built up."

"How many drinks have you had?"

"Just three. It started this morning with Marat telling me all about his problems as he always does. He never wants to hear anything about me. I could be bleeding to death right here in front of him, and he would continue talking about his own problems. Do you know what happened? It was a bad night for everyone on Saturday. I'll never go to the disco again. You know about Zhana, of course. Marat was there with her, and he had told his wife some story about having to help his brother with something, but she knew it was a lie. So she came down to the disco and caught him there with his mistress. Little meek Natalia did that, came down and caught him cheating. Found him dancing slow with her. She turned around and was just going to leave, but stupid old Marat saw her and thought he could explain everything with his lies. He tried to tell her that his brother made him come to the dance and that Zhana was just a client of the station. Marat can make up lies like a politician, just like that, *vot tak!* That's probably what he'll do once Gennadi comes to his senses and fires him.

"Natalia wouldn't listen to his lies. She's had enough, and she screamed at him right there that she is pregnant, and how does he expect her to feel with him cheating on her when she's just found out that she's having his baby. Isn't it terrible? It's all so sad. Everything has just built up, Connor. Do you know what he does when I try to talk to him? He treats me like a child. He acts as if my problems are ridiculous. That they're just nothing." Tears rose to her eyes.

Just then a man and women from the news department exited the bathrooms and walked by. Alina hung her head and spat at the table. "On at six," she said loud enough for them to hear. "What do you think they were doing in there together?" She sighed and then told me, "I've only had three beers, but I took some pills."

"Are you trying to kill yourself?" I asked.

"I don't think so." She sputtered a laugh. "Do you know what I'm upset about? I have rheumatism. I'm a young woman, but I have this condition, and it causes me terrible pain." She began to cry. "The only thing I can afford to do is get these horrible injections that are even more painful. There are pills I could get, imported medications, but I can't afford them. I'm not going to get the injections any more. I won't. I can't stand it." She humped over the table and bawled.

"What kind of pills did you take? Should I call your doctor?"

"I don't want to stop crying, Connor. Tell me something, are you more concerned or embarrassed?"

"Alina, you can't stay here like this."

"I can do as I wish. I have some other pills for my pain. I should take those, too."

I saw her purse on the floor and picked it up and put it beside me.

"Are you going to protect me from myself? Isn't that nice of you. I've done it before, you know. Maybe I have. You'll never know." Something came to her mind, and she started crying afresh. "Connor, I know you think I've had sex with many men, but it's not true. Not many. I can't stand that you think that. It hurts me so much. How can you think that about me? Do you want to know about the German? Do you want me to tell you the truth about everything? Maybe you will say that you will not think less of me for it, but if that were true, there would be no reason to want to hear it. That is a trick people play on you, *da?*"

She took a quavering breath and began, "I told you other people had left me. About a year ago, I went to Munich to meet a German man I was corresponding with. We were pen pals. I met him through a service I found in a magazine. We had so much in common, I thought. I was thinking, 'that's it, I've found this man.' We said we loved each other, and we arranged to meet. We spent four days together in a hotel room in Munich, then I had to go home. After that, he stopped writing. Do you know how I felt? He'd told me that he wanted to get married. He wrote one last time. He told me he was sorry. He loved me, but he wasn't good enough for me. I deserved better, he said. Do you know how I feel? I was a whore that he felt guilty for not paying." Tears were in her eyes. "See? So it's not just you that has to be careful of what words we use.

"It's something you should tell your children, *da?* A bad choice will stay with you for all your life. It remains a truth about you, and if you ever want to be truly intimate with someone, you will have to tell it, and he will think less of you. Everything is so sad to me today."

"Alina, you don't need to tell me this."

"Encouraging truthfulness doesn't dilute it when it comes, *da*, Connor? Don't think this is just for you, that I'm trying to embarrass you. I'm the one that's going to have to live with it. Have a beer with me, Connor. There are no hard feelings. I think you are glad to have made me cry. It shows that I finally have understood you. Isn't that true? Don't worry about leaving me, if it comes to that. I'll be better for the experience, like you said. I'll always take heart in knowing there is a kindred spirit on the other side of the world."

She was calming down now. She wiped her tears, tucked her bangs behind her ears. I began to plan my words, a suggestion of bringing her home, maybe calling a taxi. Before I could speak Marat appeared at the top of the stairs. He motioned to us that he would join us after going to the bar. He came back with beers for us all. Alina sighed loudly, nearly a groan.

"It's so pleasant to have the bar here, isn't it?" began Marat. "We can drink during the day, drink away sorrows, instead of doing our work. What's she upset about, Connor? I think she needs to stop drinking on the job and get back to work."

"Have you ever seen me drink during the day before, Marat?" Alina hissed back at him. "Maybe you should ask yourself that. Maybe you could pull your head out of your ass and have a look around."

"*Ladno, ladno.*" Marat cowed and looked over his shoulder. Attempting to recover, he said to me, "Connor, Sergei tells me he is waiting for you to finish something."

Alina rolled her eyes. "Listen, Marat," she said, "we were just discussing your little *problema*. I thought Connor might have some ideas for you."

Panic flew across his face. Without looking at me, but again checking over his shoulder, he whispered, "That is very sensitive information, *devuchka*. You can't simply tell anyone. Of course, I trust Connor. I meant to talk to him myself."

"Everyone knows, idiot," she mocked him.

"Your work performance has been very poor."

"*Pushol ti chortu.* You're not my boss."

"Marat." I interrupted, attempting to be calm. "I don't think this is a good time to talk to Alina about work, since she's obviously not feeling well. I think I'll take her home."

With an executive nod, he concurred.

"I don't want to go home," Alina drawled and drunkenly flapped her hand at me. "I shouldn't be by myself."

Just then, with shoes briskly tapping up the stairs, Nikolai swooped in on us. Without acknowledging Marat or me, he sat close to Alina and began talking to her in low, cooing tones. "*Alinichka*, what's happening here? Are you alright? Let me see your eyes." He touched her lightly on the arm.

Outranked, outclassed, and appearing concerned about being blamed for something, Marat drained his beer, got up, and quietly left.

"Come walk with me," Nikolai said to her. With a slight glance at me, he took her by the arm and helped her out of the chair. I watched him lead her into one of the nearby classrooms and shut the door. I sat and finished my beer and hers. I knew my part in this wasn't over.

Alina had been crying again when Nikolai brought her back to the table. "Don't think badly of her," he said. "She's a very good woman. You shouldn't think badly of her because of this. Sometimes we all have little breakdowns. You can bring her to her friend's house. She'll tell you where. It's nearby." With that, Nikolai tucked his tie into his jacket and clacked away down the stairs.

"I'll get our coats," I told her gruffly. "Wait here."

She met me at the bottom of the stairs, eyes downcast and holding steady to the railing. Once outside, my thoughts swirled between despair and fury. I walked supporting her on my arm. I attempted blankness. We staggered over the wet March ice to the bus stop. Few others were there in the middle of the day. Tanya's apartment was only three stops away.

"If she's out shopping, you can leave me. I'll wait for her," Alina said as I led her up the stairwell. Tanya opened the door at my first knock. Nikolai had perhaps called. Alina laughed when she saw her friend as if she'd stood there drenched in mud or dressed as a clown. She gave me a dry-lipped kiss. "Don't be mad." They immediately started speaking too fast for me to follow. I waved briefly and turned to go.

I had to go back to the station. I dreaded it, so first I stopped at a kiosk, bought a couple beers and a pack of cigarettes. I went and sat on a park bench, hoping I wouldn't meet anyone coming back from the *stalovaya*. I inhaled deeply as Pavel did. A non-smoker, and likely a dog, gets quite a buzz.

Chapter 13

Actual spring came slowly and lasted an age of dripping eves and icy walkways made more treacherous by being wet. The warmer weather brought enormous slush puddles that set everyone detouring around them out into the roads, except, that is, for rubber-booted boys who charged right through. More than once, I saw little waders lose footing and take a plunge into the pulpy gray guck. They'd scramble to shore to empty their *botinki* only to be clucked at by *babushki* and laughed at by friends.

From the snow emerged patches of fragrant mud and crumbling cement. The sense of smell was reborn. Spring flowers and sprouts of new grass appeared above the underground pathways of the city's hot water pipes, a roadside preview of spring, an unexpected benefit of wasted heat. Suddenly there was parsley and dill from Georgia for sale all over town at sidewalk stands and in the bazaar. The bunches of green fronds, startlingly bright, leapt up with fragrance and color from stacked-up boxes. I ate herbs with cheese on bread. I tossed them in pasta with garlic and oil. Parsley, dill, and spring onions, I put them in omelets and in anything else I could think of.

Winter's retreat, as welcome as it was, also left Tomsk littered and coated with scum like the stump-pocked bottom of a drained reservoir. It would stay like that, I thought, having become cynical through the winter, until the rain comes to wash it away. Thankfully, I was wrong. The inhabitants of Tomsk emerged with twig brooms and set to piling up and burning trash. There were fires everywhere, raging in dumpsters and smoldering in heaps for days. Around the clock every one of them was attended by an eager boy coaxing it with a stick. I wanted to do the same, to burn the trash. 'Give me a rake, comrade *malchik*. Let's get it all into the fire.' For weeks the air smelled of burnt plastic.

With spring also came construction. Cranes sprang up like stems of asparagus. Workmen mixed and spilled concrete, piled and pointed bricks. I was struck, nevertheless, by the shoddy quality of the work and the building materials. No wall looked plumb; the new bricks were cracked and brittle; the mortar was chalky.

One afternoon Sergei, Marat, and I picked our way along the path to the *stalovaya* for lunch. Marat declared, "I saw Old Man Winter himself leaving Tomsk the other day. He had a long gray beard and rode a bicycle through the slush in rubber boots." Marat huffed at his joke. "He had a shovel in his front basket because he was going to his *dacha* for the summer to grow potatoes."

"*Vot*," said Sergei pointing to the ground ahead of us, "He left his dog." Beside the trail was a corpse, its fur dampened by the melting snow.

"A feral dog starves all winter only to die in the spring," philosophized Marat. "That should be a proverb. Right up there, Connor, with 'even a dog doesn't smoke.'"

"Yesterday I saw a drunk man in a three-piece suit in that exact place," I told them. "He was crawling on his hands and knees and looked at me like he'd never seen another person before."

"He died and turned back into his true self," chortled Marat. "This walk has become a literary occasion, *da*?"

"*Nyet*, I know this dog," said Sergei sadly, and Marat and I laughed at him. "What?" he responded, "I do. I like dogs."

"I'd like to meet a Russian that doesn't like dogs," I said.

"They've all immigrated, Connor," declared Marat. "Or else you can tell them by the *shapkas* they wear." Sergei walked on mournfully. "Was it your family pet, Sergei?

"No, just a stray."

"As the snow melts, Connor, you will see many more drunks on the street. The cold at least keeps the streets clean of them for a few months. Wait until a holiday, *Ivan Kupala* for instance, all the benches in the park will have a drunkard on it passed out with pissed pants. We should do a story on public drunkenness that day."

"People have to cope," said Sergei, still glum over the dog.

"That's not coping. I wish we'd kept Gorbachev's prohibition on vodka," Marat asserted righteously.

"Dog shit," Sergei and I answered simultaneously.

"Ha, no, you're right," grinned Marat, wet-lipped. He then announced, "Gentlemen, I have an idea for a change of plan. Instead of going to the *stalovaya* for lunch as we have done all winter, let's find a *shashlik* stand."

This immediately put Sergei in a better mood. Tempted beyond any deliverance, he assented gleefully, "*Shashlik, bladt!*"

I'd noticed the homemade grills that had popped up on street corners, but I hadn't braved entering the circle of *hooligani* that usually surrounded them. These young men, almost invariably dressed in shiny tracksuits and occasionally mohair caps, stood next to their chosen fires, day and night, chewing gristly meat from aluminum skewers. Otherwise, they squatted nearby cracking pine nuts in their teeth and spitting the shells, sometimes taking a break to throw wet snowballs at dogs.

We easily found a stand. "Sergei has a sixth sense for finding food of any kind," laughed Marat. "There's a kiosk over there. Connor, go get us some beers." We ordered six skewers for starters. Most stands, I learned, had their own marinades and homemade sauces. There was usually some combination of garlic and vinegar, but sometimes tamarind and sometimes hot sauce. Some shashlik stands, manned by Georgians or Armenians, seduced the Siberians with herbs they'd never tasted.

"We'll make a game of it, Connor," proposed Marat. "Every Tuesday we'll go to a different *shashlik* stand. We'll taste them all." To that we raised our beers.

"What kind of meat do you suppose this is?" I asked naively. "It's not beef, I don't think. It's not pork."

"It's just meat," said Sergei, chewing. "Better not to ask."

"Do you suppose, my friends," laughed Marat with his mouth full, "that there is a *shashlik* cut on the cow or the horse or whatever this is? Do you think that on a butcher's chart there is a part of the animal labeled as '*shashlik*'?" We chuckled and chewed and drank the warm beer.

"How does it feel, Connor," began Marat as we headed back to the station, "that you are no longer the most important American advisor at TV-N?" The station had been recently granted a Soros adviser, who had arrived a week prior.

"Connor's not an adviser," protested Sergei with some distaste. "He's simply one of us."

"*Da*," laughed Marat, "he's one of us, so we have to pay him. Whereas Soros pays for the other one. So what do you know, Connor, that Yanek does not?"

The advisor's name was Yanek Witschak. He was a Hungarian émigré to the U.S., just as Soros himself. In his thirty years as a television journalist, he'd worked for news agencies all over the world, specializing in Eastern Europe and the former Soviet Union. Yanek was a stocky and energetic man in his fifties with gray hair. He chewed gum constantly, having recently quit smoking, and that, along with his tendency to pace and sigh loudly when displeased, gave him the air of a veteran coach. He was an impressive guy, and although he hadn't arrived with the equipment Gennadi had hoped for, he instantly won the respect of all the staff. Even Ilya hung raptly on his every word.

When I'd first been introduced to him, he'd laughed, "So you are their American," the inside joke being that he understood the absurdity of my position at the station. Perhaps further, I'd considered, he'd thought of me as a willing mascot, maybe a charlatan. The night before our *shashlik* lunch, however, Yanek had invited me to his hotel in *Academgorodok* to discuss what I knew of the business of the station.

"I thought it'd be best if we met here, so we can speak openly," said Yanek as he opened his room door and shook my hand. The room was lit, colored, and scented in shades of nicotine. I sat in a golden pleather chair, and he launched into the debriefing from the corner of the bed. He leaned forward with his hands held monk-like and his elbows on his knees. "I'd rather you wouldn't discuss our meeting, if you don't mind. I'm not trying to keep or find secrets, I just don't want to ruffle any feathers, and I thought you could save me a lot of time. It's not an ideal way of doing business, but I don't have much time here, as you know. I can see the state of the news department by watching the tapes. What I need to know is if the station itself is viable or on the verge of collapse. So what advice?"

I considered what to tell him. Whose side was I on?

"I know they won't tell me anything they perceive as embarrassing," said Yanek, noticing my pause, "but that could be exactly what I need to know."

I told him I thought the station was viable, that the leadership was sound, but that there were outside conditions that had them under siege. "Every time they run a story about organized crime or official corruption, they get threats." I told him how male members of the staff took turns guarding the station at night, about how word had leaked that TV-N was getting money from the States, and how Ilya had been beaten.

"Advertisers don't pay their bills. They send crates of oranges and buckets of meat instead," I went on. "The burglar alarms don't work; no equipment is secure unless it's locked down. I never find out anything directly from any kind of chain of command. The grapevine is the only way anyone knows anything."

"It is a remarkably effective method," Yanek joked, his gray eyes smiling.

All the while I vented, Yanek nodded calmly, apparently unsurprised. I worried that I was going too far on the negative points and started talking about Gennadi's commitment to the station and the staff. "He's a hero to the staff. They'd do anything for him."

"Relax," he chuckled. "You've made their case well, but also given me some important information that I doubt otherwise would have been forthcoming." Yanek sat back for a moment and looked at a notebook on the bed beside him. "I would offer you something, but I try not to drink on most occasions. Smoking, drinking, I've given it all up. That and more." He chewed gum and bounced his knee. "Yes, the story of the station is very inspirational, but I just want to teach them to report the news before the government tries to shut them down."

"Do you think that will happen?"

"Who knows? I don't know what will happen. Maybe they'll like democracy, maybe they won't. Maybe someone will come along and speak like a Democrat but act like a Soviet."

"Right now I don't think it's about much more than getting money for yourself," I put in. "Out of necessity." Yanek looked up at me, and frowned as he put his hand over his chin. There were things I wanted to ask him, and I think he was aware of it.

"What about you?" he asked. "Is there anything I can do to help you? It must be challenging living here by yourself."

With formality giving away my discomfort, I asked him, "Do you consider yourself a Russophile?" He looked at me puzzled, making me say more. "Do you love it here?" I asked him, feeling ridiculous. "There are great people and great stories and all kinds of craziness, but I don't particularly like it here. I'm finding that it holds no magic for me. It should be intriguing to me, but it's becoming less and less so. I don't feel the way I thought I would feel." The smile returned to his eyes. He had me in school now, and he would be my advisor, too. 'And I am a stupid boy?' I thought to myself.

"Maybe you're starting to feel like the people who live here. Now you can understand why so many of them wish to emigrate," he said with some twitch of indication, an invisible wink. "I am not, as people say, a Russophile," he went on. "I come here because I am a journalist. I came initially because I spoke the language and others did not. It gave me a competitive advantage, so I ended up doing a lot of stories about Russia. Probably you will, too, now that you're learning Russian. That's the way it works out. You learn to do something useful and people want to pay you to do it." Yanek had changed his way of speaking, I noticed. Instead of the consummate professional, impatient and curt, which is how I'd seen him at the station, he took on a nostalgic tone, if not like that of a father, then of an uncle.

"To me this place has the best and worst of everything. You have the best people and the most ruined, lost people. Interesting stories are never hard to come by. Russians defy homogenization. They defy the logical West. They always have, and I hope they keep on doing it, to some degree. At the same time, this country is full of madness. I'll tell you a story: One time, not far from Moscow, I ended up covering a large chemical explosion. I happened to hear on the State radio station that there'd been a 'small fire' at the city exposition grounds. That the radio even mentioned it meant that it was serious, so I went to see for myself. I'd been to the exposition grounds before, but now it was a completely different place. There was no sign of a fire, and what had been a giant field for tents was now a paved square with kiosks and trees planted in tremendous raised beds. I talked to some people and found out that a local chemical plant had been using the field to park tanker trucks filled with chemical waste. There'd been a huge fire, the trucks exploded. It had gone on for days. So what did they do, with poison gas filling the air and chemicals seeping into the ground? Did they evacuate the area? No. Did they section it off to be decontaminated? No. They called in the military to cover it up. They brought in a squadron trained in setting up airstrips and paved the whole place over. They brought in full-grown trees from the forest."

Yanek paused for a moment and shook his head in amused disbelief. "As crazy as the government is, I think, the whole of Russia, or the crazy part of it, is made up of individual lunatic microbes. Insane cells that make the insane whole." He chuckled. "Here's another story: I once met a woman who lived above the arctic circle and ate nothing but chalk. No other food, she told me. Her daughter, who was a teacher, stole it for her. 'It's hard to find good chalk,' she told me. Her family was undisturbed that the woman only ate chalk, except that she was a picky eater." He burst into laughter. When it subsided, he took a deep breath and went on, "We can thank them for not bringing down the rest of the world with them, for not holding us all hostage to their failure. Imagine if the U.S. was in the same situation. What would it do if all it had left was its weapons? Would it admit to itself that it had failed and quietly attempt to rebuild? I don't know, but the cynical journalist in me thinks it would only allow itself to go out with a furious bang. It would hold the rest of the world hostage."

Back on the path to the station after our *shashlik* lunch, I answered Marat, "Probably Yanek knows more about just about everything than I do."

"Ha," he laughed, and pounded me on the shoulder. "I don't think he knows as much about breaking the hearts of our beautiful *Sibirski devotchki, da?*"

I had not broken it off with Alina after the scene at the office, although I'd been sure that I would. When I'd come home that evening late from work, I found a note wedged in my door:

Privet, papa. I'm sorry about today. I was very silly. I slept all afternoon at Tanya's. Don't be too mad.
Poka, Alina

I'd been so ridiculous, I knew, towing her by the arm, frowning about my naughty girl. The next day at work she showed up wearing an absurd pair of bug-eye sunglasses to cover her puffy eyes.

"Do you think less of me now, Connor?" she whispered to me in the hall.

"I think differently," I said.

We talked more later. Should we change something, she wanted to know? Should we back up? By turns she was concerned, direly serious, and would look me in the eyes passionately as if trying to force herself into me, then she would appear amused, and tease me for my timidity.

"Do you know what is wonderful for us at this time, Connor? We can do anything we want to do. The world was wide open for us. We could do anything. Well, not anything, *da?* That's right, you told me. That's something I like about you, maybe it's because you're American; you are always telling me the truth. Connor, try not to worry so much. I don't care about these things. I don't know what you're bothering yourself about. Why shouldn't we enjoy what we have now and worry about other things when we come to them? It's okay. I give you permission. Why should you have to apologize for not being Russian? You won't have to look up any more words in the dictionary for me." She paused and smiled. "What were you thinking about me that day?"

"That you were right, that you do have the heavier side of all this."

"So what do you want to do?"

"I want it just the way it is," I returned. "I want it to be even worse."

"Good," she said, "then that is what you will have."

Alina and I attended Easter mass at the newly-opened Tomsk Catholic Church.

"Why do you want to go to church?" she'd asked when I suggested it.

"Just to see," I started, but saw in her face that vagueness would not suffice. "When I was a kid it made me feel better after something bad happened."

"You feel guilty, *malchik*," she cooed. "Will you confess?"

"*Nyet*, I never believed in that, not even the first time they made me go."

"I should tell you something about that church," she said with a grin. "During Soviet times it was used as a planetarium, and we went there on school outings every year. When I walked in the door somehow I felt at home. I have always wanted to be a Catholic."

"Or maybe an astronomer."

"You're getting better with your jokes."

"I knew the word because of Fest."

"*Da.*" She kissed me in reward.

In the morning before mass, I walked to Alina's flat to meet her. She opened the door and told me she was scared. She had big childish eyes for me and wore a beige dress that made her shapeless. A sinners smock, I jokingly called it. "Why are you scared?"

"I once went to an Orthodox wedding in the Crimea," she told me coyly, "and there were a bunch of old ladies crossing themselves over and over again as if they were possessed. They reminded me of the fervent Communists saluting and marching and clapping in unison. It was frightening. I was just a little girl. The priests, all in black, even now when I see one on a bus, they make me nervous. I feel guilty, even though I am just an ordinary girl. I'm no worse than anyone else. I have no reason to be ashamed. I don't believe in their God, but still He somehow has the power to condemn me."

As a virtuous and chaste couple in their Sunday best, we walked hand in hand to the bus stop and paid our fare downtown. By the time we came to the base of the small hill below the church, almost all our fellow pilgrims were old women. "Probably these *babushki* had Catholic parents who held secret masses," whispered Alina conspiratorially. "They secretly taught their children the beliefs of the Church. Think of what they risked. Maybe for these people, the collapse was worth it."

The green-painted house of God held on its single spire a cross made from two scraps of bare wood. Though dilapidated, it was majestic on its hill, overlooking the uncared-for rooftops of the town. A smiling usher held the door for us as we entered. We thought it was a good start and gave each other a brief smile. We stood at the back. We were a bit late, and the place was packed.

The procession began. The priest in his robes, eyes fixed forward, held the bible as if it were a magnet pulling him to the lodestone of the altar. Behind him a choir of peasant-like *babushki* bellowed heavy Russian hallelujahs; behind them, shepherds to the newly-recovered sheep, were three nuns wearing the white and blue saris of the Missionaries of Charity.

"Hallelujah, hallelujah," wailed the devout.

The priest, once at the lectern, looked out over his eager congregation and began, "I know many of you are here only because it is Easter. You don't come every week. You come today and maybe on Christmas. To you I say, you either believe or you have already died." A bit after that I stopped trying to follow him but frequently caught the repetition of the word for death, *cmert.*

I looked for an escape route, but we were packed in. I watched Alina stare ahead blankly. She turned to me, "Connor," she said pleadingly. There was no way out. We suffered through it. "I don't see how that could have made you feel better about anything," she grumbled once we'd fled.

"*Da*," I agreed. "Even when I go back home, I'm reminded of why I don't go more often."

"Did you pray?"

"Only to get out of there."

She chuckled and took my hand, our feet falling heavily before us as we descended the holy mount. "You are an ethnic Catholic only, Connor. The priest built a wall for us, *da?* You believe or you're already *cmert*. There's no room to grow into it. If there was a small opening, if there was just a little welcome instead of condemnation, I might have gone back. Who were those nuns?"

"You know Mother Teresa, *da?*

"*Vot*, Tomsk is with the lepers!" Alina exclaimed with a laugh and a skip forward. "The Catholics aren't the only missionaries we have in Tomsk, you know. We have the Moonies, too. There is a Canadian with thirteen children. They pretend to give free English lessons. I know what we can do, now, Connor, to salvage the rest of the day. This is one of the nicest spring days yet, *da?* We can walk to the river, eat shashlik, drink beer, and watch the ice break up and float away north to the Ob."

"*Vot*, that's religion!"

"*Vot!*" she'd laughed back at me, the new spring sunlight on her vibrant pale face, her eyes beaming joyfully. "Now that I've attended a religious function with you, oh so devoted American man, you can attend a Communist one with me. Let's go to the May Day demonstration next month. It's *my* old religion."

Someone smashed the glass front door at TV-N. The shatter-proof glazing launched inward, frozen in the path of the projectile. Cubic bits of glass lay still on the floor, scraped by the side of someone's shoe into a hasty pile. I knew why it hadn't been swept up; they were waiting for the cleaning ladies to do it. "Who smashed the door?" I asked Gasha as I walked in.

"Somebody smashed it over the weekend," she said.

"*Da*, that much I can see, Gasha. Who?"

"*Vot, tak*! Such cheek!" cackled Israelievitch from his post on the lobby couch.

"Nobody knows," sneered Gasha, withholding information.

"You did it to sabotage us," Kolya joked as he passed, slapping me on the shoulder. "You're C.I.A. We all know it."

"Never mind that," said Israelievitch, putting his paper down to shake my hand. "I just read a story about a Russian girl your age, Connor, whose family moved to America when she was ten. She came back to Moscow last year to go into business with a relative. Within a few months she had a nervous breakdown. She couldn't take our blessed heaviness. Back home in California, they have her in a sandbox for therapy." The old man put his hand over his vest buttons and chuckled. "You don't feel yourself slipping, do you Connor? Maybe we should bring you to a psychologist. You have a psychologist at home, *da*? You all do!"

"I'll find myself some sand," I told him. Israelievitch clapped his knee, sending his paper to the floor. With a groan, but still laughing, he bent to pick it up.

"Tomsk is much nicer than Moscow," put in Gasha.

"I don't know about that, *devuchka*," said Israelievitch dismissively as he fluffed his pages before him. "I don't know about that."

Kolya, coming back through reception, said, "the honorable Israelievitch here is our very own Ministry of Information. *Da, pravda*! He does everything he can to prevent its spread." Kolya chuckled playfully and strolled back out past the broken door. Israelievitch grunted and continued reading. Gasha lowered her head as if afraid of being implicated in the irreverence.

I went on a hunt for information. I popped my head into the marketing room to see if Alina was there. That morning I awakened to find she'd left, as was the norm when she spent the night. She'd wake before me, bathe, and then go back to her place to change and walk Otto.

She wasn't at her desk. Marat caught me looking and said, louder than necessary, "She's having a special meeting with Yanek, but nobody knows where, since they're not at the bar."

"Spy," shouted more than one person in the crowded room.

"I needed to ask her something," Marat protested.

"Why are you working in here, Marat?" I asked him, although I knew the answer. Snickers followed. Sergei had told me that he was being transitioned to a new job in marketing because he'd done so poorly directing the studio. He would lose his office, but not until Yanek departed.

"Anyone want to tell the American C.I.A. agent what happened to the front door?" I asked the room.

"It's war, we've taken a shell, just like in Sarajevo."

"We'll be massacred like Rwandans," added Misha with standard caustic irony.

"I brought my machete," chimed in Yana without looking up from her monitor. "Nikolai is giving us all a talk," she added.

Marat prescriptively cleared his throat.

"*Nu shto?*" said Yana, sounding uncharacteristically annoyed. "Is that a secret? How are we supposed to know to go to a meeting if it's a secret, eh?"

"It's not a secret, Yana," answered Marat, taking on his official tone. "But Connor's attendance is not required."

"*Pochimu nyet?*" came from several in the room. "He works here, too."

Holding up his hands, Marat answered, "We need Connor to distract Yanek, *da?*"

"I'll tell you everything afterward," sighed Yana.

"I'm sure I'll hear everything before the meeting starts just like the rest of you have," I cracked to a few laughs and an absurdly disappointed frown from Marat.

"Sergei," I intoned with joking inquisitiveness as I stepped into the editing room. "Who smashed the front door?"

He motioned me to shut the door before saying, "Leto did it."

"Leto? How do you know?"

"I saw the car drive away, the one they say he stole from us."

"Who said?"

"Nikolai."

"When did it happen? What were you doing here?"

"Late last night. I've been sleeping here," he admitted, looking embarrassed. "My wife and I…"

"*Yasno*," I said, sparing him the explanation.

"Everything is going crazy right now. There's some kind of fight going on with Leto and the station. They say he stole your TV from Marat's office. Leto also has one of the company cars and won't give it back. Somebody's threatened to kidnap Gennadi's children, too, but that can't be Leto."

Ilya entered suddenly, and having caught the last of what Sergei had said, added hotly, "In my opinion it's that stupid fucking hemophiliac that's threatened to kidnap the kids. *Takoi idiot!* What's the point? They're just going to send the kids away now. Great timing with all this, right when we've got the Soros advisor here. Fucking Leto, eh? Crazy idiot, *bladt.*" Ilya threw himself in one of the ragged, squawking office chairs and began to roll up his sleeves. Points of sweat beaded on his forehead. "How much do you know?" he asked. "Do you know about the oranges?"

"Leto's oranges?" Sergei and I followed.

"*Da, da, da,*" said Ilya, and with the sigh of one at the outset of an unpleasant task he began. "We gave Leto money to buy equipment on his last trip to Moscow. We gave him a money order. He was going to buy oranges, of course, *bladt,* more fucking oranges. We thought he was doing us a favor, since he could bring back our equipment with the oranges, and we wouldn't have to pay for shipping. We had already arranged for the equipment on the black market so we wouldn't have to pay the tax, which is one hundred percent. *Nu*, Leto wasn't going to buy our equipment. He was going to buy more oranges and send them to Krasnoyarsk. He thought he could borrow the money and buy the equipment later. Somebody found him out or he got drunk and told someone because Gennadi got an anonymous call. So he called the bank and had the money order canceled. Leto showed up at the bank in Moscow, *bladt*, and went crazy. He kicked over desks and attacked the clerk. The guards pulled their guns on him and took him outside for a beating.

"Then he had to go see his Greeks and tell them that he didn't have the money for their oranges, so they beat him, too. He was in the hospital in a coma for two days. We didn't know what happened to him. Nobody heard from him until yesterday. He walked into the station—he has the keys and knows the lock codes—and he stole a TV from Marat's office, and one of the company cars."

"Wait! Marat told me that somebody stole my TV a couple months ago," I said.

"It was a second TV, *bladt*," said Ilya.

Then I asked, "No one thought to change the keypad codes?"

Ilya resignedly shrugged, "We can't change the codes, *bladt*. We had a fight over the costs with the company that installed them, and they won't do anything for us until we pay what they say we owe them."

"But why wouldn't Gennadi have someone chain the doors closed, if nothing else, if he knew Leto might try something?"

"We thought Leto was in Moscow. There were people in the station when he came in, *bladt!*" Ilya exclaimed.

"I was here," admitted Sergei. "Nobody knew what had happened, so it wasn't unusual to see Leto. Nobody tells anyone anything."

"I didn't even know," raged Ilya. "After he got what he wanted, he threw a brick through the front door with a note tied to it saying he took the car and TV as compensation for Gennadi ruining his business and made threats to do certain things if we tried to get them back. A brick with a note, *bladt*, just like a fucking Van Damme movie."

Sergei and I chuckled halfheartedly.

"He could have walked right in and put the brick on Gennadi's desk," Ilya went on. "He could have stuck his note there with a knife if he wanted to pretend he's in the movies."

"What did he threaten? Has Gennadi called the *militia*?"

"*Nyet.* He can't call the police. Leto knows that. See, even though Leto hasn't worked here in a year, the car is registered to him. He legally owns it. All the company cars were registered to the drivers or the cameramen personally, so that we could avoid paying the crazy business taxes. That is what got us here! Leto could reveal it, and it would end up costing us way more than just one car." Ilya sighed, "He was a friend, but I always knew he was capable of something crazy like this, *bladt.* I heard stories about things he did in the Army. Crazy things." With that Ilya got up, hailed us curtly, said "I've got to go," and left the room.

"*Vot tak*," said Sergei in conclusion.

A bit later Nikolai asked. "Connor, can you please take Yanek up to the bar for coffee?"

"Of course, but Nikolai, can I ask you a question? Where's Gennadi today?"

Begrudgingly he answered, "He's taking his wife and children to their dacha. It will take him all day. The roads in the villages are still muddy. He had to borrow a 4X4."

Yanek was waiting for me at one of the mezzanine tables. "Are you with OVIR?" he smiled, referring to the Soviet-era keepers of foreigners. "So what's this meeting about, the front door?"

"They won't let me in the meeting either," I shrugged.

"You know."

"I know a disgruntled former employee broke the door."

"I don't care, honestly," Yanek exclaimed in his slightly accented English. "They are afraid of embarrassment, or more importantly, of losing funding. But I couldn't be shocked by anything. What they don't know is that I've seen it all."

"I think they're worried that if they appear to you to be dealing with the mafia, they won't get the Soros money. No bribes, no corruption, it's one of the rules, right?

"I know how things operate here," said Yanek. "What they are doing is so much more important than that. When I see their broadcasts, it's hard to believe they aren't shut down. Only a few years ago, their lives would be ruined by reporting such things. It's nothing short of amazing. They have nothing to be embarrassed of. It's the waste of time that I'm concerned about. They need to learn as much as possible. They should put aside all other concerns while I'm here."

"Somebody's threatening Gennadi's kids."

"I'm not surprised," he said, though he raised his brow.

"That's the rumor," I added.

"Nicely qualified, kid," he chuckled. "Do you really understand the importance of what they're doing, the miracle of it?"

"I think I have a pretty good idea," I said defensively. "What's a miracle, though? A dysfunctional government collapsed. From what I've seen, the biggest threat to the station isn't the remnants of the old government, the KGB, or the police, but the society around them, the anarchy."

He nodded, paused for a moment. "I'm reminded of a Czech expression, 'You can't make a whip out of shit, and even if you could, you couldn't make it crack.' What your friends have done here is make a whip out of shit."

Four Sundays from Easter, the everlasting spring crept on. The snow and ice were vanquished, but the deep continental chill remained. Nonetheless, Alina and I threw aside our *shapkas* and winter coats to attend the May Day demonstration. She had a robin's egg blue jacket that lit her up with youth. "It's still too cold for it, but it makes me feel like spring," she said. It came as a sweet revelation, too, to see her hair loose and fluttering in the breeze. By now she'd grown out of her German-fashion-magazine hairdo and had it trimmed at shoulder length.

"No one will make the mistake of thinking you're from Tomsk," she kidded me, indicating my bright fleece jacket. "You're finished trying to fit in, *da*? That's a shade of green I don't think we've ever seen here. What's that material, it's so soft?"

"I'm a member of the Green Party."

"Do you have a Green Party in America?"

"*Nyet.*"

"Only green for dollars, *da*? Well, I am wearing nothing red," she said with mock defiance. "We have visited your old and discarded religion, now we will pay a visit to mine. Ruined old ideologies of death, of all in or all out, good riddance!" With that she hooked my arm, and we walked sprightly towards the rally.

As we approached the designated public square, we heard soviet marching music echoing over loudspeakers, filling the air with tinny, antique militarism. A highly elated old man came down the sidewalk, smiling and waving his hands at us like a conductor. He burst into song, and Alina joined him, swinging her arms to the beat of the march. He smiled all the more, and they sang together at the top of their voices until he passed us. He went away still singing, and Alina, too, sang on for a step or two before turning to me and blushing.

I wondered, right then, did my brief smile give her comfort? The song, clearly, had recalled for her a lost feeling of innocence and joy. Did I look at her like a friend, like someone who loved her and wished to drink her in? Or did she catch me feeling sorry for her, for her tiny lapse and outpouring? Luckily her good mood was durable to my looks.

"I miss singing out loud," she smiled. "Why can't you sing out loud anymore. If you did, people would think you were drunk. I noticed, Connor, that you didn't sing in Church. Was it just because you were unhappy with the priest? Do you usually sing? Let's sing now, I'll teach you the good Communist songs." She laughed. "Your C.I.A. will be waiting for you when you get off the plane. We'll have to keep you here. You can be the second American buried in the Kremlin Wall. Picture me as a Young Pioneer, Connor —a little red tie, the sash of badges." Then she snickered, "Probably you find it terrifying to think of me as a little girl, *da.*"

The rally was in a concrete plaza surrounded by low metal and glass fronted shops with polished wood doors. There were close to two hundred people gathered, some with Soviet flags, a couple of banners held on poles. I saw no families or young people, only old women and old men.

In a moment of seriousness, Alina said, "Probably very few of them have been paid in a long time or got their pensions. If you were to ask them, I'm sure that is what they would say, 'at least under the old regime we got our checks.' You can't argue with that, can you? For them it is true, and that is all that matters. What they worked for their whole lives is gone."

Alina listened to a dry speech that I didn't bother trying to follow. I snapped a few pictures of the crowd and in return was looked at askance, as if I was there to gloat. I looked back at Alina, took her picture. In that crowd of old coats and gray gripers, she stood out as something altogether separate. In her blue jacket, with her fine hair shining, she was a fresh, new, blue, waiting, wanting egg.

Chapter 14

It was somebody's birthday, so as was the custom at TV-N, the staff gathered in the 'journalists' room,' for cake and champagne, and often vodka, depending on whose birthday it was.

Yanek, to no one in particular, corrected, "Newsroom, we say."

No longer impressed by our Soros advisor, Kolya joked, "*Vot*, we even don't know how to speak, friends. Make way to the *Newsroom*, we are having cake for Grigory's birthday." He had already opened the vodka.

In the usual course of affairs, the birthday celebrant supplied the refreshments and all but their closest friends stayed no longer than for a quick toast and a wobbly slice of custard cake. Whether to impress Yanek with our intra-office camaraderie, or to give the nerve-wracked staff an opportunity to unwind after weeks of threats against the station, today was special. Gennadi had shelled out for much cake and alcohol, and he and Nikolai had personally approached almost everyone in the office to insure that they would attend. They even asked Gasha to wash the teacups.

"But there are roaches in the sink," she protested loudly. Gennadi had hurriedly hushed her and begged in a small plaintive voice that he rarely used. Unfortunately for him, Marat was in earshot and had immediately begun singing to me, as I'd also been in the lobby, "*La cookarahca, cookaracha!* Connor, do you understand me? *Eto* Spanish." Marat smiled and smacked his lips.

"Marat," said Gennadi harshly. "Go clean the roaches out of the sink for Gasha."

Marat, oblivious to most things but not his current standing at the station, snapped to it. "*Da*, boss."

In the *newsroom*, Gennadi made an enthusiastic toast to TV-N's current course of success, but omitted mentioning the threats against the station and to his own family, or the nightly vigils by male staff. He thanked Yanek profusely and ended up forgetting to mention the birthday boy. A situation that Gasha unceremoniously corrected by piping up, "And to Grigory for whom I washed our disgusting teacups."

After a welcomed laugh, and three cheers of *Oorah!* for Grigory, Feodor opened the champagne. The bottles of vodka, at least what remained after the pilfering of certain staff members, he left on the floor.

Ilya stood next to me in the cake line. "We've got to get this guy back to his hotel so we can start drinking vodka, *bladt.*" He jerked his head toward Yanek, whom Gennadi and Nikolai appeared to be insulating from the staff by standing close around him. Alina, too, hovered there.

"Feodor, when do we get vodka, *bladt?*" asked Ilya.

"You know," mumbled our social director. "Three bottles have already gone missing."

"Kolya's got one," said Ilya.

"Sam has another," I added. Feodor nodded and sighed.

"*Vot,* listen, Connor," Ilya said suddenly and clapped me on the shoulder. "It's a long weekend coming up, *da.* We are going hunting on the taiga. A holiday."

"I'm going hunting with you?" I asked, stumbling on the Russian.

"*Da, da,* Connor."

"Magic words, Ilya."

"*Tak,*" he chuckled. He tracked an imaginary duck across the ceiling and pulled the trigger. "*Boom!* We'll drink lots of vodka then." Ilya collected a piece of cake for our Soros advisor, and I followed with cake for Alina and champagne in one of the station's few water glasses, which I'd been hiding for myself in the editing room.

"I'm such a lucky girl," Alina smiled at me. This caused Nikolai to look down at his shoes for a moment, always the nicest shoes in the office. Alina winked. "And champagne in an actual glass."

"Are drinking glasses hard to come by?" asked Yanek in good humor.

"The drinking glass mafia buys them up and keeps them from us," joked Alina. Yanek chuckled, but even the seemingly innocuous joke deepened Gennadi and Nikolai's unease.

"I bought three jars of German mustard in mini beer steins just for the glasses," I said. "But the mustard is too good to dump. I can't bring myself to do it."

"With that much mustard, you must be planning on staying a while," returned Yanek.

"Empty it into teacups," put in Gennadi, attempting to lighten up.

A few moments later when the others had begun talking about something else, I whispered excitedly to Alina, "I'm going hunting with Ilya."

"When?" she asked as if concerned.

"This weekend."

"The long weekend?" she said disappointedly. "Well, I've got our travels to plan, *da*." Alina and I had decided to take a trip together in the summer. She had friends in Barnaul, a city in the Altai region, that did a lot of hiking and camping and had written to them for advice. Whenever we spoke of the plan, we referred to it somewhat ominously as 'our travels'—*nash puteshestvovat*. "It's good, Connor." Alina continued. "Get some fresh air on the taiga. You need to get out of Tomsk for a bit. I'll look forward to you being revived."

Without her mentioning it directly, I knew she was referring to me having missed a day or two of work recently. Spring somehow hadn't been enough for me. There were days I couldn't get out of bed. I offered no excuse, and no one asked me about it.

Abruptly Losha broke through the protective circle around Yanek. "My Yankee friend," he roared with vaporous breath.

"Your journalists don't say what they think, but not because the State won't let them. It's because they won't let themselves. I ask you, how is that free press?"

"*Tak*, Feodor!" called Ilya. "I know who took the third bottle."

Yanek laughed and appeared to welcome a frank discussion. Knowing that even he was unlikely to get anywhere with a drunken Losha, but not particularly caring if he did, I went looking for other company. As if reading my mind, Marat reached out and steered me into his circle. "Ah, Connor, I hope you're ready to stand guard tonight. You and I will stand watch, *da*?"

"What's that?" said Oleg who stood with a bottle of beer. "I thought it was me and Kolya tonight."

Marat laughed as if amused by a child's gullibility. "Well perhaps Connor and I will keep you company. We can all fight off Leto, hemophiliacs, white slavers, and the mafia."

"White slavers? That's a new one to me," I said.

"Oh, yes," asserted Marat, "they're the ones we think are threatening Gennadi's children."

"No, it's not them," said Oleg. "We haven't heard from them since last year."

Ignoring information contrary to his story, Marat went on. "You see, Connor, a few months ago we ran a commercial for a company that called itself an escort service. They gave us a spot they'd produced in Moscow, very professional."

"*Eroticheski*," croaked Kolya, "little *devushki* in bikinis."

Oleg shook his head. "It's that jailbird hemophiliac that threatened Gennadi's kids."

"When Gennadi saw the commercial," continued Marat, "he had us pull it off the air because he thought the girls looked underage. Once he asked around a little bit, he heard what these guys were really up to. They didn't like getting their ad pulled, even though they got a refund, and they started coming down here and making threats. So that was the last time we had someone sleeping at the station. So just think, Connor, we can document the whole thing for your film —the dark night, the danger. We'll get a case of beer and drink all night."

"That's my plan," said Oleg, nodding to the crate on the floor beneath Feodor's hospitality table.

"I'm tired of the vodka hiding," grumbled Kolya. He stepped over to the table and reached for a bottle. As he opened it, he looked over to Gennadi, who assented with a quick nod. In a moment we all had sloshing-full teacups.

"Kolya, since you're in charge of security, tell me something," I said after a hot gulp or two. "I see all the windows and doors are wired with alarms."

Kolya shook his head. Marat and Oleg chuckled and looked around to see who was listening. Alina, I saw, was keeping an eye on us.

"They're not hooked up to anything," said Kolya loudly. "There was some kind of fight with the alarm company."

"The lock company and the alarm company?"

"Same company," answered Oleg, nodding at the absurdity of it.

"There are bars on the windows," I said.

"That doesn't stop them from throwing a Molotov cocktail."

"Okay, so the men sleeping at the station will call the fire department if someone tries to firebomb the place?"

"*Nyet!* The fire department won't do us any good, *bladt.* We have to put it out ourselves."

I answered smugly, "Well I guess you better drink a lot of beer, and maybe some tea, too."

"*Shto?*" said the three men.

I sprung the trap. "I haven't seen any fire extinguishers in the building, so I guess you'll have to piss it out."

Genuinely embarrassed, Kolya questioned, "A fucking American is the only one that can think of these things?"

Marat laughed and slapped me on the back. "We'll drink enough beer to piss out a volcano. Let's get started."

"You can laugh," Kolya shot back at me angrily.

"I'm not laughing," I answered, looking back at him. Putting down his drink, Kolya walked over to Gennadi. Pointing vigorously to the alarms on the windows and then to me, he grew heated and red in the face. Gennadi calmly put a hand on his shoulder, and with an unperturbed glance at me, said something quietly. Kolya was assuaged.

Alina followed him back over to me. "That wasn't very nice," she said.

"*Nyet,*" I agreed.

A little later, after Yanek had headed off to his hotel, and I'd had several cups of vodka, I went to apologize to Gennadi. With a mellow smile, he told me not to worry. Then, putting his hand on my shoulder and leaning in closely, he said, "You know what American book I love? *Catch-22*. That book made me realize that Americans are just as incompetent as us." Then he chuckled, "*Nu,* perhaps I was wrong about that."

The morning we left for the hunt, Friday, was misty and mild. I waited outside my apartment building with my pack. I sucked in the creamy, mild air and enjoyed it all the more for the trace scent of coal. Two army jeeps suddenly careened up onto the curb. Not recognizing the drivers, I backed away before Ilya rolled down a window and called to me. "*Vot,* our convoy."

The driver got out to open the back for me, which was packed with equipment and supplies. His name was Igor, he told me as he shook my hand. He had a mashed nose and squinty, bloodshot eyes. He looked like a boxer. I slid into the back seat next to Ilya's father, Danil Sergeivich, to whom Ilya introduced me from the front. The father was a slightly broader and wiser-looking version of the son. He struck me as a powerful man, yet thoughtful and kind. With some people you can get that from their eyes.

"The drivers came with the jeeps," Ilya explained jocularly. "They say if we get into any trouble, they'll protect us."

"In case we meet up with some negative ducks?" I joked, flubbing the Russian.

"The duck mafia," Ilya chuckled through his cigarette smoke.

"We're just out of the military," said Igor defensively, unsure if he was being made fun of. "This is our new business." His partner, Sasha, drove the other jeep. I'd find he looked about the opposite of Igor. He had feathered sandy hair, pretty features, and a neatly-trimmed mustache. Cousin Alex was also in the other truck, along with Uncle Maxim, whom I hadn't met before.

Underneath our seats the shotguns were stacked like firewood, and they clattered as we drove. Through the quivering water droplets on the windows of the jeep and through the thick fog that obscured the city, I watched as we drove out of Tomsk. The towering gray slab housing of *Kashtak*, which reminded me of wartime footage of Beirut, was erased and reformed as squat wood houses as if we'd gone so many kilometers in a time machine. Then the muddied human hives vanished entirely, and we flew alongside hazy stands of birch and straw fields flattened by the winter.

Leaning back from the front seat, Ilya called over the droning engine, "You know what the good thing about me getting beaten up was? It showed that I could take time off. Ha! They can do the news without me. This will be the first vacation I've taken since we opened the station three years ago."

"I was just thinking, Ilya," I called back to him, "what's Yanek doing this weekend?"

"I invited him, but he declined. That's why there's an empty spot in the other jeep. Gennadi invited him out to his *dacha*, too." Smiling, he joked in English, "his safe house, *da*? But Yanek declined. He said he wants to see more of Tomsk. Alina said she would show him around."

I nodded. That was the first I'd heard of that. Sitting next to me, Ilya's father said, "This mist will clear up." I nodded again and turned back to the window. It was too loud to talk. We drove west across the taiga to the river Ob.

"We're almost there," announced Igor after an hour or more. "Here's the proof." Ahead on the road a man was waving us over to the side. "It's the night before the opening of hunting season. They want to check the licenses for the guns," he hollered as he pulled over.

"Let's go stretch our legs," said Ilya. The guns would have to be unpacked and have their serial numbers compared to the licenses. "Look," he said pointing across the road, "let's go walk over to that cemetery while they sort this out."

I followed him but asked, "Isn't it unusual to be pulled over by men with no uniforms, who show no form of ID, before asking for your guns?"

Ilya gave a high, disbelieving laugh, "Why would anyone want to pretend to be *GAI, bladt.*" Then he coughed, and said, "To collect bribes, I suppose. They'll be in for a surprise if they try to get a bribe from Maxim. Know why? Because he's ex-KGB." Ilya chuckled, "the real thing, *bladt.*"

"Is he Alex's dad?"

"*Nyet.* Maxim is my father's sister's husband. Alex is from the other side of the family. I don't think they've ever met before today."

We stepped over a crumbling low wall into the overgrown cemetery. "Our old religion," said Ilya, crunching through the dead grass. He knocked on a monument made, like all the others, of welded sheet metal affixed with a red star. It donged like an upended garbage can. "Is this a cemetery or a junkyard? Is there a difference? Ha!" We walked between the graves silently for a time. Some graves included small oval photographs behind glass, most of which had long since faded in the sun or been destroyed by moisture. "It's funny that Soviet cemeteries existed at all," Ilya said. "It's entirely a religious concept, *da*? It's not a good use of land; it's not a good use of materials, not if you don't believe in any kind of afterlife. Maybe that's why the graves are such junk; it's a half-hearted effort, a concession. It's one bit of tradition they couldn't take away from people. Of course, the Soviets adopted all kinds of religious methods, iconography and so forth." Just then, the shrill honking of the jeeps called us back.

"I've got to take a piss," said Ilya. "Tell them I'll be right there. Now let me see if I can find a Communist Party member."

Arriving back at our mini convoy, I found our paperwork had been in order, the guns were re-packed, and we were free to go without paying a fee, fine, or bribe. Once Ilya returned, and we got underway, the roads became smaller, the woods thinned out, and the landscape was spotted with ponds.

Igor spoke into the two-way radio he wore on a strap across his chest, "Are we ready to get off this road?"

"Go," came Sasha's voice from the jeep behind us.

"Get ready," Igor called to the rest of us. Danil Sergeivich gripped the door handle, and I followed suit.

As if to make the change of terrain as eventful as possible, Igor sharply veered off the road and down a steep slope into a field. We lurched forward and were thrown against the slack in our shoulder belts. The gun barrels crashed beneath us. My head hit the roof.

"*Ne nado*," reproached Ilya's dad calmly. "*Eto ne nado.*"

"What are you trying to do?" fired Ilya.

Surprised at the criticism, Igor apologized. He rolled down his window and motioned to Sasha to slow down. Still, we flew through the fields at considerable speed, the grass lashing the tires and the thin sides of the jeep. All of us, now, were exhilarated. We were on the taiga.

Up ahead we saw horses. "*Tushonka*," said Igor for my benefit, referring to a kind of canned meat. He turned around in his seat to grin at me.

"*Vot tak*, watch what you're doing," hollered Ilya nervously, and reached for the wheel. Ignoring his reprimand this time and nodding to me as if I'd egged him on, Igor drove at the horses and set them running.

After another hour of bouncing through fields, Ilya was fed up. "Won't we be arriving at the Atlantic soon, *bladt*? Shouldn't we have come upon a suitable pond by now?" Just as he spoke, we crested a rise and saw before us another small herd of horses and an old man mounted on a horse that had one hoof raised.

"We'll ask him," said Igor, braking.

The old man, who wore a patchy grizzled beard and a greasy cloth hat, watched blankly as we climbed out of our jeeps and greeted him.

"What's wrong with your horse?" Igor asked, squinting up at him.

"He has a sore foot," the old man replied. "Do you have a cigarette?"

Igor proffered a smoke. Uncle Maxim, who looked the part of a charming veteran gangster in a Scorsese film, called magnanimously, "*Dedushka*, how about we share our beer with you for your help in finding a place to hunt. We'll even share with your horse, maybe it will help him with his foot."

"I should sell him for *tushonka*," griped the herdsman.

"*Vot*, just like I said," grinned Igor, flicking my shoulder.

Sasha unloaded a wooden crate of beer and the old man dismounted to accept one and look at our map. Maxim passed the tepid beers around to the rest of us. Everyone dug for their cigarettes.

"You're smoking now, *bladt*?" Ilya asked me.

"Only when I'm hunting on the *taiga*."

"*Tak,* then let me give you a light."

Igor unrolled a large topographical map on the ground. The old man squatted, puckering his toothless mouth around the end of his bottle to drink. He turned the map around a couple times before standing back up and pointing over our shoulders to the west. We left him with a couple more cigarettes and another beer.

At last we found a sizable pond, and in the middle of it sat a solitary black duck.

"Load the guns," said Igor.

"The season doesn't begin until tomorrow," Ilya pointed out.

"The ducks aren't waiting," Igor responded. Yet as we stood surveying the area for a campsite, before a single gun could be unpacked, we saw two men circling around the pond towards us on a motorcycle.

"Could be officials, leave the guns in the back," said Ilya's father mildly. As the pair came closer we could see that they were not officials.

"Genuine peasants," joked Ilya.

Pursued by a swarm of mosquitoes that became a column above them as they slowed their sputtering bike, the raggedly dressed men pulled up to us. "We've been feeding these ducks," said the driver.

"That's very thoughtful of you," said Maxim.

"They're ours," said the rider.

"We've been circling the pond all day."

"That must be the one deaf duck in the flock," chuckled Maxim imperiously.

"*Nu ladno,*" interjected Ilya's dad, "we'll go somewhere else."

"*Nash* duck," repeated the rider.

It was late afternoon by the time we found another pond. The grass bordering it had been burnt back several meters. The birches in the burn zone stood stunningly white, their lower trunks bearing the sooty shadows of the flames. "A black-eyed pond," joked Sergeivich.

"Probably to keep hunters away. Nowhere to hide, maybe. But we're too stupid, so we'll stay," chuckled Ilya. "We all care less about hunting and more about having something to eat."

"To drink!" added Maxim, and his words were borne out as we unloaded our provisions onto a tarp on the ground: two bottles of vodka per man. Alex claimed his, opened it, and drank straight from the bottle. In addition to the alcohol, we had lots of potatoes and onions, bread, cheese, sausage, garlic, a few apples long-stored in a root cellar, carrots, a cabbage, and numerous cans of the wrongfully maligned *tushonka*. It was the best canned meat I'd ever had. Each can held an unprocessed chunk of stewed meat in a greasy jelly of broth and usually a bay leaf or two.

"Where are the tents, *bladt*?" exclaimed Ilya once the jeeps were emptied. "I see one."

"That's mine," answered Sasha. "For Igor and me."

"You said you provided equipment."

"*Nyet*, just the jeeps," said Sasha.

"We have equipment," added Igor. "We have jeeps and radios."

"Did you tell them we provide equipment?" Sasha asked him calmly.

"Just for transportation. Transportation, I said. Jeeps and radios. They have their own guns; they should have their own tents."

"*Ladno, ladno,*" put in Maxim. "Nothing is going to make tents appear."

Ilya looked around angrily. "Let's go over here and discuss this," he said, and led the drivers behind one of the vehicles.

Meanwhile, with a small pointed shovel, Alex began digging a fire pit. Reinvigorated by his drink to the point of fury, he dug like a dog tied to a tree.

"Alex," grumbled Maxim amusedly. "What are you trying to do? Dig a hole to bring our friend here back to America?"

Looking up dazed, Alex stepped out of his hole, dropped the shovel, picked up his bottle, and headed off into the woods.

"All day he's half-dead and now you couldn't stop him with a Kalashnikov," mused Maxim.

Returning with the drivers, Ilya announced. "We'll sleep by the fire. If it rains, we'll sleep in and under the jeeps. Connor, you'll sleep in the tent with Sasha." The men nodded. I accepted my due. It wasn't my fault they forgot tents.

Alex returned with a huge armload of wood, threw it in the hole he dug, and sloshed it with petrol from a jerrycan. He threw his cigarette at it, but it failed to ignite.

"What's this?" said Maxim, pointing to the can of fuel, which itself was splashed with gas, as well as the ground around it. He shook his head, as if at a disappointing student. "Move that can away before you blow us all up." Alex silently obeyed his superior before lighting a match.

Danil Sergeivich unpacked a hatchet and with a few sharp strokes cut down a birch sapling as thick as my wrist. He stripped off the branches and trimmed the end to make a spit for cooking. The rest of us nursed beers and watched while he sunk rebar posts with welded brackets into the ground on either side of the fire to hold the spit. "*Voda*," he said to Ilya, jerking his head at a pair of galvanized buckets. Ilya handed me a pail, and we walked down to the pond.

"This is safer than any water in town," said Ilya as we filled up.

"We didn't just forget drinking water?"

He sputtered a short laugh and flicked his cigarette in an arch over the dark water. When we returned to camp, Danil Sergeivich threaded the buckets onto the sapling and suspended them over the fire. Then, as the finishing touch, he hung a flowered lacquer spoon on a notch he'd carved at the end of the spit.

"I'm taking a nap," declared Maxim.

"Outstanding idea," followed Sasha, and he and Igor accompanied Maxim back into the jeeps.

Mechanically Alex continued adding wood to the already large pile he'd amassed by the fire. On his knees on the tarp, Danil Sergeivich wiped a jackknife on his jeans and peeled potatoes, throwing the skins on the fire to crackle and throw an earthy, roasted smell into the air. Ilya knelt next to him and began scraping carrots, likewise flicking the muddy orange dross into the flames. Sergeivich dropped a handful of garlic cloves into the buckets, which were now beginning to steam. He opened four cans of tushonka and plopped two hunks of the fatty meat into each of the pots, leaving bits of bay leaves floating on the surface of the water that was rapidly becoming soup. Alex's wet wood sizzled and coated the outside of the buckets with soot.

"Nothing I can do to help?" I asked Ilya, dropping my empty bottle into the wooden beer crate.

"*Nyet, nichevo ne nado,*" he said musically.

"I'm going for a walk."

"*Sheslivi puti.*"

I set off crunching through the cinders to the edge of the burn zone. Then I walked headlong through the grass as if I had somewhere to go. The wind and the misty spitting rain raised rippling specks on the surface of the water. It was a long steady wind, having retained momentum since it was thrown down the slopes of the Urals, a thousand kilometers away. The breeze brought everything to life. It seemed every bird and bug had been blown in and was setting up shop. The thawed birches were budding and held a blurry greenness at the drooping tips of their whip-like branches. On the ground shoots of grass worked their way up through the husks of the year before.

"Alina would enjoy this," I involuntarily said out loud. I wanted to take a break from her, but here I couldn't say her name, even to myself, without producing anxiety and energy.

On the burnt shore, I saw a birch that had grown out over the water. The trunk of it reached out over the pond like a goose's neck and then split into a Y, making a throne. I bounced out on the narrow trunk and perched in the notch. I had a sketchbook with me and thought I would try to capture something of the dark water and blackened border, but after only a few pencil strokes, I felt a tickle on the back of my neck. I slapped at it and pulled a tick away. It must have just landed, since it came away easily, but I worried the spot, rubbing it, trying to figure out if the tick had broken the skin. I squeezed it, thinking I could flush the bite with blood. I checked my pant legs, pulled my socks up over my cuffs, and headed back to camp.

"Find any ticks?" asked Maxim by the ashy glowing fire.

"Nobody told me about the ticks," I answered, trying to sound amiable.

"Japanese Encephalitis," added Ilya's father, who was squatting to stir the soup with a cigarette in his mouth. "You've got to watch out for them."

"I'd read it was only in the southern areas."

"This is Southern Siberia, my friend. It may not seem like southern anything, but it's all north from here," Maxim snickered, much unlike a friend.

"I'm glad I'm not the one sleeping on the ground," I returned.

"*Nyet,* it's no problem," said Maxim dismissively. "They only fall out of the trees."

"Come over and have a drink with us," invited Sergeivich. "Have some *salo.*"

"*Eto shto?*"

"Salted pig fat. Try it."

Unable to resist Sergeivich's pleasant calm, I took the sugar cube-sized bit of fat and skin he offered me on the tip of his jackknife. "Bite it off the skin like this," he said, and demonstrated snipping fat from skin with his incisors as if separating a melon from rind.

"Have some vodka first," offered Maxim.

"Health food," I said, chewing the salty raw fat.

"*Salo* and vodka are what's going to keep us warm sleeping on the ground," said Ilya. "As long as you only eat it when you're hunting, you won't turn into a pig yourself."

"It will give you tits and ass," said Alex, already drunk. We ignored him, except for Maxim, who studied him with a look of angry concern.

As the sun set, we sat on blankets and tarps over the rain dampened grass. The fire glowed and Danil Sergeivich served his steaming soup in painted wood bowls. Taking up lacquered wooden spoons, we ate. Fatty and salty from the *tushonka* and a measure of *salo*, the soup was delicious. The potatoes were soft and steaming and infused with garlicky broth; the carrots, onions, and cabbage were sweet and fragrant. Sergeivich sat next to me and ate with a clove of raw garlic in one hand, which he nibbled between swallows of vodka and mouthfuls of soup and bread.

After eating we dropped the bowls into the empty pails and set them aside to be washed in the morning. Two open bottles of vodka twinkled in the firelight as they circulated and were tipped into metal cups, each man pouring for his neighbor.

"*Nu, ladno,* this is good," said Maxim, settling back. "You should have a woman as part of your outfit to cook and clean," he told the drivers. "Although it'd be hard to find one as good a cook as Danil Sergeivich. It's too bad you're so successful at building mansions for our new millionaires, Sergeivich, you'd make an excellent wife."

Ilya's father scoffed, "I may end up cooking for them yet. They're driving me crazy. I may end up broke. Everybody wants things they can't afford, more rooms, more garages, more things to impress their friends. I have more than one house sitting half built and less than half paid for."

"Charge them one brick at a time," added Ilya.

Maxim chuckled, as if someone more knowledgeable. "They've learned how to get money, but not how to keep it."

Igor stared intently across the fire, clearly impressed by the wealth he was hearing about. "How do they get the money?"

"Are you asking me?" said Sergeivich with a modest smile. "I just build houses for them. I don't do their finances. It's a question for my son, the journalist."

"*Xuyu znayet!*" cursed Ilya glibly, chucking back the last of his drink.

"It's not right, the way some people have taken everything," growled Alex, darkened in the shadows, looking directly at Maxim.

"What are you looking at me for?"

"You worked for the government," he answered, slurring his words.

"We all worked for the government."

"You were KGB, *da?*"

"I don't have one of those houses."

"*Ladno,*" Ilya said, breaking it up. "I have a lascivious story to change the subject."

"Let's hear it," cheered Sasha.

"Connor, do you remember my friends Olga and Ivan?" asked Ilya. I nodded. A couple weeks prior he and I had sat in their kitchen eating frozen raw beef with salt and pepper and drinking beer. "They seem like a perfectly normal young couple, *da?* But they are not. Ivan's father is trying to kill them."

"*Pochemu?*" gasped Igor, breathless like a child.

"Olga is Ivan's stepmother."

Igor blinked for a moment while he calculated the affair. Sasha's eyes widened, and he laughed along with the other men.

"Ivan's father is rich," Ilya went on. "His wife, Ivan's mother, died a long time ago. He married Olga when she was twenty-six, while his son was twenty-four. Olga is beautiful, blonde, tall, and has a nice figure. Connor can vouch for it. The inevitable occurred. The son lusted for her; he went after her for months whenever his father was away or asleep or passed out drunk. Bit by bit he wore her down, and they started sneaking around on the old man.

"I've known Ivan for a long time, and he's a sympathetic guy, but not very ambitious, which drove his father mad. His father was always angry with him. So now he was getting even. *Nu*, his father isn't dumb and soon starts suspecting them. They both knew that if the father found out, he would fly into a rage. He's a violent man. Olga told him she wanted a divorce and moved in with her mother. Ivan tried to move out as well, but his father caught him and beat him badly. He locked him in a room and chained him to a radiator for days. His father gave him a bowl of water and a bowl of potatoes, and a bucket to piss and shit in. He told him that he was going to behave like a dog, then he'd be treated like one.

"Eventually Ivan escaped. He was able to get the chain over his hips after losing weight. I won't tell you what he used to lubricate it."

"What?" begged Igor. "*Davai.*"

"Use your imagination," Ilya scoffed. "The father hired a man to hunt for Olga, to grab Ivan if he saw him, and to kill them both if he found them together." Ilya went on describing the affair and the couple's brushes with both the father and the hit man. Danil Sergeivich smiled as his son spun the yarn, seeming to appreciate his son's ability.

When Ilya had taken me to see Ivan and Olya, he explained by the fire, they'd managed to secretly get an apartment together. "You probably didn't notice, Connor, but I took a very circuitous route to get there, just to make sure we weren't followed. They chose that apartment because it's on the top floor, and there are no other buildings facing them, nowhere the hit man could shoot at them."

"They must trust you," said Maxim, like the old spook that he was.

"*Bladt,* and I thought my love life was a mess," expelled Igor and then with awe added, "Fucking your mother."

"She's not really his mother, *durak,*" groaned Sasha.

"I know, but your father's wife," said Igor, wide-eyed.

"You can mess up your love life and your family life in one go," joked Maxim.

"The old bastard was greedy," slurred Alex from the shadows. One bottle, I'd noticed, had stopped circulating the fire and now rested empty on its side in front of him. Another stationary bottle stood there as well, already half gone. "He was after the young stuff."

"Tell me the father's name and maybe I can mention it to one of my old colleagues," offered Maxim.

"It won't help them. The father has *cvazi* of his own," answered Ilya. Then, turning to me and filling my cup, he suggested, "Connor, why don't you tell us about your friend the *garmushka* player?"

Now sufficiently loosened up, I took a shot at it.

At the story's end, Maxim spat, "Bah, he deserves it. He killed his wife, *bladt.*" Just then, Alex let out a moan as if he was going to be sick and got up to leave the fire.

"There goes your lovely *tushonka* stew," hollered Maxim after him and laughed. We listened for Alex's retching but instead heard him crunching through the grass and then the sound of branches cracking when he reached the trees. "When was the last time that fellow was sober?" asked Maxim, shaking his head. He looked to Danil Sergeivich, who did not respond. "He acts like a prisoner getting ready to try to escape, confess, or slice his wrists. I should know, *da?*"

"Quick, someone tell another story," coughed Ilya, having just lit another cigarette with the glowing end of a stick.

Igor then, in his gruff but appealing voice, told a crass story about catching his sister sleeping with one of his friends, about how he'd watched them several times before he'd confronted them. The men laughed at him. "It sounds like you liked watching, *bladt*," guffawed Maxim.

"That's what I said when he told me the story," added Sasha, "and he hit me."

Igor shook his head in dismay. "It's my own sister. I couldn't believe what I was seeing. She's only fifteen." At this we all burst out laughing.

"Does she look more like she's fourteen or more like she's sixteen?" said Maxim, and we laughed all the harder. As the ruckus died down, we heard Alex in the woods bellowing. It took a moment to recognize the sound. Was he calling for help? Was he in pain? No, he was simply bellowing, nearly howling like a dog.

Maxim sputtered in disgust. He hollered back, "What in hell is wrong with you?" We waited. The next bellow came with the crack and crashing fall of a dead tree. "Did he turn into a werewolf, *bladt?*"

"*Da, nyet,* he just likes to fight with trees when he gets drunk," Ilya chuckled. "He has a whole forest to defeat. That should sober him up."

"Probably he'll kill us all in our sleep," said Maxim. "Our bodyguards will have to protect us from ourselves."

Soon the wind picked up again and flicked us with rain. I was spinning from the vodka and had reached the end of my ability to speak Russian clearly. I excused myself to go to the tent. "Enjoy the environment," I said.

I heard Alex roaring in the woods, now farther away, and chuckled to myself.

The tent smelled of old canvas, of military surplus. Sasha had not only thought to bring a tent, but a pair of cot mattresses as well. Softly groaning with pleasure, I rolled out my sleeping bag and fell quickly and soundly to sleep.

When I woke, I found Sasha passed out next to me reeking of vodka and with an unopened beer laying next to him as his morning remedy. Around the smoldering campfire, I found Ilya and Igor splayed out on the ground as if massacred. Vodka bottles lay around them like the empty shells of the munitions that wiped them out. The steamed up windows of the jeeps indicated where the older men slept. I fed the fire and went for a walk.

Thinking I'd take advantage of the privacy afforded me by the morning, I undid my belt and squatted with my back against a tree. Instantly I was rained on by ticks. They popped off my shoulders and bounced in the crotch of my underwear as if on a trampoline. I yelped, cursed in Russian, and hopped around with my pants around my knees slapping at the bugs that clung to me.

When I got back into camp, Ilya was standing by the fire drinking a beer. "Breakfast of Champions," I said in English.

"Crazy night, *bladt,*" he said hoarsely. "*Chort,* those drivers can drink. Alex went crazy and ran off into the woods. You didn't see him just now, did you? We could hear him crashing around and howling like a madman all night." Ilya shook his head. "He's really going out of his mind, I think." After a pause. "My father and Maxim went to sleep in one of the jeeps but the rest of us kept drinking. I think your husband Sasha was the only one that made it to a bed of any kind. The rest of us passed out in the grass. I'm freezing. I can't shake the chill."

"You get any ticks on you?"

Making a dismissive sound through his teeth, he said, "Agh, I don't know. I suppose I should check." He pulled up his pant legs and checked under his socks. "None there." He checked around his waistband. "*Oi, bladt,* here's one." He pulled a fat round tick from his lower back. "*Eyob tvoyu matz,*" he cursed and burst the insect, spraying blood over his fingers. "Have you been bitten?" he asked me.

"I found one on my neck last night, but I don't think it bit me."

"Has the wolf man come out of the woods yet?" asked Igor as he joined us by the fire with a couple beers hooked between his fingers. He held the bottle out to me, "*Pivo budish?*" I shook my head. "Vodka? No? I've got something for you to drink. Watch this. Come with me."

Shrugging, I followed Igor, who had picked up the hatchet from where the wood pile had been but was now only a patch of bark chips and splinters. "You've got to drink something in the morning," he said like a doting grandma. "I'll show you something healthy." Casually flinging the hatched against a birch tree, Igor showed me how to chop a reservoir into the side of the trunk and sip the running sap through a grass straw. It was slightly sweet and starchy, similar to coconut milk.

Alex wandered back into camp while we were eating breakfast. "There are no ducks on our pond," he complained.

"What are we going to do if we shoot a duck in a pond, *bladt?*" returned Maxim with a steaming cup of tea held level with his big cleft chin. "Do you want to go swimming after it?"

Alex stood with his back to the fire, shivering.

"*Bladt,* you have a tick on your neck," Ilya told him.

Alex plucked the fattened bug from his skin and popped it. He stared at the blood on his fingers.

"What's the matter? Afraid of the sight of blood?" asked Maxim.

After breakfast we got into the jeeps and went hunting for ducks with the barrels of our shotguns out the window. Like a squad of rebels, a pack of bloodthirsty insurgents, we flew across the plains on the lookout for fowl.

Chapter 15

Catching her breath through swollen lips and with her cheeks burning crimson, Alina sighed to me, "Oh, Connor, that was one of our best times. The air on the taiga was good for you, I think." I laid down beside her.

"Was it real sex?" I asked.

"It's getting closer. I was so wet, I didn't even mind the condom," she said, nudging me and blowing her sweet cool breath in my face. Alina had come over shortly after I got home from the hunting trip. We'd barely spoken a word before heading to the bedroom. It was after nine p.m. now, but we could still see daylight through the sheet over the window. It was hot in my room. With haphazard modesty we half covered ourselves with the open sleeping bag. Our arms and legs stuck out at angles, touching one another, overlapping. Alina let the covering slip from her breasts as she sat up against the cool cement wall. The zipper teeth raked soundlessly over her skin and made her shiver. "Do you know what we should do? We should start a rumor that Yanek is Soros himself. People would believe it." She crinkled her nose and gave a laugh. "That idiot Gasha would believe it. Probably she doesn't even know who Soros is." She grinned at me wryly. "Stop looking at me."

I slid up next to her and kissed her thigh. "You're too beautiful for me."

"*Da*, you should be grateful, *malchik*. I see all the other women at the station in the banya, you know. None of them look as good as me. I know you think Nastia is good looking, but she doesn't have a nice body at all."

"Yes, you told me she has cellulite?"

"Her breasts are uneven, too," said Alina, demonstrating by holding her own at different levels. "Her nipples are different sizes, and she's very hairy."

"A hairy twat," I ventured in Russian.

"*Fu,*" she laughed, slapping me with the back of her hand. "Who taught you to say that? Ilya? *Doraki.* But that's what it is. She looks like she's riding my schnauzer."

I burst out laughing, bringing on a fit of coughing.

"*Dorak,* stop smoking cigarettes."

"Chuff, chuff," I barked when I'd caught my breath, which sent me giggling again.

Alina chuckled and got out of bed. "Poor Otto," she said. "You never want to come over to our house because he chewed up your clothes all that time ago." In the hall she asked, "What's this? You have a package." She'd found the post slip that had been left in my mailbox.

"It must be from my sister."

She came back into the room. "Does that mean you'll be able to stop being so conservative with your condoms?"

"That's what condoms are for."

"A play on words, *malchik,* very good. Soon you'll be talking circles around eight-year-olds." She paused and smiled. "Stop looking at me."

"Come look at the back of my neck," I said, rolling onto my side. "Do you see a bite there?"

She sat on the edge of the bed and brushed her fingers over my skin and through my hair. "Did you get a tick?"

"I remember slapping at it with my right hand, like this." I demonstrated and slapped her hand.

"There's a little mark there. It's not raised."

"A red mark or blood?"

"Just red, I think."

"You think?"

"I'm sorry, Connor, I just can't tell."

"It must have broken the skin for there to be a red mark, right?"

"Maybe."

"Would it have to just break the skin or go deeper than that to infect me?"

"*Ni znaiyu.*"

"I thought you majored in biology. Shouldn't you know these things?"

"I'm not a medic. I don't know."

"How come nobody told me about encephalitis before I went on the trip?"

Alina kissed my neck. "Poor sparrow," she cooed to me.

"Come lay down again, we'll have another one of our best times."

"Filthy hunter, what's the matter, didn't you get to shoot off your gun all weekend?" She laughed and laid back against me. I smoothed her hair and looked down at her naked body.

"What did you do all weekend?"

"Hmm, I saw Yanek," she answered coyly. "I went up to the hotel and took him out for *shashlik* and beer. We went down to the river and had a picnic. He bought me some Dubonnet. We talked quite a lot."

She waited for me to respond. "About what?" I asked.

"Oh, many things. About life. He's a very intelligent person. Mostly we talked about my career and what I can do. He says he may be able to help me get some training in America. Wouldn't that be fantastic? Maybe we could see each other. You could come see me in California."

"I live a long way from California."

"Alright, then, I could come see you wherever you are."

"What kind of training did Yanek offer you?"

"I don't know exactly. Marketing. He said there are programs. Are you jealous?"

"No. I just hope he's genuine."

"His wife left him, you know, the poor fellow. You are jealous. If you're not here looking for a wife, why should he be?"

"What? That doesn't make any sense," I said and flipped the sleeping bag over her. "He's old."

"Not so old. Tell me, Connor, is it like Yanek you want to be? You want to travel the world, learn many languages, and report to everyone how things are? I can see how you would want to be like him. He's charismatic, even powerful in a way. You can feel it from him. It strikes me, though, that you will not be like him."

"No," I said. "I don't think I will."

"You don't have his drive, in my opinion."

"No," I agreed. "I didn't grow up in post-war Hungary."

I didn't care to get out of bed the next day. Alina had gotten up early and left. I laid listening to cars pass and watched the sheet in the window luff in the breeze like a dead sail. I was like that for quite a long time. Then, like a hammer blow, there was a knock on the iron door. Hurriedly I dressed as the knocking continued.

"Who's there?"

"It's the police," said a woman on the other side. I opened up. I recognized her from when she'd come to my door a few months before.

"Alona Dmitriava, *privet*. Nice to see you again," I said, aware of how much better I sounded than at our first encounter. "How have you been?" I stood in bare feet. She looked me up and down, all business behind her thickly-applied lipstick. She held back a smile.

"Not bad, thank you. Now, Connor Chessick, I am here to inform you that you did not report to the police station after the first three months of your stay for your AIDS test as is required by law."

"AIDS test? A blood test?" I'd forgotten.

"That is correct." She handed me a paper. "This document states that you have been notified of the requirement."

After she'd gone, I placed the papers she'd left with me in a drawer with my passport, visa, and pistol. I forced myself to eat something and rinsed off in the tub. I picked up the delivery notice and headed out to the post office.

It was a dusty, high-ceilinged building that reverberated with echoes. It was bone-dry and chalky, like a giant room containing the moon. I scuffed across the floor, and for once, I didn't have to stand in line. However, that didn't mean I wouldn't have to wait. Four women sat behind the counter having tea with their backs to me. Were they real attendants or only ghosts? They ignored me clearing my throat. It was likely they hadn't been paid in months. This is what ghosts do, I thought, they occupy the place they last were whole, where they last got paid to do something. I shuffled. I coughed. "Excuse me, please."

I received my package split open with a razor. The attendant laid it on the counter, a string holding it together. I picked it up, not realizing the gash in its side. Three condoms slid out onto the counter, as well as a picture of my mother, grandmother, and sister standing in front of our house in raincoats. The attendant stared. The others doing nothing stared. I was sure they'd all perused the contents of my package. I gathered up my trifles and turned for the door.

"Wait," said the attendant. "You must sign." I ignored her and walked outside. I looked for a place to sit unobserved. Here was a package from home, the unfortunate tourist hacked open for an unwilling donation and sloppily stitched up. Gently I unpacked it. A letter had been sliced in two by the penetrating blade, likewise an envelope of photos. The condoms had been in a zip bag, but they had been dumped out. Why search every little thing?

"They want my dollars; they want my blood," I mumbled to myself.

I got on a tram and headed toward the station. It was a strangely hot day. My scalp prickled with sweat. Someone had puked in the train. It reeked. I leaned close to a window.

From the streetcar stop at Frunze, I cut through the park to get to the station. I saw Alina and Yanek on the path ahead of me walking slowly, appearing deep in conversation. I threw down my cigarette and watched them. Alina wore a sheer, red, polka-dot skirt, through which her panties were clearly visible. She didn't have many pairs, not more than ten, and by now I was acquainted with each. Today it was little girl panties with hearts or stars and elastic around the legs. The thin material bunched unattractively. I burned with embarrassment.

It's hard to find nice undergarments, she told me. It's all garish lingerie or stuff for children. "None of my clothes suit me, not even my underwear," she mourned. "I feel better in just your green undershirt than in just about any of my own clothes."

I'd seen the sheer skirt the week prior, part of her spring collection. Sergei and I had walked behind her on this same path back from the *stalovaya* (as she and Yanek were, no doubt, doing now). "She's a beautiful woman," he remarked.

I asked him how to say polka dot in Russian.

"You know it's see thru," I said to her later. She'd shrugged.

Now on the path I cleared my throat. "*Privet.*"

"There you are," Alina said, sounding concerned. "Ilya's got Encephalitis."

"Were you bitten as well?" asked Yanek brightly, chewing his gum.

"I'm not sure."

"How can you be unsure if a tick bit you?"

"It was on the back of my neck. It didn't seem to be attached."

"I don't think you were bitten, Connor," Alina said maternally. "I think you were just scratching at it. You should try not to worry about it. You said Ilya slept outdoors, drunk in the grass, and you slept in a tent. Probably you're fine."

"You might want to get the blood test, just the same," said Yanek.

"They reuse needles."

Alina turned back to Yanek. "The problem is that it's been three days since he was bitten. You have to get the prophylactic shots within two. Also it doesn't always work, and you can get the disease from the shot."

"Now you know all about it," I grumbled. "Why didn't you tell me any of this last night?" She shot me a glance, abashed in front of her benefactor-to-be.

"I have disposable needles," offered Yanek coolly. "It's always part of my kit." He added in English, "Get the test."

"More fucking blood tests," I spat in English, flushed in anger. I sighed and told them about my visit from the AIDS police.

"Fuck, fuck," Alina mocked lightly. "I think our friend Connor is having a bad day. I can tell because he smells of cigarettes. Connor, do you know that it's Yanek's last day with us? We're having a goodbye party for him tonight. Even Ilya's going to come by. He stopped by the station this morning after coming from the hospital. The shots have made him very sick. He looked terrible. He said there was something he needed to tell you, but he wouldn't tell me what it was. You'll come tonight, Connor, *da?*"

I called Pavel from the TV-N lobby to see about finding a doctor. "He has Encephalitis, too," Gasha explained to anyone passing by. To their concerned looks, I shook my head. "He may have it," she clarified. I snapped my fingers at her and made a motion for her to zip it.

"What's he doing? He's snapping his fingers at me like I'm a dog."

"*Vot,* it's the effects of his brain swelling," Yana posed seriously as she walked by.

Gasha looked suddenly conflicted and then with discovery gasped, "*Taaak!*"

Over the phone, Pavel comforted me. "*Da,* Connor, try not to worry. I know a young doctor. He is an oncologist, but he speaks a little English. Let me call him, and I will call you back. You sound shaky a bit. Yeah. Try not to worry." I sat and waited. Gasha avoided looking at me.

"Here we have Connor and his poor swollen brain," cooed Yana on her way back through.

"Yana," hissed Gasha. "It's not funny."

"He knows I'm only joking. You know, *da,* Connor. Besides, he's not sick now. When he's sick, it won't be funny." She laughed. "You know I'm kidding. I hope you're not sick."

"From humor comes hope," I said.

"There, you see?" she said to the scandalized Gasha. "I offer him hope instead of your cold clinicalism."

Gennadi came into the lobby and put his hand on my shoulder. "I heard you got a tick on the hunt. They should have taken you to the doctor."

"I told them I wasn't bitten."

"You're supposed to get the shot within two days."

"*Znayu,*" I said edgily. "I feel fine. The tick wasn't dug in. I'm waiting to hear about seeing a doctor."

Gennadi nodded with a bedside manner of his own, his hand still resting on me. "*Ladno,* Connor, let me know if there's anything I can do."

"I feel like the dying man in the room."

"*Nyet, nyet,*" said my colleagues. Yana, hearing the exchange from the marketing room, leaned into the doorway and crossed herself.

Pavel rang back. "It's okay. He can see us now. Also, I told him about your documentary, and he is interested to speak with you. Maybe you can bring a camera?"

Hanging up, I walked into the studio. "Oleg, do you need your camera this afternoon?"

"No. You can take it. It's been a while since you asked. I thought you'd retired."

"Nevermind," I told him after a moment. "I don't need it."

I met Pavel on the corner of Lenina and Kirova. We walked on to the cancer clinic. Pavel was visibly uncomfortable in the warm weather. He walked smoking with sweat glistening in his beard. "Are you feeling okay?" he asked me.

"Fine," I told him. "I couldn't get the camera." He shrugged.

We met the young doctor, named Tetarin, in a large green and white, wainscoted room. Aged medical apparatus, hulking and pale green, stood bolted to the floor like dinosaurs on display in a museum. In their midst, waited Tetarin, who was tall and dark haired and immediately reminded me of Anton in Moscow as the doctor he might have been. Tetarin's calm, friendly manner, and his open gaze instantly put me at ease.

"You speak Russian, yes?" he asked in halting English. His eyes were bright and curious but also careworn and becoming tired. He continued in Russian, looking to Pavel to translate when necessary. "I am not a specialist in Encephalitis," he said, "but I should be able to diagnose it. How many days has it been since you were bitten? Have you scratched at it? I can't tell if there's a mark. We'll have a look at you. If you don't mind, please take off your clothes, just down to your underwear."

"I can get disposable needles if we need them."

"Those are good to have," said the doctor. "They can be difficult to find. Yesterday I was in the bazaar, and I saw someone selling a whole box of them as if they were candies. I would have bought them, if I had the money."

He had me lay on my back on a padded, vinyl-covered examination table. One after the other, he gently raised my legs, bent them at the knees while guiding me with his cool dry hands. "Is your neck stiff? Your joints? I don't think you have the disease. You would be showing symptoms by now. I wouldn't want to give you the prophylactic unless I was sure you'd been exposed. You can sometimes get the disease from the pooled blood used to make the shot. You can get dressed now.

"Pavel Nikolaievich mentioned that you are a filmmaker. Perhaps you'd like to document the state of healthcare here now. There's much to talk about. Maybe you'll want to come back." With a friendly smile he added, "Or perhaps you won't want to come back, hospitals seem to make you nervous. It's a good thing I wasn't checking you for high blood pressure." He smiled gently.

"You're an oncologist?" I said, feeling relieved and more talkative now.

"I deal mainly with women's cancers, cancer of the breasts and genitals."

"I suppose rates are high," said Pavel.

"Very high," said Tetarin, sitting on the edge of the examining table. "According to the oblast oncological dispensary thirty percent of women get one or the other of them. The female reproductive organs are the most sensitive to certain types of radiation. We also have high rates of thyroid cancer and stomach cancer. And the age at which people get these diseases is dropping. Also, Leukemia in children."

"Pollution," said Pavel as if uttering the name of a god.

"So don't stay here too long, my young patient," smiled Tetarin and straightened his jacket. "The whole state of medicine in the country is a disaster. Maybe not as bad as you in the West are led to believe. It is not third-world, certainly. It's not as bad as it was a few years ago in 1990. There were severe shortages then. I heard stories of surgeons using razor blades to operate and certain procedures, abortions for example, being done without anesthetic." He shook his head again, sagely detached. "It didn't get as bad as that in Tomsk, but we've learned to make due with old and sometimes poor equipment." He motioned to the machines around us. "I've seen doctors adapt and do extraordinary things with old pieces of junk. We've learned not to rely on technology."

"But it's getting better?" I asked while tying my shoes.

"I don't think the situation will change, it won't get better, for the next ten years. Not for public healthcare. The rich can get what they want, but ordinary people will get nothing more. It will be all we can do to keep from going back to 1990. Even now, the life expectancy for males is decreasing. Last year the death rate exceeded the birth rate."

"People are emigrating," added Pavel.

"One day they'll have to pay people to have children. I would like to be one of those émigrés."

"*Donu?*" exclaimed Pavel.

"I was ashamed of it before. I didn't tell anyone, but now I've accepted it. I want to get better at what I do. I am interested in research. Here there is nothing for me to do but damage control. There is no growth. How can a person be expected to do just that? For a feeling of national pride? I suppose I care more about medicine than about nationalism. We are all so dependent on our government, on their foolish ideas. We never know what they will do, you can't be sure."

"The country needs good doctors like you," said Pavel.

"If Russia cares about good doctors, she must show it. Don't look at me as though I've betrayed you, Pavel Nikoliaevich. Many of my colleagues feel the same. I for one have applied to take courses in Britain. Perhaps, Connor, you can help me with some of these letters I must write."

We left the hospital. Upset by Tetarin's declared intent to leave Russia, Pavel mournfully shook his head as he lit his cigarette. "It's a great pity for us," he said. "You know, Connor, he reminded me that I also wanted to ask you to help me with some letters. Yeah? I would like to have my band go on a cultural exchange to America."

"No problem, Pavel" I said, "And since you've been so helpful solving my medical problems, I wonder if you'd help me with something else?"

"Anything, Connor, really," he said, talking with his cigarette dangling from his whiskered lips. I filled him in about that morning's visit with Alona Dimitriava.

"Ah," he said, inhaling deeply. "You're unlucky to live so close to the police station. We had a problem with Graham, too. In the end, he had the head of the university where he teaches call them up and tell them to leave him alone. Maybe Gennadi can call them. Your news department can do a story about it." He smiled and exhaled out of the corner of his mouth, away from me.

"I don't think TV-N is in the good books with the police, right now," I said. "Did you see the last episode of *Gob-Stop Camera* that everyone is talking about?" I was referring to one of the station's shows that involved a journalist riding around town with the cops. "They wanted us to pull it, but Gennadi refused, so now the police have backed out of the series."

Nodding, Pavel said, "I saw it. They break down the door of someone's apartment, but he's not there, only his wife and two kids and a dog. They shoot the dog when it comes after them, and then slap the woman when she screams." He shook his head and chuckled. "I guess Gennadi doesn't have any favors due him at the police station."

"That episode is also at the top of the list of theories why we're getting bomb threats."

"Maybe you can fake a document that says you've already taken the test. It's easy. I do it for Boris all the time. You can copy things through the fax machine to make it look like it was sent in from America. Yeah?"

"I'll do it," I laughed suddenly. "There's an emblem on my immunization card that I could copy to look like letterhead."

"Perfect. It will work, Connor, don't worry about it. You can always pay a bribe, *da*. Maybe that's why this police woman keeps visiting you. She's looking for a bribe of some kind," he giggled and lit another cigarette, "maybe not money."

The party for Yanek was in the mezzanine bar. I found Alina alone at a table. "*Nu*," she said glumly. "You're not sick?"

"*Ni bolal nyet.*"

"*Slava Bogu*, let's drink," she half-smiled. She told me she was waiting to have one last meeting with Yanek to discuss her career.

"Can I get you a beer?" I asked.

She nodded. "It's a pity they don't have any Dubonnet. Connor, in your package from home did you get any pictures? Let's see." After fetching drinks, I jogged downstairs to retrieve the envelope of photos from my bag. Yanek, I saw, was meeting with Gennadi in his office, a bottle of vodka between them. I returned to Alina and flipped the opened envelope onto the table.

"They opened it, *da*? That's shitty. Poor *malchik*." She looked through the photos, easily recognizing everyone. "Look at your grandmother," she said, holding the photo that fell out at the post office. "She's no *babushka*; she's simply a proper woman, a lady. Our women get fat and hunched and waddle like ducks." She sighed, "I want to be like your grandmother." She looked up at me and then around at the others who were starting to fill up the other tables. "I don't belong here. I was born in the wrong place. I've always felt that." Almost to herself, she added. "There's nothing here for me."

"Why did you wear that skirt today?" I asked, recalling the anger I'd felt in the afternoon.

With a slight smile, pleased, I thought, by what she perceived as jealousy, she answered, "Why not? It's warm enough."

Taking a moment to formulate my response in Russian, I said, "So when it gets warmer are all of your clothes going to be see-through?"

"What?" she snickered. "You like it when I put on the see-through green shirt. Be nice and maybe I'll put it on later at your place. Are you jealous?" Then, after a pause, she became tearful. "You shouldn't make fun of my clothes. You know how I feel about it." She tried casually to wipe her eyes. "I understand you've had a bad day, but please don't take it out on me."

Despite her crack-up a few months back, she hated for people at work to see her get emotional. Her enemies ate it up, her former lovers, she thought. When we were alone, Alina cried openly in front of me. She didn't get up and go into another room or hide her face. She let her tears pool up between us.

"You're right. I'm sorry," I said.

"It's so easy for you to say that, not like a Russian man."

"I was wrong."

"*Da.* You're still wrong." We sat silently for a while. I drank my beer and watched her pull herself together. I was as detached from her pain as if I was watching a wounded animal through binoculars. "You seem refreshed, Connor, now that you've made me cry. I guess the required blood has been spilled, Russian blood, *da*? The source of your frustrations. Why don't you go sit with someone else? I'm waiting for Yanek."

As she said his name, he appeared. Yanek may have given up smoking, but he couldn't hide the effort it took him to climb the stairs. Restraining himself from gasping for breath, he nodded to us and came to sit down. "It's career day, I see," he said loudly as he exhaled, vodka on his breath.

Alina looked to me to leave, but I chose not to. I would intrude. Something had changed in Yanek's manner toward me. It had started before the hunting trip but now was more pronounced. I wondered what she had told him. "We'll start with you, Connor," he said. "What kind of filmmaker comes halfway around the world without a camera?" He laughed and looked me in the eye like an old wolf.

"One who can't afford one," I said, feigning good humor.

"If you put together enough for this trip, you must have been able to save for a camera."

"I thought working in a television station, I'd have access to equipment. I didn't want to delay the trip."

"The home electronics shit is all you have access to here, anyway. You could have bought that."

"I didn't know that ahead of time. I've always been able to borrow equipment."

"Listen to yourself," he said. "You're blaming the world." Then in English he added, "You sound like a Russian yourself." He laughed, and so as not to be rude to Alina, switched back to Russian. "I'm only joking with you. I'm sure you'll get your documentary made."

"Connor," Alina began, showing some relief herself now that I'd been flayed. "Why don't you ask your sister to buy you a camera." She held up a photo of her, which Yanek took to examine. "Or your grandmother," she said, holding up the other photo.

"I was just talking to Gennadi about it, and it's rather a surprise to him as well," added Yanek, looking through his glasses at the photo. "That you're a cameraman without a camera."

"I didn't have the money before I left, and I don't have it now," I shot back.

"I'm always impressed how much better your Russian is when you are angry," said Alina, now looking at me sadly. "I'm just trying to help. Maybe you could have asked your family for a loan. Why won't you let your family help you? When you talk about them it always sounds like you have such a good situation, so why not let them help? You wouldn't want to look back and think that your time here was a waste."

"It's not an opportunity you'll want to have missed," agreed Yanek.

"How did we start talking about me not having a camera? I don't remember asking anyone's opinion about it. Besides, it's too late now."

"We might be able to arrange something," smiled Yanek.

Just then Ilya came to the top of the stairs, and everyone got up to wish him well. He was pale and looked like could use a hand, but he refused help when I got to him.

"You're alright?" he asked me.

I nodded. "I saw a doctor this afternoon."

"I'm not supposed to drink, but I need a beer," he said. I went to the bar for him while he sat down next to Yanek to thank him for his mentorship and once again make the case for new equipment.

"I'm convinced," hollered Yanek, holding up his hands in surrender. "If you ask me, it's money well spent. I've only got to convince the Soros people, as you call them, and I'm sure your work will go a long way towards that."

I stood next to Sergei and drank. He and I rarely talked about anything other than editing. We occasionally exchanged a bit of gossip, but otherwise, we stuck to a series of endlessly repeated inside jokes that had arisen between us. "Nazareth," I said to him with a flash of devil horns.

"Nazareth," he snarled back to me and clinked my bottle.

A bit later I sat down alone with Ilya. Alina and Yanek, I could see, were still sitting together and talking. She sat by his side as each person in the station came by to bid him farewell and offer their overblown, supplicatory thanks. Later she would dance with him and look round to see if I was watching.

"You're lucky you didn't have to get those Encephalitis shots, *bladt*," Ilya groaned wearily as he leaned forward on the table. "It's awful. I've never been so sick. They told me it would be like the worst hangover I've ever had, but for three weeks."

"It's better than having brain damage," I offered.

"Maybe not. I think I'd risk it. If I ended up brain damaged then maybe everything would be easier, *bladt*. We drink and smoke to accomplish the same thing. Why not make it permanent, *da*?" He noted disturbingly, "I feel like I'm going to die." His young face, usually embarrassingly rosy to him, was ashen and deflated.

"But speaking of death, I have something to tell you," he said. No one was around us, but he looked to see if anyone was listening. He sighed. I had never seen Ilya like this; I knew him as cynical and brassy, but here he was purely distressed. "You know my cousin Alex. You know he's a madman. This time he's in real trouble. He's on the run from the police. He's killed someone. I should have known something was happening. He's always crazy, but on the hunting trip he was crazier than normal. It turns out that two days before, he'd killed his neighbor in the village where he lives. With an ax, *bladt*! I'll tell you how it happened: he was drunk and sitting on the porch. His wife came home and told him that the neighbor had just called her names, swore at her. Alex went crazy and went over with an ax. He didn't just kill him, he cut him up into pieces. His wife stood there screaming. The next day Alex turned up at my father's house in Tomsk. He didn't tell him anything, and when we invited him to come hunting, he accepted. The night we got back town, the police came looking for him, and he jumped off the balcony of the flat and ran. Nobody has seen him since."

Ilya sat back shaking his head. He took a drink. "So now you can say you've been camping with an ax murderer, *bladt*."

I sat wide-eyed, and he nodded to me. "He'll be shot if they find him. He's too crazy to surrender. He went to military prison once before and said he'd never go back. *Bladt*, this beer is making me feel worse. I've got to go, but I need to tell you something else as well. You know how we talked about a trip to

Baikal? I'm not going to be able to do that. By the time I get back to work, I'm going to be so behind."

"*Ponyatno!*" I said, having expected as much.

"You mentioned that you might be going horseback riding with Vodopyanov, out to old gulags, *da?*"

"*Da,* maybe," I said, not wishing to bother him with my disappointment that Boris had also canceled our tentative trip. Pavel had told me that afternoon that his boss would be away most of the summer. Pavel had also told me that Boris thought that I hadn't gone out to the village to practice my riding enough to be ready for such a trip, which was probably true.

"Are you alright to drive?" I asked Ilya.

"Of course! Why do you always ask that?" Ilya did his rounds, saying goodbye to Yanek again before leaving.

"Don't be angry with me, silly," Alina said to me. "Come dance with me. Yanek can't keep up." She smiled, beautiful and always sly, and held her hand out to me. A slow song came on, and I held her in my arms. After a few moments, I told her what Ilya had said about Alex.

"*Interestno,*" she said dispassionately. "How many murders have you met now? The *garmushka* player, now a duck hunter. Just think how you can brag to your friends in America." After a pause, she added, "Let's not talk about it."

I told her about the collapse of my travel plans. "I always knew they would," she said. "It doesn't matter because we're going to go on a trip together, *da?* I'll never let you down."

Like most parties, this one began to degenerate at a point. The drinking had become excessive. The dancing had become inappropriate. Those who knew better had long since left.

Yanek cornered me and drunkenly told me, "You can't just do it for them. You need to show them how to do it?"

It took me a moment to decipher what he meant. "Yes, sir," I said. "I've been trying."

"How is it then that you and Sergei are still splitting duties? He could do it himself."

"There's not enough equipment for the both of us, and we've worked out a system that gets things done faster."

"This doesn't seem efficient to me." He shook his head. "You should work on something else."

I chuckled, "I've already got one guy mad at me for taking his job."

"So you've resigned yourself to being a mascot?"

I shrugged, having long since prepared myself for the charge. "I've suggested numerous projects to them, but they're stretched to the limit with the daily news. I'm collecting clips and footage where I can. I'll put it all together when I get home."

Suddenly, Yanek demanded, "What are you going to do with the girl?"

"I'm not going to do anything with her," I answered shortly. "She's free to do what she likes."

"Then you won't mind if I take her from you." He paused and smiled wantonly. "I'm only joking, son. She's too good to be left here, to be used up and ruined. You know that." He put his hand on my shoulder. "Not to mention your own opportunity. That's all I have to say."

In the morning Alina got up early to see Yanek to the airport.

Chapter 16

On the morning of July seventh, just before daybreak, I was awakened by the sound of a man retching beneath my window. I listened to him cough and spit and then heard his shoes scuff as he began to walk away. It was quiet for a moment. He'd fallen, I thought. Then a car came fast down the street and skidded to a stop. The doors opened. I thought it must be the police and jumped out of bed to watch. From the window I saw a shiny new white Volga sedan. Even in the predawn half-light, it was sparkling white. Two men in black leather coats laid somebody out on the back seat of the car. I couldn't see him. They closed the doors, got in, and drove away. I don't know how they'd picked him up and got him into the car before I got to the window. Who was that drunk? A mafia boss, a politician? I imagined him in a ragged tuxedo, tie missing, his shirt unbuttoned and stained with drink and sweat. To my sleepy mind, it was like a dream. I had a thought: the drunk had thrown up a moment too late and had died;it was in the back seat of a white Volga that God took Siberia's drunks to heaven.

Today was the Day of Ivan Kupala, a holiday related to the Feast of John the Baptist in the Orthodox Church. Marat had given me a vague warning. "You'd better bring a change of clothes to work tomorrow, motherfucker." I'd long since grown accustomed to ignoring him, but on this occasion, I should have paid attention. On this day, as was the tradition, children sprayed adults with water.

The people at my bus stop that morning stood together as if under siege. Overnight the city had changed. Some ugliness had been released and was now masquerading as harmless fun. A rangy, greasy-haired boy in a floppy sweater, of maybe twelve, circled us with a plastic pop bottle filled with water before dashing in to spray a woman in a purple blouse. The bottle crinkled as he squeezed water through the hole in the top that he'd put there with a nail. Yellow-toothed, he smiled as the stream made a pissing sound against her plastic shopping bag, which she successfully held up to deflect it. He aimed higher and got her sleeve. An older man chased him away as if shooing away a scavenger.

"I despise this holiday," said the woman as she swatted water off her bag with the edge of her hand.

Maybe in better times, these baptisms were carried out on a more willing populace, maybe with greater mercy, but on this day in 1994, the bus ride to work was a trip through a city engaged in a simulated massacre. The boys of Tomsk had something pent up, some grudge, and appeared just barely willing to open taps instead of veins. Most were armed, like the little scab at my bus stop, with a pop bottle with a hole in the cap, but others had traded up entirely. I saw older boys with large inner tubes filled with water slung over their shoulders like molded cannons. With one end of the tube tied off, they held the other, straining at the weight of the water, with their clenched fists as triggers.

The bus stopped at a light. From my window, I heard an old woman in front of a kiosk plead, "*Malchik*, please." A pair of grinning teens stood on either side of her with their water bazookas coiled up on their shoulders. She held her hands up to them, but they let loose on her, drenching her as if with full buckets. The man from my bus stop hollered at them, and they turned what ammo they had left in their bladders towards the bus. We slid the windows closed and took the stuffiness of the humid morning over being soaked.

"You see how the little cowards stick to splashing women," said the man.

I got off at my stop and immediately attracted the attention of another skinny kid with a water bottle. He circled, dancing towards me to get within squirting distance. "Fuck off, you little shit," I bellowed in English. He ran off, but when I looked behind me, I saw him hanging back with two other boys. I flipped them off and got to the station doors before they caught up with me.

Israelievitch cackled from behind his newspaper. "Get wet?"

"I'm not walking to the *stalovaya*," announced Sergei at lunch time. "Ilya, drive us to the *stalovaya*," he called across the studio.

"Beat the hoodlums, *bladt*," responded Ilya. He'd been back to work a couple weeks, now, but still hadn't made a complete recovery from the Encephalitis treatments. He looked tired, aged. Additionally, his cousin Alex had been arrested and was being tortured by the police, or so he had heard. The news crew had tried to do an interview with Alex while he clearly had two black eyes, but the police wouldn't allow it.

"It's a beautiful day for a swim, Seriosha," kidded Alina, who was in a cheery mood.

"Forget it. I'll drink my lunch upstairs."

Alina had tsk-tsked me when I told her about my walk from the bus stop. "You're not supposed to do that. Let them have their fun. It's tradition."

"They should cancel it until people are able to have fun again," I'd said. "This is the kind of fun a mob has with an enemy corpse."

"You're overreacting"

It was a banya day. There was little reason to go to a sauna on a hot summer day, other than that the company was paying for it, and it was an excuse to leave work early. The drivers took us to avoid being out on the street.

"My friend, you are all alone," bellowed a naked steaming Kolya. I was sitting on a bench with a towel around me and an open beer before me on the plank table. I'd come out of the heat a few minutes before. It was my second time around from the sauna to pool to shower to beer, but I was out of sync with the others. Most of the people I usually socialized with weren't there:

Ilya, Sam, even Marat. Sergei, of course, was there, since his wife still hadn't taken him back, and this was his one chance a week to get clean without begging for a flat key from someone.

"Are you tired of us, or are we tired of you?" Kolya amiably asked me as he slapped open a beer against the scarred edge of the table. "*Nu?*"

"I guess my circumcision isn't the novelty it once was," I responded, and then he laughed heartily as he sat his bare ass down on the creaking old bench.

Raising his bottle and his eyebrows, he told me, "I'm sure your Jewish pecker gets all the attention it needs." We heard splashing in the pool, and a moment later we were joined by Feodor. Kolya repeated his joke, and he and Fedya had a laugh. Again we raised our bottles. Kolya was a creature of the bathhouse. He was no Russian bear; he was a hippopotamus with his bulbous belly protruding and his back striped with the welts of birch branches. At the station he mostly kept quiet. 'I'm just a driver,' I'd often heard him say when asked his opinion. But at the banya he was animated and social, even brotherly.

"This is the safest place to be today," declared Feodor, sitting down. "We're already wet."

"And if you're going to be wet, it's best to be warm as well," said Kolya.

"The warmer the better."

"*Drusyei,*" I said to excuse myself with a quick salute. I dressed in the tiny change room amid the shoes and piles of clothes of my colleagues, the smell of men and their laundry.

Alina met me outside the banya. She stood in the evening sun with leaves casting fluttering shadows over her face and hair. She had her wry smile for me and wore the green silk shirt, the translucence of which I'd had to accept.

"*Nu*, Connor," she said sweetly, making a song of my name. "How was the banya? Relaxing?"

I took her hand and gave a repentant kiss at the corner of her mouth. We'd gone through another rough patch the last couple weeks, another condom argument, but had come through it.

"You're in a better mood now, *da?*" she teased. "I thought we could walk down to the river. We could get something to eat, a few beers, maybe light a fire."

"Sounds perfect," I told her.

"Probably the hooligans are tired of splashing people by now. We won't let them bother us. It's too beautiful an evening to let them take it away. I have something I need to talk to you about. A couple of things. Enough time has gone by, *da?*"

We walked by my apartment so that I could lob my wet towel up onto my second floor balcony.

"When you're gone," she said. "I can see myself walking by here and thinking of all the nice times we had up there. But you will be missing."

"Will you be more glad for them, or sad that they have ended?"

"Both, I imagine. I don't want to think about that now, *malchik.*" Alina curled her cool hand around my wrist, and we walked towards the river on our usual paths between buildings and back allies. We walked on Lenina, which was lined with government buildings displaying the strident blockiness of the Soviets, but also the ornamental wood houses built one hundred years prior. Both types were equally in disrepair, but the street was wide and lined with trees and small parks, and that made it pleasant. Above us was the web of trolleybus lines. The street was mostly empty.

"Look there," said Alina abruptly, pointing to an old yellow, white-trimmed building. "That's the women's clinic. What would you do if I became pregnant?"

I faltered. "I don't know."

Becoming serious in her sudden and powerful way, Alina said, "I never want to go in there, Connor. Women go in there when they don't want the baby. Do you understand me? They butcher women in there; they make it so they can't get pregnant again. Some of them even bleed to death."

I looked at her strangely but said nothing. We walked in silence for a while.

"So how did it go with your phony AIDS documents?" she asked finally.

"They're beautiful," I answered. "I should be a spy."

She smiled. "You are a spy. How did you know what the documents should look like? Have you ever had an AIDS test?"

"No, I've never had one. I'm not in what you'd call a risk group," I told her. "I doubt the Tomsk police have any better idea what an HIV test results document from the U.S. looks like anymore than me. So I just made it up. Do you want me to get the test?"

She shrugged, "Yanek left you his needles."

We took a few more steps together before I said, "So now I'm a dirty foreigner, *da*?"

"Does the United States make foreigners take the test?"

"Yes."

"Then it's simply political," she said definitively. "What will you do if they say you have to take the test?"

"I was thinking about it," I answered. "It's such a ridiculous requirement. You already have AIDS in Russia. Even if I did have it, I'd be no real threat to public health. Maybe I'll leave in protest."

"Well, then, that will be that," she said with detachment.

At that moment, two bare-chested teenage boys with bottles of water came around the corner. They smiled as they spotted us and readied their weapons.

"Do it, *bladt*, and I'll beat your asses," I growled. I expected Alina to scold me for cursing or slap me on the arm.

"We're not in the mood, boys," she said instead.

The two scooted around us and let fly a quick stream, nothing too soaking, but it set Alina off. She lunged after one of the boys and slashed her nails across his back. He arched his shoulders in pain and ran forward.

"What?" he protested, "You're not supposed to..."

"Scorpion!" she hissed triumphantly. She came back to me holding her hands up as claws and baring her teeth. She laughed, "You're a wimpy fish, but I'm a scorpion."

"You're a strange girl."

We sat in the park on a slope of mowed grass that overlooked the River Tom. Alina had on shorts and stretched out her long smooth legs on the grass. She looked down at them. "I need to sunbathe. I like to sunbathe in the nude," she grinned. "Maybe we should go find a more secluded spot."

"It's too late in the day. The sun's too low; you won't tan now," I said.

"I suppose you're right. Too bad for you that you won't get to watch."

"Would you really sunbathe nude down here by the river in a public park?"

"I've done it before," she smiled. "I don't like tan lines."

"I like them," I said, grinning back.

"What! How can you like tan lines? They show you how pale I am the rest of the year."

"They highlight what's most covered. Tan lines make you even more naked."

"*Durak*," she chuckled, and complimented me, "That was good Russian there." Alina laid out on her side and rested her head on my thigh. "It's been such a while since we've been together, *malchik*. You must be feeling a little tense, *da*? After all," she teased, "I'm a biologist. I understand how your eggs are producing sperm all the time and that it needs to be released one way or another." After our last mid-sex condom argument, two weeks prior, we hadn't been intimate. The times that she'd spent the night at my apartment since, she'd asked that we sleep next to one another, 'like children.' I'd been irritated at her for pouting.

"*Nu,* have you been busy?" she smiled now, plucking at the grass.

I made a face and nodded.

She laughed. "What do you think about?"

"The last time I was with you, usually."

"When do you do it?" she asked with a smile.

I shrugged. "Sometimes I do it before you come over, so that I can last longer with you."

"Hmm, I'm not sure if that always works so well." She laughed and rolled onto her back. "Do you want to know about me? I do it. I have my own special way. I'm not going to tell you about it, but maybe sometime I'll show you, if you're nice to me." She looked at me doubtfully. Alina sat up. "*Ladno,* now on to business, Connor. I want to ask you something. Did you sleep with that stable girl? You've been acting strange. I don't think you did, but I have to ask."

Last weekend, I went out to the village to see Olya for a riding lesson. I'd run into Vodopyanov recently, and though he'd canceled our gulag trip, he'd said that if I practiced, we might be able to take a shorter trip in the fall once his schedule freed up. "Once the mafia children are back from their English camps," he joked.

I'd put a condom in my duffle bag and taken the bus out to the village. I found Olya in the coral with a foal. She'd walked it on the end of a rein with a bit in its mouth, on which it chewed and slobbered. She was in jeans and a thin t-shirt. Her small breasts sat up pert and sporting, giving only the slightest pop as she moved. Olya smiled and waved at me. She blushed. Pursing her lips, she reeled in the horse and beckoned me to approach. She stood petting the animal's nose as I climbed between the beams of the fence.

"A new horse?" I said.

"*Da*, we've even named him that, *Novesti*."

"*Privet, Novesti.*"

"Give him an apple," she said, indicating a bucket of small misshapen fruit hanging from a nail on the other side of the fence. "Get two," she instructed, smiling. "I want to give him a treat, too."

I held the apple in my open palm for the young horse to pluck with his upper lip.

"So you've come back for more riding lessons," said Olya. "Do you want to go out on old Mikhail again? Maybe he'll be nicer to you this time. I need to take the crazy old guy out for some exercise anyway. Now you can help me. Olga's not here today, so I'm glad you came. Come help me with the saddles."

A few moments later, the smiling Olya, with a smear on her cheek from the new horse's snout, held the reins for me as I launched myself into the saddle. She had small, babyish teeth.

"I forgot to close up the stable. I'll be right back," she said. As soon as she was out of sight, old Mikhail trotted over to the gate and nudged it open with his nose.

"Whoa," I protested, thinking I was either going to be whisked out to the taiga or else promptly flipped off his back. Instead, he casually clomped to the side of the road and began feasting on wild hemp. "Is it alright for him to be eating that?" I asked when Olya returned.

"*Da*, it's his favorite. Besides, maybe he won't mind you riding him so much." With a shy look, she chuckled. "It's not strong. The village *babushki* make tea out of it for their arthritis." As we got underway, Olya said, "Remember, don't let him intimidate you. You're riding him, not the other way around." The horse tolerated me for a while, and Olya and I carried on a pleasant conversation. "Your Russian is much better," she smiled. She asked me about TV-N's various on-air personalities and what they were really like. I started to tell her about Bogdan, whom she swooned over, but Mikhail dashed my hopes of coming off as cool. We came to an open field, and off he went as if from the gates of a Siberian derby. I'd stiffened, bracing for the fall, but ended up getting bounced side to side and flailing like a puppet.

"Relax, go with him," shouted Olya, galloping next to me. Her lovely breasts nosed up and down like dolphins charging through a bay. "Mikhail loves to gallop. Just stop him before the trees."

"How?" I cried.

"Pull hard on one rein," she shouted, and then pulled away from me as if Mikhail might suddenly crash into the ground with slashing hoofs. I pulled with my right arm. Mikhail pulled back and galloped on.

"Harder," called Olya.

I yanked savagely and at last the horse responded, veering to one side and bringing us to an abrupt stop.

"*Molodets*," huffed Olya, cheeks rosy. It was a hot sunny day, and in the open green field, we both broke a sweat. The horse, I could feel in my legs, was hot as well. "Let's get them some water. There's a stream over there. You'll want to lean back when we go down the bank. Way back. Then when we come back up, you want to lean forward. *Ponyatno?*"

After a frightening lunge down the steep bank, we splashed through a broad shallow creek, then led the horses a few paces upstream to drink. Olya and I sat on the mossy bank and threw a few stones as the animals filled their bellies. The air near the water was cool.

"We can drink this water, too," said Olya. "It's very clean."

"Do you want to go for a swim?" I asked.

"It would be very cold," she answered sheepishly. We sat awkwardly silent for a few moments. Then the horse flies found us. The animals twitched their ears and flipped their tails. We swatted. Olya smacked one on my back, biting me through my shirt. She cut us both a birch switch with a jack knife in her pocket. The horses wandered casually back from the water.

"We could tie the horses and get away from these flies," said Olya, nodding toward the water. "Maybe it's not too cold." Before I could react, something strange happened with the horses. Mikhail swung his head around to nip at a fly on his belly and caught the bottom row of his front teeth on the stirrup. He was hooked to his own saddle and reeled around and around like a dog chasing its tail in reverse.

Spooked, the other horse trotted away. Olya took off after him, leaving me to try to help Mikhail. I snatched the reins but couldn't keep hold of them. The power of the whirling horse easily whipped them from my hands.

Olya tied her horse to a birch tree and rejoined me. We looked at each other hopelessly. "What do you do with a spinning horse?" I asked helplessly. Mikhail was growing tired and began tripping over his own feet. He was going to fall.

"I'll try to slow him down," Olya said finally. "You grab the bridle. I'll push from behind. We'll squeeze him," she said, and motioned like a strongman bending a bar. We took our sides and with a nod, Olya lunged at the animal's haunch, slowing him just enough for me to catch the leather straps around his jaws. She pushed, and I pulled. The horse came unsprung and threw us both onto our backs. Mikhail kicked and bucked, and we covered our heads with our hands. At last he calmed down and fitfully started nibbling at the grass along the creek.

Olya laughed, hopped to her feet, and brushed herself off. She cautiously approached Mikhail to check his mouth for injury, something he was in no mood for her to do. "I've never seen anything like that," she said, still catching her breath. "He doesn't seem to have been hurt."

"Must have been the pot," I joked in English.

She smiled and added nervously, "Please, don't say anything about this to Boris Mikhailovich."

"Everything is fine, *da*? The horse is fine."

"Just the same," she'd pleaded, "please promise not to say anything."

"*Ladno,* I promise."

"I didn't sleep with her," I told Alina in the park and related the story about the horse.

She chuckled. "Maybe if you hadn't had so much trouble with the horse, you would have slept with her, *da?* A roll in the hay."

"Probably not. She's more cute than beautiful, but she's very cute and has a kind of sexual energy coming from her."

Alina nodded, "I know what you mean."

"You're like that, but in a different way."

"I know. Are you going out there again, Connor?"

"I don't think I'll have much time to go before you and I leave on our own travels."

"You know, Connor, when we are together like this, I think it's nice to have you around. You're a good guy, and I enjoy spending time with you. But when you're not around, I don't miss you. I don't feel that I need you." She sat in the grass with her legs crossed. She looked at me as if there was a part of her I had given up trying to understand, a look of disappointment. "Sorry to have gotten so serious, but many things are on my mind, since you came inside me the other night."

"What?"

"I was surprised you did it. I thought to myself, 'Poor boy, if he wants to wear a *preservativ,* let him.' I shouldn't have pressured you, and I guess I'm not so brave as I thought."

"Alina," I stuttered. I panicked for an instant that my own judgment and memory had betrayed me. However, I didn't have to try to remember; it was close to my mind.

"When it's good like that, my kitty wants more," she'd said shortly after we'd first had sex. She turned around and stuck her ass in the air. "From behind," she said and wagged her tail. "You don't need a condom," she added as I sat up, "not for the second time. Just go wash yourself."

I went to the bathroom and washed. I then rolled on another condom. She stayed in position for me, her shoulders down on the bed, back arched, one arm cast over her head, the other extended between her legs, rubbing herself. We rubbed together. We put our fingers inside her. She perched at the edge of the bed. I stood. "Connor, Connor," she'd spoken ecstatically. She reeled her hips, and I kept slipping out of her.

"Alina," I started again in the park. "I was wearing a condom."

"You didn't take one from your drawer," she said, starting to blush.

"There was one in the bathroom."

"I didn't think you were wearing one."

"So you couldn't feel it?"

"This is embarrassing, Connor." She looked as if she might cry, and I put my arms around her and embraced her solidly.

"For the last two weeks you thought I came inside you? Are you late?"

She sighed. "*Nyet*, Connor."

"But you were worried that you might be."

"Talking about sex makes it feel lonely and far away, Connor."

"*Ladno*, we can talk about something else. We can talk about our trip, our travels."

"*Ladno*, let's talk about our travels," she said with sad eyes. Nevertheless, we sat silently.

"Who's going to take care of Otto?" I asked.

"Tanya, I hope."

"She's a good friend to you. How come you don't see more of her?"

"That's the way it is with my close friends, Connor. We don't need to do little things together," she said dismissively.

"Do you want to go home?"

"*Nyet*, let's talk about the trip. It's coming up soon. We need to get ready." Alina had told me that her friends in Barnaul had agreed to host us for a few days and direct us to suitable areas for hiking in the nearby Altai region. "I was thinking that we should get hiking boots, Connor. You don't have any, do you? I don't. Last time I went hiking I borrowed a pair from a friend, but we're not close anymore. I went down to the clothing bazaar last weekend. I don't think you've been there. It's a big warehouse full of every kind of clothing. Most of it is *fuflo* from China. There are a lot of knock-offs, I think. The label will say Reebok, but it is not Reebok. You can see that it's bad quality. They had good hiking boots but very expensive. Around a hundred bucks. I can't spend that much. Can you?"

"*Nyet*."

"*Nu, ladno*, Connor. I was thinking we could buy running sneakers. They should be nearly as good, *da*? I'm going to borrow a pack and sleeping bag from my father. You have yours."

"Ilya is going to loan us the tent he forgot to bring on our hunting trip."

Alina smiled. "This trip is coming up fast."

The evening sun had left us. It was cooling off, and Alina rubbed her legs.

"You mentioned that you were worried about asking for the time off from work," I said.

She sighed and flipped her hair with a finger. "Nikolai says that he can't guarantee my job will be here when we get back, but he's just being a goat. I told him about our trip weeks ago, but now he tells me, 'After all the station has been through, Alina, we can't afford to have a busy salesperson go away for two weeks.'"

"It wouldn't be worth losing your job," I said.

He's jealous, Connor, *prosto tak!*" She gave a satisfied sneer. "He's impotent. He can't fire me. I have their biggest accounts, and my clients love me. I could easily get another job. My clients ask to hire me all the time."

"TV-N isn't just any job," I said. "Don't you think?"

"I'm not ideological about it," she answered. "Why should I be?"

"I think Yanek would encourage you to stay in independent media."

"*Da*, of course. He's with the Soros people, after all. Did I tell you about the courses he thought I could take? Yanek told me that I should understand my worth at the station. They can't do what they need to do unless the operation makes money. He said Gennadi understands that, and he should be willing to have me go for training. I was thinking of something else he said, too. He told me, 'The world loves to see a beautiful woman fail.'" She grinned and she looked down at the grass for a moment.

"Enough about Yanek," she continued. "I know you're jealous of him, Connor. I'm only looking for advice from him, but you'll always see it as something else."

"I just wonder what his motivation is."

"Connor, the man came all the way to Siberia to help us succeed as a news company. His motivation is that he cares about free journalism. It just happens that I work for TV-N. It's an opportunity, just that. You never know what is ahead, Connor, *da*? There's no reason to pass up an opportunity as far as I can see. What if I went to California for the courses and was able to get a job there? Maybe with the Soros people, *da*?"

"Now you sound like a real Western *devochka*."

"Don't make fun of me," she frowned coyly. "Will you try to borrow a video camera for our trip?"

"I'm sure I won't be able to," I sighed. "I'm tired of bothering Oleg about it."

Alina began again, "I don't think I'm going to stay at TV-N for much longer. When you go, I don't know if I'll be able to stay there." Then she said disdainfully, "I don't care what happens.

Despite what Yanek said, I've been thinking that TV-N is dog shit. What are we doing there? Everyone talks about bringing independent news to people, but that's not what it's really about, Connor. Not even for Gennadi, our holy icon. It's about making money, *da*. It's about charging our clients enough that we can play with their money and keep a good bit of it for ourselves."

"*Vot, Kapitalism!*" I said. "We don't have to go on the trip."

"*Nyet*, Connor. This is something we're always going to look back on. I'll never look back on this job and think it was something special. Besides, they're not going to fire me. They're my friends. We've known each other since we were Pioneers. Nikolai and Gennadi were older than me, but I remember them. I remember them in their uniforms." Alina curled her lip. "I remember them flirting with the young girls, or else ignoring us. Nikolai still loves me, and Gennadi likes to look." She stood and brushed herself off. "Do you know what I'm thinking, Connor?" she said, looking down at me in the grass. "When we get up into the mountains, we'll fuck like butterflies." With the swift flash of a blush, her lip still bent facetiously, she turned and walked away.

<h1 style="text-align:center">Chapter 17</h1>

We left Alina's apartment early for the train station, and riding a city bus with the seller women commuting to their sidewalk posts, our travels began. Alina and I stood with our packs on and gave each other tiny expectant smiles. She held our tickets in her hand as if they would otherwise be lost. At the *vokzal*, the attendant told us the tickets were for a train that didn't exist.

"I waited in line for two hours," argued Alina.

"No such train," barked the agent. "You have to take the commuter line to Tayga, and from there you can get the afternoon train to Barnaul."

We had plenty of time to go back to the apartment, but we stayed at the station. "It's like starting something exciting and then having to stop, *da*, cowboy?" Alina smiled and nudged me. "Who knows? The train could be early."

We bought a bag of oranges from a vendor outside and sat on a bench peeling them onto the ground. It was a couple hours past daybreak. Drunks staggered around the plaza, drifting in and out of the waves of smoke from a dumpster fire.

"They're dancing," I joked.

"*Da*, staggering is a traditional Russian dance," Alina smirked tiredly. Wearily vicious, she sang, "Here, watch, '*kalinka, kalinka...*'"

We arrived late at Tayga and learned we'd be spending the night there. The next train to Barnaul was at five in the morning. We couldn't, however, simply buy our tickets and then find a quiet corner to sleep in. The snarling ticket seller informed us that she never knew how many seats were available until the conductor on the train called from one town over. If we wanted tickets, we had to stand in line all night. There were already some thirty frowning people queued up, trying to configure their luggage into cots and chairs.

I took the first shift while Alina went to call her friends in Barnaul and to find us something to eat. With my back to the wall and our packs around my feet, I yawned at a day of doing nothing, save for sitting on wooden train seats and having made little progress toward our destination.

The walls of the station had once been light blue but were now turned gray. Black soot swirls were etched in the paint in a corner where electric wiring had caught fire. On the front wall, above the doors, hung a crooked and battered Soviet-art diorama of the railway system, each major city represented with a pressed-tin coat of arms. All lines ran to Moscow. "The decrepit network and its retarded brain," I mumbled to myself.

An old woman shouted that her suitcase had been robbed. No one responded. A fight broke out between drunks: A group of three followed a man around the station, who held a bottle in defense, and then chased him out the front doors. There were other ticket lines, too, none moving, each fronted by a snarling head of Cerberus, a ticket agent, a tortured angry mammal in a cage.

Alina returned with warm beer and cold cabbage *pirozhki.* "You don't look very happy," she said.

"Just trying to fit in."

We ate and slapped mosquitoes. I got up to find the bathroom. The pit toilets were filled and piled up, filth splattered on the walls, piss in the sinks, maggots, rats.

"Don't take it out on me," Alina preempted when I returned. "What do you expect?"

Speaking loud enough for people around us to hear, I said, "I wonder if Yeltsin has to hold his breath when he goes to the bathroom."

"I hope so," she said and then whispered to me, "If you're going to be a baby every time something unpleasant happens, this is going to be a miserable trip. Why don't you take the bags over there and relax for a bit." She pointed out a vacant spot against the front wall between the doors. "It's my turn to stand in line."

I went and sat on the floor, leaning back on our packs. I drank a couple beers and watched as the sky of the station was pulled toward the darkness of the one scorched corner.

"Connor, wake up," said Alina, crouching next to me. It was dawn. "We got tickets."

I sat up suddenly. "You waited in line all night? Why didn't you wake me?"

She smiled wearily. "I tried. Look, I threw kopeks at you." She stood and scattered the worthless coins with a light kick. I apologized, hugged and kissed her. "It's alright," she said, "but I really might have killed that ticket agent if she'd told me there were no seats."

The air outside was cool and humid. Alongside the track we found a buffet kiosk displaying a variety of food, most of which looked as though it had been left out for days. Nonetheless, we stared hungrily through the dusty glass. "Are the cutlets fresh?" Alina asked the attendant. The woman sucked on a gold tooth, scratched the dark roots of her dye job, and shook her head. "The eggs?" Alina inquired. Another grimace and head shake.

"Ask her why she's selling rotten food to people," I grumbled.

"You ask her," responded Alina. "I already know." We bought more *pirozhki*. The woman wiped her hands on her already greasy coat before dropping our breakfast into a bag and sliding it through a slot in the glass.

It was hot outside and hotter in the train when it arrived, but despite the heat, the windows in our car were up and locked. The wagon was packed. People sat fanning themselves. They stripped their pale little children down to their underwear. One car over was nearly empty. Alina and I found a seat near the one open window and immediately fell to sleep.

We were woken at Novosibirsk by a skinny young man in a conductor's outfit. He examined our tickets and told us we had to go back to the other car.

"It's full."

"There are free spaces now. I just came from there. This is where I sit." He grinned a small-toothed, gummy smile.

"Tell me, please," Alina began, sleepy and puffy-eyed, her voice creaky and irritated. "Why don't you open any of the other windows?"

Grinning on, the conductor reached over our heads, pushed up the window, and locked it with a key. "You have to stay in the wagon on your ticket." Speaking to Alina, he said, "I'd like to make an exception for such an attractive young woman, but the rules are made for a reason. Maybe if you were on your own I could help." He glanced at me.

Alina's face reddened, but before she could speak, he continued down the aisle. "That frizzy haired little Uzbek," she growled as she picked up her pack. "I don't care about racism, Connor. I hate *xhatchi*. Uzbeks are dumb as sheep. You can see it in their eyes. Their brains aren't capable of anything other than selling fruits in the market. You give them a uniform, and you see what happens. He thinks he can get women to have sex with him for an open window."

"Let's just go between the cars until he leaves, and then we'll come back," I suggested. "What can he do? "

"He can have us thrown off the train. If he puts in a complaint against us, we won't even be able to take the train back to Tomsk." Alina scowled and headed back to the other car.

At last we arrived in Barnaul and everything improved. Alina's friend, Oksana, met us at the station. She had dry blond hair and cat-like features. She was in her mid-thirties, and while neither fat nor thin, she appeared soft-bodied and a bit hunched, slowly transforming into a *babushka*. Tears came to her eyes when she saw Alina. She talked to keep from crying.

"Oh, ho, you are here at last. Is it a law that trains are always late? Someone should tell the people who make the schedules so that they should compensate for the perpetual lateness. Uh huh. But it's not your fault, lovely. Look at you. I haven't seen you in so long. It's so wonderful of you to come and see your old friend. Uh huh. Well, have you got all your things? Come this way."

Oksana led us onto bus after bus and then a tram and another bus. She talked almost non-stop. Every time she did stop, tears again welled up in her eyes as she looked at Alina.

"It's so wonderful to see someone from home. Life becomes so strange, Alina, doesn't it? Uh huh. Oh, sometimes it can be hard. You have come to us at one of those times. You will see how we are living. I don't complain. It is simply a fact. Uh huh," she affirmed. "Then you see someone from a past life, and it's almost not like a memory, more like a dream. That is how it is for me to see you, now. You'll have to forgive me. Yes, you can hug me as many times as you wish. I hope your boyfriend won't mind.

"We had such high hopes for Barnaul, Alina. It's a nice city, but we've had bad luck. Have you met my husband, Karim? Oh, yes, you met him that one time. Wait until you see little Toma. He's grown up so much. He's ten now. So handsome. He looks just like his father, my first husband. I'm so much happier with Karim. He's a wonderful man. This is all so hard for him. He's started smoking, but I try not to bother him too much about it. I hope you find a man like him. I couldn't get through all this without him. You know we had to leave our little baby back in Kazakhstan with his grandparents. Uh huh. It makes me cry if I think about it. Things were going so well, we thought we'd be able to bring him here. But not now.

"Karim misses his little son so much. I can see it on his face when he is thinking about it. Things were so bad there, we had to leave. The economic situation is bad, terrible, and there's all kinds of nationalistic things going on. The atmosphere was very bad for people like us, you know, a couple of different races. I was teaching there, but they wouldn't hire Karim, and the only work he could do as a geologist was make stone jewelry to sell at the market.

"But I should tell you what happened here. Uh huh. I haven't been able to bring myself to write to you about it. You know that we had a position at the city botanical gardens as caretakers. Does your boyfriend know I am a botanist? It was delightful there at first. We had a nice little house in the gardens. All the time we were surrounded by the beautiful plants and the smell of the soil. I think it was the best job I ever had. Karim and I both also teach, but you know, we don't always get our money. Sometimes they pay us and sometimes they don't. As long as we were at the gardens, it was never a big problem. We grew some of our own food. I wish we could go back there, but it was cursed. We should have done nothing, maybe, but how could we?"

"Oksana!" Alina interjected through her friends rambling, "what happened?"

"Well the director of the gardens was a pedophile. Filthy. Horrible. Uh huh. He'd offer schoolboys a job and then get them drunk and bring them back to his flat to have his way with them. He was corrupt as well. He charged universities and researchers for use of the gardens and then pocketed the money for himself. We had to do something. A snake in our garden. Uh huh. I was worried about Toma.

"It was terrible. One day I came home and there was a boy of about twelve, drunk and crying beneath a bush near our house. It was a terrible fairy tale, like Baba Yaga in the woods. Uh huh.

"Karim confronted the director and that was that. He made something up, said we were stealing from the gardens by growing food, and threw us out. We tried to go to the police, but he had paid them off. They told Karim that if he wanted to stay out of jail, he'd better keep his mouth shut. Now we are living in a dormitory, and you will see for yourself what that is like."

"We were cast out of the garden into this," Oksana half-joked, half-lamented as she led us up a dark moldy stairwell littered with trash and broken glass. On the fourth floor, she showed us the kitchen and bathroom she shared with a neighbor. Water leaked from wherever there were pipes. The place smelled strongly of leaking gas, sewage, and mildew.

Indicating a small spattered table on which sat an aluminum fry pan, a spoon, and a knife, she said, "That's it! That's almost all he owns, our neighbor. I'll introduce you. Put down your packs.

"There he is, Borya," she said, sweeping her hand through an open door. On a mattress on the floor laid a white-bearded man with his mouth open. "Don't worry, we won't wake him. He's a drunk. He looks like Solzhenitsyn. Uh huh. Borya here once had a two-room flat, but he sold it and bought this room so he could spend the rest of his money on vodka. Not a bad situation for a drunk. Occasionally he smashes bottles, but mostly he's harmless. He sings to us while we have our breakfast."

"Are you sure he's alive?" asked Alina.

"*Nyet*," chuckled Oksana. "I guess if he is dead, we'll be the first to know. I shouldn't be so negative. I should be more welcoming, of course. It's just that I can be myself with you, Alina. I don't need to put on appearances. I can speak my heart. It's therapeutic for me. I try to be the optimistic one. Karim needs me to be that. Before I go back to being optimistic, though, let me show you our beautiful bathroom. *Vot,* a sink, a toilet, no bathtub, no hot water. You can heat up some water on the stove, if you want. Usually we get soaped up and then use this bucket to dump water over our heads. There's no drain, but the water runs down through the floor. Uh huh. Now let's go into our rooms; it's much nicer in there."

Karim sat smoking at a table. He was a thin, dark man, tightly muscled, with a trimmed black beard and bushy coarse hair. He shook my hand and kissed Alina on the cheek.

"*Pkew, pkew.*" The boy, Toma, exploded from the bedroom, where the TV roared, with a kung fu kick, pistol-pointing fingers, and spittle-lipped sound effects. "*Pkew, pkew.* Momma, I saw a new kung fu movie. Kung fu! I can do it. Watch!" Forgoing introductions, Toma showed us his fighting style. Oksana's first husband was a Tartar, Alina had told me, and her son bore the Mongol look, except for the feline mouth identical to his mother's. "What's for dinner?"

As Oksana prepared dinner, Karim unrolled several topographical maps on the table. "Karim has been to the Altai many times," called Oksana as she peeled onions. "He'll find something for you. Uh huh."

Stony calm amidst his chatty wife and hyperactive step-son, Karim placed books at each corner of the map to hold it open. "I have a couple options for you. I need to know a bit more about your level of experience and what you're looking for." He looked me in the eyes for the first time. They were dark and tired, but still he wore a look of concern. "I assume you're not looking for anything technical. No ropes."

"*Nyet,* no ropes," I said emphatically, feeling a twist of nervousness.

After a quick, simple dinner and a little time in front of the TV with Toma while Oksana and Alina caught up, we turned in. Alina and I slept on the floor in the main room, laying our sleeping bags over folded blankets for padding. We listened to Oksana chatting in the next room, talking nervously, relentlessly. Then we heard the television and smelled Karim's cigarettes. Then silence. We were exhausted but could not sleep. I heard Alina's breathing next to me, heavy, somehow turned on. "Let's have sex, Connor," she whispered.

"We can't," I said. "The bathroom's in the hall. My condoms are packed."

She kissed my neck. "You understand nothing." She guided my hand, arching her back. She panted, "Connor, please." She pushed the covers off of herself. She pulled her t-shirt up and her panties down. She squeezed my hand hard over her breasts, pushed my fingers into herself. I shushed her as I traced and painted with wetness. She bucked against the floor, then shivered and told me with portent, "Almost never that hard."

In the morning Oksana was up early and off to her classes. Borya sang from his room while we had tea and bread. Karim gave us a list of provisions for our trip and directions to the market.

It was sunny and seventy-five degrees. Barnaul struck me as nicer than Tomsk, calmer and greener. There were more factories and fewer kiosks. A sign on one factory wall read 'The Factory Named Lenin.'

"I wonder if there's a 'Grocery Store Named Lenin' or a 'Shashlik Stand Named Lenin,'" I joked to Alina.

"Connor, why didn't you want to have sex with me last night?"

"A Sausage Named Lenin," I continued glibly, but I had laid awake wondering the same thing. "I was tired, maybe a bit overwhelmed by your friends' situation. Seeing educated people living in poverty isn't a turn on."

"You're too sensitive," she shrugged. "It's not such a big problem for them. It's temporary."

"So long as the building doesn't collapse or explode from leaking gas."

Alina sighed, annoyed.

"You think it can't happen?"

"She's made some bad choices that have put her there. You want to know what turned me on? I was thinking that could never happen to us, either one of us. Then I started thinking about how we are doing this together. At TV-N we just happen to be together. We're just doing our jobs at the same place at the same time. At parties we drank some alcohol and danced and then ended up sleeping together. In Tomsk most of what we do together is run errands. We do the same things that we would otherwise do alone. Sometimes we do something special, something just for us. This is bigger. We are creating something together. It's much more than just spending idle time together. I was thinking about that."

I nodded and squeezed her hand.

That night Karim took us to see some friends of his to consult about our trip. We decided on a route. Karim wrote us letters of introduction to men he knew in the mountain rescue service. The next day I went to OVIR, the tourist authority, to get a stamp on my visa so that I could legally travel in the region. I'd gotten one in Tomsk to get this far, and I would need another stamp in Gorno-Altaisk, the capital of the newly formed Altai Republic. We bought our bus tickets.

The evening before our departure, Karim helped us organize our supplies and pack while Oksana quietly looked on. She was strangely sullen. Despite having been ecstatic at Alina's arrival, Oksana had become burdened by our presence.

"Are these the only shoes you have?" Karim asked incredulously. He went into the bedroom and came back offering his and Oksana's boots —good, worn leather hiking boots. But they didn't fit. Karim asked me to come out to smoke with him in the hall. "I'm not telling you not to go," he sighed, "but it could be dangerous. This could be a reckless adventure. You don't have the proper equipment. Also, they've had violence against Russians there. I would go with you if I could." He took a deep drag and exhaled. "If anything bad happened to her, I would feel terrible."

We arrived in Gorno-Altaisk and were glad for the cool air of the hills and the calm demeanor of the town. Right away we went to the address of one of Karim's friends. A neighbor heard us knocking and told us that the man had broken his leg mountain climbing and was in the hospital.

Before we could consider other places to stay, I needed to register with the police. For a town a tenth the size of Tomsk, it had an exceptionally large police station, which consisted of two buildings next to one another. The attendant at the first station told us we should go to the second. The officer at the second station told us we should go to the first. "We were just there, and they told us to come here," I said. The young man nodded his head, got up from behind the reception desk, and ran next door to the other office.

When he returned he told me that they would have to call someone in to register me, as it was after eight p.m. He asked politely if I would wait. Alina and I sat in the lobby and ate apples and pears, happy to kill time since the only other place we had to go was the bus or train station.

My registrar turned out to be a huge, muscle-bound man with an Uzi slung over his shoulder. He stormed through the front doors as if called away from a terrorist standoff and asked me to approach the counter.

"Your passport," he commanded. "Yours as well," he said to Alina.

"I'm all Russian, comrade," she responded sarcastically.

He looked at her sharply, then grinned. "You don't look Russian to me."

"Just listen to me speak, then. Do I sound Russian?"

"*Da*," he conceded. "It's just that most of the Russian women I see aren't quite as attractive."

"Are all Altai men quite as forward as you?"

"I'm Altai and Russian," he answered. "You're traveling with this American?"

"*Da.* I thought I would show him some mountains."

"Are you sure you're Russian? Do you have your passport?"

"No, I didn't bring it."

He shook his head. "The Altai is an independent republic, you know."

"I didn't know that. Are you going to send me back to my homeland?"

"No. You don't need a passport to travel here, but you'll need it to get a hotel room."

"We're not planning on getting a hotel room."

He nodded. "That's alright. The train station is reasonably safe at night."

We left the police station and headed towards the *vokzal* on the town's dusty central road. "We may as well find someplace to have a picnic before we go back to the train station," Alina said airily. "Now that we're really underway, it's more relaxing. Don't you think? We have only one more bus ride, and then we'll be on the open steppe. We'll be like nomads; we'll walk for days and days. I could skip for joy," she said and then did, smiling at me around the corner of her full pack.

We came to a school building, shut down for the summer, with a row of auditorium chairs and an old desk in its portico. We sat. On the desk, we set out our meal of walnuts and raisins, bread, and two cans of gin and tonic cocktails I'd picked up at a kiosk. We silently sipped our drinks like an old couple enjoying a nightly ritual. Alina's composure and calm enthusiasm set me at ease and drew me closer to her. She'd been right about this. It was something more than tracing out the workday.

We were startled suddenly. Someone said, "Are you students?" A man stood in the doorway behind us. He emerged from the building with a spotted dog on a lead and holding a garden hoe with a yellow handle. "Don't you know school's out?" he smiled. He was a big, round guy with a jack-o-lantern smile.

"We are travelers stopped for a picnic," Alina explained.

"That's fine," he said amiably, pulling the door shut behind him and locking it. "I'm the night watchman. You can help me watch," he chuckled. "I've got some gardening to do. If anyone comes looking for me, tell them I'll be back in twenty minutes, if you don't mind. Enjoy your picnic," he said and was off.

Unlike the watchman, several passersby looked at us strangely, but before long it was dark, and they couldn't see us there. "There's no reason to go to the train station now," I said. "It's a warm evening. We have our own watchman to keep an eye on us." Drowsily, we laid back in the wooden chairs and closed our eyes.

"You're still here," the guard said some time later, again startling us. "Are you sleeping here? Don't you have anywhere else to go?" He didn't sound annoyed, only puzzled.

Without speaking, I got up and lifted my pack.

"Please," said Alina. "We're not doing any harm here, and if we go back to the train station we might get robbed."

"What robbed?" said the watchman as if insulted.

Alina explained our situation, and the man smiled broadly. "You can't stay out here," he said, shaking his head. We resumed collecting our things. "I'll take you back to my flat. You can sleep there. I have a daughter of my own who goes to university in Tomsk, and I wouldn't want anyone letting her sleep out on the steps of a dark building. Was that little snack I saw you having all that you've eaten? My wife will make you a proper dinner. I'm Vasily Sergeivich, pleased to meet you."

Alina and I shared a look that said, 'Found Treasure.' Sergeivich smiled and beckoned us to follow him. He apologized for not carrying Alina's pack and explained that he had a bad back. We eagerly trailed our night watchman, whose smile was visible even in the dark as he turned back to check that we were still with him.

"You're from America, *da*? You've come a long way. Our little flat isn't much, but it's better than the front steps of the

Pedagogical Institute. My wife will be asleep by now, but she won't mind getting up and fixing you something to eat."

"Vasily Sergeivich, *eto ne nado*," protested Alina. "Please don't wake your poor wife. We've had enough to eat. We just need to sleep. We've got to catch a bus early in the morning."

"She wouldn't hear of it. I'd be in trouble if I didn't wake her up for pleasant young guests such as yourselves. What time is your bus? I'll wake you when I get off my shift. I can take you down to the station."

Alina smiled and nudged me victoriously. One of her beleaguered countrymen had come through for her with the famous Russian hospitality. Her face told me, 'now I've shown you.'

The flat was cramped and cozy in the Russian way with each piece of furniture serving multiple purposes, each shelf carefully organized to display favorite books, photos, and mementos. Our Samaritan's wife greeted us tiredly, understandably less enthusiastic than her husband was to have guests. We apologized and thanked her as we watched with watering mouths as she made us potatoes and eggs. As we ate, she folded out the couch and made it up for us.

Vasily Sergeivich returned to his duties, his wife returned to her bed, and Alina and I tucked ourselves in. I whispered to her, "This is incredible."

"This is the real Russia, Connor, the one I know it will always be."

A cool breeze came from an open window, and we fell asleep.

In the morning we had bread and cheese and dark sweet tea before Vasily Sergeivich led us to the bus depot.

"So long then," beamed our watchman. "You're welcome to stay with us on your way back."

We bought tickets according to Karim's instructions and boarded a mini-bus. We were lucky to claim the last two open seats. Less fortunate passengers sat on their luggage in the aisle. We rode on the shuttering, jolting short bus for twelve hours, stopping occasionally for bathroom breaks at rundown, filthy rest stops. Then, suddenly, we came to the mountains. Splintering gray stone peaks jutted up on all sides of us. This was the Altai.

The bus groaned as it chugged up steep hills and haltingly negotiated sharp turns along precipitous drops. Mesmerized by the view, Alina and I forgot everything until we saw a sign for the village Karim had written down for us. We called out to the driver. In a moment, we watched the bus whiz away through the valley, and we were alone in the mountains.

"We've got to go all that way," said Alina to the jagged horizon.

I turned slowly in a circle attempting to take it all in: the steppe, rolled out by glaciers and framed by mountains, pitched into the sky. The incline induced a kind of reverse vertigo. Close to us was a strange little wooden bus stop covered with bright green moss. A gravel road led to a dusty village of wood cabins and a low cement-block building or two.

As we walked through the village, we heard sounds of habitation but saw no one. "It's just as well we don't see anyone," said Alina. "We don't want them coming after us." It was late in the evening by now, but still light out. "Now that we're here, Connor, I'm finding myself a bit nervous. I'm thinking about Karim's warnings, and I'm anxious from all that sitting on the bus. Let's walk fast."

Before long, we were out of the village and came to a wooden bridge over a small river. Not knowing when we'd next be able to get water, I climbed down the bank to refill the plastic bottles we'd drunk on the bus.

"Let's keep walking," Alina protested. "Those mountains are covered with melting glaciers. We'll find plenty of water."

"It'll just take a minute," I told her as I held a gulping bottle beneath the cold, silty runoff. I would filter it later. On the other side of the bridge, we passed through the line of birches that grew along the river and began a slight incline onto the steppe. 'You'll follow the path west for a day and a half,' Karim had told us. 'Then it will fork, and you will go south toward the mountains. It's a full day hike up the mountain, so you'll want to camp at the base the night before. Don't go too far up the slope or you won't find anywhere comfortable to sleep.'

We walked on a single-track road of stony rubble and packed dust. On the centerline grew scrubby grass and wild thyme. On either side of us waved tall golden grass in the breeze. We followed the trail along a low ridge that sloped down toward the birches along the river, about a mile away. The sky was clear and open, its brightness fading now that it was after eight p.m.

We sang each other bits of songs loudly in the openness, secure in our solitude as if at sea. "I wouldn't live there if you paid me," I sang from the Talking Heads.

"*Dozdje...*" Alina sang from DDT.

"Other people's problems..."

"*Gloopi sticki...*"

We stopped, realizing at the same time that we'd heard an engine, something large. After a few moments, a dump truck appeared on the ridge coming towards us. We exchanged worried looks. We were ready to run.

"Probably they see hikers all the time," I said.

We moved into the grass on opposite sides of the track. Then I quickly crossed to where Alina was. Not wishing to encourage the driver to stop, we did not turn to look as the truck approached. Nonetheless, it skidded to a stop beside us, throwing up dust and stones that pelted our shoes. Alina walked along as if she hadn't noticed.

I stopped and looked up at the man on the passenger side of the truck. His eyes were on her. She was wearing the green silk shirt and from their perch they could see the bob of her breasts as she walked past them. Maybe right now, I thought, she wishes she wasn't wearing it. I caught up to her with a long step or two and took her hand. As we halted and turned around, the driver stepped down and slammed his door. The passenger sat with his elbow out the window, silently looking down on us.

"Where are you going? Where are you from?" the man asked brusquely, squinting his eyes. "Get in, we'll give you a ride."

"We're hiking; we like to walk," Alina calmly told him.

"It's a long way. Get in. We'll drive you," he insisted. "Come back to our camp with us. We'll have a party. Are you students? Do you want to have a party?"

Reading menace in the word 'party,' Alina braced her jaw and replied, "We're not interested in a party or a ride with you. We're hiking and we have a long way to go, so you'll excuse us, please." Shooting me a look, she started to walk again. I followed.

I saw the man smile from the corner of my eye. He sensed our fear. "Maybe we'll see you again. Maybe you'll change your mind." The passenger took his arm inside, prepared to jump down if the other requested it. Instead, the driver got back in the truck and revived its monstrous engine. They roared past us and made a grand, dusty U-turn through the grass.

Alina was shaken. I squeezed her hand. "I forgot to tell them that I'm American," I joked in vain.

"I don't know what we're going to do, Connor," she said, her voice quaking. "They are going to come back, and we're going to be out here in the open. I'm afraid. They're going to be looking for me. Do you understand? There won't be anything you can do."

"Let's go down to the river," I said. The trees there were too dense for the truck to get through. She nodded, and we charged through the grass. We came to the tree line at dusk. The old yellow light of the day filtered through the trees like a slow shower of dust. We moved further upstream to get away from the trail we'd left in the grass. We had just enough daylight left to set up our tent and look for defensive sticks and stones.

"If they do come back and find us, we must not get into their truck, no matter what," said Alina.

At that moment, I wished dearly that I'd brought Ilya's *bolonchik* pistol. I'd decided against bringing it because it was illegal for me to have it. If I'd been caught with it, I could have ended up in jail. Right now, the risk seemed like nothing.

Silently in the dark, we ate bread and canned fish.

"What is this trip? Why are we doing this?" Alina said as we laid in the tent. "I'm not saying that I wish we didn't come, Connor, but things could get bad for us."

So it has all become desperate, I thought. We'd been desperate to get away from the station and from Tomsk. We were desperate to make the most of this trip, our travels together. Most of all, we were desperate to break through to each other or break apart. This could do it.

Before long we heard the truck. We got out of the tent and crouched behind a fallen tree. The dump truck, we could see by its waving headlights, was going back and forth over the ground we'd covered. Our pursuers worked their way to the trees and stopped. They were off at an angle from us, near where we'd entered the woods. We could hear them talking. There were more than the two guys we'd seen before.

"They're hunters, trackers probably," Alina fretted. "They know we're in here."

We heard the doors of the truck opening and closing. We heard the sound of the engine accelerate. Alina and I waited in the darkness for a bit, measuring our breaths. I walked to the edge of the trees and watched the rear lights of the truck disappear over the rise in the steppe.

At first light, we packed up and headed out, opting to stay along the trees near the river for as long as we could. By midday we had to return to the trail up above us or else be separated from it by a ridge. We were nervous at first, but as the afternoon wore on, and we grew tired of our stress and from the walking, we eased up.

"Sunscreen is not something I thought to pack when I came to Siberia," I pondered loudly, as if to convince myself that we'd regained perfect solitude.

"It's hard to find," Alina answered blankly.

"I asked Lubomira to help me find some, but I don't think she'd ever heard of it before." For sun protection, I had on a ball cap and a bandana draped over the back of my neck, but it didn't quite provide the protection that Alina's head scarf did for her.

"Poor sparrow," she said to me, "your ears are blistering."

By late afternoon the mountains were closer, and it seemed, an impossible expanse of steppe behind us.

"Somehow we think we're going to climb that," I said. We stopped for water and to take photographs of each other with the insurmountable range of rock threatening our backs. As we started back on the trail, we heard a strange raspy yapping sound. 'Hap, hap.' We turned in circles scanning for the source of it. 'Hap, hap.'

"A Steppe Fox," said Alina, pointing to a little ridge north of us. "Don't worry, mama, we're only passing by." The gray and white fox, nearly as large as a coyote, trotted to within fifteen meters of us and followed along. 'Hap, hap. Hap, hap,' she barked, agitated but not threatening.

"I guess we don't know if we're getting farther from her den or closer to it," I said, but after a few minutes she turned away and headed back to the ridge.

"I don't know why, but I'm no longer worried about the men in the truck," said Alina. "It's behind us."

Midway through the long summer evening, we veered off the road and onto a smaller trail that headed straight into the mountains. We made it nearly to the tree line just as the light was fading. We set up our tent, had something to eat, and boiled water for tea. Alina picked wild thyme and added it to our cups with a palm measure of sugar to make a warm, aromatic, sleep-inducing liqueur. We slept soundly and uninterrupted.

We woke up early and immediately began kissing and taking off the clothes we'd slept in. Alina's skin was salty and grainy with dried sweat. I kissed and sucked her nipples and saw that I was removing a film of dust. I licked a clean trail to her vagina and licked her there. She writhed urgently. I dug in my pack for a condom and entered her roughly. Our filthy bodies smacked together with the hard ground beneath us, and both of us were free to give voice to any sound we pleased.

"I wouldn't usually let anyone touch me when I'm so dirty," she told me as we lay catching our breath. "Especially not go down on me, but I couldn't help it." Embarrassed, she smiled and pulled the sleeping bag around her. "When we get to the research camp, we'll get clean and have lots of sex. I want to have as much sex as we can."

I unzipped the tent to drop the condom outside and found myself looking into a stand of brown horse legs. There were three mounts, one ridden by an Altai boy and the others by old men with rifles slung over their shoulders. I was relieved, at first, to see that they were not the men from the truck and that they were smiling. Then I realized the reason they were smiling.

"It's a nice morning to wake up in a tent," said one of the men.

"One moment," I said and zipped back up.

"Who is it?" asked Alina as we gathered up our clothing.

Now that I had seen them, I could hear the horses' breathing and feel their presence towering over us. We quickly got dressed and sprung cheerfully from the tent to bid good morning to our neighbors.

While they asked us the same questions as the guys in the truck, they clearly meant us no harm. They were hunters from the village and were out for a few days. They'd work their way up the mountain and would maybe see us at the research camp, since they usually stopped there for a cup of tea. We were on the right trail, they confirmed and left us feeling good, if still embarrassed.

"Probably they thought they were coming up on wild animals mating."

"*Fuu,* Connor."

We headed into the forest surrounding the base of the mountains. We stopped at a creek to filter silty glacial water. The trail rose steeply and became a single track, impassable to vehicles. Ascending through the pines, we worked up a sweat and were soon surrounded by Eurasian-sized horse flies, droning and dive bombing us like mini MIGs.

By late afternoon the trail leveled off a bit and the trees became more sparse, lower to the ground and twisted by the wind. Further on, as we came out of the woods, we saw swaying green grasses and wildflowers. Above us we could see the glaciers and the stone mountains' cathedral peaks.

We reached the rescue camp around eight p.m. At the front of a small compound, there was a little tin-capped cabin on stilts against a hillside. "*Allo,*" Alina called from the foot of the steps. We heard a chair squawk inside, footsteps, and the screen door was pushed open with a familiar and vaguely welcoming squeak.

"*Privet,*" said a shaggy red-haired man. Beside him stood a thin dark-haired man with sharp, boney features and a mustache. "Are you with the university?" We explained ourselves, and the redhead, who eagerly introduced himself as Yevgeny, took us to a dormitory cabin with eight rooms. Next to it was a long hangar-like laboratory building.

"I can't wait to get into that banya," Alina whispered to me, indicating a small outbuilding with a fuming smokestack.

All of the buildings, Yevgeny explained, were owned by the University of Tomsk but were currently not in use. "Once you get settled in, you should come back to our cabin for dinner," he offered with a smile. "Also I'll stoke the fire in the banya. We've got to get clean to have the company of such a lovely lady."

Alina gave me a sly look, as if to say, 'With this guy, I can have whatever I want.' To him she said, "If you would do that for me, then I will cook dinner for all you good men."

Yevgeny stood gobsmacked as if he'd received the most exquisite offer he could imagine. With a short, royal giggle Alina added, "We brought some food to share as well."

"I hope you've got some fish," Yevgeny panted.

Now with a full laugh, Alina answered, "We have tinned fish."

"I love fish," he said, and hurried off to tend the fire.

The front room of mountaineers' cabin consisted mostly of a cramped kitchen with a gas camping stove and a sink basin for water carried in from a cistern. There was a two-way radio on a shelf, and from the walls hung many skeins of colored climbing rope. We sat at a creaky table and drank tea. Yevgeny immediately recovered his conversation with Alina about how much he liked fish. "Dried fish, canned fish, it doesn't matter, *ya tak lyublyu.*"

Valery, the other mountaineer, was not much of a talker. Most of my initial questions to him he answered with nods and slight gestures. "We're volunteers," he said, when he finally spoke. "We get paid a little, but not much. The hiking season is from May to September. You can serve half of it, ten weeks, or all of it. I've done it all for the last few years. Yevgeny here is almost at the end of his ten weeks. He's ready to go."

"I miss my wife," put in Yevgeny, interrupting his ode to fish.

"I like it up here," Valery went on. "We just have to keep the buildings standing and wait for emergency calls. We haven't had any this year. People are staying away because of the violence in the region. Maybe nobody has money for travel. Maybe the people that do go to the Alps now. *Ne znayu.*

"The way I look at it, I'm hiding out on top of a mountain until things improve down there. Everything here is the same as it's always been. Provided that our supplies arrive every month, I'll stay here and let the time pass. Call it 'history,' but I'd prefer to let it take its course before I rejoin it."

"You'll have to excuse me now, boys," said Alina. "I'm going to go to the banya and clean up." She gave me a wink. "Then I'll make dinner while you do the same."

"Ah," sighed Yevgeny, "it's so fantastic to have a woman here. I wish my wife was here. I'll come with you to make sure you have everything you need." He glanced quickly at Valery and me as if scanning for objections. We watched him go.

"Is he alright?" I asked Valery after a moment.

"He's alright," he replied. "He means well. He's harmless." When Yevgeny returned a few minutes later, Valery kidded him, "You make sure to check the walls for holes?"

Blushing, Yevgeny replied sternly, "I was just checking that there was enough wood for the fire. I would have cleaned up more if I knew we were going to have a female guest."

We opened a bottle of vodka I had brought as a gift and sat talking. Alina entered the cabin a bit later with wet hair and cheeks flush from the hot bath. Into the cabin with her, she pulled a steamy scent of soap and wood smoke. She smiled. "*Ladno,* boys' turn."

The banya was a two-chambered cabin. In the first room was a plank table and pegs on the walls for clothes. The second room contained the wood stove with a water tank welded to the top of it. There were benches on risers against the back wall, the wood of which was stained black by steam and soot and the oils of bathers' bodies.

We undressed in the dim light. The mountaineers were lean and muscular. Yevgeny flipped the latch on the stove with a bit of wood and threw a fresh log into the glowing embers. He dipped an empty *Tushonka* can into the water and splashed the hot stove again and again until the sauna was filled with poaching hot steam. We washed quickly, taking turns with soap and a bucket. We sat on the risers and sweat.

"She's very beautiful, your girlfriend," said Yevgeny. "You should marry her. You're not going to find one prettier. My wife is very beautiful as well. I knew that a guy like me wasn't going to do better than her. But your girlfriend there, take her back to the USA with you. Maybe you already have a wife at home. I hope that's not the case because this one is lovely."

I nodded but didn't reply. Valery ignored the conversation and watched fluid bead up on the backs of his hands. "You came at a good time," he said after a few moments. "Our supply truck is scheduled to be here at the end of the week. He parks at the bottom, across the creek. We go down to bring everything up. If you get a ride with him, you won't have to spend two days hiking back across the steppe." The bus to Barnaul comes only once a week, so we'd be risking missing it, but Valery encouraged me to not worry. "The driver is Russian, not one of the locals. He's very reliable."

"You can help us bring up supplies to pay for your ride," put in Yevgeny.

When we returned to the cabin, Alina had made us mackerel with kasha and potatoes. Very filling. Yevgeny was immensely satisfied with the fish and helped Alina wash up. He told her that he could take us up the mountain the day after tomorrow. Tomorrow, he garrulously explained, he had to help Valery with a new cabin they were building. However, since there was only one chainsaw, there was only so much he could do. Generally, he told us, he didn't have much to do.

I sat at the table talking to Valery, who appeared happy to have Yevgeny distracted. He opened up once he had a couple drinks and talked about politics and history in an intensely interesting and well-informed way that I'd happily found in many Russians.

Alina said she was tired and excused herself, giving me a wink before she left. Yevgeny sank into his chair and bemoaned his loneliness. On my suggestion, we opened another bottle of vodka and the mountaineers shared rescue stories. After an hour, I knew I was remiss and excused myself. Coming down the cabin steps, I realized I was quite buzzed. The beam of my flashlight veered ahead of me, exaggerating my staggering. I was drunk and exhausted. I could hardly stand.

The room was dark when I entered. I turned off the flashlight. The moon was bright and shone through the window. Alina was in her sleeping bag. I took off my sneakers and listened for her breathing.

"You shouldn't have kept me waiting so long, Connor."

"I thought you'd fall right to sleep."

"I'm never too tired for sex," she said coyly, needfully forgiving.

"I'm so tired," I groaned in English.

"Come over here and give me a kiss goodnight, then."

I leaned over to kiss her, and she swept back the cover, showing herself nude. She pulled me to her and guided my hand over her breasts and stomach and between her legs. "Take off your clothes," she purred. "I can tell you're not too tired."

Instantly my heart was pounding as if in a panic, and I was feeling around in my pack for the condoms. "You don't need it, Connor," she panted hotly, as always. "Come and have sex with me."

I sat on the edge of the bed to roll on my shield. I could hear her rubbing herself, her wetness making tiny licking sounds in the darkness. She moaned softly. I hovered over her and she rubbed me against her, inhaling desperately. I wasn't going to be able to give her what she wanted, only she didn't know it yet. I tried to fuck like a butterfly but came like an underage boy. She began to cry.

"Why would you do that?" she wept softly in my ear. "It's as if you set out to disappoint me."

"*Ni Znayou*," I said, my Russian failing me. I could explain nothing, even as she quietly sobbed. I went to my own bed and fell asleep.

In the morning Alina was gone. I went to the mountaineer's cabin for breakfast and tea. She'd already been there and left, they told me. I took my time eating. I wasn't worried. I went back to the dorm and rehearsed what I would say. I looked up words in the dictionary as usual. Later, I went out for a walk. Yevgeny had told me to feel free to explore up to the foot of the glacier but warned against going higher. Along the trail I found a mock gravesite of piled stones decorated with a ram's skull and a cracked orange climbing helmet. On the headstone was painted, '*On prerekelcya*'—'He tripped.' I chuckled, but further up the trail, on the side of a cliff, I came across two plaques dedicated to those who had actually died climbing these peaks, one just the year before.

I was lured off the trail by a statue in the woods, carved out of a tree trunk. It was a large round Asiatic face festooned with strings of dried flowers and weather-tattered ribbons of torn cloth. I could see a clearing just behind the statue, and there I found Alina sunbathing on a large flat rock. My Siberian princess laid naked in the sun, her legs slightly parted, her breasts resting to the sides of her chest, her eyes closed. She had folded her clothes neatly in a pile, her bra set to one side, the cups tucked into one another like spoons. I admired her for a moment, but then looked around to see if Yevgeny was somewhere doing the same.

"Are you in shock, *malchik*?" she said without opening her eyes. "Do you think I'm too close to the trail? That Yevgeny might come looking for me, seeing how much he misses his wife?" she said drowsily. "Did you come to find me to talk about last night? I don't know if I'm ready to talk. I suppose you want to get it over with, and you already know what you're going to say." She propped herself up on one arm and held her other over her chest. "What happened, Connor? You were so passionate in the morning, and I wanted you so badly. How could you leave me waiting?"

I didn't answer right away, so she continued, "I have a theory. Listening? Yesterday morning you made a mistake and let yourself go. You were still in the world of dreams, and you were warm and relaxed from sleep. You found me next to you, and we had the sweetest sex despite that we were covered with dirt, and both of us would have felt disgusting at any other time. Instead it was beautiful. Then, I think, you started thinking about it and decided you had given me too much. Even if you didn't think of it consciously, that's what was going on inside you. So in the evening you held back. Why do you always want to hold back from me?"

"You know the reason, Alina," I said, abandoning my prepared speech. "Maybe the truth is somewhere in the afternoon."

"You always talk about being honest, Connor, but maybe you're not so honest with yourself. We are good friends, you and me. I think we can be sure of that, don't you? Other things we're not so sure of. Maybe we should stay closer to what we're sure of."

"No more butterflies?"

"We keep trying, but we never get there," she said. "Maybe we can be friends and still be butterflies, too. Now, you go climb the mountain, and I'll lay in the sun." She uncovered herself and spread her arms wide as she laid back down. "Do you know what I think?" She smiled with her eyes closed. "I am definitely before lunch."

I climbed to the foot of the glacier and stood on a boulder at the intersection of rivers flowing from separate peaks. One was gray, the other chalky white. Where they met, they flowed side by side, each shade distinct until a rapids churned them together.

In the evening, I sat and watched Valery work on the new cabin. He had cut and dragged trees out of the woods one at a time with ropes and belt straps over his shoulders. Now, he cut them into shape with the roaring saw, and the wood dust covered the ground, smelling richly of pitch.

"I don't want to finish it too quickly," Valery joked, standing by me in a sweat-through shirt. "Then I'll have nothing to do but sit and wait for the radio and listen to Yevgeny talk." He stopped work and brushed the wood chips from his shoulders. We drank warm beer, and he talked about how he would construct the roof. Then, in the distance, we saw the Altai hunters Alina and I had encountered the day before outside our tent.

"Here come the Apaches," said Valery as he waved to them. "They come for tea."

The next morning, Yevgeny came to get us to go on a hike. We were just getting up when he knocked and then abruptly opened the door. Alina was naked and had been digging in her pack for something. As she dashed for the blankets to cover herself, I watched his eyes follow her. "We need to get going," he said, without acknowledging the intrusion.

"*Vot*," Alina snickered after he'd left, "his payment for the day has been collected."

Yevgeny led us to the glacier. "In Altai, the name of that peak means Black Stone," he said. Alina and I tested our running shoes' footing on the ice. "The other peak is Red Stone." We climbed along the edge of a glacier for a mile, Yevgeny directing us away from crevasses. The top layer of ice crumbled as we walked, but the grip was good. Scattered along the way were angular shards of red rock. In the snow rested white and black butterflies.

Yevgeny talked constantly, even when we were too far behind him to hear. He reminded me of a golden retriever I'd had as a kid, I told Alina.

"*Da*, he is like a dog in his inability to suppress himself." She wrinkled her nose in a grin. "But also in his friendliness and eagerness to please."

"*Tochno.*"

The higher we climbed, the more the mountains seemed like a different world. No plants, no trees. This was a new planet or one newly destroyed. There is something riveting about cataclysm and debris. I was nearly giddy. This was a beauty and geological drama that you ought not to be able to reach without ropes and training, without risking your life. This was the payoff. We'd come a long way; we'd taken some risks, but not enough to deserve this.

"I've never seen you so excited," said Alina.

I tried to explain.

"I've seen better," she said.

"Where?" I questioned dubiously.

"With my friends. We went to Kazakhstan a couple years ago. This is nice, but that was better. But I'm glad you like it."

At the top of the glacier, just before the final rise to the mountain peak, we came upon a luminous milky blue-green lake and a tiny cabin. Alina said she wanted to stay there while we continued to the top. She wanted to sunbathe.

"You brought your suit?" asked Yevgeny.

"No," she smiled.

Yevgeny and I started up the loose gravel slope to the top. The going was slow and onerous. Frequently we stopped and cast back glances to spot our naked girl, but we didn't find her.

Coming to the top, for me, was a near revelation. It was as if I'd stepped into a realm of unfamiliar physics and might fly off into the sky. At our backs was the majesty of waste, the rock and ice. Here before us was a sheer drop and then the green expanse of the steppe, undulating in shades of green and gold to the limits of sight. It was a vastness that confused perspective. The horizon was farther away. There was more of the Earth to see. With my first breath from the top of the mountain, my chest opened to the wind, my ribs dried and chilled. There, that expanse, not only does it exist, and I have seen it for myself, but I had covered it; I had conquered it in some small way.

We lingered, caught our breath, and turned to go back down.

Chapter 18

I was late getting to the station the first day back from the trip. I avoided the lobby and went straight into the studio. I found the front room there empty and poured myself hot water from the samovar for instant coffee. I sat and drank the whole cup without anyone coming by. That was unusual. I could hear people in one of the editing rooms. I silently opened the door to peek inside.

Sergei, Oleg, and Ilya were crammed in. They didn't notice me. There was the smell of nervous sweat, anxiety, and cigarette smoke on damp clothes. Their faces were lit red by the monitors. There was something horrible and bloody there. I saw skin, hair and dark clothing. It was a dead body being probed by the camera as if in an autopsy.

"Horrible, *bladt*," said Ilya. "Oleg, why do you film such things? You know we can't use them."

"Better to get everything," Oleg replied coolly. "Bear witness, like Yanek said."

"I don't think this is what he had in mind," said Ilya as he turned away from the screen and saw me. "*Vot,*" he started, jumping out of his chair to take my hand. "Turn that off," he said to Oleg. "A nightmare," he said, turning back to me.

"What is it?" I asked.

"Hasn't heard," Sergei whispered almost to himself.

"*Bodje moy,*" Ilya spoke witheringly. "That's Fest!"

Sergei paused the video and looked down. Oleg stood up and commanded, "Sit."

"He doesn't want to see that, *bladt*. They were friends."

"It was a contract killing, *absolutno*. An assassination. Rewind the tape, Seriosha. Do you want to see it or not? They got him early this morning while he was out in his garden," Oleg rattled off. "He was pulling weeds. He had dirt on his fingers."

Ilya explained, "Oleg got a call from a contact in the police station at five-thirty in the morning and instead of calling me, he went with the camera by himself."

"I tried to call you. The phones weren't working, " Oleg protested. "You see, Connor, there are good reasons that I can't loan the camera to you."

"Sorry to welcome you back with this."

"I loved the guy," put in Oleg, "but he must have known that he was in danger. Why make himself so vulnerable? He's out gardening like he's a regular person."

"Better he should live in fear? Stay behind an iron door?" Ilya hollered. "Shouldn't public officials remain part of the public, *bladt*?"

"Maybe have a bodyguard."

"How? Unless he's taking bribes, a politician still gets his money from Moscow."

"Can you rewind it?" I asked Sergei, although I could have reached out and pushed the button myself. Ilya and Oleg stopped arguing. Ilya crossed his arms and turned to the screen: there was a whir of motion as Oleg hoisted the lens to his shoulder. In the blue early morning light, he hustled across a street to where police cars were parked in front of an old wooden house. After weaving through the cars and the shoulders of policemen, one of them demanded, "Who told you about this? This is a crime scene, you can't be here." Oleg continued towards the garden gate, behind which two officers stood over the body. "*Nilzya!*" one hollered. "Don't come any closer." Ignoring him, Oleg swung a leg over the gate, grunting as he strained to keep the camera steady.

"Tore my pants," said Oleg next to me, then pointed me back to the screen. "Watch this."

"*Oi,*" he called to the cops, "did you see this?" He turned on the flood light and directed it down into the weeds Fest hadn't gotten to pull. Two pistols lay side by side. The cops strode over.

"Don't touch anything."

"Stay back."

Oleg used the opportunity of their distraction to go over to the body and get his close-ups. It was unmistakably Fest. There were bullet holes in his face. All but his lips and the tip of his nose were covered with blood. There was something else wrong that was not immediately evident. There were loose whiskers stuck to his face, as well as in the dirt and trampled among plants around him.

"They cut off his beard," said Oleg. "Whoever killed him didn't like Jews."

"He wasn't a Jew," I said. "He was a Mennonite."

"A what? I thought he was a Jew."

"*Bladt,* you're not the only one, *bladt.*"

On the screen, Oleg panned the area around the body, the blood on the leaves leapt up at the camera in the bright light. The blood soaked into the dirt cast a ghastly ruby-black reflection. One of the cops approached. "Get out of here. Who called you? I can charge you with meddling in a crime scene." Oleg started to put down the camera, but happened to pan over the man's feet, revealing blood and more than a few of Fest's whiskers stuck to his boots.

"Is that what you're doing," asked Oleg impudently, "keeping the crime scene pristine?"

"*Bladt,* you put that on the air, you'll end up like him," growled the cop as he wiped his boot in the weeds.

"*Bladt,* you shouldn't fight with them like that," said Ilya, his face lit blue by the screen.

"Smart of him to threaten me on camera, *da?*" beamed Oleg.

When the picture resumed, Oleg was back on the street side of the fence, filming the body being taken away. "I thought it was a dead dog in the garden," said a woman off-camera.

The tape stopped. We took a moment to recover. I went out for a smoke with Ilya.

"How was your trip?" he asked feebly.

"What happens now about Fest?"

"Gennadi made a statement on air. He didn't want anyone on the news team to seem speculative, but he wanted to address what everyone must be thinking." Ilya paced in the doorway. "This is something big. We've had politicians assassinated before, but it was because of their own black business dealings or because they'd been paid a bribe but didn't deliver. Fest was clean. He was killed for what he said, for his politics.

"We're going back to the house to film the opening of the report, interview neighbors. We've got Kolya and Tanya down at the Duma to interview colleagues. The police are giving a statement this afternoon. We have everyone working on this. We've already run a 'breaking news' spot," Ilya said distractedly, saying 'breaking news' in English. "Do you want to go? I've got to make a few phone calls, speak to Gennadi. We could use your help editing. We've come to rely on you, *da*?" Ilya thumped me on the shoulder. "I'm going to do something with this."

I rode with Ilya and Oleg to Fest's house, where we again filmed the garden and the blood on the plants. One of his neighbors, a woman in her fifties with a green scarf in her hair, told us angrily, "Somebody told them he was a gardener, that he liked to garden early in the morning. He was used to getting up early from his days as a sweeper. Probably someone in this building told them. Someone here has blood on his hands." She had tears in her eyes. "We were proud of him. All those years they made him sweep the streets, but he rose up. He showed that something good could come from all this." She covered her face and turned away from us.

Later at the police headquarters, in which everything was painted gray-blue (the walls, the floor, the ceiling and most of the furniture), we set up the camera on its tripod before an expansive black metal desk. A crew from the State station did likewise, purposefully ignoring us.

"They don't love us," chuckled Oleg. "We spoiled their party."

"Sssh," joked Ilya, "the police don't love us either."

In a near goose-step march, an officer in a stiff gray and red uniform strode into the room, followed by two men in suits.

"KGB, FSB, same thing," Oleg mumbled to me.

With a short nod to the cameras and the newspapermen with their notebooks, the officer removed his hat and placed it on the table as he sat. The spooks stood against the wall behind him with their hands clasped behind their backs.

"Good day," he began. "We are here to discuss the circumstances of the death of Peoples Officer Warner Fest, who was found shot to death outside his place of residence this morning. Officers were dispatched just before six in the morning after neighbors reported hearing shots. In addition to Fest's body, officers discovered two *bolonchik*-type pistols that had been modified to fire live .25 caliber rounds. We wish to assure the public that this crime will be solved in short order. That is the end of the statement."

Ilya immediately piped up, "This appears to be a political murder. Can you comment on that?"

"*Nyet,*" said the officer. He stood and picked up his hat.

One of the men in suits stepped forward and said, "There are no political murders in Russia."

"Say your name please."

"Deputy Prosecutor-General Kolesnikov."

"And I thought he was just KGB," mumbled Oleg next to me.

"This crime will be solved in short order," repeated the officer, looking back at Kolesnikov.

"Are you saying you intend to investigate this murder without taking into consideration that it may have been politically motivated?" shot Ilya.

"I have no reason to," answered Kolesnikov. A groan rose from the room, even from the State crew. The officials left the room.

"Welcome to the new Russia, same as the old Russia," griped Oleg.

"But with more orange juice," added one of the other journalists.

After the evening's newscast, we headed for the bar. My eyes stung from the hours I'd spent in front of the monitors, but it was some of the best work I'd done. We'd accomplished something tasteful but shocking. Hard news. I was buzzing and worked up from the tension of the day. All day I'd been choking back the taste of instant coffee and stomach acid. I'd had hardly anything to eat, and now the vodka was open.

I ran into Alina on the stairs. It was the first I'd seen of her all day.

"Poor boy," she said, reaching for my hand, "I'm sorry about your friend, Fest."

"Why do people keep telling me they're sorry," I snapped inadvertently and pulled away. "I barely knew the guy. He's your elected official, your loss."

"*Ladno,*" she said tiredly, "I'm going home."

In the bar everyone was buzzing. The vodka was going around, and the bartender was smiling at all the overpriced Danish beer he was going to sell. Most of the news department was there, everyone smoking heavily. Ilya was more energized than I had ever seen him. He'd done the best interviews and come up with the best lines of the broadcast that day, and now he was basking in it.

"Do you remember that big speech Yanek gave to us?" he said, holding out his cigarette. "It was about raising the public to its higher ideals, starting the conversation with a focus on a positive outcome rather than with a tone of commiserating cynicism, as we often see." He took a long drag. "The optimism in this report was somewhat embarrassing, but it inspired me despite myself. I thought today, 'This is what Fest was talking about.'

"Contract killings aren't so uncommon these days, *da*? So they've become part of what people are willing to accept. People could say, 'here was a man who was trying to stop the corruption, and it got him killed. So much the worse for him.' They're vindicated in their defeatism, their lazy helplessness and fear. But couldn't they be outraged instead? If we describe it the right way, I think this could push people beyond what they are willing to accept, especially if we show that there is something to do. Stage a protest. Vote against corrupt officials."

"Isn't that just propaganda?" asked one of the other journalists.

"The right kind," joked Uncle Sam.

"It's not propaganda, not if we're just showing possibilities, rather than advocating them." After pausing for a drink, Ilya answered further, "It's no more propaganda than taking a cynical approach to everything. I'm not talking about painting Fest as a national hero, *znachet*, Yuri Gargarin, *bladt*. He was maybe overzealous. He'd been stripped of his university position and been made a street sweeper. It couldn't all have been about his desire to serve the public. He had something to prove. Sure, he must have known he was putting himself at risk, too, and you can't serve the public when you're dead. If you think Fest had hubris to pay for, think of those who spoke the words 'we want this man killed,' an elected official. They took out their wallets, and they paid someone to obtain disposable weapons, to shoot him in the head in his garden, drop the guns, and walk away."

"*Vot!*" called Gennadi from the doorway. He put his hand on Ilya's shoulder as he squeezed past him to sit down. "Fest and his killer aren't the only ones with hubris to pay for, my friends. I'm afraid we're on that list as well."

"What's happened?"

"More threats," he sighed.

"What do they want?"

"They want the story to die, of course."

"What do we do?"

"Find out why they want it to die, why they wanted Fest to die." Putting his hands out to the room, Gennadi asked, "Who wants to spend the night in the studio?" The room responded with a groan.

"Let the drivers."

"Sergei? Has his wife taken him back?"

Ilya leaned in to talk to Gennadi. "We assume that Fest was killed for something he said, or something he was proposing, but I'd like to try to find out exactly what it was. I'm thinking we need to go through the records, all the transcripts of the Duma sessions, every measure he proposed."

"Good. And you'll have plenty of time to read while you spend the night in the studio."

Ilya chuckled, "*Bladt,* get the drivers to do it."

Gennadi looked around to see who was listening before saying quietly, "These threats keep getting worse. They're threatening my family again."

Ilya shook his head in solace and responded, "have one of the drivers stay at your place."

With a wan smile Gennadi stood up. "I've got to get home. Will you make sure someone stays the night? Interesting affairs, *da,* Connor? *Nu ladno, dobre.*"

Over the next few days the TV-N news team sifted through what public records it could acquire. Fest had said plenty to put him at odds with several murderous groups. There was hardly any element of society Fest had not criticized for its graft or acceptance of it. His primary target was the corrupt Communist officials who'd used their power as the regime collapsed to make themselves rich and had since become a powerful class of oligarchs.

"Just as I have worked for the truth about the purges," Fest had pronounced on the floor of the Duma, "so am I committed to the truth about the thievery that occurred as Communism was breaking up. The corruption of Communism, even with its dying breath, has left us not with a new Russia but with the old corruption and a new name. If we are truly to have a new Russia, we must extract the elements of our society that caused Communism to rot from within. We must take seriously the crimes committed against the people of this country. These treacherous men that we now call oligarchs, as if that position were rightfully theirs, stole what others worked for all their lives. Most of the people of this country and of this oblast have been left with almost nothing of what is rightfully theirs. This cannot be shrugged off, explained away, or forgotten. We need to prosecute these men."

As Fest saw it, what followed from the corruption of the collapse was inherently and equally corrupt. "We call it the 'Wild East,' as if by making this out to be a Hollywood movie, we can excuse the injustice that is taking place. Some of my colleagues speak to me of growth, of allowing much of what has happened to fade into the past and focus on building better things. But I say, a tree grows from its roots! If we let these people shape our society, then we will be left with a criminal's paradise."

"You wouldn't know it to meet him," said Ilya as we were editing one of the reports, "but Fest was an angry man. I like that. The only problem I have with him is that he didn't see any difference between the Communists that plundered State resources, and the businessmen that are trying to build something of their own. He sees them all as plundering disadvantaged people. He wanted to roll back the clock to 1989 and divide up everything fair and square."

"That's exactly what Vodopyanov says," I told him. Ilya raised his eyebrows and looked back to the screen.

Later, in an interview, a member of Fest's party told Ilya that at one meeting of the Duma, Fest had named names. He'd called for the arrest of a number of local businessmen and public officials. There was no record of this in the transcripts. Off the record, the official provided Ilya with a list of the names as he recalled them. When Ilya confronted the oblast librarian, he rather nervously insisted that there were no other records. Ilya set about trying to interview everyone on the list, as well as others, to see if they recalled that day.

"Whoever says they don't remember must know that the transcripts have been removed. *Vot*, a trap," sang Oleg as we drove to an interview.

"Probably most of these guys are smart enough to know that," replied Ilya.

"Or powerful enough not to care."

With each interview more names were added to the list. Each person remembered others who were mentioned, turning the idea of the list into a sham. The interviews themselves were surreal. Put on the spot in front of an implicitly unfriendly camera, presumably clever men made insane and self-implicating statements. Most implied that Fest was working for his own interests, just like everyone else. His murder was proof that he'd had shady deals on the side. One man, a well-known criminal, according to Ilya, told us, "That's what gets people killed. Dishonesty."

"Can you believe this, *bladt*?" shouted Ilya in the editing room. "Can you believe this idiot is saying this?"

In the interview, Mr. Mafia went on, "Politicians who do not make waves —who accept, rather than extort, cash gifts— don't get killed. They try to avoid making anyone angry, but from fairly early in his political career, Fest managed to antagonize people."

"Are you saying that Fest tried to extort people, businessmen like yourself?" Ilya asked on camera.

"I am only speaking in general terms," answered the boss, with an imperial wave of his hand and a smirk.

A Communist official accused Fest's own party of killing him to make a martyr and named people who he thought might be involved. Officials from Fest's party responded by adding more names of bribe givers and takers in the other party to the phantasm of Fest's list. Vodopyanov was one of the later names.

"We can't go from this list anymore," griped Ilya once it began to snowball. "They're trying to manipulate us to settle scores. We shouldn't have mentioned it in the first place. We won't be agents of a pogrom, *bladt.* Without the official transcript, we can't use this at all. The list is dog shit."

Regardless that the list was never mentioned on air, the word was out, and the police and FSB/KGB turned up at the station to demand it be presented to them. Kolesnikov himself stormed into the station. He marched through the lobby of the *Xobby Dom,* children clearing a path for him like ants for a flame.

"*Vot,* the ghosts of the past are among us," joked Oleg as the man appeared at the reception desk and demanded to speak with Ilya and Gennadi. His presence in the station was that of a monster in a schoolyard. We were enemies, that was clear. He ushered our sainted founder into his own office as if cornering him. Ilya straggled hesitantly behind, uncharacteristically timorous.

Being that it was the end of the day, the staff gathered in the bar to wait for the spook to leave, all except Gasha, who was keeping watch. When Gennadi finally joined us, he held up his hands and exclaimed, "He wants a list that doesn't exist. Now he wants the tapes of all the interviews we've done. I told him we don't have tapes. We reuse them. We only archive what goes on the air or might otherwise be useful. I told him we decided that this cycle of accusation was useless for us and so we taped over whatever we had. He says he's going to put us under investigation."

"Gennadi was brilliant, *bladt*. I'm scared of that man myself. *Xhoyovy KGB, bladt,*" cursed Ilya. "They're all excited about a list. You know what they'd do. They'd consider it a warrant to arrest anyone mentioned and search their houses."

"Depending on who they were and how much they could afford to pay off," put in Oleg.

"*Da, pravda,* and we'd be blamed for it."

"If we'd given any more credence to the list than we did, it would have been our fault," said Gennadi.

"You could see the frustration in him, Kolesnikov. He was cursing and threatening us," said Ilya.

"He's not someone who's especially pleased about Democratization," smiled Gennadi.

"What was he threatening?" I asked.

Together Gennadi and Ilya mimicked, "You won't be exempt!"

"This so-called freedom, freedom to lie and hide things from the police, will come to an end," Ilya continued with the imitation. "And when it does, you will not be exempt."

"Another thing he said," added Gennadi, "was 'you are like children set loose for the afternoon to do as they please, but the afternoon will end, and your father will come home.'"

"What's that supposed to mean?"

"It means Kolesnikov is waiting for the return of tyranny. The people are children and are unable to take care of themselves."

"*Tochno!*" added Ilya. "Once he saw we weren't going to give him anything, he changed his tactic. He said, 'oh, I'm just a servant of the public trying to solve a murder of a man that was also of the people, a man who survived persecution under Communism and also worked to shed light on the tragedy of the purges.' *Bladt!* Do you know what Gennadi said to him? He said,

'Oh, *da*, the purges, but that wasn't a tragedy for everybody. Isn't that how your father started his career, and hence how you are also in the KGB?"

The room exploded into laughter. "If Fest was too honest to be a politician, then Gennadi has eggs too big for television," hollered Oleg.

"Idiots like him make me mad," explained Gennadi, calmly shaking his head. "Also, I happen to know that it's true. We started this station to protect ourselves from people like him."

"It's us that's under threat," answered Oleg, still laughing. "We'd better be careful or they might start assassinating journalists."

"We've got to fight," said Ilya in English with a mocking pump of his fist. He shrugged and took a drink of vodka, "who else is going to do it?"

"*Ladno*, no more of this for now," issued Gennadi. Turning to me, he said, "*Znaish*, Connor, who called me today? Ilya I meant to tell you this, too; you can put it in your next report. Lubomira Markova called. She's decided to organize a vigil for Fest on Monday night at the Duma to mark one week since he was killed."

"*Ladno*, we'll make the announcement and cover it," said Ilya. "Gennadi, I wanted to ask you, were you able to get through to the Soros people?"

"*Da, da*, that *gazyol* Kalesnikov made me forget. I'd just got off the phone with them when he showed up. They're interested! It's good news, *da*?" Ilya had suggested that we edit his Fest reports into a documentary and that I would do an English overdub. We thought we might have a good shot at making one of their international broadcasts. "Only one bit of unfortunate news," continued Gennadi. "Sorry, Connor, they said they need to translate it themselves for subtitles."

I shrugged, "*Nyet problem*."

As we adjourned, Gennadi warned us to be careful on our way home. Oleg and Kolya would spend the night at the station. Sergei was there as well, but he complained that he was getting stuck with all the watch duty and never got any sleep.

"We'll tuck you in and read you a bedtime story," teased Oleg.

"Baba Yaga," I suggested.

"*Boje*, don't tell me that one. I'll have nightmares."

I cut through the darkened park, perhaps unwisely, engulfed in a feeling of war apathy. I'd had a few drinks. As I emerged onto the street on the other side, I saw the break lights on a passing car come suddenly on. The vehicle pitched sharply into a U-turn. I was ready to run but thought I recognized the car, a nice (re-imported) GAZ. It swung to the curb, its tires brushing the raised cement. Vodopyanov reached to pop the passenger side door. "I was by your apartment, and then I tried to catch you at the station." He was energetic as always, but appeared troubled. "I will give you a ride to your flat. I want to talk with you."

He pulled quickly from the curb as I closed the door. "Terrible about Fest," he said immediately. "I knew he aggravated people, but I didn't think anyone would kill him." He paused and corrected himself, "Well, I guess the thought had crossed my mind. You want to know how people will live post-apocalypse? This is how."

"Do you know who did it?"

Boris pursed his lips for a moment. "Nah. There's no real telling. Connor, will you tell me about this list?"

I told him what I knew, including that he'd been named. I truthfully told him that I didn't know the name of his accuser.

"It's okay. I understand you work for the news station. I know who it is, anyway. You remember my business dispute, the guy that tried to rob me? His own *krysha* told him to pay up. Remember? His brother-in-law is a People's Officer. He's also his business partner. So you see, he's settling a score just like everyone else.

"What was Fest doing naming people like that? If he has evidence that someone is breaking a law, he should tell the police. If there are laws that need to be created, then that's his job, right? You can't persecute people for breaking laws that don't exist. Yes?"

"From what I understand, he thought too many people were getting away with too much, and it wasn't enough to make new laws," I hazarded for the sake of seeing what Boris would say.

"What system of government or economy starts out differently? It's funny. Fest was persecuted by the Communists, but he shared many of their beliefs. He thought we could have a utopia if everything was set up fairly. What philosopher was it that thought man's natural state was of kindness?

"It is a pity, yes, but you have to get your hands dirty in order to get by in our country right now. If you're going to accomplish anything, you have to play on the field you find yourself on. Corrupt Communists, businessmen, entrepreneurs, mafia, Fest believed we were all the same. Then he wanted to make a list, to name people? What kind of tactic is that? It sounds like what they did to him. At one time, I can tell you, his name was on someone's list. He wanted to get revenge, I think." In the dark car, Boris was closer to being angry than I'd ever seen him. "He was wrong about many things, Connor. About letting criminals shape the country: you can't start off in the mud and stay clean. It doesn't work that way. Ideals can't be achieved so easily. That doesn't mean you don't have ideals. You have to work for them when and where you can.

"What good would it do to have our corrupt officials persecuting our corrupt businessmen? We avoid that for now with bribes. That is the way it is. We need to focus on building institutions, not on going after every person that did something wrong. Everyone has had to do something wrong here. This is the way to survive. It is a privilege to be guiltless."

Boris pulled into my lot. "I didn't come to talk to you about Fest's politics," he sighed heavily. He turned off the car and put his arm over the seat and turned towards me. "I think you should be careful around TV-N, Connor. Maybe you should go on another trip. Maybe take some time off and go out to my stable with Olya. I know she likes you. You could stay out there with her. Learn better to ride," he chuckled. "Then maybe we could still take that trip to the gulags we talked about."

"I just got back from a trip. Are you pimping your stable girl?" I chuckled back.

"What is pimping? No. I was only joking. Are you too serious with your other lady? What's her name? How come you haven't brought her to see Sveta and me? We can tell you if she's a good girl for you or not. We'll be able to tell. But listen, get away from the station. This could be big trouble. I know about the threats. It's not your fight, Connor. You have nothing to gain by putting yourself in danger, so why do it? Maybe you and your girlfriend can go out and stay at the stable house. Olya can sleep in the barn to take care of the horses. Why not?"

When I arrived at the station in the morning, I found it barricaded by old army jeeps. Men in camouflage stood leaning on the vehicles and behind oil drums filled with sandbags. They were a bit old, a bit paunchy, to be soldiers. A private militia? I considered turning around.

Someone called, "Here he is! The man that saved TV-N!" It was Kolya dressed in old camos. He squeezed sideways through two barrels and came toward me with his hand extended. He pulled me against him and clapped me on the shoulder. "Here he is!"

"What's happening?" I asked, feeling childish.

"What's happening, he wants to know." Kolya looked around at the other men. He appeared to be in charge. "They tried to burn us down, that's what! They pushed the air conditioner through in the studio and threw in a petrol bomb. It hit the samovar but didn't break. Sergei put it out with one of your fire extinguishers!"

"Really?" I said, suddenly smiling.

"*Da, da,*" replied Kolya and chuckled, "You should ask Gennadi for a raise."

"But what's all this?"

"We are the *Afgansy,* the veterans. We're protecting TV-N. If these mafia idiots think they can get past us, they're welcome to try."

Ilya came down the front steps of the building smoking a cigarette. "Crazy, *bladt,*" he laughed. "We've got the Afghan vets guarding our videotapes. I'm afraid you're not going to get your Nescafé this morning. They bombed our samovar, *bladt.*"

Inside the studio, the scene was frenzied. A welder was fixing an iron frame and bolts to the old air conditioner. The place reeked of the fumes from his torch and perhaps the petrol bomb as well. There were scorch marks on our wallpaper beach. The dry chemical dust from the extinguisher had drifted into the corners and against the walls. The flimsy metal samovar sat on the table, bashed on one side.

"We should have that samovar bronzed," said Yana, who had also come in to inspect the damage.

"We should get it fixed, so I can have my coffee," said Ilya.

"We should get a real coffee maker," I put in.

"*Vot,* Americans and coffee."

"*Vot,*" I mimicked. "I was right about the fire extinguishers." Yana laughed and punched Ilya on the arm.

Gennadi joined us and Yana repeated my joke for him. "*Da,* I guess it paid off. You've made a fool of me," said Gennadi with a weak smile. This was taking a toll on him.

"Not at all. You bought them."

"Poor *Gennadichka*," Yana consoled. "Where's our hero, Sergei?

Gennadi answered, "I sent him to my flat for a shower and a rest. When he wakes up, my wife is going to cook him the biggest breakfast he's seen since his wife threw him out."

"Now that's gratitude."

Gennadi shrugged. "The least I can do. How long has he been sleeping here?"

"Since I've been here," I said.

Gennadi shook his head in sympathy.

"I was going to suggest to him that it's time that he got a flat," said Ilya, "but..."

"*Da*. Good you didn't."

Despite the ugly circumstances, it was a pleasure to talk casually with Gennadi, since he rarely stood still long enough to say 'hello.' While we each made an effort to keep the conversation going, it was distressing to see how the stress of the past months had worn him down.

"Who do you think did it?" I asked.

"Take your pick," he grumbled. "We've got mafia angry about the attention we're putting on them manipulating politics; politicians angry about being exposed for taking bribes; our new oligarchs don't want to be hassled with having to explain how they came to own everything, and the KGB doesn't want us to talk about any of it.

"Speaking of which, we've received official unofficial word from Kolesnikov that we're not to say anything more about a politically motivated assassination of Fest. He says it's still technically against the law for us to do anything that he says not to do. It's ridiculous, of course, and we'll continue airing what we see fit. I told him we were preparing a story for international distribution. He just about choked. Then he asked me if the Soros people were helping to fund our 'private army.'" Gennadi gave an exasperated laugh.

"I didn't know you could be in the KGB and have a sense of humor," said Ilya, holding himself back from cursing in Yana's presence.

"He's an attack dog that doesn't know what to attack anymore."

Just then, Alina came through the door. With a smile she strolled over to me and gave my hand a squeeze. "*Nu*, you saved us, *Amerikanits.*"

Gennadi gave us a hesitant look. "*Da,* thank you again, our rational friend," he said. "I should go see how our *Afghansy* are doing."

Ilya and Yana left us as well. I took Alina's hand again and kissed her.

"Your major accomplishment," she kidded.

I answered, "I'll take it."

The night of the Fest vigil was cooler than it had been, and for the people of Tomsk, it was a relief. Lubomira scheduled the event for eight pm. That way, she said, people could go home first and eat. It wouldn't be dark yet, but in the long-lasting dusk, the candles would still show.

I met Alina at her apartment for a small meal. "We're rallying for democracy, so we'll have hot dogs for dinner," she announced cheerfully as she opened the door for me. "I couldn't find any of those buns that are just so. We can have them with bread." She shepherded Otto down the hall and into the kitchen with her knees. "And all I have is German mustard, but I found some more of that Texas beer that isn't very good, but at least it's from Texas. Of course, these are our sausages, so you have to peel the plastic off. Otto *lubit* hot dogs?" She laughed cutely as she peeled steaming franks and tossed them to the dog. Otto wolfed them down, despite that they burned his mouth and made him slurp air and bare his teeth.

Earlier I'd tried to dissuade Alina from coming to the vigil by saying that I'd be helping Lubomira and wouldn't be able to stand with her.

"I don't mind," she replied. "I'll bring Otto."

As we left the apartment, Otto trotted merrily along, appearing aware that something was going on. "This weather makes me think of autumn, Connor, my favorite season. Going out to the countryside, collecting mushrooms and berries, it's the best. The smell in the air. I can't wait for us to be in the woods together and to have that smell around us. What do you think this vigil will be like? Maybe like the demonstrations we used to have. I don't know why I'm so excited. It's nice when people get together for a reason, something worthwhile. We're not just lining up to buy something. Although, I did have to line up to buy candles. They're not so easy to find. Maybe we should have gone back to your Catholic church and seen if they had any candles for us."

There were few sounds as we walked, other than the occasional car and the dog's huffing as he strained against the leash. When we came around a corner onto Fest's block, we were surprised to see a large crowd gathered around the low garden gate. The many candles stood out as sharp points and set their keepers out of focus, making their faces ghostlike. The old carved wood house loomed before them as a dark-shadowed monument. The TV-N crew was there, and the spotlight on the camera combed the crowd. I saw it settle onto Lubomira.

"Should we light our candles now, *malchik*?" asked Alina.

"I'm going to go say hello to Lubomira," I answered, and started to move into the crowd.

"Is it alright if I come with you?" she said, keeping up with me. "Are you afraid that your *Sibirskaya babushka* won't like me?"

"Of course not."

"Or maybe you don't want to introduce me. It's okay, I understand."

"No. Nothing like that. Come on."

Lubomira stood as matron to the mob, with her back to the garden and facing into the camera's light. Looking somewhat like the uniformed ladies on the Trans-Siberian, she wore a long form-fitting skirt, a jacket of the same color green, and a ruffled blouse. Her teachers from the English department, her ladies, flanked her as generals.

I overheard Tatyana from the news team tell Oleg behind the camera, "We should wait a bit. There may be more people, still." She called to Lubomira, "*Ladno*, we'll wait a few more minutes." Oleg killed the light.

"*Privet*, Marion," I said. She held her hand before her eyes.

"Is that you, Connor? I can't see from that light. Just a minute." She blinked. "Oh, there you are. Oh, that's a big dog."

"Otto, heel."

"Now you know, Connor, you can speak to me in English or Russian, but not a mix of the two. There's no point in it." She ostensibly said this to me, but looked directly at Alina. "I am Lubomira or Marion, but never both at the same time. This must be your Russian girl," she said.

I introduced them. Alina said formally, "*Stratsvitsya*," as if she might curtsy.

"We've seen each other at the TV station, I'm sure," Lubomira answered casually with a youthful flip of her hand.

"You've attracted quite a crowd," I commended her.

"I'd rather be organizing tea parties, of course, but I'm glad to be useful. You can see the outrage in people, something needs to be done with it."

"I see you've recruited all your ladies."

"I didn't draft them, they volunteered," she chuckled. The women circled her, fulfilling various roles, their voices high and singing out to one another. They laughed excitedly and touched one another as sisters. Behind them, behind the garden fence, I noticed something covered with a tarp.

"What's that?"

"This may be a somber affair, Connor, but still there will be surprises."

Alina stood awkwardly by as Lubomira and the ladies and I spoke in English. She felt like an intruder, she would tell me later. "You have real camaraderie with those women. You've made friends with them, Connor. Will you write to them? Will you send them books for their English classes, I wonder."

"I think we'll get started now," Lubomira told the TV crew, and Oleg snapped on the light. We all backed away, leaving her alone in the pool of light. Tatyana stepped up to her, held out the microphone, and began the interview.

Lubomira answered questions to the camera at first, but then, with a veteran teacher's ability to know how to get a group's attention, she switched to her classroom voice. The crowd listened to her raptly. "Tonight we honor a man who survived the oppression of Communism, who never gave up despite the undeserved punishment that was heaped upon him. He worked for our Russian democratization in action, and was killed by those working against it. His murder is a message to not just the political classes of Russia, but to all of us, that anyone who crosses the red flags of the existing powers may be killed. Instead, we will take inspiration from Mr. Fest. They can have their fear back!" Applause began, but Lubomira raised her hand and pushed her voice still further out into the crowd.

Tatyana, by now, stood to one side, though she still held out the microphone.

Lubomira, standing on her tiptoes as if to address the back of the classroom, called out, "To pay tribute to Mr. Fest, we will finish the one small piece of his work that we can in one night." With that, Lubomira nodded to her ladies, who pulled the tarp aside to reveal several wheelbarrows and numerous hoes and shovels. "We will finish his gardening!"

As the crowd cheered, "*Hoorah!*" Oleg swung his light over the tools. Hands reached, but once again, Lubomira restrained her class with a slight gesture.

"We will take the garden to the Duma, and plant it in the doorway so that all that enter there may remember Mr. Fest and what he was working for," she called out, her voice now starting to strain. "And may those responsible for his death see that we have sided with Fest, and we are not afraid of them."

The ladies began to hand out the tools, laughing and saying, "These are all borrowed, so please be sure to bring them back to us."

"Yes, we are going to do a little gardening this evening."

"We've spoken to the neighbors, they say it's alright."

"Some of them are even glad to have it dug up, since they now believe it's bad luck."

Flustered by the turn of events and the enthusiasm of the crowd that had shouldered her aside, Tatyana held out her mic to Lubomira's ladies and asked, "How did you get those wheelbarrows here?"

"We brought them on the bus, of course, *devuchka.*"

Otto was anxious in the press of people, and Alina held him by the collar. We followed the gardeners to the Duma and watched as they recreated Fest's flowerbed in the doorway, complete with the fence around it. On the way home, Alina joked, "I've never felt so righteous in my life. I even have some of the sacred soil on my hands, look. Otto enjoyed the digging, anyway, didn't you, Otto?"

"I heard people arguing over what was and what wasn't his blood on the grass and how best to preserve it."

"We know how to commemorate things, *da?*"

"You know what Oleg said to me?" Doing my best to imitate his snarl, I said, "'Russian people know how to mourn, *bladt.* That's something we're very good at.'"

Chapter 19

Sitting before the glowing monitors in the editing room, Gennadi beamed, "This work could take us to a new level." He'd just seen the Fest report we'd completed for the Soros people. "We'll have an international audience with this." He smiled, stood, and slapped his hand on Ilya's shoulder. "When we first started this station, we got by on our good looks. But this! We'll show them what independent journalism is." Turning to me, Gennadi said, "Our friend Ilya here is becoming quite the celebrity, Connor. Did you hear the *Tomsk Weekly* thinks he should run for office?"

"When you're a politician, you don't get to edit the tape," Ilya scoffed. He took a cigarette out of its pack and held it between his fingers.

"Becoming a priest would suit you better," I joked.

"*Tochno,*" he chuckled.

"The State station even praised Lubomira Markova for organizing the vigil," said Gennadi. "Of course, they can't say anything about us."

"Naturally. Independent media is a passing fad," Ilya answered sarcastically.

"So how are we getting this tape to Moscow?"

"A friend of my father is going to take it tomorrow morning. I'll take the tape home tonight."

"*Nu, ladno,* have a good weekend. I'll see you Monday."

"*Tak.*"

Gennadi returned to his office, temporarily pepped up. I followed Ilya to the front of the building and stood with him outside as he smoked. "Any plans for the weekend?"

"*Nyet.*"

"Not going to see Alina?"

"Don't know."

"Maybe you want to get together on Sunday. Drink some beers. Do you like playing cards?"

"Sure, sounds good."

"*Ladno*, I'll come by your apartment Sunday afternoon sometime," he proposed, and we said goodnight.

"So you're shoving me out so that you can drink beer with Ilya?" Alina said late on Sunday morning.

"You can stay if you want."

"I don't want to." Alina was naked and walking around my apartment, looking for a key that had fallen out of her pocket as we'd gotten undressed the night before. Her hair was mussed; her feet scuffed softly on the dry, rough floor. "I haven't seen much of you lately, Connor. Are you trying to diminish me? Are your feelings fading?"

"I've just been busy."

"You volunteered for the extra work. A couple weeks ago you told me that you were tired of being an editing boy."

"I was, but the Fest murder stirred things up. I'll have a credit on the Soros piece."

"*Da*, it's good." She smiled at me and bent to pull on her underwear. She quipped, "I just want to make sure you're not enjoying sitting in those little rooms with stinking boys more than getting in bed with me."

When Alina had gone, I straightened the apartment. By six o'clock there was still no sign of Ilya, and I went out to get myself some beer.

On Monday morning, I walked into the office and greeted two or three people before I ran into Alina, who immediately said, "Did you hear about Ilya?"

"He didn't turn up yesterday."

"He was attacked on Friday."

"Again?"

"He's unconscious and in the hospital."

I turned and looked back at those I had just spoken to, each now looking in some other direction.

"That's all anybody knows," said Alina.

"Gennadi?"

"He's in his office. The door is closed. Ilya's father called him."

"He must know more than that. Is he on the phone now?"

"What are you going to do?"

"I'm going to knock."

"*Nyet*, Connor. Why don't you wait? Maybe he'll come out in a little bit and tell us."

"Okay, I'll wait," I said and then mumbled to myself, but loud enough for everyone to hear, "Why does everyone hoard information?" I sat on the couch next to Israelievitch, whom I'd greeted a moment before. "Do you know anything about what happened to Ilya?"

He shook his head. "In my opinion they came after him because of the reports."

"Who?"

"*Vot*," he croaked slowly, "the mafia, the KGB, who knows?"

I sat back, crossed my arms, and slung one leg over my knee. Alina stood for a moment looking puzzled before coming over and sitting next to me. She exchanged a quick nod with Israelievitch.

"Connor, I don't understand what you're upset about. You suppose that Gennadi knows more about this, but he might not."

Just then, Losha stormed into the lobby. Shaking his fists, he declared, "They think they can intimidate us? That they can beat us?"

"*Tak*," croaked Israelievitch, "What have you heard?"

"I've heard nothing! I know all about it! It was political, of course. It was payback, just like Fest." With two wide strides, Losha stood before Gennadi's door. "Is he in there?" he asked.

We nodded. Losha crossed his arms, sighed, and turned back to us. He stood in the middle of the room mumbling to himself like a sulking wizard.

"This is ridiculous," I said. I got up and knocked on the door.

"*Da?*" Gennadi answered. He asked me to close the door behind me as I went in. "I'm very concerned, Connor," he said dourly, his eyes dark rimmed. "He's very badly hurt. They cut up his face. He's still in a coma. He's the only one who knows who did it." Gennadi sighed.

"People are assuming that it was political."

"I can't help assuming the same. What else can we assume? We had the threats. I've got to figure out what we can say on the news."

"How about the staff? Shouldn't they know what's going on before it airs on the news?"

"You're right, of course. I'm so shaken; I didn't want everyone to see me like this. I thought I'd give it a little while. Maybe we'll hear something more. He went in for surgery this morning."

"Was he alone?"

"*Da,* he'd gone out to the brewery outlet. His father went looking for him when he didn't come back. He found him lying in the street next to his car unconscious." Again, Gennadi sighed. "Terrible."

Ilya woke from his coma the next day. It wasn't political, he told his father right away. It was *hooligani.*

I asked about going to visit in the hospital but was discouraged. Apparently that wasn't done. Despite the attack, the Fest tape made it to the Soros people in Moscow. They loved it and would give it to all their member stations to air worldwide. Yanek sent an email of congratulations. Gennadi wrote a cheerful response without mentioning the attack.

More than a week passed before anyone saw Ilya. Then he and his father showed up at the bar one evening at our usual gathering time. Much of his face was still covered in bandages. Both his eyes were purplish black. One ear was bandaged. There were stitches visible in the middle of his upper lip. There were stitches on one cheek and several on his back, where he'd fallen on glass, he told us. Everyone came to pay respects and get a look at him.

Ilya drank beer through a straw. Danil Sergeevich drank vodka, as did most everyone else once they saw his son's condition. Gennadi was very disturbed, nearly reduced to tears. He held his hand over his mouth and paced back and forth. "*Bodje moy*, Ilya."

"Gennadi, *bladt*, sit and have a drink with me," said Ilya, his voice nasal and distorted by his swollen lips. "It wasn't a planned attack. It had nothing to do with the station or the reports about Fest. It was my big mouth and a gang of marauding drunks. They didn't know who I was, even though some of them should have known me. I know who they are."

Gennadi sat on the edge of a bar stool. "You've told the police?"

"The police say they all have alibis. It's my word against theirs."

"We'll have alibis as well, *bladt*," growled Ilya's dad, inaudible to most people in the room, but I heard and Gennadi did, too. Danil Sergeevich stood and took Gennadi's place pacing, his anger supremely palpable.

"I should have had the *Afghansi* with me to get beer, *bladt*. To protect me from myself."

"Tell me what happened," plied Gennadi, his eyes pained and urgent.

"I went to get beer. I stood in line with two pickle jars under my arms. I got them filled, and as I was walking back to my car I ran into a group of guys, all of them drunk, four or five of them. They said, 'give us your beer.' I told them, '*eyob tvoyu mats.*'

They beat me. One of them had a spike, the kind you hold in your fist. He stood over me and hit me three times. The first time I rolled and it tore through my ear lobe. Unfortunately, I rolled onto broken glass from the jars. He hit me again here, on my upper lip." Ilya lifted the bandage so that we could see the star-shaped wound between his lip and nose, the size of a fingertip. "Then he hit me again through my nose. It went into my sinuses. They could have killed me with that thing. I don't think they cared one way or the other."

Danil Sergeevich broke in, "Can you imagine? I found him lying in a pool of blood and broken glass, with his face beaten to a pulp."

"Still, I'm lucky," answered Ilya. "*Nu*, I don't suppose I'll ever be pretty enough to go back on TV."

Gennadi stood up and again put his hand over his mouth. After a pause, he said, "You'll be back on." Then, fighting tears and anger, he joked, "So long as you're no uglier than Yeltsin."

I stayed at the bar and drank. I listened to the story repeated. Alina asked me if I would go home with her. No, I said. "You're getting drunk to show your love?" she asked.

"*Da.*"

"I think something bad is going to happen," she warned.

Around nine o'clock four big guys in mafia coats showed up. "Tonight," I heard one of them announce to Sergeevich. "We know where they are."

The remaining people from the station left. I stayed. Sergeevich began giving me looks. "He should go," he said to Ilya.

"I want him to come. He can stay with me in the car," Ilya slurred. "He's American. He understands how these things are done. It's the wild east, *da*?"

"This is private business, understand," Sergeevich said to me vehemently. He guided his mafia men into a corner and whispered to them.

Ilya, high from the mix of booze and pain pills, leaned over the table and apologetically told me, "It's not just for me. *Moy Otetz* has a reputation to uphold. He can't let something like this pass. They'd walk all over him, understand?" He sat back with an exaggerated sigh. "I preach about democracy, *da*. I say we have to break ties with these new lawless elements, but look at what I am doing. Am I outraged?" he asked loudly. "Are you outraged?"

"I'm outraged, *bladt*," shouted his father, turning towards us, "that you were beaten almost to death for nothing. Here is how I show my outrage."

"Things were not always this way," quietly said Ilya. "But this is how it is now. A culture in crisis, *bladt*. Maybe it will get better. Maybe not. And what are we to do in the meantime? Do you have an answer? I will tell you: survive."

I nodded dumbly. I believed. I wanted more to drink. I wished to survive.

In the car we had more vodka. Ilya took a slug or two before his father stopped him. "*Ladno*, I'm not going through this so that you can overdose on medication and alcohol." We followed the thugs' car, hanging in the glow of their tail signals as if on a tether of light. Ilya looked sickly out the window. He had turned some corner. He had separated himself from what was going on.

I was spinning. I hadn't eaten. The red lights ahead pulled at my eyes, giving me a feeling of vertigo. The lights in our side windows, the shops, the streetlights, all swirled furiously like sparks from a chop saw.

Ilya's father looked ahead. His jaw was set, his eyes deadly focused, grim. The angry creases in his face sloped and intersected as shadow and light cascaded over his profile. He may have been a small man, and he'd always struck me as stoic, but now something had turned in him as well. This was vengeance. He was prepared not to stop.

Ilya sat up and took a deep breath. "How horrible this is. I can't keep quiet, can I? I never can. I haven't felt this wasted in a long time, not even on our drunken hunting trip. I haven't felt this bad since I was in the army. Have I told you about the pot train, Connor? You know how there are marijuana plants along the roads in Tomsk? You told me about that horse that eats it in the village with the pretty stable girl, *da*. That stuff is nothing. Nobody bothers smoking it. When I was in the army, *bladt*, one time we were taking a train through Kazakhstan and suddenly we saw that we were going through a giant field of marijuana. Men hung out the windows with their comrades holding onto their belts. Since everyone had tried to do the same, they only got sticky bits of leaves and pieces of bare stem. I went to the front of the train, *bladt*, and jumped off. I ran along and cut down whole plants, which I slung over my shoulder. When I got on the last car of the train, a friend was waiting to pull me back on board. Our officers went on a search to confiscate it, but we hid it too well for them in the walls of our cabin. There was one officer, he nearly went crazy with anger at us. 'I saw one of you out there harvesting it like a peasant stealing corn. I can smell it, *bladt*! I will find it and you will be court-martialed.'" Ilya chuckled weakly under his breath. "We had enough for the rest of our tour of duty. We got very sick smoking all that marijuana."

Sergeevich in the front seat cleared his throat. "That was not worth the possible consequences, son."

Following a pause, Ilya questioned carefully, "This is?"

"There is no choice."

We were driving out of town, now. It was pitch black, and then suddenly I was staring at the flashing lights of the airport runway. We pulled into a large, dimly lit, and mostly empty parking lot. We slowed and cruised through it, traversing the length of the terminal building. At the far end was the bar, marked with a blurred little sign, flickering as if illuminated by candles. I could hear music inside, the drums going pap, pap. I thought of Pavel in a groove, shaking his beard like an indie rocker.

The thugs got out of their car, leather coattails flicking like bat wings. One after the other, the four of them passed through a side door, presumably into the kitchen. Each threw the door roughly aside, assaulting it with their shoulders.

"Are they going to shoot in there?" I blurted out. "My friend Pavel works here."

"No shooting," Sergeevich answered sharply. I sat back once more. Out on the tarmac, a vehicle trolled by as if in a bay, its lights flashing. Momentarily our mafia reappeared, each pair clutching a man who looked nearly identical to themselves. They pushed them up against the side of our car. Ilya's father rolled down the window.

"This them?" asked the lead thug.

Ilya looked and nodded sullenly.

"Check his belt, *bladt*," said one of the thugs. They roughly pulled up one man's shirt. "Look at that. It's on his belt like a buckle." They pulled at the weapon, turning his pants side to side, almost comically. "You, take that thing off. Give it here." The man complied. "*Vot*, look at that. You want this?" The thug held the weapon with the star-shaped point out to Ilya.

Ilya shook his head.

"If you don't want it, I'll have it," said the thug. "Maybe we'll use it on him. Give him a scar to match the one he gave you, d*a*?"

"Remember my instructions," said Sergeevich.

"Of course, don't worry. They'll still be breathing when we leave. They'll still be breathing tomorrow." The thug sneered at his captive. "It'll be hard at first, but every day you'll breathe a little easier. You'll keep at it, won't you?"

Reaching a panic as he was taunted, the man still wearing his belt cried,

"We didn't know. We didn't know who it was. We were drunk. Anything. Anything we can do. Money. Anything. Don't do this. It was an accident. It was him that hit you with the knife. It wasn't me."

"And now we'll watch you be beaten the way you watched him," snarled Sergeevich.

"And we're drunk, as well," said Ilya.

One of our thugs went back to their car. He reached behind the seat to retrieve two hardwood batons, the same kind the police carried. The other men dragged the two attackers away from the bar, over to where the dumpsters stood perpetually full. There was a flood light there. They started right in.

"Pull away," said Ilya. His father started the engine and looped back into the parking lot. Safely in the dark, at a comfortable distance, we observed. It was like watching sharks attack their prey in deep water, soundlessly illuminated by a spotlight, itself nearly powerless in the weight of that dark, that pressure from above. The sharks tore, thrashed, and circled back for more. Every blow, with shocking force, took life away, every movement crushing.

I turned away. In my state, I was afraid the men would burst open, would suddenly spray us all with blood, betray the entire scene with the reality of what is hidden inside. They would dance there in the dim light with their guts glistening. Smash only the outside. I didn't want to see it. I didn't want to smell it. I didn't want to have it on my hands.

Sergeevich said, "I told them, 'beat them until they stop moving, but not until they stop breathing.'"

A few men came out of the bar, but they quickly turned their backs. I imagined Pavel putting down his drumsticks. He wouldn't come out. He would have a cigarette and wait for his audience to return.

Our thugs walked back to their car.

"Blood must come off those track pants well," I said stupidly.

Ilya answered only, *"Bladt!"*

I looked to my side and found that there was still vodka in the bottle. I had a drink and handed it up to Ilya's father. He took a drink as well.

Back in my room I could not sleep. I cried. This was all over now. Whatever I had been doing here, it was over. Ilya had said to me, "You are a voyeur on a very nasty scene. Everything, a nasty scene." Then, drugged and weary, he said as if sending me away, "I envy you, my friend. If I could pack up and get away from here, I would."

Chapter 20

I called the airline and made my reservation. The end was ahead of me, and I plummeted towards it. I kept my plans to myself for a few days, then I told Pavel. I was having dinner over at his place.

"You're going back to America?" asked Vika, looking up from her plate, her brown eyes wide. "Goodbye," she followed, as if expecting me to get up and go at that instant.

Pavel smiled and reached across the table and took my hand warmly. After dinner, he clapped me on the shoulder and guided me to the balcony for a smoke. "We will miss you," he said. I stayed with him until late in the night, talking casually. When we parted, there was no pretense about writing and exchanging addresses. Our paths had crossed and would now diverge.

When I told Alina, she cried and told me she didn't want to talk to me for a while. She was upset that I'd waited until a morning after we'd had sex to tell her.

"It's like a lie, Connor. You've disrespected me with that. You've treated me like your..." She didn't finish. She cried fiercely.

"I wasn't sure. It wasn't planned," I blubbered in realization.

"Every minute," she stuttered.

I talked to Lubomira on the phone. "We must have a party," she said, and after a quick pause to check her calendar, she gave me a date and a time.

I hadn't visited the English club in quite some time, and going back there I had a feeling of returning to my own elementary school. It was a sentiment both fond and fretful, but I entered that world and floated through it. The students clapped for me when I arrived. Somebody told a Russian joke that was made nonsensical by being translated into English, but everyone laughed. They had the good *Altaiskaya* beer, just for me, and there was gelatinous custard cake. Marion presented me with a certificate in English that read:

> *This is to certify that Mr. Connor Chessick has visited the city of Tomsk on his own will, showing ardent enthusiasm, great courage and outstanding persistence in covering immeasurable expanses of Russia and Siberia to reach this remote settlement of bear-hunters and snow-eaters.*
>
> *This further certifies that he is unanimously elected an honorable member of the Friends of Tomsk Association and is hereby authorized to enjoy all the privileges of Siberian food and hospitality offered to individuals coming to this land of cedar pines and transact business partnership, respect and live between nations.*
>
> *Finally this certifies that he is entitled to a direct access to our hearts, souls, and Earth's bowels."*

After an hour or so, most of the class had left. I stayed for help with translating my letter of resignation to TV-N. Lubomira corrected my draft and told me, "Any books that you could send us, especially ones with lots of pictures, even magazines, would be very helpful."

"I will," I promised.

"Hmm," she hummed in doubt. "I invited Graham to come tonight, but he called to say he couldn't make it. Strange that the two of you have never met. You must before you leave, Connor. He has something he wants to ask you. I suggested next Thursday at seven p.m. He will come by your apartment. I told him where you live."

"Okay," I agreed, sensing little choice.

I left my letter on Gennadi's desk while he was out. Alina saw me as I came out of his office. We stood awkwardly for a moment.

"Are you going to tell people," she asked. I shrugged. "Is it okay if we talk for a minute?" We went into the *Xhobby Dom*'s small theater, as we often did to talk, and stood between the stage and the first row.

"What made you decide? Was it something I did?" she asked, attempting to look at me dispassionately, but with an edge in her voice.

"Partly it was what happened with Ilya?"

"What happened?"

"I'm not supposed to talk about it."

"Did they kill the *hooligani*?"

"No, they didn't kill them." I sighed at the uselessness of keeping the secret.

"What have you got at home that makes you want to go back so much?" she asked.

"My life. I want to get on with it. It's not here."

"Neither is mine," she answered.

"There's nothing I can do about that."

"Would you stay longer if we weren't together?" she asked.

"Possibly," I said honestly, "but I wouldn't want to be here without you."

"At home you don't mind?"

"It's not as simple as that."

"No? Maybe." She sighed.

Later that day, I received a phone call from Vodopyanov. "Pavel tells me you've decided to go. I've been saving something for you."

When I next ran into Alina, I told her with a smile, "Uh oh, Vodopyanov has a surprise for me that involves going somewhere with him, but he won't tell me where. Call the embassy if you don't hear from me." She looked at me coldly and walked away.

Boris picked me up in yet another new-looking, re-imported GAZ. As we headed out of town, he told me, "It was between this and bringing you to see the icons in the museum. My wife's brother is the curator there, and he could have taken us on a private tour. Maybe, still, it's something we can do, but I thought this would make a better story for you. Didn't you bring a camera? Too bad, you're going to wish you had."

We drove past wood-cabin villages, between the plots where horses, cows, and sheep grazed. The late summer grass was thick and long.

"You are very quiet, Connor," commented Boris after we'd driven for a time. "You are all out of questions." Just then he spotted a sign and made a quick right turn. "Did you catch that sign?" he asked, then chuckled and added, "Just wait." We drove down a narrow road into the woods, branches overhanging. We came to a stop at the corner of a windowless brick building that was built close among the trees.

Boris turned to me. "You have seen how the mafia does business. You have seen what happens to honest politicians. You know what a Russian girl is like in bed." He chuckled, pleased with making me blush. "So what better thing for a Russian to give such an American than a dose of radiation?" He pointed to a plaque at the narrow entryway. It took me a moment to sound out the Cyrillic. It said, 'Nuclear Reactor.'

"This is part of the Nuclear Technology Institute in Tomsk. There's nothing like it in the world. It's a test reactor, and it has something very special." He nearly giggled as he opened his door, "Let's go."

"*Seriozno?*" I asked as we climbed the stairs towards shiny steel doors.

"Yes, of course."

Inside, the foyer was enclosed by barricades. To the right sat a woman in a white lab coat at a metal desk. She glumly considered us for a moment before two men appeared behind her to greet us.

"Boris Mikhailovich, I'm so glad you could pay us a visit," said an older man with a close-trimmed white beard.

"Vladimir Vasilevich," Boris hailed casually, as if he knew surely in his mind that he was the dominant of the two of them.

"Welcome. This is my assistant, Igor," he said, gesturing to the man at his side. Both men wore white lab coats, but Igor also wore what looked like a chef's hat and held a Geiger counter. "Please take a coat from the rack," he directed us, motioning towards a pair of lab coats hanging on the far wall. The one I picked up had a blue stain over the breast pocket, as if from a burst pen. I touched it to make sure it wasn't wet before putting it on.

We were allowed through the barrier and then followed the two men up a few stairs to another set of doors.

"Do you carry that around all the time?" I asked Igor about his instrument.

"If that thing starts to beep, turn around and run," Boris joked and laughed loudly.

Vasilievich smiled over his shoulder and answered for his assistant, "Not at all. Only when we have guests, to reassure them that everything is safe." We entered a dim corridor. "Igor is going to take you on the first part of the tour. I will join you for the second part. I hope you'll excuse me, Boris Mikhailovich." Vasilevich gave a slight deferential bow before entering a room to the left.

Igor, appearing more at ease, led us up a stairwell to the reactor's control room. On the wall near the door hung a large, cartoonishly illustrated sign showing how to properly handle radioactive materials. Boris joked, "Study well, Connor, they'll be handing you a chunk of uranium at the end of the tour."

Igor smiled. He set down the Geiger counter and cleared his throat. "The facility was built in 1967," he began, "however most of the equipment was updated about ten years ago." I looked around at the panels of buttons, dials, switches, and flashing indicators, which lined the pale green walls of the room, as well as a raised semi-circular helm in the center of the room. There were also a number of instruments protruding from the walls at eye-level. With needle-thin arms, they scribbled on scrolling sheets of graph paper.

"This reactor runs on a potent isotope of uranium," Igor said plainly. "If it was much more potent, we'd be dealing with a bomb. Of course, it is only used for research." Just then an alarm sounded. Igor strode to a control panel and dispassionately flipped a switch to silence it. "There has never been a serious accident here," he said, as if on cue. "There have been times when the emergency systems have had to kick in. Fortunately, all of them have worked."

Another man, this one with a bushy black moustache, came into the room. "This is the captain of the shift," explained our host. The man nodded to us curtly as he checked the instruments. Igor then went on to explain the function of nearly every device in the room.

Boris nodded seriously, appearing interested. It was impossible for me to follow, and my mind wandered. The control room, I speculated, could be for just about anything, a submarine, a freighter, a dam, a sewer plant, a missile silo, a spaceship.

"On this screen we can visually monitor the core," said Igor, catching my attention. On a small black & white closed circuit TV we saw an uneven glowing blob, like a telescopic view of a far away star. Again an alarm sounded, and I jumped.

Boris chuckled and put a hand on my shoulder. "Calm yourself, now."

The crew chief saw to the controls, and Vasilievich rejoined us. "Do the alarms worry you?" he asked. "It's part of normal operating procedure."

"A bit like having a firecracker for a doorbell," I said in English.

"No jokes about explosions around here," Boris laughed.

The scientist smiled tolerantly. "Are you ready for the next part of your tour?"

"Now for the good part, Connor."

"This is the only functioning nuclear reactor in the world with a window," said Vasilievich. "There was one other, but I understand it is no longer in use." Motioning to the far side of the control room, he said, "Through that door, we'll be able to view the functioning core of the reactor. This is a rare opportunity, of course, one you will likely never have again in your life. It is my duty to tell you, however," he added with a slight smile, "that this opportunity is not without risk. The radiation level behind the door is many times what is normal, approximately one thousand times more. But it's perfectly safe."

Boris guffawed. "One thousand times?"

"How can that be safe?" I asked.

The scientists smiled at each other, as if playing a prank on a child.

"You'd be in trouble if you slept on the glass," noted Igor.

"We'll spend only a few minutes inside, but it is safe to have as much as eight hours of exposure over the course of a month. We each go in there regularly. We wear these monitors," he said, pointing to what had looked like a pen in his lab coat breast pocket, "to ensure we don't exceed the safe dosage."

Igor flicked his monitor and told us, "I've reached my limit this month."

"So I guess that whoever last had your coat, Connor, got too much radiation," kidded Boris, pointing at the ink stain. Igor chuckled. "Pow!" went Boris.

"If you have doubts," said Igor, "look at Vladimir Vasilievich here. He's been working in this facility since 1967. He is healthy, his children are healthy, and his grandchildren are healthy."

Vasilievich nodded. "As I said, we'll only go in for a short time. You can reduce your exposure by staying in motion, as well. When we reach the viewing platform, circle around it rather than standing in one place."

"So what do you say, brave American, are you gonna go?" smiled Boris.

"This is something few people have seen with their own eyes," Vasilievich encouraged.

We stepped through the door and onto a catwalk suspended high above the dark cement floor. We were in a large dark room, much like a hanger, illuminated only by a few yellow safety lights. Out in front of us was the containment cylinder of the reactor, rising forty feet from the floor. It was twenty feet in diameter. "Remember, when we get to the viewing area, circle around it. Keep moving," said Vasilievich as he led us across the chasm to the top of the cylinder. "You don't have to move quickly, just steadily." Our footsteps echoed over the iron grate. When we reached the top of the reactor, we saw a handrail ringing a large glass porthole in the center of the thick iron and cement tank. We peered down into the reactor. The tank was full of water and lit bright blue. The core, the source of the light, was suspended in the center of the tank by cables and pipes. There it was, the radioactive core in its cooling bath. It was a bundle of rods, four feet long, two feet in diameter, and from the gaps between the rods came the light, glowing electric blue. It was a quality of light I had never seen before. It was dense, more than light alone. It appeared to have substance that you might be able to pluck from the water like thick plasma. It was surreal to see it, to encounter true magic.

"Atoms, Connor, are being split beneath the soles of our shoes," said Boris, as wide-eyed as me. "Keep walking."

"This is called Cherenkov radiation," said Vasilievich.

When we emerged from the reactor room, the scientists gathered around us, smiling as if we'd gone through a rite of initiation. "How do you feel?" asked Igor.

"Actually," said Boris, "I have a bit of a headache, just behind my eyes, like I've been staring at a computer screen."

"*Da.* Me, too," I said, just realizing it.

"Probably psychosomatic," answered Vasilievich. With that our tour was over. Igor led us back to the lobby.

"Your wives will be pleased with you when you go home to them," he forecasted slyly.

"Thank you, Boris, that was the coolest thing I've ever seen," I told him as we got into the car.

"Worth, maybe, a day or two off your life?" he laughed, very pleased. "When you meet the woman you want to marry, don't tell her about this. She'll worry about your sperm."

"How do you know Vasilievich?" I asked.

"Simple. He came to me for a loan to buy some cases of figs and dates for his wife to sell in the market. It's a good thing he's not out there selling something, eh?

"Do you think he could do that, sell uranium?"

"I think he could do what he must to feed his family." Boris shrugged and started up the GAZ.

"I think you are more yourself now, Connor," he said as we drove away. "It will be good for you to get away from that TV station and all its problems. Don't let all the heaviness weigh on you once you leave. It's not your own. You will see. You are an optimist, I think. It is always good to meet one. I am also an optimist, Connor, and I don't mean in the way like the Russian joke. Do you know that one? But do you know what else? I had a bet with a friend that I could get you into that reactor." Boris chuckled. "You really should have brought a camera. You could have taken pictures. They would have let you. Nobody cares about it now."

"The *other* American, so we meet," Graham said ironically, shaking my hand and walking into my apartment. His voice, his open broadcast of American English, echoed in the hall as I pulled the iron door closed behind him. He had a scruffy beard and wore jeans and a t-shirt.

"Lubomira's wishes are fulfilled," I answered automatically in the same tone. I led him out to my balcony and gave him a beer.

"She tells me you've decided to head home."

I nodded, took a drink. "I've had enough. How long are you going to stay?"

"I'm not sure. My teaching contract goes until the end of the year. I'm thinking of applying for law school back home, but I may put it off for another year."

We sat silently for a moment. "What do you think Lubomira supposed we'd talk about?" I asked.

"We could talk about her," Graham suggested cheerfully. "It tells you something about the endurance of generosity, Lubomira. Or maybe this is where real generosity is born. How does someone who was thrown on a prison train as a child and sent to Siberia with her whole family end up being so generous? I'd like to ask her if there was some moment when someone was nice to her in the prison car, some stranger. It must have happened, don't you think? I'm sure she remembers it."

I nodded, though unsure what he meant.

"I've never met anyone like her. Not even my own family is as generous to me. Everything with them comes with strings attached. Lubomira gives without caveats."

"I don't know about that. You guest-star in her classes, don't you?" I pointed out. "She helps me translate, I help her with her classes, pretty straight-forward exchange."

Looking like I wasn't getting him, Graham went on, "What I mean is that I feel unburdened by personal politics here. Don't you? Everything is about relationships. It's refreshing. Maybe it strikes me because I've always had a crappy relationship with my family. Are your folks divorced? It's like each parent hates you for the ways you're like the other one. When my parents got divorced, my brother and I were right in the middle of it. They fought over us and through us. Everything they did had ulterior motives. Here, I feel like when people are your friend, that's all there is to it. You're on the inside, and they keep an eye on you and help you out. Conditions are tough, but you help each other through it."

I nodded slowly. "At the same time, I get the feeling that if you fell down a manhole, no one would help you unless you were a personal friend."

"That's true, too," he shrugged. "People have a hard exterior, but the closeness you have when you break through —it's made me realize that I never really trusted my friends, that they always had specific motives of their own. When you were a kid, you'd go play with one kid because he had a pool or another kid because he had a ping pong table. Your parents teach you that's how you do things, and it stays that way. Everything is a transaction. One guy likes you because you let him use your computer, the other because you give him pot."

I chuckled, sounding to myself like Boris. "Don't you think that just by being an American here, you are the kid with all the good toys? That's your novelty, your worth. It's what makes people want to be your friend."

"Maybe at first," he said, perhaps put down. "Whenever I start a new class, I make a point of going through all the stupid things I always get asked, just to get it out of the way. How many rooms in your house, how many TVs do you have, et cetera? Some kids think it's funny, but some are embarrassed. Have you ever noticed how embarrassed people get here? It's not just a little blush. They're blushing for everyone in the room and beyond."

"Have you ever felt that way?"

He hesitated. "As an American? Not at this moment in history, no."

"We've got Bush Legs to be proud of."

"Ha, and Clinton brand cigarettes!"

We went on joking. People on the street could look up and see us yammering and laughing and be able to tell that we were not Russians, that we didn't really live here.

"How do you find the women?" Graham smiled at me through his whiskers. "Beautiful, aren't they? All those mixes of people exiled out here. Do you have a girlfriend?"

I nodded and returned a question. "Do you date your students?"

"I try not to. I often get invited over for dinner, so I usually end up meeting siblings. I've had the best luck with that. Although that's the one thing I'm not very happy about, my relationships with women. They all seem to be trying out for the part of the perfect demure wife."

"The Russian bride."

"I'm not into that. I'm amazed by how so many of the girls dress exactly the same, same black miniskirt, same white blouse. It's as if somebody told them that looking like they work in a restaurant was the pinnacle of fashion."

"The Russian Bride Café."

He laughed, "Bar, grill, and human trafficking."

"If you like your waitress, you can get her to go."

I got up for another round of beers.

"But seriously, you try to have a conversation with these girls? They nod and agree with everything you say," Graham continued when I returned. "Even when you tell them that you're not looking for someone to play sidekick, they do it. It's what they've been taught, I guess."

"Traditional society," I say in Russian.

"I have a cycle worked out. First I'm drawn in by a beautiful girl. I ignore the black skirt. She might be a conformist (like how people clap in unison here, which weirds me out), but she's still a hotty. There's nothing like lifting up a short black skirt and pulling down a pair of white panties. It's a classic." He laughed and went on. "Things escalate after a few dates. She's quiet, but you think maybe she just has to get to know you better. The sex comes before the conversation. And she likes sex! She acts all demure and shy, but she's surprisingly uninhibited in bed. That's a good thing, you think. But then you realize that she's doing in bed what she thinks you want her to do (maybe she's seen it in a porno movie), and at the end of it she's waiting for her answer: 'Are you going to marry me and take me to America or not?'"

I sat back. I asked, "Do you think you could ever give one of those girls the answer she wants to hear?"

"I could, absolutely. I'm open to it. I'm looking," Graham said resolutely. "You said before that you think they want something we have. I don't think so. Maybe it's me that wants something they have. I just keep hitting this obstacle of obsequiousness," he said, tripping over the words. He shrugged, "with women back home, you're both trying each other on for size. If it's not something that's going to last, you both enjoy it for what it is and while it lasts. Here, there's urgency in everything."

Deciding to contribute a story of my own, I said, "My last girlfriend in the States warned me that she was falling for me. She gave me notice. She didn't just come right out and say it. She told me that 'maybe I was a person she might fall for.' I told her, I wasn't sure if I *might* feel the same way, so we split up. How businesslike of us. How sensible. That was one of the things that made me decide to take this trip. The way you were trying to escape family politics, I was running from dispassion or blandness." I chuckled, adding, "And now that I've succeeded, I'm running back home. What you've described about your relationships with women here, my girlfriend is nothing like that." I told Graham about Alina.

"So what are you going to do about her now that you're leaving?"

"I told her. She's not talking to me. Everything is all about her now. It's all I think about. If I stayed, I don't know what I would do. I don't see how we could break up. We work together. I don't want to break up, but to keep it going is just digging us in deeper and deeper. She's a great girl, and if I was going to stay here, or if we were seeing each other back home, we'd stay together. I don't know what would happen. Maybe it would work out in the end, maybe it wouldn't. But it doesn't matter because we don't have any more time."

"You mean you're not willing to take the chance?" posed Graham.

"No, I'm not willing. And it just so happens that it's up to me. I got into her world on my own power, and I'll get out the same way. She's stuck here. She has no such power. I didn't make it this way. We were all born into it. I've been honest with her, although I'm not sure that counts for much. Intellectually I should be at ease, but these things don't always meet up. I'm sick with guilt over it."

"You're letting it get to you, but like you said, you didn't make things this way," Graham said with a therapeutic tone. "If I'm sleeping with a girl, I know on some level she might want me to marry her and take her back to the States, but I'm not going to do that unless I want to, and I don't feel bad about it. It's not as if I'm holding auditions or lying to anyone. If she wants to sleep with me to see if she can get to America, then, you know, I'm into that." He laughed. "The expectations are her own, not anything that I've given her. Membership has its privileges or whatever. If you like her, just let things take care of themselves. One day at a time and whatnot."

"It just isn't working out like that," I said. "I feel like I'm doing her more harm than good. Maybe she's playing to what I want more than I realize. I tell her things, you know, that she's smart and beautiful, American things, maybe, that she can have what she wants in the world, that she's capable. These are things, I think maybe, she never dared to imagine about herself."

"What's the harm of that?"

"Those are things I don't think people say to girls here, man. So she asks herself, 'if I'm so smart and beautiful, why doesn't he want to marry me?' The answer, 'because I don't want to get married,' doesn't go anywhere. She sees it all as a betrayal. It's all lies, and I'm using her." I drained my bottle, and pronounced, even to my own surprise, "At home there are things you like and things you don't like. Here there are things you love and you don't know how you could ever live without them again. There are also things you hate so much you think they might take over your life and destroy you."

"Heh," scoffed Graham after a pause. Then, sitting back, he joked, somehow without nastiness, "If I could marry all these girls and just have them around to screw now and then, you know, I would. If they're so eager, why not? 'Sure you can come back to America, sweetheart, and so can your sister, and her friend, and her, too.' You can all come and be part of my happy harem with a full mod-con kitchen."

I got up to get us a couple more beers.

"Maybe this is what Lubomira really wanted us to talk about," Graham called out. "I've told her about my frustration with women. Maybe she knows you're about to leave a good one behind. Maybe you should introduce us."

I smiled weakly, suddenly nauseated. 'Okay, let's stop,' I say to myself. 'Let's have some beers and tell some jokes.'

Shortly thereafter, I heard the gong of the security door. There was only one person it could be, and I was surprised by my own desire to see her just then. She knew I was meeting with Graham today. I'd mentioned it at work.

She was there with her beautiful sly grin. "Don't let me interrupt, boys. I only wanted to see what it's like when you Americans get together. On TV it seems you always have a good time. Give me a beer, and I will sit here quietly while you talk. Don't worry about me, I understand very little English. I won't know what you're talking about. I just want to watch."

I introduced her and got her a stool from the kitchen. "Go ahead and talk in your own language," she instructed us. "It will help take you away from me."

I was happy to oblige her, although Graham was uncomfortable. He launched into a made-up line of conversation as if we'd just left off. "...So maybe it's my dysfunctional family that makes me appreciate how close families are here. Maybe you have more to look forward to back home."

Ignoring his cue, I explained, "She says when she sees me speak English I seem like a different person, that she doesn't really know me."

"It's good she realizes that," said Graham, again in his therapist's voice.

"I can't blame her. She only has so much to go on. I don't say the things in Russian that I normally would. I don't do the things I normally would. I'm an idea to her, as much as anything."

Graham bashfully stole a glance at her. Alina winked at him and took a drink. "Do you like our Russian beer?" she asked him.

Graham raised his bottle to her. "I don't. I like the imports better."

"Me too," she said.

When Graham had gone, Alina said, "He was interesting."

"Nah, he's a typical hippy," I answered inadvertently in English.

Alina smiled at the word and repeated, "*Xhiiippy.* It's like you've known each other all along. It's easy for you to laugh at whatever you want. It's nice."

"It was good to laugh. Lightheartedness isn't something I've experienced much in the last few months."

"*Nasha bednaya, tedjolaya Russiya,*" she goofed.

We were still outside on the balcony. It was dark now. I lit a cigarette.

"You still look stupid with a cigarette, Yankee." She watched with quiet amusement as I smoked, then asked, "So, Connor, are we still together?"

"I hope so."

"I was thinking we should cut it off, for practice, maybe. But then I thought, 'why stop?' So, now, I think for the rest of the time you are here, I want us to be friends like you and Graham. I want us to laugh and have fun. Of course, we can do other things as well. Guess what else I've decided, Connor? I'm coming with you to Moscow. No further, don't worry. I'm going to Belarus to visit my mother and sister after that. I'm going to take some time away from TV-N. Don't look so pale, sparrow," she laughed. "Let's go back to my apartment. I have some food. I found some Georgian wine at a kiosk on Komsomolski Prospect. We can have that."

We walked back to her place, holding hands, trying to be at ease when there was simply no way.

We ate largely in silence.

"Otto's very relaxed," I commented.

"I told him you're leaving, and he's happy."

We had a glass of wine before we started kissing. "Let's take things slow. We'll take a bath together. My hot water is back on." We didn't undress each other. She removed her jeans and socks, unbuttoned her shirt, undid her bra, slid her panties down her legs. She stepped into the large claw-foot tub, as the water was still heating up.

"Let's do this," she said as I stepped in beside her. "Close the curtain around us, turn on the shower." Unlike in my flat, Alina was able to hang her showerhead on a fixture on the wall. "It's like the rain, *da*, warm." We sat facing each other with our legs tangled, watching the water splash over us. I smoothed the warm water over the cool spots on her skin with my hand. I felt her shiver.

"*Nu, ladno*, Connor, sit back." I might have thought she had something serious to talk about, if it wasn't for the look in her eye. "I have a surprise for you that you'll like better than the one about me coming to Moscow."

"*Nyet*, I'm glad you're coming," I protested, but she waved me silent.

"Reach through the curtain there behind you, down in the hamper, down deep. Feel something?"

I got up on one knee and forced my wet hand through her laundry. I grasped something, "*Shto?*"

Alina giggled and put her hand out to receive her improvised sex toy, a large carrot in a condom. She laughed, "Do you like my vegetable?" She sat back against the rim of the tub, adjusted herself, and opened her legs. She looked at me with an eyebrow raised as if requesting assent. She held the narrow end of the carrot, the condom tied in a knot at the tip. She rubbed the thick end over her vulva, pushing down on it. Adjusting her hips and slowing her breathing, she pushed it into herself and sighed. She closed her eyes as she did during sex. Her labia cupped the root, flaring over its contours as she moved it in and out, making soft noises only slightly distinguishable from the splashing water. She opened up her mouth and the water splashed at her lips. She then spit a stream at me and laughed.

"Would you like to?" She offered me, touching the tip of the tusk lodged inside her.

"*Ne nado*," I said breathlessly, and she laughed again.

"You like to see. But now that's it; now I'm in the mood for the real thing. Let's get dried off and get into bed." She nonchalantly waved the carrot under the shower's streams and handed it to me.

"You're trying to kill me with this," I said.

"*Tochno.*"

I kissed it.

"Carrot lover," she said.

"Who loves carrots?" I exclaimed.

"There, now we're laughing."

Jittery and eager, we dried off. She hurriedly put Otto into the steamy bathroom, with the quip, "It'll be good for his curls." We laid down on the bed, which she'd pulled out and made prior. Her skin was soft and warm.

Outside, the summer was over. It was just August but already cooling down. A slight breeze from the open window had us pull the sheets up over us, itself like a dry puff, a thin warm veil.

"Look at this, *malchik*," she smiled as I lasted past the five-minute mark. "It must be your little dose of radiation."

"Maybe my little dose of carrot," I whispered, and she snickered.

"Still, we're laughing. Don't lose your concentration. I want more."

I reached to touch the bead of the condom. It had come off. I pulled out suddenly, and she opened her eyes.

"Well?"

"The condom came off."

"Well?"

I sat up on the edge of the bed and reached into her with two fingers. I pushed up past my knuckles and fished in circles until I caught hold of the filmy latex.

"Mmmm," she hummed. "For a minute there, we were really having sex, Connor. Did you finish?"

"There's always a little."

"Poor boy, put on another condom and finish."

"Isn't there something you should do?"

"*Nu, ladno,* I'll go wash. You shouldn't fret. Your good American condoms have spermicide on them, too."

Otto sniffed around while Alina was in the bathroom with the water running once again. I held the condom in my fist.

"Now we'll have to think of something else to laugh about," Alina said gently as she climbed back into the bed. "Don't get yourself worked up."

I softly shushed her.

After a few moments, she said, "Your mind has left Russia already, I think, Connor. You've carried some of our weight around. I don't know why. You're not used to it. It's harder for you. So now I think it's enough. Enough Russia for Connor. It's time for you to go home, *maya lasichka*."

Chapter 21

I packed up a couple boxes and bags for Alina. They contained the knife and cutting board that she'd brought me, some half-used ingredients, such as vinegar, sugar, Lubomira's rice, the brown-brick laundry soap, and mustard in a beer mug. I also left her my stash of condoms, minus a few for the trip.

Alina's father came to help us move my things to her apartment in his little red Lada. He took time off from work, she pointed out. Before he arrived, she'd warned me, "My father is a military man. He won't trust you."

"He doesn't have to trust me," I said in English. "He just has to take my shit over to your place."

He was a big man. He had a big moon face, like this daughter. I shook his hand. He reached for the box with the condoms before I could hide them. "Papa, those are my good *Amerikanskiy* condoms," said Alina. "Put them down."

Without looking up, her father grabbed a different box from the floor and headed out to the car. Alina grinned and shrugged. "He tells me he's worried for me," she whispered. "Dog shit."

After we'd carried down all the bags, Alina said, "This apartment was never much to look at, but I hate to see it empty."

"I'm going to stay and sweep up," I told her. "Do you mind doing the unloading with your dad? I'll meet you there in a bit." I glanced casually away from her. I thanked her father.

Alina and I parted at the steel door for the last time. We waited for her father to go down the stairs before lightly kissing. She gave the door a little rap with her knuckle and turned to go.

I went back inside the room and danced the broom over the floor. For one of us, it was a happy evacuation. Moments by myself, now, became times I was no longer present in Tomsk. For her, though, I'd wear the look of burden and stick around for as long as I could.

There'd been a party for me at the station the day before. Following the model of birthdays, cake, champagne, and vodka were served after work. Alina missed it.

Sergei had made a toast. "Connor, I tried to buy you a gift. My wife said a Matryoshka doll, or something made of lacquer or birchbark. I try not to argue with her since we got back together, but I couldn't do it. 'I'm not buying something for a tourist,' I said. So, I bought you something I think you'll actually enjoy, a Nazareth CD."

"*Vot*, love hurts," saluted Uncle Sam, and he downed his vodka.

Ilya made a brief appearance, although he had not yet come back to work. It was the first time I'd seen him since witnessing the payback. He looked better but still was plainly mauled. He awkwardly came up to me, his eyes alternately downcast and searching my face, expecting judgment. He said finally, "I found something I'm not too ugly to do, *bladt*. I'm going to go to Chechnya to report on this war we're having. That way I can claim these are war injuries." He'd chuckled sheepishly and drank. "*Vot*, a war correspondent. Chechnya, *bladt*."

After wasting as much time as I could in my empty flat, I headed over to Alina's place for our last night together in Tomsk. "*Privet*," she said breezily as she let me in, but her eyes, too, searched my face for something.

Wishing to keep things casual and distant, I tried small talk. "*Bodje moy*, you look like your dad."

She put on her pained tone, as if I'd dropped some crushing weight on her. "Please don't say that to me, Connor."

"*Nu*, he is your father. It's reasonable that you resemble the man."

"You don't understand, Connor."

"No, I don't," I said in English. Then I gratuitously added, "clearly I do not." After a few moments, I tried again, "Otto's quiet tonight."

"*Da*, you know why."

Alina and I stayed up late, drank tea, and talked. When we got up to go to bed for a couple hours before the train, she held me tightly. We slept next to each other like little children.

A small crowd showed up at the train station to say goodbye. Gennadi and people from the station were there, Lubomira and people from the English club, Vodopyanov and Pavel, a couple of Alina's friends I'd met once or twice, and her friend Tanya. Alina's father was there. He would take care of Otto while she was gone, since Tanya wasn't able to. "I don't trust him to take care of Otto," she'd told me earlier. Nevertheless, she gave him the keys to her flat, and he gave her a small package for her sister in Belarus.

Gennadi approached and gave Alina's dad a warm, familiar handshake. Alina gave a start of surprise, almost disgust. "You know each other?"

"We've spoken a few times," Gennadi said elusively.

"I'll ask him about that later," Alina hissed in my ear.

"So you are taking her with you after all," said Lubomira in English. She smiled, but I felt her pragmatism and sorrow looking through me.

"Only as far as Moscow," Alina corrected her tersely, as if there was a long-standing tension between them.

"Well, Connor Chessick," exclaimed Vodopyanov, grandly holding out his arms like a statue of Lenin. "All this and more!"

At last came the moment to board the train and then the slow extraction of the train from the station with people waving at the windows. Alina and I flopped down on opposite sides of our berth, which for now we had to ourselves. "I'm glad we didn't have to say goodbye to each other in front of all those people.

Why do you think they came to see us off?" She wearily answered her own question. "They say, 'We're not looking away,' *da*, Connor? But we say, 'We want simply to leave, enough formalities. We don't want what other people want.'"

"Let's listen to music," I suggested, and fished out the tape player with the spliced-together headphones. I put on a much-shared cassette, and we watched the familiar scenery roll away. Before long, Alina fell asleep.

The *Tomich* —it was the same iron road I'd come in on in January, but now the woods alongside it were lush and green. The great gray sky sprinkled rain, and it was pleasantly cool. Thinking back, I could barely remember the naked branches and the blinding snow.

Our train passed an engine pulled over in a side branch of track. In the open control room, I saw three engineers in blue coveralls sharing a meal on a crate. They were far enough away so that I could watch them for several silent ticks of the electric poles flashing by like frames of film. Recognizing my own hunger, I set out a meal.

After our journey to the Altai, Alina and I knew how to shop for these kinds of things. We had hard boiled eggs, yogurt, bread, sausage, cheese, apples, preserves, and vodka. I waited for Alina to wake up to eat. I watched her peaceful sleeping face.

"I'm glad we took the train," I said when she awoke. "We could have flown, but then Moscow would have been undeserved. It would have been an insult to Siberia. You have to watch Siberia as you back away from it, as if from a king, slowly, respectfully."

Alina looked at me with tired eyes, aware that I'd spent considerable time composing these flowery Russian words. She brightened when she saw the food arranged on our small table.

On the second day the sky cleared for a time and woods along the tracks were patrolled by mushroom collectors, sometimes whole families making a picnic of it.

Said Alina, "Look at this little girl waving to us. Her village clothes are stained with berry juice. Her mama is wrapped in scarves. *Vot*, our Russian soul. Their heart strings are strumming and sounding like *balalaikas.*" She gave a short chuckle and steamed up the window before her.

We shared our berth each night with other passengers. I didn't speak to them. Alina and I stayed close but spoke little. By the time we crossed the Urals and were closing in on Moscow, I had said hardly a word in twenty-four hours.

Alina spoke up, breaking the silence. "The days are going by much quicker than I would have thought. I think I could be on board for another three days before I would really start to have cabin fever or before I would grow tired of your sullenness. Tell me what you're thinking, *malchik?*"

"I'm thinking mostly of the one thing," I answered, my voice croaking at first.

"*Da*, I'm not interested in hearing about that." After a pause, she said, "Since we're not living up to our plan of laughing, I'm going to tell you a sad, sad story. I've almost told it to you before, but then changed my mind. I don't know why I want to tell it, but here it is."

She spoke dispassionately at first, lighting out on a narrative, enjoying the roll of it, a piece of her own life. "When I was a little girl, and we lived in an apartment building on *Kievskaya Prospekt*, we had a dog that became pregnant. I was very excited, and in preparation, some friends and I set up a bed for her in the basement storage area. Tanya was one of those friends.

"The day came, and the puppies were born. We watched them nurse and stroked their tiny furry bodies. After a few days, their eyes opened and they became more playful, but they never strayed far from their mama and the bed we'd made them. We checked on them several times a day, whenever we could. In the morning before we went to school, we went down, then again as soon as we got home." She paused and took a breath.

"Then one morning we went to check on them, and we knew right away that something was wrong, terribly wrong. We all went cold with fear as we came down the steps. Usually the puppies were fairly silent, but today they cried and cried. The mama cried, too, like a moan. She lay among her crying pups, helpless to do anything for them. You should have seen her eyes, Connor.

"We couldn't tell what it was at first, even so, we started to cry. Some of the pups were wriggling in pain, some of them had stopped moving and only cried, some were barely alive. I picked one up to try to see what was wrong, and then I realized. I picked up another and another. Every one of them had broken legs. All of their legs were snapped. Someone had picked each puppy up and snapped all four of its little legs." She looked at me solidly, but with eyes reddening, that little girl reawakened.

"Of course, we were innocent of such things. We didn't believe that someone could do that, and we wondered how it could have happened. We cried and cried for all this hurt we had found in our own home.

"I went and got my mother, but I wouldn't go back into the basement with her. Mama came back up the stairs saying there was nothing we could do. 'Some terrible man has done that,' she said. The puppies died one by one over the next couple days.

"I came to believe that it was my father who did it. I have no evidence. I never had any evidence or a real reason to suspect him, but I always did. Maybe it's how I put him away from me, since he didn't love me.

"*Nu*, did I do it, Connor?" she said, crying and laughing. "Did I get through? Are you sad for me now? This is what I'll do, I'll tell you all the sad little stories in my life, and that will keep you here with me instead of off in the distance, racing ahead of the train to where you will at last be able to put your bags on a conveyor belt and board a plane."

We arrived at Moscow's *Kazanskaya* station in the afternoon of the third day. We stood dazed on the platform. The other passengers rushed past, ramming through the surge with their luggage. We took the metro to a housing development outside the city center. It was pleasant and green, and as we arrived the sun cast a golden glow that made even the concrete honeycomb of apartment towers appear inviting. We entered a building and rode an elevator. We knocked on a door, and it was opened by Alina's uncle Vanya, who was a jolly, red-cheeked man. "What, are you married now?" he exclaimed upon seeing us.

"*Nyet,* Uncle Vanya," Alina said coyly, her voice constricted as her uncle hugged her.

Behind Vanya was a plump, bubbly woman, his rosy-cheeked twin and wife, Auntie Alyona. They bustled and welcomed us and reached out to help with our bags. After a moment, Alyona took her niece aside and said, "My dear girl, we don't have enough beds for the two of you." Without a hint of embarrassment Alina told her that it was quite alright for us to share the fold-out couch.

We had a large meal with all the Russian treats I had come to love: salty cutlets, potatoes with meat gravy, many salads in mayonnaise and sour cream. "Eat, eat," urged Alyona. "You are both too thin. You'd think people out in Siberia would have to have a little more flesh on themselves."

"They spend all their energy chasing after caribou, dear Alyona," laughed Vanya. "Carving ice into houses."

Both husband and wife, I learned, worked in a nearby defense plant and were lucky to still be receiving their paychecks. Closer to Moscow, perhaps, it was easier to get money from the Kremlin than in Tomsk.

Vanya and I polished off the customary bottle of vodka over the meal. After my months of practice, I could accomplish this and still stand, but I needed a good walk afterwards. Alina and I got back on the metro and went to Red Square to prove to ourselves that we were in Moscow.

As we strolled in the darkened square, Alina told me, "We can only stay with them for tonight and tomorrow. They are going to their dacha to go mushroom hunting. They're meeting people there and can't delay. Of course, they didn't tell me this when I called two weeks ago."

"They won't let us stay in the apartment while they're gone?"

"It wasn't offered. I don't want to ask unless I have to. Can you see if Vodopyanov will let us use his flat?"

"*Da*, I'll call Masha."

"Ah, young lovers," said a man with a camera, "You want your pictures taken?"

"*Nyet*, we don't."

When we arrived back at the flat, Alina's relatives had turned in, leaving the couch in the living room made up for us. Alina took off her clothes and laid out on the bedspread.

"I don't think we should," I whispered tiredly.

"You'll regret it," she sighed, "Or maybe not." She pulled the blanket over herself.

After two nights of heaped-on hospitality, we moved to Boris's flat for our last night together.

"The Russian way of life is wonderful, isn't it?" beamed Uncle Vanya as he pumped my hand goodbye. "You've been here long enough to know."

The flat was exactly as it had been. The fridge rattled like a tractor and the faucets leaked. We didn't see Masha. She'd left the key for me in the police station downstairs and asked that I drop it in the mailbox when I left.

Alina and I were very nice to each other. We bought little gifts. I handed over anything that could be useful to her, the cassettes and player and headphones, my medical kit.

"Of course I can keep the green shirt, *da*?" she smiled. In the evening, she said, "I'm sorry to say we can't *do* sex on our last night together, Connor. You just keep winning, my Yankee. I'm having my period. God must love you. I tried to tell you the other night. Haven't you figured out my cycle yet, *durak*? You are relieved, *da*? I know what you are thinking."

We kissed and undressed just the same.

"I've never taken you all the way like this before," she whispered secretly with my come on her hand. She got up and went into the bathroom.

When she returned, I asked her, "What took so long?"

Her answer was, "It's hard to wash off, silly."

We got up early and had breakfast. The plane was scheduled for three-thirty. We left at nine-thirty and arrived at Sheremetyevo by eleven. Alina brought her bag with her. She was leaving for Belarus on a train at eight and had nowhere to go until then. We waited in line for a while and talked a bit.

"Do you know that beer in the green bottle, Connor?" she asked, pointing out the Heineken for sale at a news stand.

"Of course. You've never seen that before?"

She stepped out of line and bought a couple. We drank as we stood there, shuffling ahead, a few steps every so often.

"I don't think you can come with me past customs," I said to her as we finished our beers.

"*Da*, we may as well part here," she said. With a glance of understanding to the people behind me, we stepped out of line.

"You've been very important to me."

She began to cry. "See, you did this." She smiled through the tears. My eyes burned. My stomach cramped.

"*Ladno*, Goodbye." She picked up her bag and walked away.

An idiot's farewell, I thought. I got back in line, and I thanked the people behind me for saving my spot. I started up a chat. We were on the same flight.

An hour passed without movement. What was going on? A family, a whole village, people who had butted in front of me in the first place, Russians were holding up the line. They had giant canvas bags filled with silverware, antiques, family heirlooms, things that weren't allowed out of the country. The silver had to be counted and cataloged, every spoon.

I'd tried to keep them from butting in line, but I'd been roughly pushed back by a rangy punk in a tracksuit. Let them go ahead, I'd thought. Plenty of time. I don't need a fight.

And now the customs agent seemed deliberately slow. "Open another line," I shouted in Russian and then in English.

We stood waiting and waiting. I could see the Helsinki Air desk, the attendants in blue uniforms. One woman attendant came over and asked if anyone was going to Helsinki.

"Yes!" There were six of us, at least.

"Can't you open another line?" she said to the customs officer, a woman in a bulky brown uniform. The woman looked up with a silver fork in her gloved hand and shrugged.

The Helsinki Air woman looked back to her desk. There, another blue-suited woman crossed her forearms in an X. "Oh, they've closed the gate," said the attendant and walked away.

The American woman behind me, a lawyer married to a soft-spoken Russian man, shouted, "What are you talking about? You're closing the gate? There's still more than a half hour until the flight even boards. There's a group of us here." She led her husband to the front of another customs line, spoke rapidly in fluent Russian, and was immediately allowed through.

I was next in line, so I tried to get their attention. I pounded my fist on the customs desk and shouted. The woman there with bushy dyed red hair refused to look up. She continued with forks and spoons. "Miss, my plane is about to take off," I pleaded with her.

"So what?" she snapped.

I begged another officer standing by. After a cursory look at my documents, he waved me through. The Helsinki Air desk, however, was abandoned.

Lugging bags I should have checked, I got in line at passport control. The American lawyer and her husband were already there, as well as an English couple headed to London and an elderly American pair wearing safari gear. Without boarding passes, we were turned away. The old man stuffed his passport back into his fanny pack and whined in a mid-western accent, "Oh, no, this is the third time."

"We need to find someone from the airline," said the lawyer. "We should stay together, we'll have more bargaining power."

We were a clan: Americans getting poor service. We wouldn't stand for it. We asked other airline agents to page Helsinki Air. Was there a phone we could use?

A woman from Helsinki Air showed up, inadvertently crossing our path, and we screamed at her to get us boarding passes.

"No key," she said in English.

"I'll break the fucking thing open," I roared back at her. I threw my bags down and went around into the Helsinki Air booth. I yanked at the drawers and cabinets, tearing the handle off one. Mindless and out of control, I kicked at the desk until a bone snapped.

I looked up, shocked by the pain. The security personnel looked on, unmoved. Events were unchanged.

"No key," repeated the attendant, and strolled away.

I was not going to make this flight. The admission came slow and throbbing, nauseating me.

The other passengers abandoned me. I was now a liability. They hurried off to the Helsinki Air office, hoping to be put on another flight. I had too many bags, and without Alina to help me, I lumbered along. The cheap rolling duffel I'd bought in the Tomsk bazaar lost its wheels and dragged on the floor. I fought through the exit gate, looked up, and found Alina there.

She watched me with eyes watery and red. She raised her hand and waved distantly, as if on the opposite side of a wall of glass. The last touch, the last kiss, everything had already passed.

I stopped, stunned, uncontrollably overjoyed. Here was my guide back to guide me again. "They won't let me on the plane," I said.

"Poor *malchik*." She shook her head slowly, softly. We kissed strangely. "You're crying."

"I think I broke my toe."

We found the other jilted westerners on the sixth floor, lined up along the wall outside the airline office. Three men in Helsinki Air uniforms passed by, apparently knowing who we were and told us, "Wait for the girls."

Alina whispered to me, "I'll be right back."

The women of Helsinki Air showed up with their Soviet faces on. They marched past us into the office. Holding up her hand, the one who had approached us in the customs line said, "We have no Helsinki flights over the weekend. The manager of the office is not here. He was on the flight today. You will have to go to the main office in Moscow on Monday. We cannot put you up in hotels. You have missed your flight. We are not responsible."

"We didn't miss it, you wouldn't let us on it. We were here," objected the lawyer. "Why would you close the desk when there are passengers waiting to check in? You should check people in until the flight is ready to take off. I'm sure that's the airline policy. Maybe you could look that up."

"Where did you go when you closed the desk?" I snarled in Russian. "On a coffee break?"

"Why can't you call the office in town?" argued the lawyer. "Don't tell me it's closed, it's the middle of the day. Give me the phone, and I will call them. You can't let me use the phone? Why not? I have spent a great deal of money with this airline. Why can I not use the phone?" She spoke American in perfect Russian, but it got her nowhere. She quivered with rage. She fought back tears and began to choke on her words. Her husband stood silently by, knowing for certain what was still cemented in the veins of these women. Defeated, his wife finally stepped aside. "Let's go buy tickets on another airline," she said. "We'll settle this when we get to a country where people understand things."

"You really don't understand, do you?" I growled, leaning over the counter, "you stupid fucking whores." My Russian, now, was very good, and it poured from me in a caustic torrent. If there'd been another man in the room, he'd have been obliged to belt me. "You work for a company, and we are your customers, *bladt.*"

"Are you going to tell us how to do our jobs?" snapped the one from the line.

"Yes, I will! Get a Finn in here, and he will tell you that I am right, *bladt.* I want to talk to a Finn. Get me a Finn! How can there be no Finns here?"

"There are rules in the airport. We have to obey them. We have no choice."

"Dog shit! You closed the counter because you had an excuse to take a coffee break. In your Soviet brains, power is in withholding. That is why you bitches are '*sovok*!'"

I'd done it. I broke them. "Why are you talking like this? Do you know what you're saying?"

"*Da,* I do know. Do you know what you're doing? I don't have any money to buy another ticket. I don't have a place to stay. I'm stuck here until Monday, and it's because you went on your coffee break instead of doing your job."

I left the office and found Alina in the hall, waiting for me with a couple of beers. "Terrible, Connor. A tantrum like a child! You can't talk to people like that." She gravely shook her head, but not without a hint of her grin, the curled lip of her admiration.

"Now I'm the hysteric."

We sat on the floor to drink.

"How come you were still in the airport?" I asked her.

"I missed the bus, and there was a couple hours before the next one. I came back to make sure you got on your flight." She paused, sighed, drank. "I'd wanted to see it take off, but I couldn't find a window. I was just standing there, and then there you were. I wondered if you had changed your mind. Isn't that funny?"

I plowed ahead. "I'll have to go back to Moscow. I'll have to try to get back into the apartment."

We took the elevator to the main concourse and slumped into molded plastic seats. "Poor *malchik*," Alina said again and again. "Poor *malchik*, you're still not used to this." We waited for the next bus into Moscow.

When we finally arrived downtown, Alina asked me to wait on the sidewalk while she went into a store to look at shoes.

"I'm going crazy about this key," I protested.

"I'll just be a minute. Don't worry so much. Probably it will be there."

"I'll meet you at the train station."

"Just give me ten minutes. You know I have no nice shoes. You know it's important to me." She stood and looked at me for a long moment. "You're a storm cloud, *malchik*," she said. Her eyes were still red. "We need to toughen up, Connor, I think, if we're going to get through all of this."

When we got to the apartment on *Frunzenskaya*, I tore open the locked mailbox. The key was there. Inside the apartment, I called home and left a message for my sister that I wouldn't be home until Monday or Tuesday. I nearly lost it.

We didn't have time to eat. We had to get to the train station. We sat and rested for a few minutes by the door before heading back out to the metro.

The train station, as always, was dirty, and full of people crushing and struggling, spitting sunflower seeds and tubercular wads of phlegm.

"*Nyet*," said Alina simply, and I followed her back outside.

Since we had some time, we bought sausages and beer at a kiosk and went looking for a decent place to sit. Up the street, out of sight of the station, we found a housing development and sat in the playground there. We watched two young mothers fuss over their children about one small thing after another. "The strap to your overalls has slipped off. Wipe the dirt off your hands. Don't pick that up."

A drunk man in a suit staggered through with a red rose in his hand. He paused by the jungle gym for a moment, then presented the flower to one of the children before slouching away.

"I wish I was an artist, a painter," Alina said dreamily. "Even if I could just draw. I have a friend who's an artist. Each piece he does is a perfect little bit of life, filtered through his own self, his gift or whatever it is. Good genes."

I couldn't eat. Alina wrapped the second sausage in a napkin and put it in her bag. "We are people who feel things deeply, Connor, but also we are people who can put our feelings aside," she said suddenly, wiping her eyes. "We look at things and come out with the best in them, *da*? There is a mystery to things, Connor. You pretend to have control, but..." She stopped. "We've said everything." She snickered after a bit and put her hand on my shoulder. "We can still be pen pals."

We found her track and stood on the platform to wait. The train arrived and the passengers crowded to get on and find their seats. Wordlessly we began our second goodbye. We embraced and kissed. "At last, our hearts are breaking," Alina whispered. She sniffed and wiped her eyes. "I thought the one to leave first was luckier."

We were bumped into, knocked against with baggage. "I'm going to go now, Connor. Please don't stay on the platform. You should go. There's no use in prolonging this whole thing. If you're going to stay, stand where I can't see you." Her voice caught.

There was a brackish kiss, and she stepped onboard, into the flow of the dead.

I watched her walk down the aisle. I followed along through the windows. She had to go all the way to the front of the car. She looked up at me at last, crying harder now. She forced a smile and motioned me away. She put the headphones on.

My own plan, cruelly imposed on her, was now thrown back at me. I exited down the stairs into the pedestrian subway. There the seller women lined the walls. They glared at my wet cheeks, my limping, and offered me their disgust, free of charge.

All but one.

The old woman looked at me with freckles on her careworn face and a smile in her eyes. Holding out a sample of food on a grease-spotted square of newsprint, she said, "For you, *malchik*, just a taste."

The end

Acknowledgements:

Thank you to the people I knew in Tomsk back in 1994. Thanks to Project Harmony & Marlboro College. I am grateful to my readers, Normand Côté, Marya Plotkin, Amy Heard, and Robin Archer. A special thanks to John Bate who encouraged me to keep trying to get this novel published. Thanks to AOS Publishing. Thanks and love to my wife and sons.